Includes Bonus Story of
The Magistrate's Folly
by Lisa Karon Richardson

Heart's Heritage

RAMONA K. CECIL

BARBOUR BOOKS
An Imprint of Barbour Publishing, Inc.

Heart's Heritage ©2012 by Ramona K. Cecil
The Magistrate's Folly ©2012 by Lisa Karon Richardson

Print ISBN 978-1-63409-712-3

eBook Editions:
Adobe Digital Edition (.epub) 978-1-63409-840-3
Kindle and MobiPocket Edition (.prc) 978-1-63409-841-0

All scripture quotations are taken from the King James Version of the Bible.

This book is a work of fiction. Names, characters, places, and incidents are either products of the author's imagination or used fictitiously. Any similarity to actual people, organizations, and/or events is purely coincidental.

Published by Barbour Books, an imprint of Barbour Publishing, Inc., P.O. Box 719, Uhrichsville, OH 44683, www.barbourbooks.com

Our mission is to publish and distribute inspirational products offering exceptional value and biblical encouragement to the masses.

 Member of the
Evangelical Christian
Publishers Association

Printed in the United States of America.

Chapter 1

Indiana Territory, April, 1812

Annie aimed the musket's barrel at the center of the deer hide shirt covering the stranger's broad chest and prayed she wouldn't be required to pull the trigger. At the same time, she sent up a silent prayer of thanks for the presence of her late husband's Irish wolfhound, Cap'n Brody. The big dog—whose muzzle easily reached the shoulder of the man's horse—appeared to have the stranger effectively treed, lending an extra dose of courage to Annie. She strove to keep her voice strong and steady. "State your name and purpose, *Monsieur*."

Willing her heart to slow its pace, she hefted the gun and glared down its barrel at her target. She knew all the residents of Deux Fleuves, and most of those living in neighboring settlements within a twenty-five mile radius. But she'd never seen this man, who sat unflinchingly regarding her from atop his black gelding. And she was sure she would have remembered one so comely. She guessed him to be not quite thirty years in age. Several days' worth of rusty stubble covered his angular face. His gray-green eyes held an intense look, glancing about as if attempting to ferret out additional threats beyond her musket and Cap'n Brody.

"Is this Jonah Martin's place?" His casual tone held no hint of fear, but the way he sat straighter in the saddle spoke of his respect for her weapon.

"*Oui.*" Best not to offer too much information, but allow him to believe Jonah might appear at any moment.

"I mean no harm." He held up both hands, empty palms forward as if to demonstrate the sincerity of his claim. "I'd just like to speak to your pa."

"You have not yet said who you are, or for what reason you are here." Though his words had fallen short of persuading her he was

3

harmless, he must know something of Jonah to realize her husband had been old enough to have a daughter Annie's age.

"I'm Brock Martin, Jonah Martin's nephew." He dragged off his black felt hat, revealing a shock of thick, russet hair.

The name sparked an obscure memory. Jonah had said very little about his extended family. According to Papa, there'd been some sort of falling-out between Jonah and his brother, Henry, years ago. But she did recall her husband once mentioning a nephew named Brock. She'd thought the name odd, and it had stuck in her mind. If this man was indeed Jonah's kin, he deserved to know his uncle was no longer living.

Slowly she relaxed her arms, allowing the weight of the weapon to pull the barrel downward. "I am sorry to tell you, Jonah is dead." Saying the words aloud jarred Annie, filling her with renewed sadness and a measure of the same disbelief now registering on her visitor's face. Even after two weeks, she could still hardly believe that the man she married only six weeks ago was no longer living.

"Your pa is dead?" Brock's soft voice held stunned disappointment.

"Oui. My papa *is* dead. But Jonah was not my papa. He was my husband."

Only a slight rise of his eyebrows revealed surprise at her statement.

"May I dismount? I've been riding for several hours, and I'd like to see my uncle's grave if he is buried here." He cast a wary glance down at Cap'n Brody.

"He is. Cap'n Brody, come here." At her call the dog moved away from the horse, but only far enough to allow the man room to dismount.

"You look nothing like Jonah." She voiced her thoughts while her gaze followed Brock's slow, deliberate movements as he dismounted and tied his horse to a low branch of a sycamore.

Though she kept hold of her musket, Cap'n Brody's congenial bark and happy swishing tail eased Annie's mind concerning the man's intent. Watching the dog trot over to greet Brock with a friendly lick on the hand, Annie remembered Jonah's comment that he'd stake his life on Cap'n Brody's appraisal of a man.

In his moccasin-clad feet, Brock Martin stood maybe a few inches short of six feet tall. As he walked toward her, his lean, muscular frame moved with a kind of tense grace that reminded Annie of a panther.

"Been told I took after my ma's family." His well-shaped lips tipped in an easy smile, and his gaze radiated a genuine friendliness.

"Hey, there, Big'un." He stopped to give Cap'n Brody a generous scratch between the ears, causing the dog to nuzzle his hand and beg for more attention.

Suddenly self-conscious, Annie reached up with jerky, ineffective motions, attempting to smooth unruly curls from her face. "I'm Annie—Annie Martin." She offered her hand in greeting.

His warm, strong fingers wrapped a bit tentatively around her proffered hand, as if not quite sure what to do with it. After an awkward pause, he gave it a little shake. "Brock Martin," he said with a quick laugh. "Reckon I said that already." The shy way his gaze scooted from hers reminded Annie of one of Obadiah and Bess Dunbar's little boys greeting her at church.

"I'll show you where he's buried." Hefting the musket in her right hand, she led him to the gravesite several yards east of the cabin. Despite Cap'n Brody's approval of the stranger, it wouldn't hurt to remind the man she was still armed.

Neither spoke as they waded through a whispering stand of fragrant, knee-high prairie grasses with Cap'n Brody lumbering between them. At last they stood before the row of little mounds. For a few moments, they allowed the happy chatter of birds and the constant, deep-throated gurgling of Piney Branch Creek along the ravine behind the cabin to fill the silence.

Brock stared at Jonah's fresh grave while Cap'n Brody began his usual low, mournful whine when near his late master's resting place. Annie couldn't describe Brock's look as one of grief, but there was certainly a sadness that spoke of regret.

"You've not seen him since he and his family moved here from

Kentucky?" Somehow a conversation with this man felt more comfortable with Jonah intervening, even if it be from the grave.

"I last saw him when I was five. I barely remember him." Brock's gaze remained fixed on the wooden slab bearing Jonah's name, age, and date of death. "What did he die of?"

Annie's throat tightened as she recounted how, two weeks ago, a neighbor had found Jonah dead a half mile from Fort Deux Fleuves with a Shawnee arrow in his back. Though theirs had not been a love match, she had held a fondness for her father's old friend who'd lately become her husband.

"I—I asked him to go to the fort." Annie's confession surprised her. She hadn't shared that with anyone else, even the preacher's wife, Bess Dunbar, who was like a surrogate mother to Annie. Since Jonah's death, the guilt she felt for that act had built up inside her with each passing day like a festering sore. As much as it hurt to say it aloud, it was high time she lanced it. It felt good to get it out.

She stole a sideways glance at Jonah's kinsman, wondering how he would react to that piece of information.

The sweet look of compassion on his face caused her eyes to sting. She sensed this man knew the devastating power of guilt.

He reached over and clasped her hand in his and gave it a quick, warm squeeze.

"Don't blame yourself," he said softly. "I reckon if anyone's to blame, it's old Tecumseh. He's got a good part of the Shawnee in Indiana Territory all worked up."

With a silent nod, Annie swallowed down the knot of tears that had gathered in her throat and returned Brock's kind smile. A portion of her guilt seeped away.

His attention drifted from Jonah's grave to each of the other four grave markers in turn. He stared for a moment at the weathered gray board bearing Clara Martin's name, then turned a questioning look to Annie. "What—what happened?"

Annie's gaze slid from Clara's marker to those of Clara and Jonah's three children, Patience, Grace, and William. "A bilious fever took them early last year. Losing them all at once like that hit Jonah really hard."

She shook her head and winced. "Such great sadness." It hurt to remember Jonah's inconsolable agony.

Glancing over at Brock's profile as he continued studying the grave markers, she couldn't begin to guess what might be going through his mind. "My papa insisted we stay with him for two weeks. He was afraid Jonah might do himself harm."

"Your father knew my uncle well?" His lack of knowledge about Jonah confirmed Annie's suspicion that Jonah and Brock's father had not been close.

"Oui. My papa, Gerard Blanchet, and Jonah served together in the War for Independence." Papa and Jonah had been like brothers as far back as Annie could remember. It seemed odd to know more about Jonah than his blood kin knew.

"Your father has not been gone long, then?" His gentle tone and tender look caused her to once again blink back hot tears.

"He died six weeks ago. Rabies." Annie saw the question in his eyes, yet appreciated his good manners not to ask why Jonah had chosen a seventeen-year-old girl for a wife. But perhaps because of his kindnesses, she felt compelled to satisfy his curiosity.

"That's why—that's why Jonah and I. . ."

"I understand," he murmured with a nod and look that told her he meant it.

She silently thanked the man for again rushing gallantly to her rescue.

Oddly, a measure of relief washed through her as she turned from the graves and started walking back to the cabin. Jonah was dead now, so it shouldn't matter whether or not his nephew approved of her marriage of convenience to his uncle. But she was glad that he at least seemed to have no ill feelings toward her.

Brock fell in step beside her with Cap'n Brody loping along, sniffing and nudging his hand. After a few steps, Brock cleared his throat and a tight, almost embarrassed tone crept into his voice.

"I remember Aunt Clara's letter to Ma in '05, saying the family had moved here to The Forks. I just can't rightly remember why."

Annie absently shoved her fingers into Cap'n Brody's scruffy coat. "After the war, Papa and Jonah were each given forty acres of land in Kentucky as payment for their military service."

Brock nodded. "Yes, I remember Pa mentioning Jonah's bounty land grant." His voice lifted as if happy to discover a shared knowledge.

"Papa was a trapper and trader: a *voyageur*." Annie couldn't help the pride that crept into her voice. "So he never settled on his Kentucky land. Before the war, he'd trapped here along the White and Muscatatuck Rivers and liked the place, so he came back to it. Seven years ago, treaties with the Indians opened up land here for sale."

Pausing, she glanced at Brock. Would he resent her father's influence over his kinsman? At his mute nod, she continued.

"Papa knew the land here was better for farming than what they'd been given in Kentucky. So he sold his bounty land grant there and talked Jonah into doing the same." Her words crept out slowly at first, as if testing the air. "Papa and Jonah used the money to buy land together, here."

Brock's reaction resembled nothing close to what she'd expected. Grinning, he shook his head as if in amazement and gave an odd little snort. "Reckon it runs in the family," he muttered.

When they reached the cabin's front door, Annie stopped, unsure what to do. It was impolite not to invite a visitor into one's home. Yet, for a woman to invite a man inside without a chaperone would be both scandalous and unwise.

Annie glanced about as if the answer might be found floating on the April breeze. "Would—would you like a cup of water or something to eat? I could bring something out. . . ."

"No. Please don't trouble yourself." His words rushed from his mouth as if he sensed her dilemma. He stuck his hand out toward her and a slow grin crept across his face. "Well, it was nice meeting you, Annie. I'm glad Uncle Jonah was not alone in his last days."

The confident strength in Brock's warm grasp suddenly

reminded Annie very much of Jonah. After administering Cap'n Brody's begged-for scratch behind the ears, Brock turned toward his horse, and Annie realized he'd never mentioned what he'd wanted to talk to Jonah about.

He untied his horse and, in one fluid motion, planted a foot in the stirrup and swung to the saddle with barely a creak of the leather. As he took up the reins, his gaze swept the area around them before settling back on Annie's face. "I just wish I'd had the chance to know him."

The regret in his voice touched Annie, making her long to tell him all she knew about Jonah. There was something about this man she found at once curious and compelling. Studying his handsome profile, it made her sad to think that after this one brief meeting, he would ride away and she would likely never see him again.

"Will you be staying at Fort Deux Fleuves?" The hopeful question bounded unbidden from her lips.

He frowned. Even at a distance, she could see his figure tense in the saddle. Once again, his face swung slowly around, his narrowed gaze scrutinizing the fields of infant wheat, the creek behind the cabin, and the woods beyond.

"No." The word snapped from his lips. At her raised brows, his tone moderated, and he glanced at the cabin behind her. "I–I'd hoped to stay here. . . ." His voice wilted, and a deep reddish hue suffused his features.

This time, it was Annie who hurried to Brock's rescue. "You should make yourself known to Preacher Obadiah Dunbar and his wife, Bess. There's never a stranger comes through these parts that the Dunbars don't offer their hospitality."

Annie felt pleased with herself when a look of interest lit his face. With the afternoon waning, he wouldn't want to be benighted without the protection of a sturdy cabin around him. And tomorrow was Sunday. She'd never known Bess to allow a guest to leave without partaking of their Sabbath meal.

"Besides," she said with a grin, "Papa, Jonah, and Obadiah would talk for hours about the war and their younger years. I imagine Obadiah could tell you stories about Jonah I haven't even heard."

She gave him quick directions to the Dunbar place, hoping she'd convinced him to seek out the preacher's homestead.

Brock's gray-green gaze seemed to study her face for a moment, making her stomach flutter as if it were filled with a swarm of butterflies.

"Much obliged, Annie. Believe I'll take your advice." His lips stretched in a lazy grin, and he nodded and tipped the brim of his hat at her. Wheeling his horse around, he kicked it into a canter in the direction of Obadiah and Bess Dunbar's farm.

Cap'n Brody's sorrowful whines echoed Annie's feelings exactly. She watched until the horse and rider disappeared over a hill, a herd of questions crowding her mind. Why had he just now come to see Jonah after all these years? And what exactly had caused the rift between Jonah and Brock's father in the first place?

Other more troubling questions crept to the front of her thoughts. Why had he seemed so skittish, especially when she'd asked if he planned to stay at Fort Deux Fleuves?

Heaving a sigh, she burrowed her fingers in the thick hair at the dog's neck. "Maybe Obadiah will convince him to stay for Sunday services tomorrow, and we'll learn more then, Cap'n."

The dog licked her hand in response, then slinked back into the cabin.

Annie continued to stare at the empty rise awash in the gold of the dipping sun, her doubts of ever seeing the man again growing with the shadows. Nothing in Brock Martin's conversation had suggested he was a Christian. Most likely, by dawn tomorrow, he'd leave the Deux Fleuves settlement behind.

She turned and stepped into the cabin. Still, no harm in freshening her best Sunday frock.

Chapter 2

Brock fidgeted on the split-log trestle bench, one of several that, on Sunday mornings, transformed the building from a garrison house and trading post into a makeshift church. According to Obadiah Dunbar, the building also regularly housed in its upper floor the occasional passing troop of soldiers. At the thought, beads of sweat broke out at Brock's hairline, though he'd been assured no such troops were presently about.

He rubbed his suddenly damp palms along the tops of his thighs. His every instinct screamed for him to bolt from his seat and race out the building's open door. Had he lost all reason? Why had he allowed the genial preacher and his wife to secure his promise to attend Sunday worship service here? Worship service. At the last moment, he managed to stifle a snort. He had no interest in worshipping a God who'd done nothing but take from him. Seven years ago, God had taken Brock's parents, leaving the sixteen-year-old orphan to bury his mother and father alone. And now fate—or God—had played a fiendish trick on Brock, stripping him of his second family, the army.

It seemed incredible that three short weeks ago, Brock had honorably held the rank of sergeant in the army of these United States and territories.

The events of the fateful evening that brought that life to an end for Brock played again in his mind like a recurring nightmare: Lieutenant Driscoll's arrogant sneer and the moonlight flashing on his sword as he lunged at Brock with the weapon. Brock falling backward onto the ground and instinctively lifting his six-inch sheath dagger in defense. Then the stunning swiftness of the next horrifying moments. Driscoll smashing his foot into a pile of horse manure, falling forward, and impaling himself on Brock's upturned dagger.

Willing himself not to shudder, Brock squeezed his eyes shut, trying to expunge the terrible vision of the lieutenant's stunned expression and wide, lifeless eyes staring into Brock's face. Brock might have remained there, frozen by shock, if a soldier hadn't happened upon the grisly scene and raised the alarm.

Never a favorite of his commanding officer, who was the dead man's uncle, Brock's choices were clear—flee or face a firing squad at dawn. So he'd fled. And the army, which had been his home and family for the past seven years, was now Brock's enemy.

Desperate for an ally to help him cheat the hangman and maybe even salvage his military career, Brock had sought out his war hero uncle for solace and counsel. But again, God had yanked that hope away as well. So why was he still here?

The answer strolled through the garrison house doorway, quickening Brock's heart to triple-time cadence. With her riot of mahogany curls, bright agate eyes fringed by long, sooty lashes, and alabaster skin decorated by beguiling freckles, Annie Martin simply took his breath away. He'd thought her fetching yesterday in her faded calico frock and bonnet with the spring wind playing through her lovely curls. Though pretty as a spring blossom, she'd appeared more child than woman as she struggled to hoist the brown Bess. Not today. Her black dress hugged her appealing curves, leaving no doubt it clad a woman grown. Her lively cinnamon eyes sought Brock, and her freckled cheeks tinted pink, causing a deep ache to burrow beneath his breastbone.

His mouth went dry. Yes. He knew why he would sit here through a sermon he didn't want to hear, risking capture should a troop of soldiers happen by. She flashed him a smile, and his mind went to mush. Answering with what he feared looked more like a silly grin than a smile, he knew he'd happily risk his life to spend a Sunday with Annie Martin.

Maybe today I'll get some answers.

Annie entered the garrison house knowing it wasn't answers she wanted from Brock Martin. What she wanted was exactly what she was receiving—smiling admiration from his handsome, now clean-shaven face. Her own face warming, she shot him a quick return smile and crossed the puncheon floor of the log structure.

With a nod of greeting to Bess Dunbar, Annie silently slipped into the rough-hewn pew beside her on the ladies' side of the room. For the next hour, with her open Bible on her lap, she strove to follow along with Obadiah's chosen sermon text.

She stared at God's Word, brightened by a beam of sunlight shafting through an open window, and felt ashamed. Normally, her spirit eagerly drank in Obadiah's sermons. But this morning, her attention kept drifting from the preacher's words.

Thoughts of Brock Martin made focusing on the scriptures difficult. She couldn't help wondering if he was a Christian. Glancing across the room at him, she noticed how he fidgeted in his seat, clearly uncomfortable in the gathering. Obviously, he was not used to attending worship services. The thought saddened her.

After Obadiah pronounced the benediction, Bess lifted her head and turned to Annie. "You comin' for Sunday dinner, Annie?"

Annie dragged her gaze from Brock, who now stood talking to Obadiah, back to Bess. "Yes." She hoped her bright tone didn't sound too eager. "If I'm not a bother."

"You know better than that, Annie." Bess's rosy cheeks pushed up, and her eyes glinted merrily as she bent to tie four-year-old Ruth's bonnet.

"It'll give you and Jonah's young kinsman a chance to become better acquainted. He seems a fine young man." Sending off her little daughter with a playful swat to the child's behind, Bess tilted her head up at Annie and gave her a teasing grin. "We thoroughly enjoyed his company last evening. I haven't seen Obadiah's spirits so lifted since before Jonah's death."

Annie's already warm face grew hotter. Bess considered herself something of a matchmaker. Although she'd voiced her concern about the thirty-four-year age difference between Annie and Jonah, in the end she endorsed their marriage. But for reasons Annie never fully understood, the preacher's wife had actively discouraged her friendship with nineteen-year-old Ezra Buxton, Annie's previous beau.

Bess glanced over at Brock, and her look grew pensive. "He seems a wanderer, though." Her teasing smile returned. "You ask me, he's just lookin' for a reason to put down roots." Her pointed look kept the fire stoked in Annie's face.

Though unable to deny her attraction to Jonah's nephew, Annie had hoped it didn't show so plainly. On the other hand, having always valued Bess's motherly advice, she found an odd comfort in the woman's attitude. The man had spent the night at the Dunbars' home and had obviously won their approval. Annie resisted asking Bess what she and Obadiah had learned of him, assuming his past would be shared later over the Dunbars' dinner table.

Bess clasped Annie's hand, and her eyes took on a look of entreaty. "If you could hurry ahead and check the dinner on the hearth I'd be much obliged. I promised Abbey Graham my croup remedy for her babies. I fear before I'm able to get home, that venison ham may be burned on one side and undone on the other."

"Yes, of course." A quick smile lifted Annie's lips. She was always glad to repay in some small way the charity Bess and Obadiah had lavished on her since Papa's and Jonah's deaths.

When Bess bustled off to coo over the Grahams' two-year-old twins, Annie turned toward Obadiah and Brock. She would give Obadiah a word of appreciation for his sermon, then hurry on to see about the dinner.

Across the crowded room, her gaze linked for a moment with Brock's. He sent her a smile that scared up another swarm of butterflies in her stomach. Their beating wings fanned the flames in her cheeks as she again felt a flash of attraction.

Espèce d'imbécile! The French words leaped to her mind as she called herself an idiot. Bess had said he seemed a wanderer. *By tonight he will be gone. And good riddance.* The last thing she needed was for him to stay and join the chorus of those trying to convince her to sell her land.

She turned away to hide her blush and found herself staring into Ezra Buxton's scowling countenance.

"Ma says you're welcome to Sunday dinner." Ezra glanced at Brock then back to Annie. His stormy features cleared a bit. He shifted his slight frame and brushed a straggling lock of sandy hair from his face. "She's fixin' to fry up a passel of spring rabbits me and Pa snared."

Annie had always liked Polly Buxton. Once, she had happily anticipated becoming Polly's daughter-in-law. She looked over at the slight woman whose pinched features seemed to disappear within her gray bonnet.

When Annie turned back to Ezra, it was the prospect of his mother's disappointment that tinged her voice with genuine regret. "Tell your ma thanks, but I've already accepted an invite from Bess Dunbar."

The thunderclouds returned to Ezra's lowered brow. He glanced in Brock's direction, then turned back to Annie. "Ma said she reckoned you might want to visit with yer kin."

His shoulder lifted in a quick shrug. But despite his attempt to show indifference, Annie saw disappointment flicker in his light blue eyes. "I understand he's jist passin' through. Reckon me and you'll be spendin' plenty of Sundays together soon enough."

Annie's back stiffened at Ezra's self-assured tone. It rankled her that he assumed they would take up their relationship where they'd left off at Annie's marriage to Jonah. Though she didn't understand exactly why, her feelings for Ezra had decidedly cooled.

She lifted her chin and gave him a chilly stare. "Monsieur Martin is *Jonah's* kin, not mine. And how I spend my Sundays is of my own choosing." Ezra needed to know he was not entitled to her affection. He'd have to win it. Whirling away, she stomped toward the front door. But before she could step outside, Brock's bright voice halted her.

"Annie, it's nice to see you again—especially without a musket in your hands." A grin parted his lips. The twinkle in his eyes suggested he found her agitated demeanor amusing.

Still perturbed by Ezra's earlier self-assured arrogance, she blurted, "Since men are so pigheaded, a loaded musket may be the only way a woman can get their attention."

His gray-green gaze seemed to melt into hers. "Annie Martin, you'll never need a musket to get a man's attention."

The quiet reply set her insides quivering. Flustered, she turned and hurried through the garrison house door without stopping to compliment Obadiah on his sermon. She almost wished she'd taken Ezra up on his offer of Sunday dinner. At least she knew how to handle Ezra, and he didn't do funny things to her stomach.

The Dunbars' two-story cabin sat only a few hundred yards outside Fort Deux Fleuves. Piney Branch, the same little creek that meandered through the stockade, rippled along the cabin's westerly side. The Dunbars laid claim to fifteen acres—not much on which to support a family of eight. But in payment for his preaching, Obadiah's faithful flock never allowed the family to want for anything the settlement could provide.

Annie lifted the leather latchstring affixed to the cabin door and pushed the heavy barrier open. Inside, a delicious bouquet of rich aromas, including roasting venison, corn bread, and a mixture of spiced apples and sassafras, greeted her. Her stomach growled, reminding her of the breakfast she'd decided to forgo.

As always, she was struck by the roominess of the Dunbars' cabin, nearly twice the size of her own. A great fireplace seven feet wide and nearly five feet tall surrounded by a cat-and-clay chimney dominated the back wall.

She swept the tidy domicile with an admiring gaze. Bess, with help from her thirteen-year-old daughter Dorcas and nine-year-old daughter Lydia, kept a remarkably neat home. Since her marriage, Annie had striven to achieve the same degree of domestic order in her own cabin. Once again, she felt the familiar stab of guilt-laced sadness. She wished she'd had the time to prove to Jonah she could be a good, industrious wife.

She stepped to the hearth and gave the spit holding a large venison ham a half turn. Juices dripped from the sizzling meat, sending up tiny puffs of gray ash as they hit the glowing coals below. A mess of dandelion greens and pork hocks bubbled in a kettle hanging from the crane built into the fireplace. A telltale *hiss* told her the kettle's contents were dangerously close to boiling dry.

On the floor near the hearth, she spotted a bucket of spring water with a dried-gourd dipper floating atop it. She ladled several gourd-fulls of water into the kettle, then began stirring the contents with a long-handled paddle.

The sound of voices outside pulled her attention to the front door. In a wave of chaotic merriment, Obadiah and Bess, along with their six children and Brock Martin, spilled through the cabin's doorway.

Brock gave Annie a smiling nod that sent her heart thumping, then joined Obadiah and the two older Dunbar boys at the maple table in the center of the room.

Bess bustled to the hearth, trailed by her three daughters and youngest son, Isaac.

"Oh, thank you for seeing to the dinner, Annie." She puffed out the words as she snatched a wooden paddle and raked the hickory coals from the lid of the footed spider skillet. Then, grabbing a scrap of linsey-woolsey from a hearthside hook to protect her hand, she lifted the skillet's lid and gingerly tapped the golden-brown corn bread. "This looks perfect," she said, shooting Annie a pleased smile.

Throughout the meal's preparation, Annie inclined an interested ear toward the conversation between Obadiah and Brock. But when they all gathered around the table, she realized Brock had said very little about himself. Instead, he'd chosen to share stories his father had told him of Henry's and Jonah's boyhood escapades. And as entertaining as the stories were, Annie realized they shed no light whatsoever on the man seated opposite her.

Well into the meal and still with no answers forthcoming to any of the questions buzzing around in her brain, Annie's curiosity at last broke free of its constraints.

As she drizzled honey onto a piece of steaming corn bread, she glanced over at Brock. "Monsieur Martin, you never said for what reason you came to seek out Jonah after all these years."

Brock visibly squirmed. His gaze refused to meet hers, and he seemed to study the hunk of pork hock nestled in the pile of dandelion greens on his plate. "Reckon I just thought it was time to mend some family fences," he murmured.

To Annie's ears, his answer didn't ring entirely true. But neither did it ring entirely false. That he was orphaned as a youth, something Annie had learned some years ago from Jonah, was the only tidbit about himself Brock readily volunteered.

"And in what sort of work have you employed yourself since?" Getting information from the man was like boning a minnow, slippery and tedious to the point of exasperation.

"Oh, a little of this and a little of that, I suppose." With the unsatisfactory answer, he avoided her gaze and forked a chunk of venison into his mouth.

Unlike Annie, Obadiah and Bess Dunbar seemed perfectly happy with whatever crumbs of information the man cared to offer. Annie had always admired the Dunbars' willingness to accept all who crossed their path, regardless of their pasts. But at the moment, she wished their curiosity more closely resembled her own.

When all had eaten their fill and the children were excused from the table, Obadiah's attitude turned quietly thoughtful. Without saying a word, he rose and crossed to the wall-peg bed nestled in a corner of the room. He knelt down, reached beneath the bed, and pulled out a small, wooden box, then raised his robust frame with a soft groan.

As he carried the box to the table, Annie couldn't guess what it might contain.

Obadiah removed the box's lid and lifted out a folded square of yellowed paper. His expression somber, he unfolded the paper and regarded first Annie and then Brock.

"I'm glad you are both here, because I have something you need to see." Obadiah handed the paper to Brock.

Brock's eyes widened and his face paled as he scanned the document. After a long moment, he held the paper out to Annie.

Curious beyond endurance and a little frightened, Annie snatched the missive from Brock's frozen hand and began reading.

"I, Jonah Martin, being of sound body and mind, do bequeath my lands and earthly goods to my surviving wife, Annie Blanchet Martin. And equally, if he yet lives, to my nephew, Brock Martin."

Chapter 3

"The chimney will need to be fixed." Annie's tone was matter-of-fact as she led Brock into the tiny trapper's cabin.

Her chilly demeanor hadn't thawed one iota in the three days since they'd read Jonah's instructions concerning the land. The realization saddened Brock, but he had no idea how he might remedy it.

After getting past the initial shock of learning he'd co-inherited his uncle's land, Brock's first inclination was to turn his back on the bequest. But a barrage of emotions, some he understood and some he didn't, kept him here.

Leaving a helpless girl alone to tend land that was half his responsibility didn't sit well with him. Besides that, he had no clear idea of where else he might go.

He could probably head west, disappear beyond the Mississippi River and take his chances in the wilderness as a mountain man. Since Lewis and Clark returned from their expedition into the Unknown half a dozen years ago, many men had done just that to escape a bad marriage, the law, or, as in Brock's case, the army.

But Brock had no intention of spending the rest of his days branded as a deserter. All he needed was a little time to figure out how to prove his innocence. And Deux Fleuves settlement seemed as good a place as any to do the figuring.

Obadiah Dunbar had suggested Annie move in with them while Brock stayed in his uncle's cabin to tend the crops. A grin tugged at Brock's mouth as he remembered Annie's reaction to the notion.

Stiffening to her full height of barely five feet, she'd planted her hands firmly on her trim hips and glared at both Brock and Obadiah. Her agate eyes flashed dangerously, and even the honey-colored freckles marching across the narrow bridge of her pert little nose seemed to stand at attention. After a volley of caustic-toned French that Brock only partially understood, she declared, "Monsieur Martin may stay wherever he likes except my cabin. Jonah may be dead, but I'm still his widow, and I am not leaving my home!"

Obadiah Dunbar had, from their first meeting, impressed Brock as a wise man. His surrender in the face of Annie's immovable stance only bolstered Brock's initial opinion. The preacher had rushed to calm Annie, who'd looked for all the world like a bantam hen with her neck stretched and feathers flaring angrily. Obadiah had then cautiously ventured an alternative suggestion. Perhaps Brock could stay in the little trapper's cabin Gerard Blanchet had built about a half mile from Jonah's place.

The proposal proved a favorable solution to both Annie and Brock. It would be far enough away from Annie's cabin to satisfy propriety, yet close enough for Brock to tend the crops.

Brock enthusiastically seized upon the plan. The notion of being viewed an usurper left a bad taste in his mouth. And, he had to admit, he'd be tempted to forgo shelter altogether if it might help him to wriggle back into Annie's good graces.

He ducked into the dark interior of the little log structure. Tamped smooth, the dirt floor bore an almost slatelike hardness. A dozen or so iron traps hung from the east wall along with a few small animal pelts. Only a couple of stools and two straw pallets covered with buffalo hides served as furnishings. The place smelled of animal skins, earth, and neglect.

Annie walked to the hearth at the cabin's north end. She looked up at the cat-and-clay chimney where Brock could see several large cracks.

"The earthquake damaged it back in December," she said flatly. "Papa got sick before he had a chance to fix it."

Brock panned the room, wishing he could think of something to say that might ease the tension between them. Discontent niggled at him like an itch he couldn't quite reach. He hated that his inclusion in Jonah's instructions regarding the land had soured

Annie toward him. Why his uncle named him as cobeneficiary would most likely forever remain a mystery.

His first inclination had been to assure Annie he had no long-term interest in part ownership of his uncle's land—or in farming. However, something halted him from rashly voicing that thought. It was clear that, unless compelled to do so, this stubborn girl would resist any assistance with Jonah's farm. Brock's partial claim to the land forced her to accept his help. But other, more selfish reasons lurked in the shadows of his mind, preventing his outright withdrawal from the claim.

Brock joined her at the chimney. Reaching up, he ran his palm across the cool brownstones, then poked his head into the fireplace and peered up at the chimney's interior. Other than a half-dozen or so sleeping bats, he saw nothing amiss. Despite the fissures in the structure's facade, he detected only minimal damage.

"It looks sound." Ducking out of the chimney, he rubbed soot from his hands onto his pant legs. "I have to commend your pa on a right solid job of building this cabin. I'd say a little clay to fix the cracks is all that's required to set it right."

She rewarded his compliment with a smile that sent unexpected heat marching up his neck.

"Was the quake not so bad here, then?" Brock asked to cover his unease. He remembered the widespread destruction the earthquakes had done to the area around Newport, Kentucky, and Cincinnati, Ohio, last December and January.

Fear flickered in Annie's eyes. "The shaking was awful," she murmured somberly, hugging her arms around her body. "*Je vous dis la vérité.* I thought the earth was going to swallow us up before it quit." A little shudder shook her slight shoulders. "I remember thinking I was going to die in the same cabin I was born in."

The vulnerable look in her eyes evoked a feeling of protectiveness in Brock. For all her starch, Annie was but a girl left all alone in the wilderness—too naive and stubborn to know just how scared she should be.

Brock resisted the impulse to wrap her in his arms. The action would more than likely be misconstrued, and the last thing he needed was to feed his undeniable attraction to his uncle's young widow. Instead, he gave her a solemn nod, then quirked a grin. "It near flattened Newport Barracks. Threw me plumb out o' my bunk, and sent seasoned soldiers runnin' from the barracks out into the winter night barefoot, dressed only in long johns."

Annie perked up. The look of surprised interest on her face alerted Brock to his mistake.

"You were in the army?"

Sometime in the future he would need to tell her—make a clean breast of it all. But not now—not here.

"I did a bit of scoutin' for the army out of Newport Barracks, just across the river from Cincinnati," he murmured, hoping his true but meager reply would sufficiently slake her interest.

The wrinkle knitting her trim dark brows together told him it hadn't.

Before she could lob another volley of uncomfortable questions at him, Brock decided to apply the time-tested military strategy of diversion. He walked to the window, feigning interest in the piece of greased fawn hide covering it.

"You said you were born here. Is this where you and your pa lived before you married Jonah?"

Annie walked to a pile of straw covered with a buffalo robe and plopped down, sending up a little puff of dust. "Oui, but up until two years ago, we mostly lived on the riverside in camps along Papa's trapline."

Sensing a thawing in her attitude toward him, Brock lowered himself to the floor and sat cross-legged, hoping to encourage her conversational mood.

Her uplifted face turned as she took in the cabin's interior. "Papa was a squatter on this place when it was still Indian lands, long before it was opened up to white settlers. He built this cabin for my mama before I was born." An appealing dimple appeared at the corner of her mouth. "Papa liked to tell how some months before I was born, Mama got powerful tired of traveling the rivers.

One day she got her Irish all up and said, 'I'll not be havin' me wee one born out in the open like a savage, Gerard Blanchet! You'll be buildin' me and the babe a proper roof o'er our heads, or I'll build it meself!'"

Brock couldn't help a chuckle. Obviously, the daughter had inherited her mother's fiery spirit.

"Your mother was Irish?" From what he'd heard, trappers more often chose Indian women for wives.

"Oui." Annie's eyes glistened with unshed tears, making Brock sorry he'd probed the painful subject. But after a few brave blinks, a smile lit her face, and she seemed happy to expound. "Papa met Mama at a trading post on the Wabash River just north of Vincennes. She'd been brought over from Ireland in 1791 as a bond servant to a well-to-do English family."

Brock knew that Fort Sackville near Vincennes had been an English possession before Colonel George Rogers Clark defeated the British, but he thought the English had left after that.

"I thought Clark and his boys rousted the British back in '79."

Annie nodded. "Most of them, but a few stayed on after the war and settled there."

A dark look crossed her face, and her voice hardened. "The family who owned Mama's bond treated her cruelly, so she ran away. She got as far as one of the trading posts just north of Vincennes when her bond master caught up with her."

Her eyes held a distant look as she gazed out the cabin's open door. "Papa had been trapping along the Wabash. He'd brought a season's worth of beaver pelts to trade when he came upon Mama being beaten by her bond master."

She turned back to him and smiled, displaying again, the fetching dimple he'd noticed earlier. Pride laced her voice, which lifted with her brightened demeanor. "Papa traded away every pelt he had to buy Mama's freedom."

Both surprised and pleased that she should share such intimate family history with him, Brock began to hope he and Annie could at least be friends. He sat transfixed, beguiled by both the story and its charming narrator. "I think I would have liked your papa very much," he said at last.

Her answering smile ignited a warm glow that radiated all the way through him, while stoking his hope that they could, indeed, become friends.

As their gazes locked, a lovely pink hue suffused Annie's cheeks beneath the golden dappling of freckles. Suddenly she stood and turned her full attention to swiping dust from her faded brown calico skirt.

"Well," she said, sounding a little breathless, "you've seen the cabin, and I should be getting back. I left Cap'n Brody guarding my mule and cow, but he can't very well do the milking now, can he?" A hint of nervousness warbled through her little laugh.

Brock scrambled to his feet, his heart soaring at her obvious attempt to cover her disconcertion. It told him she, too, had felt a connection during their shared look. Even if she didn't consider him a friend, perhaps she no longer viewed him as a foe.

Annie turned and kicked at the straw pallet with her bare foot, plumping up the indentation she'd made sitting on it. *"Aïe!"*

Reaching down, she rubbed her toe, then lifted a shaggy brown corner of the buffalo robe, uncovering a little wooden box.

She gave a muted gasp. *"J'avais oublié!* I'd forgotten about this."

She picked up the box and lifted the lid. Her eyes brimmed with tears. One clung for a moment to her lashes like a drop of crystal morning dew before a blink sent it meandering unheeded down her cheek.

The sight pricked Brock's heart.

"These were Papa's treasures." Her solemn voice sounded breathless as she fingered through the box's contents.

Feeling somewhat like an intruder, Brock watched silently as she reverently touched each article.

She unrolled a piece of paper on which the shadowlike profile of a lady had been drawn in charcoal. The name *Fiona* was visible beneath the picture.

A fond smile tipped Annie's lips. "A silhouette of Mama," she explained. "Papa traded a traveling artist six beaver pelts for this." That musical little giggle Brock found so captivating bubbled out as she lifted an auburn coil of hair from the box. "My baby hair," she said before dropping the clipped tress back into the box.

Suddenly her mood changed. With a look Brock could only describe as pride, she held out her open palm in which lay a yellowed cotton twill chevron.

Brock needed no explanation for the scrap of V-shaped cloth. It was the insignia worn on the left sleeve of an American soldier who'd served at least two years of exemplary service during the War for Independence.

Annie's chin lifted an inch or two. "Papa earned this by running through a volley of musket fire to drag four wounded men, including Jonah, to safety."

Respect for both the father and the daughter bloomed inside Brock. From what he had just learned of her parents, Brock better understood the glimpses of bravery and spunk he'd witnessed in Annie.

"Your papa was a true hero," he told her with a smile.

Annie nodded, dropped the cloth back into the box, and snapped the lid shut. "Papa always said, '*Les soldat combattent, mais les poltrons s'enfuient.*' A soldier fights, but a coward runs."

Brock's heart dropped like a stone to the pit of his stomach. With that one statement, all hope of winning Annie's friendship and respect withered. He had no doubt that when she learned what he'd done, the only sentiment Brock would be able to generate in this daughter of Gerard and Fiona Blanchet would be contempt.

Chapter 4

"*C'est inutile!*"

The French words expressing her useless efforts exploded from Annie's lips on a burst of frustration. She had tried three times to harness the mule to the plow without success.

Fighting the urge to sob, she watched the mule lope toward the grassy creek bank, its harness traces trailing behind.

She kicked at a clod of dirt with her bare foot, scattering it in a shower of sandy loam. How was she to get five acres of corn planted if she couldn't even hitch the mule to the plow?

Leaning backward, she pushed her shoulder blades together to ease her aching back, and looked at the field unmolested by the plowshare. The gray-brown stubble of last year's corn crop dotted the land. Poking up amid weeds and prairie grasses, they seemed to mock her efforts to bury them beneath the soil and prepare the ground to accept a new crop of corn.

Although not raised to farming, Annie was well aware that the couple of acres each of wheat and oats Jonah had sowed would not be sufficient to keep her and the animals through the winter. How many times had she heard Jonah say, "A farm fails or succeeds on its corn crop"?

With Joel Tanner's new grist mill on the Piney Branch, a good corn crop would be like gold. Proving she could bring in a decent crop would silence those folks, however well-meaning, who continued to urge her to sell the land.

The appearance of Jonah's nephew intensified her need to make the land pay. Jonah's instructions had sent a chill whooshing through her like a January wind. She knew little of the law. Brock was Jonah's blood kin—and a *male*. Over the past seven years, Papa had allowed Jonah to clear and farm the most fertile, level acres of her father's land. Plenty long enough for Jonah—*or Jonah's blood*

26

kin—to stake a claim to the property.

Thoughts of the man sent worrisome emotions swirling through Annie. She hadn't seen Brock since she'd shown him the trapper's cabin three days ago.

Remembering the day, Annie's face grew warm. She regretted having shared so much of her family history with him. And allowing him to see her tears.

What could this land mean to a drifter? It was true he'd shown genuine respect for Jonah's and her father's military service. But Annie could hardly imagine such a man feeling obliged to keep Jonah's land and pass it on as tribute to an uncle he'd hardly known. Papa and Jonah placed this land into her keeping, and nobody was going to rip it from her!

Stiffening her back, she lifted her chin in defiance. She *would* plant this field. *God help me, I must plant a corn crop!* The scripture she clung to like a lifeline leaped to the front of her mind and vaulted from her lips. " 'I can do all things through Christ which strengtheneth me.' "

Renewed vigor surged through Annie's aching muscles on a wave of determination. She tromped toward the stupidly content draft animal munching on Indian grass. Paying scant heed to the throaty barks of Cap'n Brody who romped several yards away, she grasped the mule's harness lines. The sound of beating wings told her the dog had flushed another bevy of birds from a nearby thicket.

"Right nice o' you to unhitch the mule for a rest, but it don't look like she's done enough to deserve it yet." Brock's teasing tone yanked Annie around.

Her heart fluttered at the sight of him.

Espèce d'imbécile!

Scolding herself, she decided her rapid pulse was the result of him startling her. "Don't you know better than to sneak up on folks?"

Musket in hand, he scanned the area, a habit she'd noticed before. "I did no such thing. Cap'n Brody, here, announced my arrival while I was still several yards away." He reached down to rub the dog's brindled head. "Didn't you, Big'un?"

Cap'n Brody, his tail swishing with glee, nuzzled Brock's hand until he received the desired scratch behind the ears.

"I suppose you are an expert at farming." Annie met Brock's maddening grin with a scowl and felt heat rush to her face. Was this his plan? To convince her she couldn't handle the farm?

Squinting, he glanced at the sun riding high in the pale blue sky, to the grazing mule, then back to Annie. "Reckon I'm more expert than you. Don't you know how to hitch a mule to a plow?"

Annie fixed him with a glare. "I was about to get her hitched." She pushed against the mule's haunches in a desperate attempt to position the animal in front of the plow. Her efforts only elicited a bray of objection from the unmovable beast.

"Of course you were." Brock's grin widened. He laid his musket on the ground and took the harness lines from her hand.

Annie's indignation at his mocking tone was swamped by the rising hope that he might actually perform the perplexing chore. To her relief, he began to do just that.

"I thought I'd come over and take a better look at the land, seein' as how it's half mine," he said as he worked.

The fear Annie had tried to squelch for the better part of the past week flared inside her. "So you plan to stay in Deux Fleuves?" She held her breath, unsure what answer she preferred to hear.

"For now." He shot her a grin as he finished the task.

Something akin to disappointment boiled up inside Annie. Just as she suspected, he had no interest in keeping the land—or passing it on to later generations.

"You may look at the land at your leisure, Monsieur Martin, but I have work to do."

She snatched the harness lines from where he'd draped them over the plow and tried to remember how Jonah and other farmers she'd seen accomplished the task. She couldn't figure out how to knot the lines together to hook them over her shoulder as Jonah had done. Holding the lines in her left hand while grasping the plow's handles, she managed to give the lines an awkward flick against the mule's back. "Sal, *marche!*"

Nothing happened.

"Uh, have you ever done this before?" Brock stood with his arms crossed over his chest and his lips tipped up in an infuriating grin.

A brew of exasperation and irritation bubbled up in Annie. She wasn't sure if she was angrier at Brock or the mule. She had to prove that she was capable of farming this land. *Dear Lord, please make this stupid mule move!* She smacked the leather reins harder against Sal's back. "Giddup, Sal!"

Unfazed, Sal stood still, nibbling at a patch of clover. The only indication the mule gave that she felt the harness line against her rump was a sweeping swish of her tail.

Brock stepped to Annie's side. "Why don't you let me do this?" He glanced down at her bare feet peeking from beneath the hem of her faded brown calico skirt. "You have no business trying to plow in bare feet. Don't you know the corn stubbles'll tear 'em to pieces?"

Annie wanted to cry. She hadn't thought of the corn stubbles. She hadn't thought of anything beyond getting these five acres plowed.

Her shoulders sagged with her heart as she reluctantly relinquished the harness lines into his hand. She'd wanted to prove she could manage this farm, but instead had proven the opposite.

"H'ya, girl!"

At Brock's barked order, Sal obediently began plodding forward.

Annie watched him follow the plow as it turned the stubble and weeds to a neat row of rich, dark earth. Practicality soothed her injured pride. He'd all but said he didn't plan on putting down roots here. What would it hurt if he helped get a corn crop in before he moved on? As he said, he *was* part owner. If he was still around when the crop came in, she would give him a generous share of the ground meal to keep or trade.

"Whoa, girl!" Brock tugged on the harness lines when he came round again to where Annie stood. Smiling, he lifted his hat and ran the back of his forearm across his brow. "First time I've plowed in ages, but I have to say, this ground's a pure joy to work."

Hope sprung up in Annie that maybe after all she could salvage her pride and show Brock she could work the land as well as he. Surely now that Sal had done a row, the mule would understand what was expected of her.

Annie lifted her chin and projected what she hoped was a confident tone. "I appreciate you getting Sal in the notion to work, but it's my land to plow. I'll put on a pair of moccasins and—"

"Annie, I have no idea why Uncle Jonah decided to bequeath half of his land to me. Nor do I have any desire to take what is rightfully yours." His look held an unexpected kindness that caused rogue tears to sting Annie's eyes.

Pivoting his gaze for a moment toward the turned earth, he paused as if measuring his words before lifting his face again to hers. "I do, however, feel an obligation to see that Jonah's crop is planted and his widow is secure before the snow flies again." His gray-green eyes shone with earnestness. "Please, Annie, let me do this. Let me feel I have, in some small way, earned Uncle Jonah's trust in me."

The plea was impossible to refuse. Annie nodded. "All right." A grin tugged at the corner of her mouth. "I suppose I'm in no position to turn down help."

When their gazes met, an understanding seemed to pass between them. Annie wondered if this was God's way of making her situation benefit both her and Brock.

She glanced up at the noonday sun. "You'll be thirsty and hungry soon. I'll bring you a bucket of water later and something to eat."

"I appreciate that." With another quick grin, he turned his attention back to the mule and plow.

Annie allowed herself one last look at his broad-shouldered form following the plow before she headed back to the cabin, Cap'n Brody at her heels.

Two hours later, she met Brock at the edge of the plowed field, a bucket of water in one hand and a basket of food in the other.

Smiling widely, he strode toward her. His wet auburn hair

glistened in the sun, and his hands and forearms extending from rolled-up sleeves, dripped with water. "I washed up the best I could in the creek."

His soft voice and shy glance did peculiar things to Annie's heart. She was glad for the diversion of Cap'n Brody, who loped up to join them. With a cursory sniff at the basket of stew and bread, the dog pranced to Brock and poked out his pink tongue to lavish wet licks on his new friend's hands.

Chuckling, Brock greeted Cap'n Brody with hearty pats and scratches behind the dog's ears before relieving Annie of her burdens. He grinned at the dog. "I might have to fight you for these victuals, old boy. They smell mighty good." Falling in step with Annie as she headed for the shade of a sycamore, he angled his grin in her direction, making her heart flutter.

When they reached the tree, Annie pulled a generous-sized hambone from the basket. "Do not worry, Cap'n. I did not forget you." She tossed the bone to a bare spot in the grass a few feet away and the dog pounced on his prize with a happy bark.

Annie and Brock settled themselves in the shade of the tree, and Annie busied herself ladling rabbit stew from a tin into two wooden bowls, hoping her halting, awkward movements didn't betray her nervousness. For most of her life, she'd dined alone with men—either Papa or Jonah. It was stupid of her to feel nervous with Brock. Yet she did.

She dipped a mug into the bucket of water and handed it to him. "You have gotten much done." Striving for an unaffected voice, she glanced at the plowed furrows.

He took a deep drink of the water and drew the back of his forearm across his mouth. "I reckon I've plowed nearly half an acre. I've worked up a right-smart hunger, and this stew sure smells good." A wide grin accompanied his compliment. He turned his focus to the bowl of thick stew cradled in his lap and lifted a spoonful to his mouth.

Watching him chew, Annie frowned. Though he might not be an especially devout Christian, it bothered her that he would so carelessly dispense with the mealtime prayer of thanksgiving. Neither had Papa been devout in his faith, but he'd always remembered his upbringing by the French nuns and crossed himself before each meal.

She glared at Brock and honed a sharp edge to her voice. "I am glad the meal is to your liking, Monsieur Martin. All the more reason to thank our heavenly Father for it, do you not agree?"

He stopped eating and his expression reminded Annie of Cap'n Brody's when she scolded the dog for lapping from a fresh bucket of milk. "Yes, of course," he mumbled, and dropped his spoon back into the bowl.

Annie offered up a short prayer, which was followed by a stretch of strained silence interrupted only by Cap'n Brody's contented growls as he gnawed on the bone and the thump, thump, thump of his tail on bare ground.

At length, Brock cleared his throat. "I reckon if the weather holds, I can get the rest of the field plowed by this time next week." He shoveled another spoonful of stew into his mouth and gazed at the work he'd done.

Annie nodded mutely and took a sip of water. Though it felt a bit like ceding her responsibility and therefore her claim on the land, she saw nothing to be gained in arguing with him about who should do the plowing. It only made sense for him to finish the task, as he could accomplish it much faster than she ever would. Besides, there would be plenty of work for her to do when it came time for the planting and hoeing.

He polished off the last of the stew. Looking more than a little disconcerted, he stood and handed her the empty bowl. "Thank you for the fine meal, Annie. Can't remember having a better bowl of stew." His lips tipped up in a gentle, almost sad smile, and the fluttering began in her chest again. "I"—he paused and glanced down as if in thought, then raised his gaze back to hers—"I enjoyed it very much."

"I am glad you liked it." Why did she sound so breathless? "I will send some with you when you leave."

"I'd like that." His gaze deepened, and she suddenly realized they were both still holding the empty bowl. She tugged it from his grasp and their fingers grazed. Heat suffused her face.

He only grinned and turned and strode to where the mule stood munching grass.

For a long moment, Annie stood watching him from a distance, the butterflies in her chest flitting madly. She must be daft to let Brock Martin's charms disarm her. She mustn't forget that if he wanted, he could take her land, at least the forty acres that belonged to Jonah. Even if he didn't, he'd be gone by the end of planting. Besides, he obviously wasn't a Christian. And didn't Obadiah warn against becoming unequally yoked with a nonbeliever?

"Annie." The male voice behind Annie made her jump, jolting her from her reverie.

She turned to face Ezra Buxton, surprise and irritation vying for dominance inside her. She thought she'd made it clear to him that she was not interested in renewing their relationship. "What do you want, Ezra?" She didn't bother to blunt her sharp tone.

Frowning, he glanced at Brock's distant figure, plodding behind the plow.

"Thought you oughta know. Folks are talkin'. Some sayin' it ain't fittin', you and him bein' out here together. I reckon it ain't any of my business, but—"

"Oui. It *is* none of your business! And we are not together." Anger flared inside Annie. With difficulty, she ignored the temptation to ask who was saying disparaging things about her. But she refused to become a party to ugly gossip. As for Ezra, he was obviously trying to be helpful, albeit in his own clumsy way. She tempered her voice. "You can tell anyone who is interested that Brock is staying in Papa's trapper's cabin. He is helping me with the farming, that is all."

"Brock, huh?" Ezra's voice dripped with disdain. He glanced at the plowed field, then down at his hands curling the ends of his hat brim and back to Annie's face. A deep sigh puffed from his lips. "Look, I jist think it might be best if we got hitched as soon as possible, that's all."

Once she might have welcomed such a proposal from Ezra. No more. Perhaps it was her marriage to Jonah. But for whatever reason, her feelings for Ezra had definitely cooled. At the same time, she could see how he would not understand such a change and would think the two of them could simply take up where they had left off before her marriage. Taking a deep breath, she strove for patience and gentled her tone. Pressing her hand on his forearm, she prayed he might understand her feelings when she didn't entirely understand them herself. "I am sorry, Ezra, but I am not looking to marry again so soon."

Frowning, he cocked his head toward the plowed field. "Is it him?"

"Non!" The word leaped more forcefully than she would have liked from her lips.

Ezra blew a frustrated sounding breath from his nostrils. "Let Jonah's kin have his share of the land, Annie. That German family homesteadin' just east of here would buy your land in an eyeblink, and they have gold." His eyes turned wistful and enthusiasm infused his voice. "Your share would bring enough money to buy us a right nice Conestoga. I hear tell there's better land than this for the takin' out west, along the Mississippi. What'ya say, Annie? Let's get a whole new clean start." He slipped his arm around her waist and lowered his face toward hers.

"Non! Don't, Ezra!" Annie pulled away, a new blaze of anger sizzling inside her. How dare he think he could force his affections on her. "I promised Papa on his deathbed I would keep this land, it is for that reason I married Jonah. This land is my *mérite des ancêtres*— my birthright. I will not sell it to the Hoffmeiers or anyone else!"

Ezra sent another narrow-eyed glare at the field, and an ugly sneer twisted his mouth. Giving a derisive snort, he clapped his hat on his head. "You jist might change your mind when word gets out to the settlement that you and that feller's been keepin' company out here!"

Chapter 5

Brock slathered another fistful of wet clay onto the chimney, and tried without success to suppress the notion growing by the minute in his brain.

With the small, flat piece of board he'd been using to repair the cracked chimney, he smoothed out the glob of clay. Yet, despite his diligent attempt to focus fully on the work at hand, the insidious thought continued to slink out to both torture and to tempt.

He flung the board down to the floor with a clatter. "It's not fair! Why does it have to be this way?" Shoving mud-encrusted fingers through his hair, he tried to obliterate the thought.

He slumped to the nearby stool in defeat and surrendered to the idea that had not let him be since it first slithered through the doorway of his mind two days ago.

When he'd learned of Uncle Jonah's death, his hope of securing exoneration for the death of Hamilton Driscoll shriveled. But now he realized, fate, Providence, or whatever one might care to call it, had provided another avenue through which he could pursue his claim of innocence.

The land. Even half profit from the sale of the land and the promised crop should more than pay for the services of a sharp Philadelphia lawyer who could competently plead Brock's case.

The thought gouged mercilessly at his heart. It most likely meant he would have to oppose Annie. As the only surviving male blood relative of Jonah Martin, Brock had no doubt he would be granted full control of the property if he so wished.

A deep groan bubbled up from some desolate cavern inside him. He had turned the problem over and over in his head—had barely slept for two days. Yet no other solution seemed viable.

The choices before him were few and grim. He could take the coward's way out and remain a deserter. He could go back without decent counsel and face Colonel Stryker and an almost certain hangman's noose. Or, he could forcibly wrest Uncle Jonah's land from Annie and sell it to pay for a lawyer who might—just might—be able to save his neck.

Brock felt sick. Desertion was out of the question. His destiny was to either die or become despicable to Annie—sweet, spunky little Annie, who in the space of a fortnight had crept into a tender, dear place in his heart.

Hope of convincing her to sell the land appeared almost non-existent. Brock found no consolation in the knowledge that she would be safer with the Dunbars or with Ezra Buxton. At the thought, something that felt like jealousy nipped at Brock's heart. He'd experienced the same feeling the other day in the field when he noticed the boy talking with Annie beneath the sycamore tree. Later when he'd inquired about her visitor, she'd dismissed Ezra as simply a friend concerned for her well-being. But Bess Dunbar had let slip that young Buxton had courted Annie before her marriage to Jonah. Likely, the boy was hoping to renew that relationship.

But Annie remained disinclined to live with the Dunbars...or to marry Ezra. And for Brock to leave Deux Fleuves and leave her alone on the land seemed as much a death sentence to Annie as Brock's returning to Newport Barracks would be for him. For both their sakes, the land needed to be sold.

A shadow sliding past the window caught Brock's eye, jarring him from his somber reverie. Instantly alert, he reached for his musket leaning against the wall. He slipped quietly out the cabin's open door, glad for the stealth of his moccasin-clad feet.

The leaves of an elderberry bush shuddered as the shadow disappeared behind a thicket, and Brock filled the musket's flashpan with powder.

"Who goes there?" He lifted his weapon to shoulder level and squinted, sighting down the barrel. As he'd done countless times during his scouting days with the army, he willed his nerves to steadiness and positioned his thumb on the cock, ready to pull it back. "Who goes there, I say? Show yourself or taste my lead."

Seeing an Indian emerge from the thicket almost caused Brock to cock his weapon. But the man raised a hand palm forward to indicate he came in peace.

Brock lowered his weapon, but kept it at the ready as his gaze traveled the length of the man.

A gray turkey feather hung from the Indian's scalp lock. Otherwise, his head was shaved. His brown print calico shirt hung to his knees, partially covering deerskin leggings that ended just above doeskin moccasins. A Delaware, from the looks of him.

"I mean no harm. I trap the creek." A hint of sadness colored the Indian's tone. "The Frenchman, Blanchet, was my friend." He nodded toward the cabin. "You knew Blanchet?"

The tension eased from Brock's muscles. If this Indian had indeed been friends with Annie's father, he most likely offered no threat.

He shook his head. "No. But I am a friend of his daughter, Annie." Sadly, Brock feared that description would not be accurate much longer. "I am Brock Martin, nephew of Jonah Martin."

Brock suspected this man knew how his uncle had died, but doubted that he or any from his tribe were involved. Obadiah had shown him the arrow they'd taken from Jonah's back, and from the fletching, Brock had determined it had been fashioned by Shawnee, not Delaware.

The Indian grunted—a response Brock could not decipher. Then he tapped his chest. "I am Gray Feather. For many years Blanchet and I hunt together, trap together, trade together." Genuine sorrow shone from Gray Feather's dark eyes.

"I'm sorry. From what I have learned, Gerard Blanchet was a good man. I wish I could have known him." Brock reached out his hand in friendship, and the Indian clasped it firmly.

Brock cocked his head toward the cabin. "Annie has allowed me to stay here for now. I'd be honored if you would come in and sit for a spell. I'm afraid I don't have much to offer, but would be happy to share some buffalo jerky."

Gray Feather nodded and followed Brock into the cabin.

He lowered himself to the floor and sat with an air of familiarity that supported his claim of friendship with Annie's father.

A strong smell of rancid bear grease hung about the Indian. Inside the cramped cabin, it became almost stifling. It was the grease that made the man's scalp lock shine.

Brock leaned his musket against the wall next to the hearth, but never moved more than an arm's length away from it. Keeping Gray Feather in his peripheral vision, he stepped to where his knapsack hung on a wall peg. He had no doubt that this Delaware brave could instantly produce a knife from beneath his long shirt and hurl it at his back in the blink of an eyelid. He wanted to avoid any move that might set him off.

Slowly, deliberately, Brock unbuckled the knapsack and drew out the slab of dried buffalo meat.

"You a soldier?" Gray Feather's dark gaze fixed on the army regulation knapsack of blue drill cloth with its red US on the flap, nestled in a circle of white.

Brock's hand paused in midslice of paring off a hunk of the meat. The notion of lying didn't sit well, so as he'd done with Obadiah Dunbar, he skirted the issue. "I did some scouting for the army a while back."

Gray Feather's short grunt gave no indication he either believed or disbelieved Brock. He took the offered meat with a nod of thanks.

Brock lowered himself to the hard-packed dirt floor to sit facing the Indian. For a long moment, the two men sat chewing the dried meat in silence. At length, Gray Feather lifted a concerned look to Brock. "Once again, the bluecoats will fight the redcoats."

Brock nodded. "Yes. I'm afraid another war with England is only months, maybe weeks, away."

"Tecumseh, chief of the Shawnee, will join with the redcoats in the war he has already begun against the bluecoats and the settlers." Gray Feather's voice was full of conviction. "Many Shawnee have answered his call to war, and that of his brother, The Prophet." A troubled look wrinkled his bronze brow. "There will be war.

Many whites will die. Many Indians will die."

Brock only nodded solemnly. The one thing he wanted to avoid was being drawn into a conversation about the army.

At length, Gray Feather stood and reached out his hand to Brock, who rose, too. "I am sorry Martin is dead. Like his blood brother, Blanchet, Martin was a good friend to Gray Feather. I would honor his spirit by calling his nephew my friend."

Brock grasped the Indian's hand. "Thank you. I would be honored to call Gray Feather my friend."

Gray Feather turned to leave, and Brock followed him to the door. Then as he exited the cabin, the Delaware paused. "Tecumseh's war in the north and east will touch this place, too. It is not good that Blanchet's daughter live in Martin's cabin alone."

Chapter 6

Annie opened the cabin door and squinted at the eastern sky where the sunrise smeared streaks of pink and gold across the horizon. In the next hour or so, Brock should arrive to help her with the planting. Her heart quickened at the thought, and she knew the warmth spreading through her had nothing to do with the early morning sun peeking over the knoll.

She was glad he had agreed to live in Papa's old cabin. Actually, he seemed content there. So much so that he rarely left the place. Just how long this mutual arrangement would suffice, Annie didn't know. What she did know was that Brock's close proximity to the farm made her feel safer. . .and less lonely.

As always, thoughts of the man set her heart warring with her mind. Her heart told her Brock Martin was courageous, good, and kind. But her mind immediately challenged those conclusions. Why did he shy away from any talk of his past? And why had he stopped scouting for the army just when the country appeared on the brink of a new war with Britain? It was also curious that he'd declined Obadiah's invitation to join Fort Deux Fleuves's militia.

She pressed her fingers against her throbbing temples and blew out a weary sigh. Her head ached with the bewildering questions. What did it matter? Brock would be gone soon. An unexpected sadness accompanied the thought.

Sighing, she turned and traipsed to the hearth where an Indian pudding baked in the spider skillet beneath a pile of glowing embers. It felt good to cook for someone other than herself, so hopefully Brock would arrive with an appetite.

With a muffled *"Ruff,"* Cap'n Brody sprang from his place by the hearth and bounded out the open door. Annie's heart jumped with the dog. She didn't expect Brock for another hour, but someone was doubtless about.

Snatching Jonah's musket from above the fireplace and the powder flask from a wall peg, she followed the dog out the door.

Brock's now familiar laughter filtered through Cap'n Brody's welcoming barks, allowing the tension to seep from Annie's limbs. "Sergeant Martin reporting for duty, Cap'n Brody." Rounding the cowshed, Brock executed a sharp salute at the big dog, who was bouncing around him like a puppy.

At the sight of Brock, Annie cradled the musket in the crook of her now relaxed arm. "I fear our captain is not much for giving orders," she said with a laugh.

A mischievous grin crept across Brock's lips. "At least he didn't meet me bearing a musket."

Annie's face warmed, remembering the comment he'd made that first Sunday about her not needing a musket to get a man's attention.

Brock's eyes narrowed in mock seriousness at the dog. "So Cap'n, how did someone who cannot give orders attain such a lofty rank?"

Annie stifled a giggle. "Cap'n Brody will not tell you, because he is far too modest. But Jonah said he named him for a commanding officer during the war who was also big and ugly."

Brock laughed—a sound Annie decided she liked very much— and patted the big dog's side. "Well, Big'un, I'm afraid I must disagree with Uncle Jonah. I think you are a right handsome fellow." Turning his attention to Annie, he smiled, sending her heart hopping. "Thought I'd better come at first light and get an early start on the planting. Hope you don't mind."

"Non." Giving a nonchalant shrug, she tugged on her bonnet, which hung by its strings at her back, hoping to hide the blush warming her cheeks. If only her heart would not bounce so at his smiles. It was important that he see her as his equal, not a silly girl. She strove for a serious tone. "The seed corn is in a barrel at the west end of the cowshed. You can pick out what looks best and fill the planting bag."

"Yes, ma'am!" He gave her a smart salute, which, despite her best efforts to maintain a somber expression, coaxed a grin from her lips.

Offering a mute nod, she turned and retreated into the cabin. Several minutes later, with her emotions tightly reined and a steaming bowl of Indian pudding in hand, she trekked to the cowshed. "Thought you might require a better breakfast than cold venison jerky before beginning the planting."

He looked up from the seed barrel, and his face brightened. "Is that Indian puddin'?" At her nod, his grin widened and he eagerly accepted the bowl she held out to him. Taking it in both hands, he inhaled the sweet aroma. "Mmmm! Much obliged. I reckon I haven't had Indian puddin' since I was a boy."

Annie's heart broke lose from its tether to dance at his widening smile. There was no sense in pretending. Brock Martin lit a glow inside her she'd never before experienced. It pleased her that this time he bowed his head, allowing her the opportunity to say a quick prayer of thanks before beginning to eat.

After he'd gobbled down the pudding, he drew his sleeve across his mouth, then handed her the empty bowl. His green-gray eyes twinkled into hers. "Good as I remember Ma's. Maybe even better."

"Merci." Somehow she managed to mumble the word of thanks as he handed her the now empty bowl. She struggled to control her raging emotions. *Stop acting like a silly girl. He is only staying long enough to help with the planting, and that is all that matters.* She cleared her throat and tried to affect the same authoritative tone Papa had used when trading pelts. "Does the corn look good?"

He nodded. "More than passable, I'd say. At least I didn't find much mold."

"Good. After I tidy the cabin, I will help with the planting."

He shook his head. "That is not necessary."

Annie's back stiffened at his dismissive tone. She lifted her chin. "Oui. It *is* necessary. This is *my* land and *my* corn crop, and I will help plant it!"

A pensive look puckered his forehead. "I had a visitor yesterday."

His abrupt change in subject took her by surprise, but she was happy not to have to argue about helping with the work. "Oui?" She *was* curious as to which of her neighbors had stopped to give Brock a hospitality call.

He nodded. "A Delaware by the name of Gray Feather."

Annie couldn't help a grin. She'd known Gray Feather—one of Papa's best friends—for most of her life. How she would have loved to have seen Brock's face at first sight of the imposing Delaware. She tried to rein her mirth to a sedate smile. "Gray Feather and Papa trapped together for years along White River and its creeks."

"So he said." Brock's serious expression held. "He also said you should not be living here alone."

Gray Feather's concern touched Annie. She should have known her father's old friend would be stealthily keeping watch over her. She grinned at Brock's serious face. Did he believe Gray Feather was a threat to her? "Gray Feather still thinks of me as a little girl."

Brock's demeanor remained troubled. "Gray Feather believes Tecumseh's influence will reach down here." He paused for a moment, then fixed her with a pointed look. "Seems to me, it already has."

Annie's smile faded. She knew he was referring to Jonah's murder. "Did—did Gray Feather have any idea who. . . ?"

Brock shook his head. "No. Or at least he didn't say." He looked past her shoulder out the back of the open cowshed. After a long pause he leveled his intent gaze back on her face. "Annie, I think Gray Feather is right. It might be best if you took the Dunbars up on their offer."

Anger flamed inside Annie. Not even someone as charming as Brock Martin could coax her off the land and away from the vow she'd made to Papa and Jonah. Every muscle in her body stiffened, and she met his look with a hard stare.

"I know everybody means well, including Gray Feather. But know this, and know this well. Nothing anyone says will change my mind. I will stay right here and keep this land Papa and Jonah earned with their service to the country."

Brock's mouth opened as if he was about to say something, but then he closed it. Hefting the gunnysack full of seed corn, he reached for the hoe propped against a corner post. "Reckon we better get started." Both his jaw and voice had taken on a hard edge.

Over the next three hours, they worked together planting the field in row after row of corn. First, Brock paced off the rows, sticking a thumb-thick piece of maple branch in the ground at one end of a row. Annie, sighting from the opposite end, did the same. Wielding the hoe, Brock made little gouges three feet apart in the soil, into which Annie dropped a couple of grains of corn. Brock then dragged dirt over the kernels with the hoe and gave each hill a little tap. They repeated this process until half the field had been planted.

Despite the shade provided by her bonnet, the increasingly hot sun sent rivulets of sweat meandering down her temples. Though half empty now, the bag of seed corn in her hands seemed to grow heavier by the minute. With each step, she shoved her bare toes into the cool dirt for relief.

Brock paused, took off his hat, and drew his bare forearm across his sweaty brow. "Whew! I'd forgotten what hard work planting a field of corn could be."

"You used to farm?" Annie snatched at the opportunity to learn something more about his earlier life.

He turned his face toward a freshening breeze and closed his eyes for a moment. As the soft wind played with his russet hair, Annie was struck again by his good looks. *Il n'est pas mal.* Not bad looking at all. Curiosity shooed away the frivolous thought as she watched his demeanor turn somber.

He curled his fist over the top of the hoe's handle. Resting his chin against the back of his hand, he stared across the field, a distant look in his gray-green eyes. "When I was a boy, I helped my pa and ma farm our little place in Pennsylvania." Bitterness laced his tone. "It wasn't like this, though. It was poor land, chock-full of stones. Plum wore 'em out till they couldn't fight off the fever that took 'em."

"I'm sorry," Annie said softly. "When Jonah and his family first came here, I remember him telling Papa that his brother and sister-in-law had died." Along with a sting of sympathy, she felt a sort of kindred spirit with the young boy, Brock, left alone after his parents' death. Although newly married to Jonah when Papa died, the realization of being orphaned was crushing. It had left a Papa-shaped hole in her heart that no one else could fill.

Annie lightened her tone, hoping to lift both their spirits. "I remember Jonah mentioning you. He thought if you'd survived, you'd gone to live with your mother's people."

Brock snorted and gave a mirthless laugh. "My Aunt Flora and Uncle Sim had a dozen young'uns and land nearly poor as ours." He shook his head. "I saw how Uncle Sim treated his boys—worse'n slaves. I wasn't about to sign on for that."

The line of his jaw hardened. "I buried my folks on the land that killed them, and vowed I'd never turn another furrow of dirt."

He gave another little snort. "Reckon I was wrong, huh?" he said dryly, and went back to gouging the soil with his hoe.

Annie silently resumed dropping corn into the freshly dug indentions. She wasn't at all sure how she felt about what Brock had disclosed. He obviously disliked farming. She assumed that was why he hadn't sought out Jonah and Clara when his parents died. She had little doubt that as soon as the crop was in and he'd satisfied some imagined duty to Jonah, he'd drift on in search of a new adventure.

One of the questions that had poked at Annie's curiosity since Brock's arrival popped into her mind. "What caused the falling-out between Jonah and your papa? I asked Jonah once, but he wouldn't talk about it."

The pained look on Brock's face made her regret having asked the question. When he spoke, his voice turned hard. "Land—that is, the loss of it." He gazed out over the rich, dark ground they'd planted. "While Uncle Jonah was away at war, a slick-tongued land speculator talked Pa into trading the deed to my grandparents' Virginia land for land in Pennsylvania. Twice the acreage and three times as fertile, he claimed." Brock gave a sardonic snort. "It was twice the acreage all right, but ten times the rocks and ground so poor it would grow only waist-high corn. That folly ripped a tear in Pa and Jonah's relationship that was never repaired and sucked the life out of my folks." Wielding the hoe, he attacked the ground with unnecessary ferocity. "So I found it somewhat amusing when you told me how your pa had talked Jonah into selling his Kentucky land and buying this land instead."

Annie was about to remind him that in Jonah's case it worked out well when Cap'n Brody's frantic barking intruded.

At once, Annie and Brock turned and looked several yards west to where the dog seemed to have something cornered on the banks of Piney Branch Creek.

Brock dropped the hoe and ran for Jonah's gun and powder flask Annie had left at the edge of the field.

When they reached the creek, Annie saw that the dog's quarry was a baby black bear. The cub, not quite the size of its tormentor, growled and swiped its paws at the dog. Cap'n Brody, apparently unfazed by the bear's defensive posture, seemed to find great sport in bedeviling the little animal.

Annie threw her arms around Cap'n Brody's neck, trying to pull him away. "No, Cap'n. Bad dog! Bad dog!"

But instead of her pulling the dog back, Cap'n Brody trotted unhindered down the creek bank carrying Annie with him.

Her bare foot hit the slippery, gray-black mud lining the sloping bank, and she slid into the water with a great splash!

At the sudden impact with the cold creek water, she gasped. But she quickly pushed herself to a sitting position and soon began to enjoy the delicious coolness rushing past her waist.

Laughing, she struggled to stand and yanked at the sodden skirts impeding her progress. Aware of the ridiculous picture she must make, she braced for the teasing Brock was sure to give her.

But when he reached the bank above the creek, she found no

levity in his expression. Instead, he looked upward and past her. And the horror she read in his widening his eyes shriveled her laughter.

Suddenly a deep, ugly roar on the bank behind her spun Annie around. What she saw froze her heart in her chest. The huge, dark form of an adult bear—undoubtedly the cub's mother—loomed above her. Its gigantic claws slashed at the air while white foam dripped from its yellow fangs.

Chapter 7

Don't fuss, Bess. I am not sick or hurt."

Sitting on the edge of her bed, Annie leaned away from the wet cloth that Bess dabbed at her forehead with. "You have young ones to tend to. You didn't need to be bothered by—"

"Brock was right to fetch me." Bess managed another dab at Annie's face. "You might have done yourself an injury when you swooned."

"I walked all the way back from the creek, didn't I?" From the moment she came to on the creek bank and Brock told her the bears had run away, Annie had resisted his help. The last thing she wanted was to look weak in front of him. She chose not to think about him pulling her out of the creek.

"Only because you wouldn't let me carry you." Brock stood at the foot of the bed, relief slowly ironing out the tense lines on his face. "You had a right frightful scare. Women have swooned over less, I reckon."

Annie's back stiffened. It rankled her that he thought she'd fainted from fright. "The bear didn't scare me into a swoon. I should have eaten more breakfast, that's all. Too little food and too much sun must have made me light-headed."

She started to stand to demonstrate that she was physically sound, but with the quick movement, her head swam again, and she sat back down.

"I heard a shot," Annie said to divert Brock's and Bess's attention from her momentary weakness. Just before everything swirled around her and went black, she remembered hearing a musket's report. "You must be a mighty poor shot to miss from that distance."

A slow grin spread across Brock's mouth and he shook his head. "I couldn't take the chance of not killing the bear outright.

48

If I just wounded her, she'd most likely have come after both of us. I just shot up in the air, then ran at her hollerin' my loudest war whoops. Apparently, she wanted no part of a crazy man. She and her cub hightailed it back to the woods."

"I reckon I'd best get some food in you, girl." Bess's worried countenance turned cheery again as she bustled toward the hearth.

"There's about a quarter acre yet to put in corn." Brock glanced toward the cabin's front door, then back to Annie. "So if you're sufficient over your fright, I'll go back to the plantin'."

"I told you I was not frightened!" She shot him a piercing glare that he answered with an infuriating grin.

"If you say so." He headed out the door before she could reply.

"Oh! *Il me rend fâché!*" Annie fumed. Realizing she'd vented her aggravation in French, she translated to English for Bess, who stood at the table spooning some of the leftover Indian pudding into a bowl. "He makes me so angry, that one!"

Bess's plump figure shook gently with her laugh as she crossed the cabin and handed Annie the bowl of pudding. Her tone took on a teasing lilt. "You ask me, where there is smoke, there is fire." She wagged her finger at Annie. "And Annie Martin, I think I saw smoke comin' out of your ears."

Heat rushed to Annie's face. Ever since Brock's arrival, Bess seemed to be sizing him up as a match for Annie.

Annie exhaled a frustrated sigh and shoved the spoon around the warm brown pudding. "What does it matter? He's not staying, Bess. And besides, he isn't even a Christian."

The corn-husk mattress rustled softly as Bess sat down beside Annie. "I see a good young man who is searchin' for somethin'. He don't know it, but I think he's searchin' for God."

She nodded toward the cabin's north wall. "There's more fertile soil than just what's out there in the fields, Annie. Christ has commissioned us to sow His Word of salvation in the world." She patted Annie's shoulder. "Sow the seeds, Annie. Water them with prayer, and watch God's blessin's grow."

After nibbling unenthused at a few spoonfuls of pudding,

Annie's stomach threatened to revolt, and she set the bowl aside on the bed.

Bess's brow furrowed as she studied Annie. She glanced at the empty doorway as if to ensure they were alone and lowered her voice. "Speaking of seeds bein' sown, do you remember when you last had a monthly?"

Annie pondered. With Jonah's death, Brock's arrival, and her worry over keeping the land, she hadn't noticed the absence of her monthly flow. "March, I think." While bundling to leave the cabin during one of the several earth tremors that month, she remembered wishing she didn't feel so poorly with her monthly.

"I b'lieve," Bess said cautiously after Annie had answered several personal questions that left her face flaming, "you may very well be with child."

Stunned, Annie wanted to refute her suggestion. But remembering the week before Jonah was killed, she knew Bess could be right.

Panic welled up inside Annie, shaking her heart as violently as the recent earthquakes. She should be happy. This was the child both Papa and Jonah had hoped would come from her and Jonah's union. But at this moment, it felt more like a burden than a blessing. How would she continue to farm this land while growing heavy with child? After that, how would she tend an infant and the farm at the same time? Many questions began roiling in her mind, but they distilled to one. "What—what shall I do?"

Bess smiled and patted Annie's hand. "God will provide. All you have to do is take care of yourself and Jonah's child."

"Please, don't tell anyone of this but Obadiah."

Brock had made it clear he felt an obligation to Jonah's land and widow. He'd also made clear his dislike of farming. She hoped he'd stay in Deux Fleuves settlement, but not because he felt bound by some sense of family duty.

Bess nodded. " 'Course. I understand. But don't you go worryin' 'bout waggin' tongues suggestin' this babe might b'long to somebody other'n Jonah. You know me'n Obadiah'll swat such ugly gossip down like skeeters."

Grateful tears misted Annie's eyes as she hugged Bess. Just knowing Bess Dunbar would be near to answer an acre of yet unimagined questions sure to sprout up over the next several months, was a true blessing from heaven.

Annie blinked back tears and fought for composure. "Thank you, Bess. As you always say, 'God will provide.'"

After Bess left, Annie still sat on the edge of her bed. Her hand went to her flat stomach. She could hardly fathom that a tiny, new life could be stirring there. But if Bess was right, keeping the land just became all the more important.

She thought about what Bess had said concerning Brock. Bess's words reverberated in her ears. *"Christ has commissioned us to sow His Word of salvation in the world. Sow the seeds, Annie. Water them with prayer, and watch God's blessin's grow."*

She pushed herself up from the bed and walked to the little table beside Jonah's favorite chair. Her fingers stroked the grainy, black cover of the Bible her late husband had read diligently each night by candlelight. By rights, it should belong to their child. But Jonah's child would have the benefit of Annie's mother's Bible.

Bess was right. Tender feelings for Brock had begun smoldering deep in Annie's heart. Even if Brock rode away from the settlement and out of her life, those feelings would never be entirely extinguished. She couldn't bear the thought of this person, who'd become dear to her, continuing to live outside of God's grace simply because she'd done nothing to alter the situation.

Annie picked up the Bible and hugged it to her heart. She would do as Bess suggested. Before Brock left today she would give him Jonah's Bible. Then water daily with prayer the seeds she'd sown.

"Coward! You're nothing but a rotten coward!" Brock's harsh self-judgment exploded from his mouth. He snapped Uncle Jonah's Bible shut and dropped it to the floor beside the buffalo-robe pallet with a thud.

He hadn't really wanted to accept the book. But Annie had beseeched him to, her delicate face still looking peaked and fragile after her swoon. He couldn't deny her. She'd also insisted that he read it, recounting how Jonah never ended a day without reading at least one chapter.

He'd reluctantly agreed. So when he returned to his own cabin, his conscience wouldn't allow him to do as he would have liked and pitch the book in the corner and forget about it.

He decided he would randomly open the book, and wherever the pages parted he would read a verse or two to salve his conscience. As luck—or perhaps Providence—would have it, the Bible fell open to the book of Job.

Thinking it altogether appropriate considering his torturous situation, Brock began to read the first verse his gaze focused on. "My righteousness I hold fast, and will not let it go: my heart shall not reproach me so long as I live."

It was as if God had reached down to chastise Brock, and the words were written specifically for him. Brock scrubbed his face with his hand. He'd always prided himself on his courage and his honor. Now, those virtues seemed to hang in dirty tatters about his broken spirit.

A painful groan billowed from the center of his being. If he hoped to restore his honor, he must make a clean breast of it and tell Annie of his predicament. And though she would doubtless despise him for it, he must tell her of his plans to sell the land.

Brock's first Sunday in Deux Fleuves, Obadiah had introduced him to Hermann Hoffmeier, the head of a German family homesteading land east of Annie's farm. The man had mentioned he hoped to buy more land to accommodate kin, who were soon to arrive from Cincinnati.

Brock pushed up from the pallet and headed for the open door. He must talk to Hoffmeier before he lost his nerve.

A half hour later, the sound of chopping met his ears, and the smell of woodsmoke tickled his nostrils. As he crested a small rise, a circle of Conestoga wagons came into view. To the south of the wagons, he could make out the crude beginnings of a cabin. Hefting his rifle in his left hand, he approached the clearing with caution. "Halloo! Anybody here?" Best to make himself known, so one of the Hoffmeier men didn't mistake him for a marauding Indian and take a shot at him.

"You are the man, Marden, *Ja*?" At the feminine voice, Brock swung around to see a young woman emerge from the circled wagons.

"Yes. Is your pa about?"

Her forehead puckered. "Pa?" Then, as understanding dawned, her pretty round face lit and she smiled. She bobbed her head crowned with blond braids. "Ah, Papa. Ja. He cut trees to make *Haus*. I will show you where."

She started in the direction of the tree line, then stopped and turned to Brock. The apples of her cheeks pinked. Smiling shyly, she glanced up at him through a fringe of honey-colored lashes. "I am Katarina Hoffmeier." She held out her hand to him.

Heat blazed up Brock's neck. With the business at hand crowding out all other thoughts, he'd completely forgotten his manners. He gave her hand a quick shake. "Pleased to meet you, miss."

At his brusque greeting her smile faded, and a pang of regret smote Brock. As rusty as he might be in the social graces, he had no doubt the girl was showing him interest. Another time, he might have eagerly returned her attention. But now only one woman ruled his thoughts, leaving no room for another. And tomorrow, Annie would doubtless hate him for what he was about to do.

The next morning, agony accompanied Brock's every step along the half mile to Annie's cabin. Meeting Katarina Hoffmeier had made him realize the depth of his feelings for Annie. It seemed incredible that in such a short amount of time the plucky girl with her upturned, freckled nose, sassafras-brown eyes, and French accent had come to own his heart. But there it was, and no amount of denial could change it.

No stranger to fear, Brock had stared death square in the face many times over during his army career. But nothing had ever frightened him like the sight of that angry bear towering over Annie. At that moment, a terror greater than any he'd ever experienced assaulted his heart.

Nettles grabbed at his trousers as he made his way through knee-high grasses, but he paid them no heed. In a few minutes, his admission, although both honorable and necessary, would, without a doubt, squelch any hope of a deeper relationship with Annie.

Brock's heart writhed. He'd rather turn himself over to Colonel Stryker than confront Annie with his plans to sell her land to the Hoffmeiers. But Gray Feather was right, it was madness for her to remain on the farm and face the rising Indian threat alone. Even if Annie despised him for it—which he had no doubt she would— selling the land would leave her with no choice but to accept the Dunbars' offer and move to the relative safety of their cabin nearer the fort.

The moment he came within sight of her cabin, his gut clenched. Cap'n Brody's enthusiastic greeting failed to ease his taut nerves.

A sad smile pulled at Brock's mouth as he gave the dog the expected salutatory scratch behind the ear. "Hey, Big'un. You'll still be my friend no matter what I say, won't you?"

As he walked to the cabin door with Cap'n Brody loping alongside, Brock wondered why Annie hadn't come out to challenge him with Jonah's old brown Bess.

"Annie," he called into the interior of the cabin, not wanting to march in uninvited.

A faint retching sound reached his ears.

Concerned, Brock stepped onto the stone slab beneath the front door and poked his head into the cabin. "Annie?"

After a few moments, Annie appeared through the open back door, pale and shaky. "Oh, Brock—I—didn't expect you today." Her weak voice quavered.

Concern for her health banished all other thoughts. Ignoring decorum, he stepped into the cabin. "Are you ill? Should I fetch Mrs. Dunbar?"

She shook her head, but her body swayed, and she grasped the tabletop.

Brock hurried to her side and slid an arm around her waist to support her. The way her little body shook against his arm alarmed him. "You are ill, aren't you?" He helped her to the wall-peg bed and set her on the edge of the mattress.

"The pork pie I had for supper must not have set well." Her explanation and wobbly smile were unconvincing.

Brock touched his hand to her forehead. Although her head felt a little warm, she didn't seem dangerously feverish. "Is there anything I can get for you—some water?"

She glanced at the hearth. "I just brewed up some sassafras tea. A cup of that might help to settle my stomach."

Glad for a chance to help, Brock hurried to fetch the tea.

"Merci." She accepted the cup with a sweet smile, setting his heart dancing like a drunken man. If only things could be different. How he would love the chance to take care of her—always.

Annie had taken only a couple deep sips of the tea when Cap'n Brody, who'd been snoozing by the hearth, jumped up. The dog began to whine and crazily pace around the little cabin.

"Cap'n Brody, what is the matter with you?" Annie handed Brock the cup of tea and started to stand up, but the cabin began to shake, knocking her back to the mattress.

Earthquake!

Brock's heart slammed against his ribcage. In the last several months, he'd experienced enough of these tremors to have no doubt what was happening. In one fluid motion he set the cup on the floor, scooped Annie up in his arms, and bolted for the cabin door. With his precious bundle in his arms, he stumbled out of the vibrating building on the heels of the barking dog.

By the time they were safely in the open, the land had stopped shaking. But he still held her against him as they sat together in the grass, waiting to see if the earth would begin its frightful dance again. In that moment, he wished it would. He longed for an excuse—any excuse—to keep her here in his arms. He hadn't prayed for years. Didn't even know if God existed. But if by chance some benevolent deity indeed gazed down upon him, he begged for an extension of these few precious moments while Annie clung to him, her trembling body melding against his, her face tucked against his chest, and her breath warm against his neck.

At that moment, she lifted her face to his, her agate eyes large pools of trust and, dare he hope, longing. All reason detached. *You can't do this. Are you daft, man? Are you daft?* It was too late. Her soft lips beneath his responded to his every caress. A new tremor shook him to his very soul. But the epicenter of this quake was not outside him but within. Her hands slipped over his shoulders, and her fingers played in the hair at the nape of his neck, sending delicious shivers through his entire body. Their kiss deepened as the universe swirled around them. He should stop this. He mustn't let this go on. To his shame, it was she, not he, who broke their connection.

Slowly, shakily, she pushed away, leaving Brock aching from the loss.

He should say something—anything. His mind refused to work. The memory of why he'd come this morning struck him like a fist in the gut. His heart twisted in agony. If there be a God, He was obviously *not* benevolent. To be given a glimpse, one sweet taste, of Annie's love only to be reminded that a deeper relationship with her could never be was beyond excruciating.

Mutely, he stood and helped her to her feet, albeit a tad unsteadily.

Stepping back away from him, she looked everywhere but his face. The skin beneath her freckles glowed a beguiling pink. "I—I think it is over—the tremor, I mean."

Her gaze shyly skittered to the edge of the cornfield. "The quakes frighten me so."

Should he apologize for his impetuousness? But that would be a lie. "As long as you're out in the open, you're safe." How he longed to tell her *he* would keep her safe. But that, too, would be a lie. "Annie." Did he dare take her in his arms again—just once more, while she still tolerated his company? By force of will he didn't know he possessed, he kept his arms at his sides and took a deep breath. If he didn't tell her now, he would surely lose his nerve. "I've been reading some in Uncle Jonah's Bible."

Annie perked up, her face shining with surprise and joy. Her happiness at his statement gouged at Brock's heart.

He forged on, into the jaws of destruction. "There's something I need to tell you, Annie. I plan to sell the land to the Hoffmeiers this fall."

She shrank from him. He might as well have slapped her full-force across the face for the pain, anger, and revulsion registering there.

"I'm sorry, Annie. I really am. But I need to—"

"Essaie un peu pour voir!" The bitter-sounding French spewed from her mouth, and her delicate little chin began to shake like the earth tremor they had just experienced. She fixed him with a cold glare as huge, silent tears slipped down her face.

"Just you try it, Brock Martin." The look of betrayal in her beautiful eyes stabbed at his gut like a dagger. "You didn't even know Jonah. I knew him, and he would not have left his land to you except for his desire to pass it on to his blood kin. Know that I will fight you every step to see his wishes fulfilled."

"Annie, please listen. . . ." Brock took a step toward her. If she would just hear him out, maybe she would see reason. "Please, Annie. You must listen. Both our lives depend on it."

Annie stepped behind Cap'n Brody as if using the big dog as a barricade. "I need to hear no more. You are *un lâche*—a coward! You fear the Indians will take your fine scalp."

The word *coward* hit too close to home, blazing through Brock like a lightning bolt. He lashed back. "Go ahead and be stubborn, Annie Martin. But your stubbornness will do you little good when your scalp is hanging from a Shawnee warrior's belt!"

"At least I will die with honor! *Allez-vous-en!* Get off my land!"

Chapter 8

"And when ye stand praying, forgive, if ye have ought against any: that your Father also which is in heaven may forgive you your trespasses."

The words from Mark's Gospel blurred before Annie's eyes. Her heart stung with remorse. Jesus had taught her to forgive—to turn the other cheek. That if someone takes away your cloak, to let him have your coat, too. But he also taught her to honor her father and mother. How could she honor Papa by sitting meekly by and allowing Brock to sell the land she'd vowed to keep?

Her heart felt as if it had endured both an earth tremor and a cyclone. The memory of Brock's kisses sent waves of shudders to her very core. While she still basked in the ecstasy of his tender caresses, his betrayal had felt like a jolt of lightning from a clear sky.

Her heart twisted with the memory. Had he kissed her to soften her up before revealing his plans for the land? At the thought, pain pierced her chest, filling her eyes with tears.

As much as she wanted to hate him, she couldn't. Indeed, she loved him. Yes, love. There was no other word to describe the emotion that filled her at the very thought of him. And he must care for her, too. No man could kiss her with such passion and tenderness and not care for her. Besides, he *had* carried her to safety when the tremor struck, not considering the hours of hard work he'd expended planting her corn crop.

She closed her mother's Bible and rose slowly from the stool as if she were an old lady instead of a seventeen-year-old girl. As much as she hated the thought, Jonah had given Brock equal right to the land. And if he *did* have feelings for her, perhaps, just perhaps, she could convince him to stay. But whether he stayed or not, her spirit would not be easy until she'd apologized for her harsh words.

She tied on her bonnet, then wrapped a linen towel around the dried-apple pie she'd baked for the Dunbars' Sunday dinner. Didn't the scriptures say, "Let us reason together?" Whatever Brock's reason was to sell the land, she at least could listen. She owed him that, at any rate.

"Come, Cap'n," she called as she headed toward the door, pie in hand. "We have some apologizing to do."

"I'm sorry."

Annie's soft voice behind Brock sent his heart bucking like an unbroken colt. His fingers halted in the midst of securing the bedroll to the back of his saddle.

He paused for a couple of heartbeats before giving the leather strap a final yank. Had she come to berate him further, or just to shoot him? He decidedly preferred the latter.

He'd reckoned if Annie forbade him to set foot on the land there would be little he could do to protect her. He might as well head to Newport Barracks and face whatever fate awaited him there.

Brock slowly turned toward her voice. She stood several feet away, near the door of the trapper's cabin he'd called home for the past several weeks. He was almost disappointed to see she wasn't carrying Jonah's brown Bess. Instead, she held a little linen-swathed bundle in her hands.

Her gaze seemed fixed on the ground surrounding her dusty, bare toes. "*Je regrette.* I'm sorry," she repeated in English. He'd noticed how, when emotional, her speech often reverted to her father's native tongue. "I shouldn't have said those things to you. The scriptures say, 'Be ye angry, and sin not: let not the sun go down upon your wrath.' I was not acting at all like a Christian."

Her gentle words smacked Brock's conscience. How could she feel she'd done wrong by displaying a natural and honest reaction to his bumbling attempt to convince her to sell the land? Her apology was altogether as amazing as it was unnecessary.

He swallowed hard and shook his head. "It is I who should be begging your forgiveness for my own harsh words to you. And you were right. I *am* a coward."

She smiled, and his insides melted. "Any man who chases away an angry bear cannot be a coward." She lifted the cloth-wrapped object. "I brought you a peace offering—a dried-apple pie."

For a split second, Brock wondered if Annie had chosen a means slower than a bullet to rid herself of him. At the merry twinkle in her eyes and the grin dimpling her cheek, he realized with horror that she must have read the wild thought skittering through his mind.

Her musical laughter, a sound he'd despaired of ever hearing again, rippled pleasantly from her. "It's not poisoned, I promise. I'd baked it for Sunday dinner at the Dunbars'."

Dried fruit this time of year must be scarce. Brock shook his head in wonder. How could he accept a gift—anything—from her? "Then that's where you should take it. I don't deserve a gift from you, certainly not one made from something as dear as apples in May. Not after the mean things I said."

"In God's eyes, there is nothing dearer than forgiveness." Her narrow shoulders lifted in a shrug. "I forgive you. And a gift is a gift."

Brock couldn't help grinning. "What is it the Good Book says about heaping coals of fire on your enemy's head by doing good to them? Well, my head's feelin' right warm about now."

Her smile faded as she turned her focus toward his horse. "Where are you going?"

His gaze followed hers to the animal packed for travel.

"Newport Barracks in Kentucky, to stand trial for desertion and murder."

Annie's face blanched to near paper-white, and her jaw went slack.

Brock reached her in two quick strides, catching both her and the pie as her limbs went limp.

He called himself every kind of idiot for blurting it out. He should have remembered she'd been feeling poorly.

With one hand balancing the pie and his other arm around her waist, he propelled her inside the cabin. "I'm sorry. I didn't mean to shock you. I shouldn't have said it like that."

Inside, he set the pie on the hearth floor and helped her to the straw and buffalo robe pallet.

She raised a bewildered face to his. "What—how..."

Brock pulled a stool opposite her and sank to the seat. He blew out a long, deep breath, dragged off his slouch hat, and shoved his fingers through his hair. "I was on my way to tell you I was leaving...and why."

Her amber eyes widened. "You—you murdered someone?" Her faint voice squeaked.

"No, but that's what Colonel Stryker will surely charge me with."

Annie's chin lifted, and she folded her hands in her lap. "Tell me what happened. I will believe you."

At her staunch support and belief in his innocence, hot tears stung the back of Brock's nose. He swallowed them down hard. "We were on the march from Newport Barracks in Kentucky to reinforce Fort Wayne against attack by Tecumseh and his Shawnee. Colonel Stryker, our commanding officer, came down with an attack of ague in Ohio a few miles shy of Indiana Territory, so we set up camp there. I held the rank of sergeant." It felt strange to say it in the past tense. Her attentive expression encouraged him to continue.

"One evening, I was securing the perimeter. When I came to the picket line where the horses were tethered, I spied the colonel's nephew, Lieutenant Hamilton Driscoll, sword-whipping a raw recruit for falling asleep at his post." Even now, the name left a bad taste in Brock's mouth. "In my seven years of service to the army I'd dealt with some nasty officers, but none more insufferable than Colonel Horace Stryker and his pompous a—, his pompous nephew."

Annie's grin at his amendment made his heart buck. He forged on.

"I couldn't watch it happen and not do something, so I tried to intervene, talk some sense into the man, but he wouldn't have it. Next thing I knew, he turned the sword on me, and I found myself defending my very life with only my sheath dagger." His throat dried. What happened next still felt like a dream, and he shook his head. "Driscoll had me backed up. My heel hit something—a tree root, I think—and I fell on my backside." He had to swallow hard before he could finish recounting the tragic events.

Annie gasped. She stared at him as if transfixed, her eyes looking glazed. "But surely the colonel would understand it was an accident. What about the soldier you protected, would he not speak in your defense?"

Brock couldn't help snorting. "Stryker despised me. He knew I didn't like the way he played favorites. When he learned I'd killed his precious nephew, I have no doubt he raised from his sickbed to lynch me himself. And the recruit took off like a scared rabbit the moment Driscoll laid into me, so he never saw the end of it. The only witness was the private who heard the ruckus and found me standing over Driscoll's body with his blood dripping from my dagger."

Feeling drained, he finished in a quiet voice. "I knew my army career had died with Driscoll beside that picket line, so I mounted the closest horse and hightailed it out. I remembered Pa saying Jonah had connections with men in high places, in both the army and the government, so I came here hoping Uncle Jonah could help me."

Annie gave a confirming nod. "I know up until a few years ago he kept a correspondence with General Clark, when the general lived down on the Falls of the Ohio."

Brock sighed. "Unfortunately, from what I've heard, the great general is now infirm, having suffered several strokes and lost a leg." His mouth tugged up in a sad smile. "Even if I thought he could help me, which I doubt, I would not lay such a burden on the man in what is surely his final years."

Annie held out her hands, palms up. "*Que faire?* What is to be done?"

Brock's gaze drifted toward the open cabin door before swinging back to Annie's face. "When I learned Uncle Jonah had included me in his will, I came to the conclusion that my only hope was to sell the land and use my portion of the profit to hire a good lawyer."

A tear slipped down Annie's cheek, but her chin lifted and her voice sounded strong. "Then that is what must be done."

Her sacrificial offer touched a deep, sweet place in Brock's heart, and he swallowed hard. He reached out, took her hand into his, and gently squeezed her fingers. "No. You were right. Uncle Jonah included me in his will to help ensure the land would be a heritage for his descendants, not for me to sell to save my sorry skin. I must return and face the charges like a man."

A look of panic animated her features. She gripped his hands. "But you cannot go back! They will kill you." The tears welling in her eyes thrilled Brock even as they tortured his heart.

He marveled at her spunk when she squared her shoulders and leveled an accusatory glare at him. "This land is your responsibility, too. You cannot leave me alone with it."

"Annie, my dear Annie." Brock caressed the tops of her hands with his thumbs. "Gray Feather is right. You are not safe there. Move in with the Dunbars. . .or marry young Buxton." His throat tightened with his chest on the last suggestion. "But don't stay on the farm alone."

"Non!" The word exploded from her mouth like a thunderclap, and her features turned stormy. A great sigh heaved her shoulders, and her voice calmed as she visibly struggled to control her emotions. "Obadiah and Bess have more than enough people under their roof, and Ezra has no interest in the land."

Her gaze captured Brock's, sending his heart into a wild gallop. "Besides, I married one man not of my choosing. I'll not do it a second time."

Brock felt as if a white-hot poker had been rammed into his

gut and twisted. Was she trying to tell him she cared for him as he cared for her? What did it matter? Annie needed a live husband, not one with a death sentence hanging over his head like the sword of Damocles.

Annie's gaze dropped to her lap and her face pinked. "Besides the vow I made to Papa and Jonah, I have another reason to keep the land. If Bess is right about my symptoms—and I've never known Bess to be wrong—I am with child—Jonah's child—your kin. So, as eager as you are to be put out of your misery, Brock Martin, it would be dishonorable of you to leave your kin unprotected." In her satisfied grin, he could almost read the silent pronouncement of *Checkmate!*

Brock stared at her, dumbfounded. For the second time in six weeks, his perspective had changed in the space of a breath. If what she told him was true, Brock knew Annie would fight to the death to keep the land for Jonah's child. And she was right. Brock couldn't let her face that prospect alone. The boys in the firing squad would just have to hold their powder a mite longer.

Annie ignored Cap'n Brody's whimpers as she loosely tied the dog to a front corner post of the cowshed. "Oh, don't whine! If I didn't tie you, you'd just follow me. I need you here to protect Sal and Persimmon."

In the past week, three families had lost livestock to marauding Indians. Just yesterday Brock told her Pritch Callahan had left his saddle horse drinking at the creek while he planted corn. When he returned, the horse was nowhere to be found.

Annie picked up the two buckets and headed for the creek. She didn't intend to become the next victim. From now on, she would need to carry the cow and mule's evening supply of water from the creek instead of driving them down to the stream and back.

She squinted westward where the red ball of the setting sun had begun to sink into the horizon. With regret, she realized she'd spent far too long planting beans and pumpkins amid the newly emerging corn and had allowed the evening to creep up on her.

Already, the chirping of crickets and the calls of hoot owls filled the gloaming, and the flickering lights of myriad lightning bugs decorated the gathering dusk. The sweet scents of wet grass and honeysuckle hung heavily on the evening air. Brock would scold her for sure if he knew she'd left the cabin so close to night-fall, especially without the musket. But she needed to finish the chore before dark, and two hands carrying water meant fewer trips.

As she rounded the cabin, thoughts of Brock and all he had revealed two weeks ago brought the familiar stabs of fear. More than once, Annie had jerked awake in the middle of the night gripped by nightmares of a phantomlike Colonel Stryker drag-ging Brock away to a firing squad. Now she understood why Brock avoided Fort Deux Fleuves whenever the occasional company of soldiers garrisoned there.

Her bare feet found the dirt path that sloped to the creek, barely visible amid the knee-high, dew-drenched Indian grass. As she carefully made her way down the embankment, slippery after yesterday's rain, she considered again the awful prospects facing the man who'd become so dear to her. But no amount of torturous pondering brought her any closer to a solution that might save him.

When Brock confessed his plan to sell the land, she'd berated him and ordered him off her place. Now, amazingly, it was she who daily begged him to embrace again his original notion. But he resolutely refused, saying he must cede his claim to the land to Jonah's direct heir.

Although she hadn't planned to tell Brock about the baby, she'd grasped at the one thing she knew would appeal to his sense of duty—keeping him here in Deux Fleuves and safely away from Newport Barracks and the vengeful Colonel Stryker. But at the same time, the revelation had killed any hope of him accepting her offer. So she did all that was left to her. She prayed that God in His infinite mercy would keep Brock safe and provide a way out of his perilous predicament.

At the edge of the water, Annie hiked her skirt to her knees, bent, and dipped one of the buckets into the swift stream.

Rising, she spied a tiny patch of red amid a tangle of nearby brambles. Hoping she'd discovered a berry bush, she poked into the thicket to investigate. When she shoved the brush aside, her heart froze in her chest. An Indian canoe—Shawnee by the vermilion markings—lay nestled in the thicket not fifty feet from the back door of her cabin.

Suddenly aware of Cap'n Brody's frantic barking in the distance, she spun around at a gentle rustling sound behind her.

She gasped to see two Shawnee braves advancing toward her. They wore only breechclouts and deerskin leggings. Their faces and bare torsos were smeared with dark creek mud. Eagle feathers hung from their blue-black hair, which brushed their coppery shoulders.

Annie remembered her father's admonition to show Indians no fear and fought to ignore the men's frightful appearance. She knew that many of the Indians spoke at least a smattering of French, so she began making apologies in that language.

They continued to advance, showing no sign that her words fazed them. The shorter and fiercer looking of the two grabbed her arm, pulled a war club from his belt, and raised it menacingly above her head.

Annie faced her death calmly as unspeakable terror melted into a sense of peace. Dropping to her knees, she committed her soul into God's hands.

But before the Indian could smash the club into her skull, the taller, more comely man grasped her would-be killer by the shoulder. *"Mat-tah!"* he said, shaking his head, and Annie recognized the Shawnee word for no. He reached down offering her his hand. She took it, and somehow managed to rise on wobbly legs.

After a brief argument between the two men in Shawnee—which Annie couldn't follow—the man with the war club reluctantly lowered his weapon.

Suddenly, a low growl drew Annie's and the Indians' attention to the embankment's summit. Amazingly, Cap'n Brody stood above them—muscles tensed, head down, and teeth bared.

Before she had a chance to decide if this was a good or bad development the dog leaped toward the Indian with the war club.

In a lightning-fast move, the Shawnee brave swung the weapon toward Cap'n Brody's head.

Annie heard a sickening *thunk* as the war club's stone head connected with the dog's skull.

Cap'n Brody yelped, then fell to the ground with a dull thud.

"Cap'n Brody!" The dog's name tore from Annie's throat in a strangled cry. Blinded by tears, she turned toward her wounded pet. But the taller Indian pulled her away and bound her hands behind her with a thin strip of leather.

Without another word, he picked her up and dropped her into the canoe.

The Indians shoved the canoe into the stream, then stepped into the little craft, one at each end with Annie between them.

Chapter 9

The midmorning sun warmed Brock's back as he guided Valor across the stretch of Piney Branch Creek bordering Jonah's farm. Oddly, he still thought of the land as belonging to Uncle Jonah.

He reined his horse to a stop and gazed at the acres of infant corn he'd come to tend. Pride welled up inside him at the sight of the rows of emerging green plants. It didn't matter that he would never reap any monetary benefits from the harvest. The land, and what it produced, belonged to Annie and his unborn cousin. Until the crop was safely harvested and Annie had delivered her child— or an army posse found him and took him away in chains—Brock would see to it that Jonah's heritage was preserved.

Thinking of the day he must leave, Brock's heart throbbed with the ache of loss. He no longer dreaded whatever sentence a court-martial might mete out. All other punishments paled when compared to his inevitable separation from Annie.

Annie.

The ache inside him deepened. Never before had a woman so completely captured his heart. Her beauty, courage, and sweet heart far surpassed that of any other woman he'd met. He still marveled at her willingness to forgive him.

The corner of his mouth drew up in a wry grin. He would have wagered that she'd find him despicable the instant she learned of his desertion. Instead, she'd offered to sacrifice the land she so desperately wanted to keep in an attempt to save his life.

He'd never before seriously considered marriage. So it seemed an excruciatingly cruel twist of fate that he should now—while living on borrowed time—find a woman who, with one flash of her dimpled smile, could entice him to the domestic life. What tortured his heart without mercy was his impression that, were he free to offer them, Annie would not rebuff his attentions.

In his frustration, he kicked his mount's sides harder than necessary, causing the horse to neigh his displeasure.

As he neared Annie's cabin, a building sense of unease gripped Brock. The absence of Cap'n Brody's eager welcome triggered alarm bells inside him. Something was amiss.

He scanned the area, quiet except for the persistent bellowing of the milk cow. Annie should have milked the cow hours ago and staked her to a patch of grass beside the cabin.

Brock dismounted and tied the horse to a sapling. Keenly alert, he slipped his musket sling from his shoulder. Always loaded, the weapon would need only a powder prime.

He poked his head in the cabin's open door and fought the fear marching up his spine. "Annie? Annie, are you here?"

Nothing.

He stepped into the deserted cabin and walked to the hearth. The fire had gone out. With the toe of his boot, he kicked at the cold ashes, which showed no signs of having been banked the night before. Above the mantel, Jonah's brown Bess hung in its usual place.

Brock's smoldering fear blazed into full-blown panic.

He raced from the cabin. "Cap'n Brody! Cap'n! Here, boy!"

Nothing answered but the bawling cow and Brock's own heart pounding in his ears. Then, as he rounded the cabin, a faint whining led him to where the land sloped toward the creek.

A sick feeling cinched his gut. Cap'n Brody lay in the high grass, his head caked in dried blood.

Brock slung the musket to his shoulder and scrambled down to the dog's side. Kneeling beside the injured animal, he stroked Cap'n Brody's scruffy coat. Gnats swarmed around a deep gash, still oozing blood, beside the dog's right ear.

"Poor fellow. What's happened here? Where's Annie?"

Cap'n Brody whimpered and raised his snout. His rough pink tongue crept out to lick Brock's hand. The big, stout-hearted dog's effort to show affection despite his grave injury pricked Brock's heart. Cap'n Brody would never have allowed harm to come to Annie without putting up a fight. And Brock feared that was exactly what had happened.

Standing, Brock scanned the area for signs of a struggle, anything that might hint at what had taken place.

A few feet to his left, he noticed a smooth impression in the mud near the edge of the creek. He ran his fingertips over the indention. Something had been dragged into the creek. Near the drag marks Brock found cut elderberry bushes and willow saplings covering a large patch of mashed grass.

His years of scouting experience told him something had been hidden here, probably a canoe.

He eyed the muddy bank closer for footprints. Two sets of smooth-soled prints suggested moccasin-shod feet. He found only one smudged, partial print of a bare foot roughly the size of Annie's.

Had Annie been taken by Indians? Fear yanked another knot in Brock's gut. It was possible Annie had found Cap'n Brody injured and had gone for help. But common sense and Brock's scouting experience contradicted that conclusion. If she had needed help, wouldn't she have come to him first? And she would never have neglected the hearth or the cow.

Cap'n Brody's soft whimper dragged Brock's attention back to the dog. Before he could search for Annie, her faithful protector needed his immediate attention.

Brock hefted the nearly hundred-pound dog in his arms with a grunt. Although the thought of carrying the big animal up the incline to the cabin was daunting, he knew the dog's great size had saved him. A lesser animal would never have survived so devastating a blow.

Inside the cabin, Brock laid the dog in his favorite spot near the hearth. He sliced off a hunk of smoked venison from the ham hanging beside the chimney and placed the meat and a bowl of water near Cap'n Brody's muzzle.

Brock knelt and stroked the dog's side, which rose and fell with the animal's labored breaths. "I'll see you're taken care of, Big'un, and the mule and cow, too."

Cap'n Brody answered with a soft whine, his brows alternately lifting and falling as he eyed Brock with a soulful look.

"Don't worry, I'll find Annie," Brock said as much to himself as to the dog. "If she's alive, I'll find her."

It was nearly midday by the time Brock approached the Dunbar cabin with Annie's cow and mule in tow. Leaving the animals in the care of the Dunbars' twelve-year-old son, Jeremiah, with orders to milk the cow, he sprinted to the family's cabin. To reach the front door, he was obliged to wade through half a dozen chickens, a spotted pig, two dogs, and three-year-old Isaac Dunbar.

Though tempted to forgo social niceties, Brock stopped at the open doorway and dragged off his hat. He poked his head through the cabin's entrance and was met by the aroma of stewed chicken and boiling root vegetables. "Please excuse me, Mrs. Dunbar, but have you seen Annie?"

Bess Dunbar stopped pushing a wooden spoon around a kettle suspended over the hearth fire. Wiping her hands on her apron, she turned toward Brock, her plump, smiling face rosy from the heat. "Brock, come in. We'll be havin' dinner soon. Won't you—"

"No. . .thanks." Brock hated being short with Bess but every second seemed precious. "Have you seen Annie today? She's not at her place. The cow hasn't been milked, and the dog looks to have been clubbed."

Bess gasped, her voice barely lifting above a whisper. "No. I haven't seen her since Sunday." Fear flickered in Bess's widening eyes. "Somebody killed Cap'n Brody?"

Brock shook his head. "No, he's not dead, but he's in a bad way. Don't know if he'll make it." He then told her what he'd found.

Bess blanched and sank to a chair. "Do you think it was Indians?"

"What was Indians?" Obadiah entered the cabin, his broad, bearded face pulled long with concern.

Her eyes welling with tears, Bess looked to her husband.

"Obadiah, Annie's missin', and somebody liked to clubbed Cap'n Brody to death."

The preacher crossed the cabin floor to his wife.

"I told her she shouldn't stay out there alone. I told her. . . ." Bess's voice snagged on a sob.

Obadiah grasped Bess's hands, then placed a kiss on her stricken face. "You mustn't fret, Bess. God is with her. You know that."

Obadiah turned to Brock. "How long?"

"By the look of things, fourteen—maybe sixteen—hours." Saying it aloud increased the urgency straining at Brock's every nerve. Instead of talking about it, he needed to be out there looking for her. He plopped his hat on his head. "I'm going after her."

"Wait." Obadiah crossed to Brock in two quick steps. He clasped a restraining hand on Brock's shoulder. "I just came from Buxton's Trading Post. Gray Feather is there warning folks of unfriendly Shawnee in the area." The piercing look in Obadiah's eyes filled Brock's chest with an almost suffocating fear. "Gray Feather said a white woman was seen late last evening, traveling south along the White River with two Shawnee. Shawnee not from any local tribe."

Annie sat in the dim light of the wigwam and tried not to shake. Three weeks of travel with her captors had brought her here, deep in the forests of Ohio on the banks of a river the men called Auglaise.

Hugging her knees tight to her chest, she pressed her back against one of the round structure's sapling supports. She strained to focus on the muted sounds outside. Though she could hear only a jumble of unidentifiable noises, nothing seemed alarming.

In the minutes, perhaps an hour, since the old woman who'd brought her into the place left her alone, Annie had retreated into herself. Fearing what might become of her, she hadn't wanted to hear, see, feel. . .think. But as the paralyzing fear loosened its grip, her senses tingled to life again, and she became keenly aware of her surroundings.

First, she noticed the smell. Not at all disagreeable, the aroma of a potpourri of dried herbs seemed almost calming. Her gaze wandered the shadowy interior of the room. She could make out two dozen or so bundles of drying herbs hanging from the wigwam's support poles. A plethora of brightly decorated clay pots dotted the space in a haphazard kind of fashion. Baskets, some covered and some left open, held various items. They lined the room's perimeter. A deerskin was stretched on a drying rack, the fur still on, but scraped clean of the meat.

Two, what appeared to be, low beds adjacent each other stretched to her left. Each was comprised of six short, forked sticks stuck in the ground—three at the head and three at the foot. Long poles rested in the forks. Over these were laid fragrant pine boughs covered with soft-looking deerskin.

A shallow, round, ash-lined pit dominated the center of the room. Blackened stones bordered its circumference. Obviously a cooking area, it was probably only used in inclement weather as Annie had seen another such fire pit filled with glowing coals a few feet in front of the wigwam.

She ran her hand along the floor next to where she sat. It was, without question, dirt. But it had evidently been pounded rockhard and somehow treated until it was smooth as polished stone.

Was this to be her home? And with whom would she share it? Papa had often told stories of Shawnee braves taking women from white settlements for wives. Was it for that propose she'd been abducted? And if so, which of her captors planned to claim her?

She ventured a fearful look at the skin-covered beds and her mind froze, refusing to fashion the unthinkable thought. Hot tears flooded her eyes.

Ne perde pas le courage. Her father's frequent admonition to never lose courage rang in her ears.

Then, like a quiet, small voice, the words from the thirty-first Psalm washed through her troubled mind like a soothing balm.

"Be of good courage, and he shall strengthen your heart, all ye that hope in the Lord." God had not left her. Whatever unimaginable terrors awaited her, she would not have to go through them alone.

Unbidden thoughts of Brock nudged their way into her mind. Would he even try to find her? It hurt to think he might sell the land in her absence. But perhaps that was why God had allowed her to be taken—to provide Brock with the means to hire legal defense. On the other hand if he simply abandoned the land, squatters could claim it.

A sudden flash of light and stirring of air shattered her musings and drew her attention to the doorway. Someone had flipped back the flap of hide that covered the wigwam's opening. Annie's heart leaped to her throat as a shadowy form appeared in the glare.

When her eyes adjusted to the changing light, surprise and relief vied for dominance in her pounding chest. A young woman about her age stood before her.

"Mot-kee-oock-tha, An-nee." The woman shook her head as she came nearer. *"N'ayez pas peur.* I forget you do not know Shawnee," she said, switching to French. I am *U-tha-wa Wie-skil-lo-tho.* Yellow Bird. I am wife of Standing Buck."

Annie sat frozen in place. The measure of relief that washed over her at the woman's introduction quickly vanished, followed by renewed terror. Standing Buck was the name of the kinder of her two captors—the man who had saved her from his more malevolent cohort, Crooked Ear, back at Annie's cabin. And during their long journey eastward through the forests and down the waterways, it was Standing Buck who had treated her with respect and kindness and often protected her from their traveling companion. So was she then to be given in marriage to the cruel Crooked Ear? She fought nausea at the thought.

Yellow Bird bit her bottom lip, and her delicate copper forehead wrinkled pensively. She muttered a string of Shawnee, then said in French, "Perhaps I did not have the French just right. Sometimes I forget."

At the young woman's worried look, remorse smote Annie. "Non," she hurried to assure her. "You said it perfectly."

Yellow Bird moved with an easy grace. Although slim and delicate looking, Annie noticed how the girl's deerskin shift stretched snuggly over a slightly protruding abdomen. Like Annie, Yellow Bird was expecting a child. Annie wasn't sure just why that knowledge calmed her, but it did.

The Indian girl lowered herself effortlessly to the floor and sat cross-legged in front of her. Without another word, Yellow Bird reached into a leather pouch attached to a belt around her waist and withdrew a few narrow leaves. One by one, she put them in her mouth and began chewing silently. After a while, she cupped her hand beneath her mouth and spat out the green wad of leaves. With her free hand she reached for Annie's wrist, still raw from the deer-sinew restraints she'd been forced to wear. Yellow Bird began smearing the green mash over Annie's injuries.

Tears stung Annie's eyes. Not from the gentle touch of the girl's slim fingers on her chafed skin, but from the unexpected kindness.

Yellow Bird stopped in her ministrations, a pained look cleaving her smooth copper forehead. *"Je suis désolé."* She murmured the apology softly in French, obviously assuming from Annie's tears that she had caused her discomfort. Her brows lowered into a scowl, and her lips smashed together. "I must scold my husband for allowing my new sister to be injured." Her brows pinched together in a perturbed look. "Before the ceremony can take place, you must be without blemish."

"Ceremony?" The word trembled out breathlessly. So she *was* to be given to Crooked Ear in marriage. A new wave of fear and nausea rolled over her. She stared at the sweet girl before her and pushed the disgusting words through her lips. "When—when will I be wed?"

Yellow Bird's soft giggle sent irritation raking down Annie's spine. She found nothing amusing about the dreadful prospect of being joined to such a frightening and disagreeable man.

Smiling, Yellow Bird shrugged and lifted her hands, palms up.

"I am not a shaman. Only the Creator knows who you might wed and when."

There were no imminent plans to force her into marriage. Annie almost swooned with relief, and her racing heart slowed. But the girl had said "ceremony." Annie licked her drying lips. "You said I needed to be fit for a ceremony. What type of ceremony?"

Tears glistened in Yellow Bird's dark eyes, and she covered Annie's hand with hers, a fond smile tipping her lips. "My sister, Bird-That-Soars, died of a sickness the healer could not cure." Her face brightened. "Our grandmother, Winter Moon Bird, will adopt you into our clan, and you will be my new sister."

Chapter 10

Dear Lord, help me. Help me to do this.

Annie lay on her deerskin bed in the darkened wig-wam she shared with the old woman, Winter Moon Bird. Every day for the past month, she'd thought of nothing but escape—escape back to Deux Fleuves. Back to her land. *Back to Brock.*

Hot tears flooded her eyes and spilled down the sides of her face into her ears. She could only pray he was still alive and well in Deux Fleuves. Her heart throbbed with the ache that had not left her since her abduction. She had respected Jonah, cared for him as a dear friend, and sincerely grieved his loss. But her heart had never fused to any man as it had to Brock. And somehow, with God's help, she would find her way back to him—or die trying.

Though she'd stayed constantly alert to any opportunity of escape, the Shawnee had given her none. Winter Moon Bird watched her as closely as a mother hawk might watch its chick, even lying across the wigwam's doorway at night. But with her adoption ceremony looming tomorrow, a renewed urgency to leave this place blazed within her.

A cool breeze rustled the reed mat a few inches from her head, drying her tears. She glanced over at Winter Moon Bird snoring peacefully on her bed near the wigwam's doorway, her back turned to Annie. This was the moment Annie had waited for all day.

Until today, the opening barred by the old woman's body had been the only way in and out of the wigwam. But with the nights turning uncomfortably warm, Winter Moon Bird had enlisted Annie's help this morning in replacing several of the bark wall panels with reed mats to allow better airflow through the cramped space.

Annie's stomach clenched. If she was to attempt an escape

tonight, it had to be now.

Holding her breath, she inched her way over to the closest mat. Over the last several weeks, her middle had begun to expand with her growing child. Was the opening behind the mat wide enough for her to wriggle through? She could only pray.

She ran her hand along the dirt floor at the bottom of the mat until her fingers touched one of the wooden pegs that secured it to the floor. The peg was pounded far too deeply into the ground for Annie to pull it out. But the twine that attached the mat to the peg could be cut. After supper, Annie had managed to steal away the small knife Winter Moon Bird used to prepare food for cooking and slipped it under her bed. Gripping the short piece of twine with one hand, she reached beneath her bed and felt for the knife.

When her fingertips found the knife's smooth deer-antler handle, a measure of courage surged through her. Her heart pounding in her throat, she extracted the knife and applied it to the twine. With constant glances at Winter Moon Bird to assure herself that the old woman remained fast asleep, she held her breath and prayed she would not be discovered.

Suddenly the twine gave way beneath the blade's sharp edge, sending a jolt of energy through Annie. She had burned her bridge behind her. If caught now, there would be no credible way to explain how the mat had come to be cut from its moorings. There was no time to think, only to do. With a flick of the knife, she quickly cut the opposite corner of the mat free.

Carefully, she pushed the mat aside causing a soft rustling sound, and her breath caught in her throat. Across the wigwam, Winter Moon Bird stirred and gave a low groan. Annie's heart froze in her chest. The old woman settled back into a rhythmic snore, allowing Annie's heart to beat again. She couldn't delay another moment. She had to move now.

Sucking in a deep breath, she stuck her head through the opening then one arm. Easing onto her side she reached out her arm, planted her elbow in a patch of dewy grass, and pulled herself forward. She was halfway through. *Please Lord, keep Winter Moon*

Bird asleep. Another push of her moccasin-clad feet against the wigwam's floor while pulling now with both forearms, and she was free.

She sat listening in the dewy grass, her ear inclined toward the bark structure from which she'd emerged. Had old Winter Moon Bird awakened? Only the chirping of crickets, the distant *rum, rum, rum* of river frogs, and the pounding of her own heart in her ears disturbed the silent summer night. The breath she'd long held whooshed from her lips. Pushing up onto trembling legs, she strove to get her bearings. She needed to find her way to the river and the spot where she'd noticed the Shawnee kept their canoes. From her earliest years, she traveled with Papa, navigating the rivers of the Northwest Territory in their old canoe. If she could get to the river, she could make her way home. Immersed in darkness, the village looked alien. Which way to go?

The deep-throated song of the frogs beckoned, guiding her steps.

Skirting the village, she made her way through the pitch-black woods, cringing at each snap of a twig and rustle of leaves beneath her feet. She glanced up at the forest canopy, wishing it were spring or even winter instead of late July. No glimmer of starlight penetrated the thick leafy foliage to light her way. On the other hand, the darkness was her ally, hiding her from anyone who might be about.

She could hear the river now, humming its soothing tune as it wended its way through the wilderness. Quickening her steps, she ignored the brambles stinging her legs and prayed she would not tread upon a viper slumbering beneath the many layers of dried leaves. Here, the land sloped, and the fishy smell of the river reached her nose.

Annie's heart sped, and jubilation bubbled up in her chest. She tamped it down. If she failed to keep her wits about her, her freedom could be short lived. It would take only one villager out to answer nature's call to spy her, and all her efforts tonight would be for naught.

Sobered at the thought, she grasped at spindly sapling willows to steady her descent down the increasingly steep incline. Gradually, the leafy carpet beneath her feet gave way to sandy soil. A half-dozen more steps and she emerged from the forest. Now in the clear, she looked up. Countless stars sparkled in the dark heavens. A silver sliver of moon offered a modicum of light to guide her steps. The braves kept their canoes hidden in a sapling willow copse near the river. But sapling willows grew all along the riverbank. She should be near the spot, but in the darkness it would be nearly impossible to determine *which* grove of trees hid the canoes.

Forcing down the panic rising in her chest, she slipped among the stand of young trees closest at hand. Her eyes were now somewhat adjusted to the darkness, but however hard she stared, she could make out nothing that resembled the long, narrow shapes of upside-down canoes.

Despair wrapped around her like a soggy blanket. Shaking it off, she emerged from the trees. She couldn't waste any more precious time looking for the vessels, but must strike out on foot and put as much distance as possible between her and the village before morning.

No sooner had she emerged from the willows, when a muscular arm grabbed her around the waist and a hard hand clapped over her mouth.

Chapter 11

Annie opened her mouth to scream, but the sound was smothered by her captor's rough palm. Struggling for breath, she strained to suck air into her nostrils. Was this where she would die? And by whose hand? Not without a fight!

Tears filled her eyes. Sobs of fury rose in her throat. The restraint over her mouth turned them to whimpers. Her attacker's other arm pinned hers to her body, preventing her from flailing, but her legs remained free. She kicked at her assailant with all her might. If she must go to God this night, she'd leave a mark on the man who sent her there.

"Annie. Annie, be still. It's Brock."

Annie's heart stopped in midbeat. Her body froze. The night began to swirl around her, and a humming commenced in her ears as if a swarm of locusts had invaded her head. "B–Brock?" She could barely breath, but not because of his hand over her mouth. For his hand had gently slid away to cup her jaw, while his calloused thumb caressed her lips.

Afraid to believe her ears, she twisted in his arms and gazed into his face. The darkness cloaked much of his features, but the scant moonlight reflecting off the stream beside them revealed gray-green eyes beneath low-riding brows.

Annie's legs buckled. He caught her in his arms. A sob tore from her throat. He pulled her close to his chest, muffling it. "Brock. Brock." His name snagged on a ragged sob as she slipped trembling arms around his neck.

A million questions flitted about in her mind like the host of lightning bugs piercing the night with their yellow-green flashes of light. None of them mattered now. All that mattered was Brock's arms holding her tight against him, his breath warm against her ear as he whispered her name over and over.

"Annie." His voice turned husky, breaking on her name. His lips blazed a fiery trail from her ear to her mouth, then lingered there.

The night, the dangers around them. . .the world all spun away leaving Annie and Brock alone, floating in a sweet cocoon all their own.

Without warning he pushed away, breaking the beautiful spell and slamming Annie back to earth with a jolt. His whispered voice turned stern. "Come. We have to leave here." He clasped her hand and towed her southward at a fast pace. Before she could ask where they were going, he said, "There are canoes a few yards from here. We can take one to where Gray Feather is waiting with mounts on the other side of the river."

The sound of excited voices advancing straight toward them stopped Annie and Brock in their tracks. Had Winter Moon Bird awakened and, finding Annie missing, raised the alarm?

"Can you swim?" Though tight, Brock's voice was calm as he tugged her toward the river.

"Oui." Annie couldn't help the hint of indignation that tinged her reply. She couldn't remember a time when she didn't know how to swim. According to Mama, Papa had taught Annie to swim before she could walk. And more times than she cared to remember, the skill had saved her life when Papa's canoe capsized in rough waters. Wading into the rushing stream, she stifled a soft gasp at the first touch of the cool water on her feet and ankles. But her skin quickly became accustomed to the water's temperature. Brock's secure grasp on her upper arm guided her through the darkness as she pushed her knees against the river's current, advancing ever deeper into the moving water.

By the time they reached midstream, the wind had whipped up, chilling Annie. She abandoned walking and began to swim through the now neck-deep water. Though they no longer touched, knowing Brock was there swimming beside her gave her courage.

Thunder rumbled overhead and reverberated through the river valley like distant cannon shot. The noise heartened her. The din of a storm could help cover the sounds of their escape. She prayed they could reach the forest on the other side of the river before the throng discovered they had taken to the water. But the instant the prayer formed in her mind, the urgent voices filtering through the thunder seemed to turn in their direction.

Angry shouts from the shore behind them sent a chill through Annie that had nothing to do with the gusting wind or the rushing river. One voice rose above the others, sending terror slashing through her like the barbs of lightning flashing around them.

"Nee-pa-wi-loo, Ann-ee!" Crooked Ear, calling in Shawnee for her to stop.

His order, punctuated by the sharp report of a rifle, had the opposite effect, spurring her on. She swam faster, pushing her burning limbs to the limit. *Please God, get me and Brock to the other side alive!*

A *whiz* and *zip* near Brock's ear told him the Shawnee had drawn a bead on him and Annie. The muscles of his arms and shoulders burned with exertion as he cut through the water with quick strokes, fighting the current as well as his sodden clothes. Had he come this far, following Annie's trail for nearly two months to now lose her and his own life in the bargain the very moment he found her?

Rage sent a burst of energy through him. No! He mentally shook his fist at whatever malevolent god found sport in snatching away the happiness he'd experienced moments ago in Annie's arms. The sound of her labored breathing as she swam beside him lent him a measure of comfort. But could she keep up the pace? If they could reach the other side of the river unscathed, they'd be beyond accurate range.

The shadowy outline of the wooded shore before them drew tantalizingly nearer. At the same time, the whoops of the Shawnee braves behind them grew louder, closer. They must have given chase in the canoes Brock had planned to use for their escape.

Annie clearly heard them, too, for her breaths, which came even quicker now, turned raspy with her increased exertion. How she managed to keep up with Brock's longer strokes, he couldn't imagine.

"I have fought a good fight, I have finished my course, I have kept the faith."

Oddly, the words from the Bible his mother had recited before she breathed her last, flashed into his mind. God may have no use for Brock, but surely Annie and her unborn child deserved to live. *Save Annie. Please save Annie.*

The thought had no sooner formed in his mind than his hand smacked against something solid poking up from the river. He grasped what felt like a branch—attached to a partially submerged tree by the feel of it.

At the speed of the bullets zipping over their heads, a plan flashed in his mind. The moment they stepped out of the water, they'd present easy targets to their pursuers. But cloaked by the darkness, they could possibly hide unseen among these branches. Annie was spent. That was obvious by her raspy, labored breaths. Not only would this tree provide her a chance to rest, but might even trick the Shawnee into giving up the chase, thinking Annie and Brock had drowned.

Reaching out his free hand, he grabbed Annie's arm. She emitted a sharp intake of breath, but made no other sound when he towed her to the log. She gripped a branch and gave a mute nod of understanding. Together they worked their way around the log, putting it between them and their assailants, while hiding amid a dense web of branches. In the dark and with only their heads above water, they should be practically invisible.

Brock slipped his arm around Annie's trembling body and held her close. She nestled warmly against him, and his heart galloped. How he longed to make her his. But that could never be. The thought strummed a poignant chord across his heartstrings. Even if they survived the Shawnee, Brock still faced certain death at the hand of Colonel Stryker.

A half-dozen Indians paddled three canoes toward Brock and Annie's hiding place. One brave in the lead canoe held a pine-pitch torch aloft. The flame danced eerily over the water. Without exchanging a word or signal, Brock and Annie slowly sank together beneath the river's inky surface. Seconds crawled by like minutes in the watery darkness until Brock's lungs began to burn. Could Annie hold her breath long enough for the Shawnee to give up and turn away? He could only hope.

Suddenly, the water above their heads began to churn and dance. Were their hunters throwing objects into the water? When he could no longer see the torchlight from beneath the river's surface, Brock tentatively poked his head up and was immediately pelted by water from above. It was raining—hard. In the distance, he could make out the shadowy shapes of the canoes drifting away, back to the Shawnee's side of the river. He could no longer see evidence of light piercing the darkness. Apparently, the rain had quenched the Indians' torch. As Brock had hoped, the searchers must have decided their quarry had drowned, leaving them with little enthusiasm for hunting dead bodies in the rain when they could sit by the fire in their dry wigwams.

Brock tugged at the collar of Annie's deerskin shift, and she eased her head up out of the water. Instead of noisily gasping a mouthful of air as Brock had feared she might, she pressed her face against his shoulder, muting her intake of breath and garnering both his admiration and gratitude. His heart throbbed painfully in his chest. Over the years he'd met his share of lovely ladies, but never one whose beauty was only surpassed by her intelligence and courage. Until Annie.

Though their adversaries appeared to have abandoned their search, Brock and Annie clung to their watery sanctuary for several more minutes, shivering while a deluge of rain beat down upon them. Finally, feeling confident enough to leave their haven, Brock motioned toward the wooded shore in front of them. Annie nodded in agreement, and they silently swam the last few yards to safety.

Fearing her jellylike legs would not support her, Annie emerged from the river on all fours and crawled up the muddy bank like a crawdad. Though now on firm, if sodden, ground, she still could hardly believe all that had occurred over the past hour or so. But the strong arm around her waist, lifting her up, gave proof that Brock was indeed here, and the place of her captivity now lay behind her across the Auglaise River.

For several minutes, they made their way through the soppy underbrush and dead leaves of the forest floor. Somewhere in the river Annie had lost her moccasins. She stepped with care to avoid slipping on the wet leaves in her bare feet. Even if she did slip, with Brock's arm securely around her, she didn't fear falling.

At length, the soft nickering of a horse brought them both up short. Like a ghostly apparition, a dark figure appeared from behind an ancient oak tree. For an instant, Annie's heart leaped to her throat, for the figure wore the long shirt and leggings of the Shawnee. But as he stepped closer, her heart began to beat again. Gray Feather! She couldn't remember when she was so happy to see Papa and Jonah's old friend.

Giving her a scant hint of a smile he gripped her shoulders and nodded, making the drenched turkey feather dangling from his scalp lock bounce on his shoulder. Without a word, he turned and beckoned them to follow. A few steps farther, he produced a pair of horses: Brock's sorrel, Valor, and a dapple gray. Brock hoisted her up to Valor's saddle, and they continued in silence for about another hour, the men leading the horses on foot while Annie rode.

At length, Gray Feather stopped at a rocky outcrop in the side of a hill. The rain had stopped some minutes ago, but Annie still shivered in her wet clothes. Brock couldn't be any less miserable in his sodden shirt and breeches. Though he, too, had lost his footwear in the river, he now wore a pair of moccasins provided by Gray Feather, which came as no surprise to Annie. That Indians often carried at least one spare pair of moccasins was something she'd learned early at Papa's side, trading with the local Delaware.

Brock helped Annie down from Valor's back, and Gray Feather cocked his head toward the rocky ledge. "We camp here." Gray Feather's quiet words were the first anyone had spoken since Annie and Brock entered the river.

A few minutes later, Gray Feather had a fire going in the midst of the alcove. How he managed to find enough tinder and dry wood to accomplish the task amazed Annie.

When the three sat down around the fire, Brock glanced at her warming her toes near the cheery flame. "You should not stay in those wet clothes."

Annie started to remind him that his clothes, too, were far from dry. Then it occurred to her that it was likely not her wet condition, but her delicate one that had prompted his comment. Heat not generated by the campfire flooded her face. She focused on the orange sparks shooting up from the flame. "The fire will dry me soon."

He stood and walked to where the horses were tethered. There he opened the leather pouch slung over his horse's neck, pulled out a brown paper bundle, and carried it to her. "Here, Gray Feather and I will see to the horses while you put this on." His voice sounded tight. He cleared it twice as he handed her the parcel, his gaze skittering away from hers. "Before Gray Feather and I left Deux Fleuves, Bess Dunbar insisted I take this fresh frock and moccasins." He grinned. "She seemed convinced we would find you."

Affection for her motherly friend welled up in Annie's eyes. "Bess would have set to praying the minute you left. And Bess knows the power of prayer." She held the package close to her chest and smiled. "And her prayers worked. God led you to me. Did He not, *mon ami*?"

"If you want to think so." Brock's sardonic chuckle filled her with sadness. Why could he not see God's hand at work before his very eyes?

"Gray Feather and I will see to the horses while you change." He turned to leave.

"Brock, what of my—our land?" She blurted the question that had rolled around in her mind since she realized he'd found her. "With no one there to tend it, do you not risk squatters claiming it?"

For a long moment he stood still, his face averted. Slowly, he turned back to her. "I did not leave the land unattended. The Hoffmeiers are living there now."

Chapter 12

Annie's face blanched and Brock's heart quaked. How would she feel about the decision he'd made?

Her eyes—those beautiful cinnamon-brown eyes—glistened with tears in the firelight. She might as well have taken a filleting knife to his chest. A brave smile quavered on her rosebud lips, and she lifted her chin. "Then you have money now to hire the best counsel to plead your case. That is good."

That she'd willingly sacrifice the land she held so dear to save him touched the very depths of Brock's soul. It took every ounce of his will not to sweep her into his arms and kiss her. Instead, he took her hands in his. He couldn't stop the widening grin stretching his lips as he contemplated relieving her mind.

"Annie, dear Annie. No money changed hands. The Hoffmeiers did not buy the land. They are only tending it in exchange for a portion of the crops."

Annie's jaw went slack. Snatching her hands from his, she stepped back. "Espèce d'imbécile!" Her face turned as stormy as the weather a couple of hours earlier. "By living in the cabin and harvesting the crops, the Hoffmeiers can legally claim the land as their own. You have given away my land for nothing!" Tears sketched down her face.

Brock stood stunned in the face of her angry volley. He'd thought she'd be pleased to know her place was being tended. Somehow, he must make her understand that her land was safe and awaiting her return. "Annie." He stepped toward her, but she took another step back and held up the bundle of clothes like a shield between them. Standing pat, Brock puffed out a breath. "The land is still yours, Annie. Katarina assured me she understood the bargain."

A perplexed frown replaced the angry one on Annie's face. "Katarina?"

"Yes. Katarina Hoffmeier. Hermann Hoffmeier's daughter. Her English is better than her parents', so I dealt with her."

The tempest returned to Annie's features. "Ah, *on commence à y voir plus clair.*" Bitterness edged the faux sweetness of her tone. "Now I understand. A pretty face and a coquettish smile turned your brain to mush and stole your senses." Now all sweetness left her voice, which turned hard and sharp as flint. "And my land!"

Brock groaned. He'd made a mess of this to a fare-thee-well. He strode to her and put his hand on her shoulder, but she shrugged it off. "It was not that way at all."

She turned her back, sending his heart to the bottom of his stomach. "Go help Gray Feather with the horses. I want to put on this dress. It may be the only thing I have left of my home."

Brock slumped to the tethered horses through the damp, ankle-deep underbrush. Frustration built in his gut until it exploded in anger, and he kicked at a fallen branch in his path. Since her abduction, he had thought of nothing but Annie. For the better part of two months, he'd tracked her with Gray Feather to the Auglaise. He'd hung his heart on every scrap of encouraging information the Delaware had managed to glean from Indians along the way, often to see his hopes dashed. His emotions had experienced the highest of heights and the lowest depths, not unlike the Ohio Valley's hilly terrain he'd traveled in search of Annie. And now she accused him of giving away her land to impress another female! He would surely never understand women.

Lifting off Valor's saddle, he gave a sardonic snort.

"My brother is angry." Gray Feather's quiet comment made Brock want to laugh. Angry. . .maybe. But of the many emotions tangling inside Brock, anger was only one strand.

He turned to see the Delaware with his familiar bandy-legged amble approach from out of the darkness. The strong smell of tobacco from the man's pipe filled the air. "I'm eager to get back to Deux Fleuves." Though he had no doubt Gray Feather had heard his and Annie's exchange, Brock had no interest in sharing his feelings about the matter.

Gray Feather emitted a faint grunt, followed by a soft popping sound as he drew on his pipe. The red glow of the pipe's embers lit the Indian's angular features. Did Brock detect the hint of a smile on the Delaware's usually stoic face? If he had, it vanished quickly, and the man's expression turned somber. "We must leave this place soon—before the moon has set. Tonight, the braves of Chief Running Wolf's village will sleep in their lodges by the fire. But when the sun rises, they will cross the river in search of Blanchet's daughter."

Brock shook his head. "Annie needs rest." Tonight she'd pushed herself to the limit. Though he had no experience in human births, he'd seen horses foal too soon when pushed hard, resulting in the loss of both the mother and the foal. He could only suppose it would be the same for people. The thought of Annie's exhausted body expelling Jonah's child far from the help of any doctor or midwife made him tremble. He'd much rather face an entire band of angry Shawnee warriors than risk losing Annie in childbirth.

"I can travel." Annie stepped up, now dressed in the blue-print frock Bess had provided. The flickering light of the campfire behind her burnished her curls to the color of rich sorghum. Though the dress hung a bit loosely about her middle—Bess had obviously considered Annie's altered figure—the sight of her in the dress took Brock's breath away.

Puffing on his clay pipe, Gray Feather nodded his agreement and ambled toward the campfire as if to declare an end to the subject. "We will rest for a time and eat the dried meat of the buffalo, then we must travel south. When we reach the place called Cincinnati, we can travel by boat down the big river, *Spelewathiipi.*"

Annie, who'd just settled herself beside the fire, cast a fearful glance between Gray Feather and Brock. "But is not Cincinnati very near Newport Barracks in Kentucky?"

Brock nodded. "Across the river from it." Indeed, that fact had rolled about in Brock's mind until he'd worn it ragged. He had found Annie. Gray Feather was more than capable of seeing her home safely. He loved Annie with all his heart, but he was tired

91

of hiding—holding his breath every time he crossed paths with a company of soldiers, fearing recognition. It was time he faced his fate like a man instead of slinking from his own shadow like a frightened cur. He likely had no future at all, let alone a future with Annie, so nothing but heartache could be gained by his going back to Deux Fleuves.

Swallowing the knot that had gathered in his throat, he gazed at her deeply, hoping to sketch her likeness indelibly on his mind. "And that is where I will part company with you and Gray Feather."

A series of emotions played in rapid succession over Annie's face, the prevalent one being anger. Standing, she strode to Brock and pulled herself to her full height of not quite five feet. Her arms stiff at her sides, she clenched her fists. "Brock Martin, you gave my land away. If you are a man of *honneur*, you will return to see that I get it back. Je vous dis la vérité! Return with me to Deux Fleuves, or I will leave this minute and go back to the Shawnee!"

Chapter 13

The smells of woodsmoke and hog manure filtering through the surrounding trees indicated they were nearing a sizable settlement. With the scents, Annie's eagerness to reach home grew. Brock's assurance that Obadiah Dunbar had vouched for Hermann Hoffmeier's honesty had somewhat relieved Annie's anxiety about her ownership of her land. Yet she wouldn't be entirely easy until she reached home and took possession of her cabin again.

"Are we near Madison?" She shifted her position on Valor's back. Every muscle ached and her bottom felt numb. Already she missed the flatboat they'd spent the past fortnight on, gently floating down the Ohio River.

Guiding Valor up a steep incline, Brock cast an encouraging smile over his shoulder. "It's just up ahead. We'll stop and rest at the inn Noah mentioned."

Annie sent up a silent prayer of thanks that they'd finally arrived safely in Indiana Territory. And that she'd successfully convinced Brock not to turn himself over to Colonel Stryker when they'd come within sight of Newport Barracks.

She couldn't help a triumphant grin at the memory of how he'd thrown up his hands in surrender at her threat to return to the Indian village. Actually, they'd seen no signs of her captors once they left the Auglaise behind. A blessing she attributed to both divine protection and Brock's and Gray Feather's skills of evasion. Brock had assured her that the closer they came to Newport Barracks, the more any danger from hostile Shawnee diminished. In truth, when the fort came into view, Annie had feared the Indians far less than the soldiers. Had a keen-eyed soldier recognized Brock, he'd likely have been clapped in irons and taken to the brig to face a court-martial.

But God had heard Annie's daily prayers and kept Brock safe.

And when they reached the Cincinnati dock, Brock had even managed to find a family of settlers bound for Madison, Indiana, willing to take the three of them aboard their flatboat in return for the men's help in poling the boat down the river. Annie felt sure her being in the family way had influenced the wife, Agnes Raab, to insist that her husband, Noah, take them on despite his obvious wariness about Gray Feather. The man's concerns, however, soon vanished, and the Raabs, especially the four children, quickly made fast friends of the congenial Delaware. This morning when they docked near the town of Madison, hugs and handshakes all around expressed the group's genuine sorrow in parting. Annie, too, was sad to say *adieu* not only to her hosts, but Gray Feather, who left them to visit relatives at a local Delaware village.

They crested the hill, and a clearing appeared. Madison spread out before them. Shops of all sorts lined a wide, dusty thoroughfare bustling with patrons both on foot and horseback. Annie's mouth felt dry as the dirt beneath Valor's hooves. Despite her eagerness to press on toward home, the chance to rest and enjoy a cool drink of water was more than appealing.

Brock stopped and dragged his hat off his head and ran his forearm across his brow. "Up ahead is the Red Horse Inn Noah Raab recommended as a reputable establishment."

At last, they stopped in front of a two-story building. The sign that angled out from above its front door depicted a gold shield with a red horse rearing up on its back feet, its front hooves pawing the air and its nostrils flaring. A man with a lady on his arm passed beneath the sign and disappeared into the inn, confirming Noah's assessment. No decent woman would enter a questionable place of business.

Brock helped Annie down from Valor's back and held her a few seconds longer than necessary. These brief moments of connection always left Annie's head and heart reeling. But what good did it do her to love Brock when he remained determined to return to Newport Barracks the moment he saw her safely back to Deux Fleuves?

She stepped away, uselessly busying herself swiping at her wrinkled skirt, which only a flatiron could make smooth. The fleeting moments of joy she experienced in Brock's arms would only make the parting more painful when she had to say adieu to him forever.

Since the kiss they shared the night he surprised her on the banks of the Auglaise, there'd been no other tender moments between them. However much she'd like to think he held special feelings for her, she knew the kiss was likely sparked simply by the emotion of having found her after a long search. And it was doubtless Brock's sense of duty to Jonah and Jonah's coming child that had spurred his search for her.

Then there was the familiar tone he'd used when he'd mentioned Katarina Hoffmeier. Annie scantly remembered the German girl, who had arrived in Deux Fleuves with her family shortly before Annie's abduction: an exceptionally pretty girl with golden hair; round, rosy cheeks; and a womanly figure that would turn any man's head. How well acquainted with *Fräulein* Hoffmeier had Brock become? An image of Brock and Katarina sharing a tender moment upon his leaving Deux Fleuves to search for Annie flashed painfully in Annie's mind. She hated the squiggle of jealousy shooting through her. Still, she couldn't help wondering if Katarina awaited Brock's return with hopeful anticipation. And if the German girl held a special place in Brock's heart as well.

As she allowed Brock to assist her up the two stone steps into the inn, Annie blinked away moisture welling in her eyes. Though it pained her to think of it, the notion of losing Brock to Katarina Hoffmeier paled in comparison to the thought of losing him to a firing squad or a hangman's noose. Worse, she didn't even have the comfort of knowing his soul belonged to Christ.

Inside, a round-faced man wearing a stained linen apron and a broad smile approached them, shattering Annie's reverie. "Welcome to the Red Horse, folks." He bent forward in a bow, displaying a bald spot at the top of this graying head. "Zeb Scroggins, proprietor, at your service."

Offering the innkeeper a glancing smile, Brock stepped to one of the several tables scattered about the dim room and pulled out a bench for Annie. "We'd like some cold well water, if you please."

Annie caught the man staring at her middle. He glanced quickly away, his face turning bright red. She stifled a laugh as he scurried off mumbling something about getting the water. She and Brock shared an amused grin. It always tickled her how the sight of a woman in the family way embarrassed men—white men, at least. She'd found it not to be the case among the Shawnee, though. Or, interestingly enough, with Brock. Aside from taking special care not to overtire her along their journey, he'd simply treated her obvious coming motherhood as a matter of fact. True, he'd learned she was with child before her abduction, but knowing and seeing the evidence were two very different things.

"You're like the Indians—it doesn't bother you." She glanced down at her folded arms, resting on the mound that housed her precious child.

Brock's attention, which had drifted to the interior of the inn's dining room, swung back to her face.

For a moment he seemed bewildered by her comment, then, following her gaze, responded with a gentle smile. "No, it doesn't."

Suddenly his smile faded and his brow furrowed. "Did they...did the Indians harm you?" A mixture of concern and remorse shone from his eyes. Until now, he hadn't asked her about her time with the Shawnee. She sensed he felt he had failed her by allowing Crooked Ear and Standing Buck to carry her away.

She offered him what she hoped was a reassuring smile. "No, they did not harm me." Her smile slipped into a grin that accompanied a soft giggle. "The one called Crooked Ear could be frightening at times, but even he never harmed me."

She went on to tell him about Standing Buck, Yellow Bird, and Winter Moon Bird, the woman who would have become her adopted grandmother. As she spoke of the people who'd taken her into their lodge as one of their family—albeit against her will—she felt an unexpected twinge of loss at her separation from them, especially her would-be adoptive sister, Yellow Bird. "I risked my life to leave them, but at times I actually miss them. It is strange, no, mon ami?"

He reached across the table and clasped her hands, sending delicious tingles up her arms. "Of course it's not strange. It's only natural that you would feel some attachment to people who treated you with kindness." His brows pinched together in a remorseful frown. "I'm glad to know you weren't mistreated, but you should never have been taken in the first place. As your kin, it was my place to protect you—and I failed." He winced, and her heart broke at his needless sense of guilt.

She gave his hands a gentle squeeze. "Do not blame your-self, mon ami. You could not have stopped it. My time with the Shawnee was God's will and part of His plan for my life." Grinning, she placed her hand on the little mound in her lap. "I will have a great adventure to tell my child."

For a long moment, they shared a smile as they gazed into each other's eyes, their hands still clasped. Annie got the sense that if the table were not between them, he might have kissed her.

"There you be, folks." The innkeeper stepped to their table breaking the spell, and Brock let go of Annie's hands. Setting two pewter tankards full of water on the tabletop, the man folded his arms across his barrel chest. "Sorry it took a bit, but I had my boy fetch the water directly from the spring out back."

Annie and Brock expressed their thanks then took deep drinks of the cool, refreshing liquid.

The innkeeper, who still hovered near the table, turned to Brock as he raked his curled fingers through his salt-and-pepper beard. "You and the missus be wantin' a room for the night?"

Warmth spread over Annie's face, and Brock's features reddened as well. Of course the man would think they were husband and wife. But before she could correct his assumption, Brock spoke up.

"The lady is my kinswoman, not my wife. I'm fetching her home to the Deux Fleuves settlement near the spot known as The Forks. We've only stopped to refresh ourselves."

"Well now, that's right curious." The innkeeper rubbed his whiskered chin between his thumb and forefinger. "See that big German boy over there?" He jabbed his thumb at the fireplace across the room. "Claims he's bound for the same place."

Looking in the direction the man indicated, Annie noticed a young man sitting alone at a table tucked in a shadowed alcove beside the chimney. Hunched forward with his head bowed, the young man's features were hidden beneath a shock of hair the color of ripe wheat.

"Poor feller." Mr. Scroggins shook his head sadly. "Been here the better part of two days now. Jist sits there most of the time. I take him somethin' to eat and drink once in a while, though he ain't et much."

"What ails him?" Brock narrowed his eyes at the man across the room.

Though the innkeeper lowered his voice, his tone sparked with enthusiasm to tell the tale. "Well, sir, he talks real Dutchy, but best I can gather his young wife somehow managed to fall into the Ohio River and drown on their way down from Cincinnati." He gave Annie a quick look. "It seems—like you—she was in the family way." He cleared his throat, his face growing red again. Mumbling something in an apologetic tone, he hurried away and disappeared through a narrow doorway.

"*C'est triste!*" The breathless expression of sadness puffed from Annie's lips. How awful to come all the way across the sea to make a new life with his family, only to be left alone.

"I wonder if he knows the Hoffmeiers?" Promising to return directly, Brock stood and pushed back his bench, making loud scraping sounds on the puncheon floor.

With hat in hand, he crossed the room to the young man. Annie could make out little of their conversation, but her heart swelled with love and pride as Brock gave the young man a sympathetic pat on the shoulder.

The prayer Annie had prayed countless times over the past months once more winged its way heavenward from her rent heart. *Dear Lord, please find a way to spare Brock. Don't let Colonel Stryker kill him.* Even if he chose to situate his affections and his life with another, it would give her heart ease knowing this kind man she loved—would always love—remained in the world.

Across the room, the young German rose and shook hands with Brock, and then the two men started toward Annie.

"Annie," Brock began when they reached her table, "this is Johann Arnholt. His family and the Hoffmeiers were friends and neighbors in the German kingdom of Hanover. He's promised to join them in Deux Fleuves, so he'll be traveling with us."

Annie started to rise, but Johann shook his head. "You sit. . . please. We all sit." A half a head taller than Brock, Johann joined him on the bench across the table from Annie.

"We are so sorry for your loss, Mr. Arnholt." Annie wanted to express her sympathy, but briefly, so not to heighten his sadness. When Papa died, even a too-sympathetic look from someone could send her into spasms of sobs.

Johann's light eyes glistened with unshed tears, and his throat moved with a swallow, but his voice was steady. *"Danke."*

He looked down at his large hands in which he wadded a dark blue wool cap. "I stay here too long, I think. Me and my Sophie, we promise *Herr* and *Frau* Hoffmeier we come to The Forks." He swallowed again—hard. "No Sophie now. No *Kind*. . . They with *Gott* now."

Johann's voice cracked, and so did Annie's heart. She wished there were some way she could ease his pain. She'd been in his place and knew there was nothing she could do except to pray and ask God to grant him peace and comfort.

Johann sat up straighter and lifted his chin. His voice took on a stronger, resolute tone. "But we make promise. So I keep promise for me and Sophie."

The innkeeper reappeared through the little doorway. Smiling brightly, he rubbed his palms together. "Would you folks like something to eat? My wife has pork pies fresh from the oven."

Brock and Annie exchanged awkward glances. Many hours had passed since breakfast and the tempting aromas wafting from the inn's interior caused Annie's stomach to grind with hunger. She suspected Brock's did, too. But she doubted he had any money, and nothing worth trading but Valor or his sheath knife—both of which he needed. She was about to say no when Johann piped up.

"Ja, we all have pies." He reached into his pocket and pulled out several silver coins. They clinked merrily as he plunked them down on the table.

The innkeeper scooped up the coins, testing one between his teeth, then with a nod, hurried away to fill the order.

Several minutes later they were all dining on hot meat pies and tankards of cold milk. Annie was glad to learn that Johann had a wagon ready to transport them all to Deux Fleuves, because she wasn't at all certain she could mount Valor after such a filling meal.

As they were finishing the last bites a man burst through the door. His wide eyes held the wild look of terror, and his face was as white as the inside of the mussel shells Annie used to gather from the riverbanks as a child. "Zeb! Zebulon Scroggins!"

At the man's loud summons, the innkeeper came thundering into the dining room. "Sam Tinchell, have you lost yer mind? What's possessed you to come stormin' in my inn and upsettin' my patrons?" He shot Annie an apologetic look. "Why this little lady's in a delicate—"

"They need to be upset. You all do." Still trembling, the man gestured wildly, waving his arm toward the north side of the inn. "Shawnee done massacred the whole of Pigeon Roost. Every last man, woman, and child from what I hear!"

Annie gasped. Pigeon Roost settlement sat less than forty miles east of Deux Fleuves, and they'd need to pass just north of it.

Dread gripped her. Did her cabin still stand? Did Bess, Obadiah, and their children remain safe? She reached across the table and grasped Brock's hands. "I need to get home."

His russet brows knitted together in a worried *V*, and for a moment she feared he would put up an argument. But as she gazed intently into his face, she saw surrender in his eyes, and he nodded.

Johann stood. "I get wagon. We go now to The Forks."

Chapter 14

It's just as you left it." Relief tinged Brock's voice as Johann brought the wagon to a stop in front of Annie's cabin.

Sitting beside Johann, Annie gazed upon her cabin for the first time in nearly three months. The scene before her eyes misted, and her heart swelled with grateful prayers. Since learning of the tragedy at Pigeon Roost, they were not at all sure what they might find when they arrived here.

But gazing over the landscape, she knew Brock was not entirely correct in his assessment. Things here *had* changed since she last saw her land. The day of her abduction, the corn the two of them planted had reached only waist high. Now the stalks stood taller than most men. Crowned with golden tassels, the plants' green leaves had begun yellowing beneath the early-September sun, while brown silks that tipped well-formed ears curled as they dried. Near the ground, splotches of orange appeared on round, green pumpkins: the gourds she'd planted the day she was taken. The four acres of wheat and oats, which three months ago had just started sporting grain heads, were now reduced to golden stubble.

"Hermann Hoffmeier and his family have taken good care of the place." Standing behind her in the wagon's bed, Brock voiced Annie's own thoughts.

"Oui." Her gaze pivoted to the cabin. All looked neat and tidy. Even the two brownstone steps that led up to the building's front door appeared swept clean. Beside the steps, someone had planted a wild rosebush and some honeysuckle vines. Although Brock had told her the Dunbars were caring for Cap'n Brody, she almost expected the big dog to come bounding out the front door. But the door was closed—barred shut.

For the first time since they arrived, she noticed the unnatural quiet. Not so much as a bray from Sal or a moo from Persimmon.

An uneasy feeling rose in Annie's chest as her gaze climbed to the top of the chimney, devoid of smoke.

Something was not right.

She sensed Brock tense behind her. He must feel it, too.

Dread tiptoed up Annie's spine, raising the hair at the back of her neck. At the worried look on Brock's face she struggled to keep her voice calm. "The Hoffmeiers must have moved to their new cabin."

Brock shook his head. "They promised some of the family would stay here until I returned."

Climbing down from the wagon, he took up his rifle and motioned for Johann to ready his own musket. "I'm going to look around. If there's any trouble, you two hightail it to the fort."

Beating back the fear rising inside her, she gave Brock a solemn nod and prayed he'd find nothing amiss. Beside her, Johann calmly loaded his musket as Brock disappeared behind the cabin. Annie wished she had Jonah's old brown Bess as well.

After a few tense moments, Brock emerged from around the building's northeast corner. Annie hadn't realized she'd held her breath until she expelled it with a relieved whoosh.

Giving a puzzled shrug, he walked back to the wagon. "They must have gone to the fort."

Annie stood. For nearly three months, she'd longed to see the inside of her cabin again. She wouldn't leave until she had. "I want to see my cabin, and I need to get my mother's Bible."

Brock shook his head. "I'm sorry, Annie, but I'm not sure it's safe to linger."

A flash of anger stiffened Annie's back, and she began to climb down from the wagon. "*Allez-y!* You do as you like, Brock Martin, but I'm going into my house!"

Before her foot touched the wagon spoke, she felt his sure grip on her waist and heard his soft sigh of defeat. "One quick look, Annie, and then we must go."

"I watch." Johann looked down upon them from his perch on the wagon, a hint of a grin lifting the corner of his mouth.

At the door, Annie fidgeted with excitement on the stone step as Brock removed the heavy wood bar. How wonderful it would be to see her own things again—to sit on her own bed.

When he finally opened the door, she stepped into a room at once familiar and unfamiliar. Objects she didn't recognize blended with her own to make a space, though homey, different from the one she remembered. It even smelled different. The scents of cooked cabbage and sausage still lingered in the air. Yet she was pleased to see how tidy the place looked.

When her gaze drifted to the table by the bed where she'd kept her mother's Bible, disappointment and sadness struck her a solid blow.

Her voice quavered and tears stung her eyes. "Mama's Bible is gone." She tried to console herself with rational thought. Brock had said the Hoffmeiers were good Christian people. Perhaps they'd simply packed it away for her.

Frowning, Brock bounced a narrow-eyed glance around the space. "They left in a hurry, that's for sure. I say we do the same."

Though she hated leaving, Annie knew he was right. Nodding, she exited the cabin, eager to see Bess and Obadiah.

On their way to the fort, every other homestead they passed looked as abandoned as hers. But Annie took solace in that they found none of the places burned or any other grim signs of attack.

As they approached the fort, someone called out heralding their arrival, and the twin log gates swung open, allowing them to enter.

Annie gazed about astounded. Only on Sunday had she seen so many people in the fort at once. And this wasn't Sunday. A buzz of excitement swelled and spread through the gathering crowd around them. Brock and Johann climbed down from the wagon first. Scanning the crowd of people for Bess and Obadiah, Annie climbed down from the wagon into waiting arms. She turned, expecting to see Brock's face. But it was Johann's smile that greeted her—Johann's arms that lifted her safely to the ground.

The disappointment squiggling through Annie evaporated at

the sight of Bess Dunbar running toward her, arms outstretched and tears streaming down her beaming face.

"Oh, my girl! My precious, precious girl!" Bess's tears dampened Annie's hair and shoulder. "Praise be to God! Praise His Holy Name. . . ." The rest of her words were swallowed by happy sobs as she rocked Annie in her arms like she was little Ruth or Isaac.

Annie vaguely noticed Johann and Brock move away to another group of people as she clung to Bess, joining her friend in a chorus of tears and laughter.

At last, Bess pushed away from their embrace. "Brock vowed he'd fetch you back to us, and he did. Praise be to God, he did! Let me look at you." Her eyes widened, and her mouth formed a little *O*. "I knew I was right." New tears sketched silently down her plump cheeks, and she pressed her palm against Annie's rounded belly. "He kicks real strong."

Annie couldn't help giggling at Bess's words. "You think it is a boy, then?"

Bess gave her an astonished look. "Why, 'course it's a boy! Look how you're carryin'—all out front in a little ball." She shook her head and brushed away fresh tears. "Jonah would be right pleased."

Annie liked to imagine Jonah grinning down on her from heaven, already aware of their child's gender. At the same time, it bothered her to think of the babe growing up without a father. Her gaze instinctively turned toward Brock like a willow branch to water. He stood some distance away with Johann, Obadiah, and a group of people she didn't immediately recognize. Then she watched Brock hug a very pretty, but obviously distraught, blond girl, and Annie's heart pinched.

Katarina Hoffmeier.

Did the girl cry from sorrow at the news of Sophie Arnholt, or in happiness at Brock's safe return? Perhaps both, Annie decided, watching Brock touch the girl's arm in a sympathetic manner that suggested a measure of familiarity. Annie hated the jealousy rising up inside her.

Before she had a chance to wonder any more about the two's

relationship, she found herself engulfed in Obadiah Dunbar's paternal bear hug.

"Our prayers have been answered, lass. We will be singing praises of thanksgiving to God tonight, my girl." Letting her go, Obadiah's happy face turned somber. "When we heard about Pigeon Roost, we feared for you and Brock and Gray Feather."

Annie glanced around at the milling throng. "Is that why everyone has come into the fort—because of what happened at Pigeon Roost?"

Obadiah nodded. "That, and because of George Kinney. They found him tomahawked to death in his cornfield yesterday."

Chapter 15

There you are, *mon chere*, with your head as hard as a rock."
At the sound of Annie's bright voice and happy giggle, Brock looked up from cleaning his rifle. During their nearly two weeks in the fort, he'd come to pay scant attention to the hundred or so voices constantly buzzing around the little compound. Mixed with animal sounds, they all blended together in an unintelligible drone that reminded him of a bee tree. Yet his ears seemed tuned to Annie's voice alone, which never failed to send a thrill rippling through him.

"Are you talking to me or Cap'n Brody here?" His heart thumped harder as she neared the east end of the garrison house porch where he sat cross-legged beside the big dog.

"Why, the cap'n, of course." She bent to hug the dog's thick, woolly neck. "But if the cap fits. . ." She sent Brock a teasing grin, displaying that delightful little dimple in her cheek he loved so much.

"I'm convinced he lived for no other purpose than to see you again." Brock hoped his voice sounded nonchalant, but doubted it. How could he remain unaffected by her nearness when these private conversations with her had become as rare and dear as gold?

In slow, careful movements, she lowered herself to the brownstone step next to the spot on the porch where Cap'n Brody lay basking in the midmorning sun. Caught in a slice of sunlight, Annie looked achingly beautiful as she settled on the rock, readjusting her brown calico skirt to better accommodate her expanding girth.

Brock allowed his gaze to roam untethered over her features, drinking in her loveliness like a thirsty man guzzles water. Her faded calico bonnet hung limply at the back of her neck, and a freshening breeze tantalizingly rearranged the walnut-colored curls at her forehead.

He swallowed down the painful knot that had gathered in his throat. Had there ever been a man so completely smitten as he. . .a heart so helplessly beguiled as his?

"There is nothing you would not do for me, is that not so, mon ami?" The golden freckles sprinkled over Annie's face seemed to dance merrily as she wrinkled her nose at the dog, who answered with a contented groan and a soulful look.

Brock longed to say that the sentiment exactly described his own devotion to her. But she must surely know that. Hadn't he tracked her from Deux Fleuves to the interior of Ohio, risking both his life and freedom to bring her home? He would gladly do it again without a moment's hesitation. How he longed to proclaim his love and devotion to her. But between his appointment with Stryker's hangman's noose and the hostile Shawnee who kept them penned up in this fort, his time on earth was quickly dwindling.

Annie offered Brock an unsteady smile. "Surely by now, Gray Feather has sent word to the rangers at Fort French Lick. Until they arrive, we must all stay as strong as our stout-hearted Cap'n Brody." A tinge of uncertainty tarnished the bright hope in her voice.

Brock rammed the cleaning rod down the barrel of his rifle and prayed Annie was right. He longed to reassure her, but giving her false hope would only be cruel. "Gray Feather will do all he can to help—you know that."

Though his statement was true, Brock feared that even if Gray Feather managed to get word of their predicament to Fort French Lick, the rangers might not believe him. Too many times Indians had used just such tricks to lure soldiers into death traps.

But something needed to be done. . .and soon. The limited food supplies in the fort would not hold out long. For the first two or three days, there'd been an almost celebratory attitude among the settlers, as if they had gathered in the fort for a wedding or a log rolling. As they had experienced on earlier occasions, they expected a company of soldiers to arrive within a day or two and shoo away the pesky Indians bedeviling them. But ten days had passed with no sign of help, and the menace lurking outside the little stockade had become frighteningly apparent.

Lately, Brock had sensed a further deterioration in the general mood within the compound. As the days passed, their frustration at being cooped up in the fort had gradually given way to a growing panic. Each time someone tried to leave the stockade, they were greeted by a musket shot or an arrow that seemed to come from nowhere. Until yesterday, they'd all been warning shots. Then, impatience and worry over the condition of his livestock at home had caused Pritch Callahan to foolishly walk out of the fort in the middle of the day. The man hadn't gotten twenty paces before an arrow whistled through the air and struck his shoulder. Brock and Amos Buxton just barely managed to get him back into the safety of the compound with their own skins intact.

Annie's brows pinched together as she rubbed the dog's head and glanced down the length of the porch toward the building's open front door.

Brock longed to still her fears. He infused his voice with as much optimism as he could muster. "Pritch didn't make it yesterday, but it was a fool thing he did, leaving in broad daylight. He's lucky he's still breathing and wearing his scalp. But I think if some of us tried it at night—"

"Pritch Callahan should have waited for the soldiers." Annie fixed Brock with a stern glare. "We all should wait for the soldiers. In another day or two—"

"Annie!" Her name exploded from Brock's mouth. His back stiffened, and he sat up straight, his musket forgotten. As much as he wanted to give her hope, he couldn't bear to hear another person say that all they needed to do was to wait another day. "We've been saying 'a day or two' for over a week now. Most of the army is occupied up north fighting the British as well as Tecumseh and The Prophet. The army doesn't have the resources these days to send soldiers to check on every settler fort in the Territory."

When Annie turned silent and went back to petting the dog, Brock blew out a calming breath and relaxed against the garrison house wall again. The last thing he'd wanted to do was fight with Annie. He resumed his work with the musket and tempered his voice. "How is Pritch?"

Annie shrugged. She seemed as disinclined to argue as he did. "Bess says if the wound doesn't putrefy, he should live." Her gaze swung toward the east perimeter of the stockade, where several farm animals grazed. "I'm just thankful the Hoffmeiers thought to bring Sal and Persimmon when they came to the fort. At least I know I'll still have my animals when I'm able to go home again. And Johann is fairly certain that Persimmon is with calf."

Brock smiled as he ran a scrap of oily cloth over the gun's mechanisms, heartened by the lilt in her voice. "Then she will be freshening in a few months, and you won't have to worry about her going dry." He decided it would be best not to mention that if the days dragged on and they remained trapped in the fort, the animals would soon be competing with the people for food.

"Johann said if Hermann doesn't buy the calf, he will." She turned a fond smile toward Johann, who was leading Persimmon and Sal to one of the few remaining patches of high grass inside the fort.

The familiarity in her voice when she spoke of their new friend set emotions warring within Brock. He'd noticed that Annie seemed to divide her time between the Dunbars, the Hoffmeiers, and Johann. He knew he should be glad if Annie's friendship with the young German turned to love. Brock liked the kind, even-tempered fellow very much. He could leave this world with his heart at peace knowing Johann would take good care of Annie and her baby. Yet the thought of her with another man—even a good man like Johann Arnholt—gouged at his heart.

Brock clicked the hammer on the gun's lock several times to make sure it didn't stick. He needed to know he could depend on his weapon if the Shawnee managed to sneak into the fort.

"You're not thinking of going out there, are you?" Her worried tone touched Brock. Perhaps she still had a soft place in her heart for him. It warmed his heart to think so.

He rubbed the oily rag down the musket's barrel, then set the gun aside. "Sooner or later, someone will have to try again, and I'd have a better chance than most. More than likely, there are just a handful of Shawnee keeping us in here."

She rose and looked him directly in the eye. "Promise me you won't go out there until the soldiers or the rangers come."

Brock's heart writhed. He wanted to do as she asked. He wanted to take her in his arms and promise her he would never leave her.

"I can't do that, Annie. If help doesn't come soon, I can't just sit here and do nothing while a few renegade Shawnee starve us all to death."

He stood and picked up his gun, his fingers convulsing around the smooth wood stock. "You once told me that your father said, 'A soldier fights, but a coward runs.' Well, I'm done running, Annie."

Whirling on him, she let go a volley of angry-sounding French words. She glanced down at Cap'n Brody, then back up to him, tears shimmering in her flashing agate eyes. "Then your head *is* as hard as Cap'n Brody's!"

His next words leaped from his mouth before he could stop them. "I'd say me and the cap'n are not the only ones with hard heads. Or maybe your time with the Shawnee has blinded you to the extent of the danger we are in."

A myriad of emotions—shock, fury, and sadness—flashed from her watery eyes. Her chin trembled, and she shot him a withering look. "And maybe you're more afraid of the soldiers and Colonel Stryker than you are of the Shawnee."

Miserable, he stood on the porch and watched her stomp away toward her mule and cow—and Johann Arnholt. A few minutes ago he'd reveled in the chance to have a conversation with Annie that he didn't have to share with anyone else. Now he'd ruined it and, most likely, the prospect of any further conversations with her.

" 'A soft answer turneth away wrath: but grievous words stir up anger.' " Obadiah's quiet voice behind Brock yanked him around.

"I reckon you heard that." Brock had trouble meeting the preacher's gaze.

Obadiah clasped a warm, comforting hand on Brock's shoulder. "Me and most everyone else in the fort, I reckon," he said with a friendly sounding chuckle.

Brock cast a sidelong glance at Obadiah. But instead of the disapproval he'd expected to see on the man's face, he found only compassion. It encouraged him to unburden his heart.

With a deep sigh, Brock shoved his fingers through his hair. "I thought she wanted to get back to her cabin—back to her land. But when I said I might sneak out at night to get help, she got her back all up."

"Perhaps she's found something more important to her than the land."

Nonplussed, Brock cocked his head and stared at the preacher, unable to deduce the man's meaning. "Since I met Annie, nothing has been more important to her than that land, and keeping her word to her pa and Jonah."

Obadiah placed a firm but gentle hand on Brock's back and guided him to the end of the porch. Motioning for Brock to join him, he sat down and stretched out his legs, resting his crossed feet on the brownstone steps where Annie had sat a few moments earlier.

Crossing his arms over his chest, Obadiah looked out toward the stockade's weathered posts. But the distant look in his eyes suggested he was seeing something else.

"A couple of years ago when Bess and I first came here, Bess was forever frettin' about not havin' any honey or sorgum for sweetin'." He shot Brock a sidelong grin.

Perched on the edge of the porch, Brock leaned forward and rested his arms on the tops of his legs. He was obviously in for one of Obadiah's famous yarns, so he might as well get comfortable.

"Well, sir," Obadiah continued, "one day while Jonah, Annie's pa, and I were out huntin' deer, we came across Gray Feather. He said he'd found a bee tree a little ways down the trail and wondered if we had an ax. Gerard did, so we proceeded to the tree and commenced hackin' it open."

Brock couldn't imagine what the preacher's story about a bee tree could have to do with his argument with Annie. But a good story would be a welcome diversion from his worries.

Obadiah angled his barrel-chested torso toward Brock, his widening grin pushing up his bearded cheeks nearly to his eyes. "Well, sir, we'd just opened up that tree when the biggest black bear I ever saw come barrelin' toward us, determined he was going to have that honey for himself." A merry chuckle bubbled from the big man. "The four of us played tag with that bear around the honey tree for quite some time, neither us nor the bear willin' to concede."

Though still not grasping the point of the story, Brock laughed appreciatively, imagining the comic scene.

Growing quieter, Obadiah scratched his hairy chin. "We finally got off some good shots and ended up with a tree full of honey and bear meat to boot."

"Reckon Bess was pretty happy about that, huh?" Brock wondered if Obadiah was trying to say Brock should offer Annie some kind of present.

Obadiah shook his head. "You'd think so, wouldn't you?" His blue eyes twinkled. "When I got home and told her the tale, Bess tore into me like I'd done somethin' awful."

Brock was confused. "But you said she wanted the honey."

"She was mad because I put myself in danger to get that honey." The preacher's voice and smile softened. "Turns out, she'd rather have me than the honey. Or the bear meat, for that matter. And for that, I am eternally thankful to God," he added with a little laugh.

Both men stood. Brock smiled and nodded, still unable to glean any kind of moral from the story. Perhaps after all, Obadiah had simply attempted to lift their spirits with the entertaining yarn.

Obadiah leveled a piercing look at Brock. "Annie loves you,

Brock. She wants to keep you alive. That's more important to her than gettin' back into her cabin."

His heart thumping harder, Brock looked with wonder across the stockade at Annie. She sat on a stool milking Persimmon and laughing up at Johann, who stood holding the cow still. Could Obadiah be right? Could Annie really love him?

Reality squeezed Brock's heart. What did it matter? They had no chance for a future together. He had no future at all. "Annie would be better off with Johann—'bout anybody but me." It was high time he told Obadiah of his predicament. "There's another reason Annie doesn't want me to fetch the rangers here. The Indians ain't the only ones after my hide."

"You're in trouble with the army." Obadiah's quiet comment held no hint of a question, and Brock experienced a flash of disappointment. Annie must have told the Dunbars of his situation.

"Annie told you?" Brock gazed across the yard to the spot where she sat milking.

"No. She didn't have to." A grin touched Obadiah's voice. "I may not look like the sharpest tool in the shed, but I can add two and two. You come here out o' nowhere, cloister yourself out there in Gerard's old cabin and stay shy of the fort, especially when soldiers are about. Didn't take much figurin' to see you're runnin' from somethin', and I reckoned it was the army."

Brock snorted a half laugh. "The way you put it, I might as well have had FUGITIVE written across my forehead."

"Care to tell me why?" Obadiah crossed his arms over his chest and leaned a shoulder against the garrison house wall.

Brock recounted the tragic events that led to his desertion. "If your conscience prods you to turn me in should we make it through this siege, I wouldn't hold it against you."

Obadiah straightened and clapped a hand on Brock's shoulder. "Son, I consider what you told me a confidence. I'll share it with no one but Bess, and she'd take it to her grave if I asked her to. It's a powerful burden you carry, for sure. I'll be praying God guides your decision on the matter."

Brock was about to thank Obadiah when Amos Buxton strode down the porch toward them, his face grim.

"Obadiah. Brock. Have you taken a good look at the creek today?" His voice sounded tight, and he drew a shaky hand across his whiskered face. "There ain't hardly more than a trickle of water runnin' through it." A look of mounting panic shone in his eyes. "Me and Joel Tanner think the Shawnee have dammed it up somewhere outside the fort to deprive us of water."

Chapter 16

Y ou gotta eat somethin'—for the babe's sake."

At Bess's cajoling tone, Annie looked up from her spot on the floor beside the garrison house hearth. She stopped humming a tune to the toddler she cradled in her arms. Her empty stomach rumbled as she eyed the johnnycake nestled in the scrap of linen Bess held out to her.

"Non." She shook her head despite her grinding hunger. This morning she'd learned that the fort's store of cornmeal had dwindled to less than half a barrel. How could she eat knowing she'd be depriving a child or nursing mother of another morsel of sustenance.

Annie shifted the sleeping, sweaty, two-year-old to a more comfortable position on her lap. Her gaze slid to Abbey Graham who sat hunched in the corner, her back to the room, discreetly feeding the twin to the child Annie held.

"Give it to Abbey. She has two babies to feed."

Bess settled herself beside Annie and set the cloth with the johnnycake on the floor between them. She reached over and gently lifted the sleeping child from Annie's arms. "Eat the johnnycake, Annie. Abbey had two cakes a while ago." She began rocking the little boy who popped a thumb in his mouth and started sucking noisily. "She's already fed little Aquilla here, and says she still has enough milk for Priscilla." She glanced at Annie's distended middle. "Your babe needs food, too."

Reaching for the piece of fried corn bread, Annie assuaged her guilt with the knowledge that Bess was right. While denying herself nourishment, she also denied her unborn child.

"Has your babe moved at all, today?"

Bess's quiet question sent a renewed wave of concern rolling through Annie. In the two days since the Indians dammed the creek, severely restricting the fort's water supply, she'd noticed with alarm, much less movement by her baby.

"A little," Annie murmured before taking a bite of johnnycake. She pressed her hand against her abdomen, praying for a kick, a twitch. . .any movement at all.

"Don't you worry none, Annie." A kind smile embroidered Bess's voice. "That babe will take all the nourishment it needs. Like the rest of us, it's just slowin' down so it can manage on less food."

Praying Bess was right, Annie rolled the meal in her mouth, luxuriating in its greasy taste and grainy texture against her tongue. This morning she'd allowed herself a sip of milk, but the fried cake was the first solid food she'd eaten since early yesterday.

She glanced around to see if anyone noticed her eating. Since her return to Deux Fleuves, some of her neighbors had begun treating her differently. Their furtive glances in her direction followed by whispers made her wonder if they believed the child she carried was Shawnee. Whatever the cause of their unfriendliness, their chilly attitudes heightened her guilt at eating even a morsel of food.

Glancing at the folks milling about the garrison house and coming and going through the building's open door, she kept her voice low. "Some treat me like I'm the enemy—or I'm dirty." She managed to swallow the bite of cornmeal that had turned to a hard lump in her dry mouth. "*C'est évident.* They think because I lived with the Shawnee, I do not deserve this." She held up the johnnycake, then dropped it into her lap.

Bess leveled a no-nonsense look at Annie, and her voice turned stern. "Anybody who begrudges you food because the Shawnee carried you off ain't practicin' their Christianity. Starvin' yourself and your babe won't make the Indians go away."

The memory of Brock's words still jabbed at Annie's heart. "Even Brock accused me of not seeing the danger we're in because of my time with the Shawnee."

Bess's smile turned kind, and she touched Annie's arm. "Now, don't you go takin' that to heart, Annie."

Abbey Graham approached, and Bess became quiet. With a murmur of thanks, the young mother took her sleeping child from Bess's arms and retreated to a corner of the room to tend her children. When she'd gone, Bess turned back to Annie with a sigh. "Brock knows you better than that. You ask me, it's the worry talkin'. Worry will cause a body to say hurtful things—things they don't mean—to the ones they care for most."

Did Brock truly care for her? As much as Annie would like to think so, she was afraid to let her heart believe it.

Cocking her head, Bess sighed. "Brock's a man, Annie. Men need to fix things. 'Specially good men like Brock and Obadiah. Brock sees you—all of us—gettin' weaker every day. He feels powerless to fix it, and it's drivin' him mad." She crossed her arms over her chest. "The sun's set a couple times now on your anger. Seems to me you need to patch up your differences before. . ." A somber tone crept into her voice. "Well, before it's too late."

Annie sniffed and swiped at her wet cheek as remorse gripped her. Several times since their angry exchange, Brock had approached her, hat in hand, a penitent look shining from his gray-green eyes. But she'd made excuses not to talk with him. Somehow, she sensed he wouldn't leave the fort without making his peace with her.

Tears welled in her eyes and slipped unheeded down her face. "I'm not angry at him, Bess. I'm scared for him. He was talking of leaving to go for help." Her tears blurred Bess's features. "He hasn't given his heart to Christ, Bess. I can't let him put his life in danger, and I don't think he will go if he thinks I'm still angry with him." Her voice hardened with her resolve. "Now that I have him here and know he's safe, if keeping him angry with me will keep him alive until the Northwest Rangers come, that's what I'm going to do."

Bess gathered Annie against her like a mother hen gathers her chick beneath her wing. "Where is your faith, Annie?" she said softly, rocking Annie like she'd rocked baby Aquilla minutes earlier. "All our lives are in God's hands. Remember the verse from Psalm thirty-four Obadiah read last night at vespers? 'The angel of the Lord encampeth round about them that fear him, and delivereth them.' The best thing you can do for Brock is to make your peace with him and put him in God's hands. Just love him, and keep prayin' for his salvation. It could even be that God will use this trial to nudge Brock into Christ's fold."

Suddenly Bess straightened and gently pushed Annie away. "I think you're about to get your chance to do some mendin'."

Annie raised her head from Bess's shoulder, now damp with her tears. She looked through the open doorway, and her heart jumped. Katarina Hoffmeier was standing with Brock and Johann on the porch. Annie's heart felt a sting when Katarina gave Brock a hug before continuing along the porch with Johann. The girl's eyes had looked red as if she, too, had been weeping.

When Brock ducked into the room, Bess rose to her feet with a little groan. "Reckon I'd best see what my young'uns are about." She headed for the door, giving Brock a bright smile as she passed him.

As he crossed to her, Annie shoved the cloth with the corn cake into her skirt pocket, scrambled to her feet, and hurriedly rubbed the remnants of wetness from her face.

Regret pulled his face long. Annie couldn't decipher the several other emotions shining from his eyes, though.

"I'm sorry for what I said to you the other day." His head hung, and his eyelids looked hooded as if weighted by remorse. He kept turning his squashed hat in his hands.

His words of contrition smote Annie with shame. As a Christian she had to forgive him and thus abandon her notion of keeping him angry at her.

She reached out and touched his hand, still scrunching the brim of his hat. "Of course I forgive you. Will you forgive me for the mean things I said to you?" Her gaze slid away from his, down to their hands. "I didn't mean them either. Besides Papa, you are the bravest man I've ever known. Will you forgive me?"

"You have my forgiveness. . .and more." A grin eased up the corner of his mouth. "I doubt you have a mean bone in your body,

Annie Martin. And you were probably closer to the truth than you knew."

The constant buzz of conversation that always filled the garrison house during the day hushed to a low hum. Annie's glance followed Brock's around the room at the many pairs of interested eyes trained on them.

"Come." He gently took her elbow and guided her toward the door. "I need to talk with you alone."

He led her outside and down the long porch, past groups of people busying themselves in various occupations. Some women sat at their spinning wheels chatting with their children, who were carding wool at their feet. Men cleaned their guns, whittled, and talked together as well. But the thing Annie noticed about everyone she passed was the common look of fear and weary desperation on their drawn faces. Only children too young to fully understand their plight failed to display the anxious expression worn by their elders—a look that seemed to teeter on the edge of panic.

When they reached the large sugar maple tree a few yards behind the garrison house, they stopped. Several head of cattle grazing between them and the building afforded a measure of privacy.

Brock's throat moved with a hard swallow, but his gaze rested unflinchingly on Annie's.

The afternoon sun filtering through the tree's leaves lit his russet hair and scraggly-bearded jaw, making them shine like burnished copper. It reminded Annie of the day last April when he first arrived at her cabin—the way he'd looked as he walked tentatively toward her, hat in hand. The memory made her heart flutter.

"Annie," he began, then cleared his throat. For an instant, his gaze faltered, sending his lashes to the tops of his cheeks. Why had she never noticed that the sunlight made his lashes look like spun gold and copper?

His eyes sought hers again. "Katarina told me you're not eating. She's worried about you, and so am I."

Annie's heart pinched as Katarina's name slipped with ease

119

from Brock's tongue. Immediately she felt ashamed. The German girl had shown Annie nothing but kindness. Indeed, Katarina had even had the forethought to bring Annie's mother's Bible to the fort in the event that the Indians might burn the cabin.

Annie reached into her pocket and brought out the cloth swaddling the johnnycake. "Bess gave me this a while ago. I've eaten a little. . . ."

"Oh, Annie." A sad weariness frayed the edges of Brock's voice.

He gently grasped her elbow and led her to a milking stool on the south side of the tree. With careful, gallant movements that reminded her of her mother's tales of noblemen, he situated her on the stool. Only when she was seated did he crouch at her side.

The pained look on his face made his features appear tired and drawn. "Katarina thinks the reason you're not eating has something to do with. . ." He glanced down for an instant to the bare patch of dirt beneath him, then looked up at her again and swallowed. "She thinks it's because some folks aren't treating you well because of your time with the Indians."

Tears stung Annie's eyes and the temptation to unburden her heart to Brock became too strong. The words tumbled from her lips like apples from a torn sack.

"I hear folks call me a white Indian and look hard at me when I take a bite of food or a drink of water." She hated the renegade tears that escaped her eyes and slid down her cheeks. "I see it in their eyes, Brock. They think my baby is Shawnee. And when they see me eat or drink, they look at me like I've taken the food from their children's mouths."

Brock's voice hardened. "Pay no attention to them, Annie. We know your babe is Jonah's, but regardless, you have just as much right to the food stores as anyone in this fort."

He swallowed again and winced. "It's been tearing at me that you might be going without food because of what I said the other day."

Annie touched his forearm, and her heart throbbed painfully. "Non. It's not because of what you said." And it wasn't. Even before

Bess told her so, Annie had known in her heart Brock hadn't meant what he'd said to her.

The taut lines in his face relaxed. "Good. Promise me you will eat your share. Promise me." The urgency in his voice and desperate look in his eyes frightened her.

"I promise." Her reply came out in a breathy whisper.

"Annie"—he took both her hands into his and gazed into her face as if committing it to memory—"we can't wait any longer. People are sickening. I won't stand by and watch you die and do nothing."

A new wave of panic rolled through her, and she pulled her hands from his. Maybe if she showed her displeasure with the notion, she could once again persuade him to stay. "You're not thinking of leaving the fort again, are you?"

He gently recaptured her hands and caressed the backs of them with his thumbs. "Annie, you've known for months that I've been living on borrowed time. If I'm to die, I'd rather do it trying to save you and everyone else here in the fort, than satisfy Stryker's thirst for revenge."

Annie's mind raced to think of something that might persuade him not to go. "But what if the Shawnee break into the fort? You're a trained soldier. We need you here."

He shook his head. "Every man in this stockade has a gun and knows how to use it. You know I scouted for the army. I'd have the best chance of making it to Fort French Lick."

Her heart writhing, she swallowed down a hot lump of tears. "But you cannot go. It is not only for your life I fear, *ma chère*, but your soul as well." Tears that would not be denied flowed in earnest now. "I want to see you in heaven one day. Promise me you will not go without putting your soul in Christ's keeping."

He smiled wryly. "Not sure God wants my ornery soul, but if you'd care to pray for it, I'd reckon the Almighty would listen to you before He'd listen to me."

Did she sense a softening in his resistance to Christ's offer of salvation? At once, hope and urgency filled her, and she gripped his hands tighter. "But God *does* want your soul, ma chère. And oui, I can pray for you. I *have* been praying for you for a long time. But *you* must ask Christ to come into your heart. I cannot do that for you. Just ask Him to forgive your sins and take you into His fold, and whatever happens, one day we will meet again in heaven."

His sweet smile clawed at her heart. "I will think on it." Then the smile vanished and he turned somber. "It has been decided. Johann, Ezra, and I will try to slip out tonight and head for Fort French Lick."

"Nooo." The word dragged out of her throat in a low, agonized moan.

"Yes, Annie." The sternness in his voice broached no further argument. "The Shawnee are most likely waiting for us to get too weak to fight, then they will come in and. . .do what they did at Pigeon Roost. This may be our only chance."

He puffed out a long breath and his voice softened. "I promise you I'll do everything in my power to bring help and get Johann and Ezra back with their scalps on."

Unable to speak past the wad of tears knotting in her throat, Annie nodded.

For a long moment he simply held her hands, his gaze caressing her face. Then giving her fingers one last squeeze, he rose and walked toward the garrison house.

Annie shoved her fist against her mouth to stifle the scream trying to claw its way out of her throat. Her teeth bit into her knuckles until she tasted blood, but she pushed her hand harder against her mouth. Brock had said he would do what he could to keep Johann and Ezra safe, but he'd made no such promise about his own safety.

A brown and white cow ambled near, its nose pressed against the ground, it's flaring nostrils blowing up puffs of dust as it attempted to nibble the pitifully overgrazed grass. Annie knew Brock was right, and she would pray for him—for all three of the men. But the life-spark inside her dimmed, for short of a miracle, she feared she'd never see Brock again.

Chapter 17

"I s something wrong, Katarina?"

The moment Annie whispered the statement she realized how ridiculous it must sound. What was not wrong? Food and water had dwindled to dangerous levels. Over the past two days, three people had died, including Pritch Callahan, who'd finally succumbed to his wounds. But as she crossed the garrison house in the predawn darkness, Annie suspected something more personal caused Katarina Hoffmeier's muted sobs.

In the dim space, lit only by the hearth's glowing embers, Annie carefully maneuvered around the many dark, sleeping forms of women and children scattered about the floor. Even with both the front and back doors open, the smell of unwashed bodies, sickness, and despair hung heavily in the air. She was grateful that the men, when weather permitted, slept on the porch or on pallets in the yard to help relieve the crowding.

As Annie neared the fireplace, sympathy twanged hard inside her at the sight of the robust German girl. Katarina's substantial frame shook convulsively as she bent to feed kindling into the hearth's glowing throat.

"Has Giselle worsened?" Annie pressed her hand against Katarina's trembling shoulder. Yesterday Katarina's mother had suffered terribly with a stomach ailment.

Katarina sniffed and ran a hand under her nose as she shook her head. *"Nein."* She angled a weak smile at Annie and patted her belly. *"Mutter* is better now."

Katarina tossed another piece of wood into the fireplace, sending red and orange sparks flying amid a puff of gray ash. She straightened and her red-rimmed blue eyes quickly swept the room as if to assure herself that the other occupants, now rousing from sleep, paid them no heed.

Turning her attention back to Annie, she pressed a hand against her chest and drew in a ragged breath. "My heart, it hurts. Afraid I am that they not come back. That they die." New tears slid down her round cheeks, making meandering little trails that glistened in the firelight.

Annie didn't have to ask to whom Katarina referred. She patted the girl's arm as a surge of renewed fear gripped her own chest. In the five days since Brock, Johann, and Ezra left for Fort French Lick, Annie's lungs had felt incapable of holding a full breath of air. Every beat of her heart was a prayer for the safety of the man she loved, as well as the safety of Johann and Ezra.

Obviously Katarina was stricken with the same worries about Brock. Jealousy slithered up from some dark, ugly place inside Annie. Her conscience rose and swatted it down. If Brock returned safely and chose Katarina for his bride, Annie would wish them well. Her wounded heart would wail out its grief and carry its scars to the grave, but she would accept God's verdict.

Annie patted Katarina's shoulder. "Don't worry, ma chère. God will protect and deliver us. Remember the words of our Lord that Obadiah read to us last night? 'Peace I leave with you, my peace I give unto you: not as the world giveth, give I unto you. Let not your heart be troubled, neither let it be afraid.'" She mustered up as confident a smile as she could manage. "The Northwest Rangers will come. We will be saved. Brock used to scout for the army. If anyone can get past the Indians to Fort French Lick, he can."

Katarina glanced around the room again, and Annie followed her gaze. Light fingers of dawn reached through the open windows and doorways, illuminating the figures that had awakened and were now milling about the place. Children cried and quarreled. Mothers soothed and chided. The constant buzz of voices blended with the jumble of noises generated by many people living in close quarters.

"Come." Katarina bent and lifted two oak buckets from beside the hearth. "Time to milk, it is now. We go milk together, Ja?" She held one bucket out to Annie, who wrapped her fingers around the stiff, prickly fibers of the rope handle.

Outside, the crisp autumn morn sent a shiver through her, jerking her fully awake. Overhead, a morning star winked at them from a steel-blue sky. She wished she could see the horizon. But the stockade's silver-gray pickets hid much of the rich, rosy-gold hues that heralded the sun's first peek at the earth.

They wended their way through the yard full of stoop-shouldered men who seemed to wander aimlessly, bowed by their despair as if they carried their hopelessness on their backs.

The livestock had grazed every bit of vegetation until there was hardly enough grass to wet Annie's bare feet with dew as they walked toward the east end of the stockade.

Near the wall of the compound, several cows stood like dark hulks in the dim morning light, tethered side by side to stakes. As Annie and Katarina approached, the animals lowed with such mournful sounds that she wondered if they, too, sensed death lurking.

Persimmon bent her head back and blinked her big, long-lashed eyes at them.

"It's all right *ma bonne fille.*" Annie ran her hand along the cow's side and winced as her fingers bumped across the animal's ribs. In another few days Persimmon would most likely go dry and have to be slaughtered to provide food for the settlers. The thought pinched Annie's heart. She loved the young cow that was little more than a heifer, having weaned her first calf last winter.

"It is just me and Katarina coming to get your fine milk, Persimmon."

They each chose one of the three-legged stools kept nearby. Annie sat down at Persimmon's right side, while Katarina did the same with a big reddish cow next to Persimmon. With Persimmon's bulk between them, Annie and Katarina set to their tasks. And for a time, the rhythmic *splat, splat* of the milk hitting the wooden buckets filled the silence.

"You think they come back, then? You think they. . .live?" Katarina's soft voice was almost inaudible over the sound of the milk squirting into the buckets.

Annie paused in coaxing milk from Persimmon's udders. "Yes,

I think they are still alive." Perhaps it was her own hope clinging to life, but Annie's heart had twined so tightly with Brock's, surely she would know if his soul had left his body.

The soft *shh, shh, shh* sound of Katarina's milking halted, replaced by another long, ragged sigh. "I *beten Sie*—pray it be so."

Sensing the girl felt more comfortable venting her worries with her countenance hidden, Annie quietly resumed her own milking.

"If he die, my heart die, I think. . . ." Katarina's words dissolved into soft sobs.

The girl's agony crumpled Annie's heart. She got up and walked around Persimmon's head, rubbing the cow's soft muzzle as she passed. When she reached Katarina, she gently grasped her shoulders, inviting her to stand, and as well as her expanded belly allowed, she embraced her.

Annie clung to the taller girl nearly twice her size, rocking her as if she were a little child. The scent of dew-drenched morning glories, fresh sweet milk, and bitter tears filled Annie's nostrils as an indescribable pain filled her breast. Why did they have to love the same man?

When Katarina's sobs had subsided, Annie pushed gently away, but continued to grasp the girl's shoulders. "I told you, if anyone can make it to Fort French Lick and back alive, it is Brock."

Katarina snuffed and swiped at her wet, puffy eyes. "Ja." Her voice sounded almost indignant. "Brock, maybe. He was in army. He know this land. But Johann. . ." Her rounded shoulders rose and fell in a helpless shrug. "Johann not know land. Not know Indian ways."

An incredible realization dawned in Annie's brain like the sun's golden rays now spilling over the stockade's weathered, gray pickets. Could she dare to believe it was not Brock, but Johann that Katarina cared for?

Katarina inhaled another tattered breath. "If Johann not come back, then I lose him *zweimal*." She held up two fingers, forming a *V*, as fresh tears cascaded down her face.

At Annie's perplexed look, Katarina offered a wobbly smile. "We finish milking. I tell you."

They returned to their tasks, and over the next few minutes, in a mixture of broken English and German, Katarina disclosed how she, Johann, and his late wife, Sophie, had been children together in their small village in Hanover. From what Annie could glean from Katarina's fractured English, Katarina and Johann had been childhood sweethearts. But when unwed Sophie learned she was with child after receiving news that her sweetheart was killed fighting in Napoleon's army, Johann married her to save her from shame and shunning.

"It was gut thing Johann do." A weak smile trembled across Katarina's full lips. "I love Sophie, too." She tapped her chest. "My heart sad for me, but happy for Sophie and Johann."

Annie nodded. She understood the girl's sentiment exactly. It was the same feeling she'd experienced only moments ago with Katarina.

Katarina's voice took a sad dip. "But Sophie and Kind gone now. . .with Gott."

Her tone lifted again. . .brighter, sweeter. "When Johann come here, *sich grämen. . .*" She paused as if searching for the appropriate English word, then patted her chest. "Hearts cry together." She brushed away another tear. "Then our hearts"—she clasped both hands together—"again."

Katarina is in love with Johann, not Brock!

The joy inside Annie threatened to bubble out in a spate of silly giggles. But she tamped down the urge to laugh in deference to Katarina's heartache.

They retrieved their buckets of milk—both less than half full—from beneath the cows. Feeling a little guilty that her affection for Katarina had grown after her revelation, Annie looped her free arm with the other girl's.

As they walked together to the garrison house, Annie tried to assure both Katarina and herself that God would hear their prayers and bring the three men safely back to Fort Deux Fleuves.

"Even Ezra," Annie said with a burst of unrestrained mirth, admitting that she and Ezra had once been sweethearts before she married Jonah.

"After being wed to Jonah and now losing my heart to Brock, I wouldn't have Ezra if he served himself up to me on a silver platter," she confided with a giggle.

A commotion erupted in the yard, and Annie and Katarina turned to see what had occurred. The sound of hoofbeats and musket fire outside the compound sent cold fingers of fear skittering up Annie's spine. Had the Shawnee decided the settlers inside the fort had grown too weak to fight and were storming the compound?

Suddenly the men stationed on the parapet walkway began cheering. In another moment, men rushed to push open the big front gates that had remained closed for weeks.

Riders streamed in and such a deluge of relief washed through Annie it buckled her knees.

"Thank You, Lord! Oh, Jesus, thank You!" She dropped to her knees in earnest now, lifting her hands to heaven along with many others, praising God for the long-awaited arrival of the rangers.

Katarina tugged Annie to her feet and they fell into each other's arms, all at once laughing and weeping.

Eager to find Brock among the group of strangers milling with Deux Fleuves' settlers, she scanned the crowd.

Katarina, too, was gazing intently into the faces of the men who'd just arrived. She gasped the same moment Annie saw Johann step away from the crowd, his head pivoting, searching.

With a little shriek, Katarina snatched her skirts away from her feet and sprinted to Johann, who caught her in a fierce embrace.

Still not finding Brock, Annie hurried to Johann and Katarina.

"Johann, where is Brock? Is he here?" Annie continued to search the crowd for Brock's face. Perhaps he had stayed outside the fort to help the rangers secure it.

Johann set Katarina aside, and his bright smile dragged down in a grim frown.

Fear balled in the pit of Annie's belly. She focused her attention directly on Johann's somber face. "Is he here? Johann, please tell me he came back."

Johann shook his head, and tears welled in the big German's blue eyes. "Sorry, I am, Annie."

Chapter 18

The faint, sweet sounds of a church bell wafted through the barred window of Brock's cell.

He gripped the bars and pressed his face against the cold iron, craving any confirmation that he was still alive. Inhaling deeply, he breathed in the scents of woodsmoke, drying leaves, and autumn sunshine. They offered only a sliver of comfort.

In truth, all he needed to do was to look inside himself to verify his mortal state. His gut still sizzled at the memory of Ezra's betrayal.

Aided by a moonless night, Brock, Johann, and Ezra had managed to slip out of Fort Deux Fleuves undetected. For the better part of four days, Brock had safely led the other two men southwest, over forty miles of hilly, thickly forested terrain to Fort French Lick. He'd thought the three of them had built a strong camaraderie, so when they finally reached their destination he was completely taken by surprise when Ezra produced a tattered and yellowed scrap of newspaper—a wanted notice listing Brock as a deserter and murderer. The notice also declared that whatever person delivered said fugitive to army authorities would be rewarded in one hundred dollars gold.

Turning away from the window, Brock pressed his back against the cool stone wall of his cell and slid down to the filthy blanket on the hard-packed dirt floor that constituted his bed. The place stank of every bodily secretion imaginable, and as he'd done countless times before, he fought the urge to retch.

The memory of the shock, disbelief, and helplessness on Johann's face when soldiers clapped the irons on Brock's wrists and ankles still twisted his insides. With no time to explain to the German the details of the events that led to the charges against him, Brock had only a moment to beg Johann to explain to Annie what had happened and to see that she was taken care of.

Compounding his treachery, Ezra, for the purpose of claiming his reward, had traveled with Brock and the contingent of soldiers assigned to escort Brock back to Newport Barracks for trial. The thought that the scoundrel might return to Deux Fleuves and marry Annie gouged at Brock's innards. But surely when she learned what Ezra had done, she'd never agree to marry him.

Brock drew his knees up and rested his chin on them. The notion of any other man but himself marrying Annie slashed at his heart. Still, if he could believe that she and the amiable Johann might make a match, he could go to the gallows feeling far easier about her future. That, however, seemed unlikely. During the second evening of their trek to Fort French Lick, Johann had confided that he hoped to rekindle the relationship he and Katarina Hoffmeier had shared back in Hanover before he married his late wife.

So, like a sweet vine, Brock's love and concern for Annie continued to grow uninhibited, twining around his heart so tightly it throbbed with the pain.

Only the absence of Colonel Stryker had delayed Brock's court-martial and, almost certainly, his subsequent execution. Apparently, the colonel had led a contingent up to New York to fight under the command of General Van Rensselaer. So for the better part of two weeks, Brock had languished here, not knowing if Johann and the rangers had made it safely back to Fort Deux Fleuves, or if Annie was safe.

Annie. She ruled his waking thoughts and nightly dreams. Was she this moment thinking of him as he was thinking of her?

The back of his nose stung, and he blinked wetness from his eyes. He should have told her he loved her. Behind the garrison house when he informed her of his plans to head for Fort French Lick, he should have told her. He should have done what he wanted: taken her in his arms and kissed her and told her that whatever happened, he loved her—would always love her.

He squeezed his eyes shut tight. Annie's image appeared

behind his lids, so clear it seemed as if he might reach out and touch her. Her voice echoed in his ears. *"I want to see you in heaven one day."*

An overwhelming desire to know that whatever happened to him, he would one day see Annie again gripped him.

Another voice sounded in his head—a dear voice from long ago. " *'I have fought a good fight, I have finished my course, I have kept the faith.'* " Those same words—among the last his mother ever spoke on this earth—had come into his mind the night he and Annie swam for their lives from the Shawnee.

Brock brushed the wetness from his whiskered cheeks. Once again, he sat at his dying mother's bedside. Her faint voice strengthened as she gripped his hand. *"Don't cry, son. You will see me again one day in heaven. It says so in the Good Book."*

For many years, he'd forgotten Ma's last words. He had shoved them back into the dark recesses of his mind, along with the awful circumstances of her and Pa's deaths, and locked them away with chains of bitterness.

Brock lifted his head and looked up at the barred window above him. Through the black wrought-iron bars he could make out a wispy white cloud drifting across the azure sky. Was Annie already somewhere behind that cloud with Ma and Pa? With Christ?

Like a beckoning whisper, her words filled his mind and convicted his heart. *"You must ask Christ to come into your heart. Just ask Him to forgive your sins and take you into His fold, and whatever happens, one day we will meet again in heaven."*

Fresh tears drenched his face. Rolling onto his knees, he bowed his head and clasped his hands in prayer as he'd done as a child. "Dear Lord. When Stryker's noose chokes the life from me I want to see Ma and Pa and Annie again. Forgive my sins, make me fit for heaven, and take me into your fold."

A peace he had never before felt washed over him. Stryker could do his worst, but because of Christ, the hangman's noose had lost its power to separate Brock forever from the ones he loved. As joy bubbled up inside him, so did a desire to get word to Annie—if she still lived—that she no longer needed to concern herself about his soul.

Footsteps and a rattling sound in the hallway outside his little cell turned Brock's attention to the locked door. Running his sleeve under his nose, he scrambled to his feet and stepped to the door. Solid, except for a tiny nose-high barred window, the heavy oak partition opened only three times each day when his meals were delivered. Brock relished these respites, however brief, from the otherwise crushing solitude.

But at this moment, despite his growing hunger, it was not food he craved, but pen and paper.

Metal rasped against metal, followed by a click, then the door creaked open less than the span of a man's hand. The savory smell of meat and cooked vegetables made Brock's stomach grind. He reached out a hand to accept the wooden bowl of lukewarm stew.

Before the fresh-faced private could slam the door back in place Brock grabbed it and held it open, overpowering the weaker youth. Stryker could return any day. This might be his last chance to get a message to Annie.

For one instant, fear flicked in the boy's eyes. His hand flew to his belt dagger hanging at his hip.

"I mean you no harm." Keeping his eyes trained on the private's face, Brock set the bowl of stew on the floor. "I need to write a letter to. . .to someone dear to me. If you could just get me a piece of paper, a pen, and some ink. . ."

The soldier scowled and shook his head, making the white tassels at the side of his shako hat shiver. "That ain't allowed. You outta know that, havin' been a soldier."

Brock kept a firm hold on the door, and the soldier kept his hand on his belt dagger. Any moment the nervous private could call out for assistance to the soldiers talking and laughing—obviously playing cards—in the adjoining room.

"It–it's for my sweetheart," Brock said honestly. That Annie didn't know she was his sweetheart didn't change the fact that he considered her so. "There are things I need to tell her before—before Stryker returns." Yesterday, Brock had overhead the private mention his own sweetheart to another soldier in conversation. Perhaps if he appealed to the young man's sense of romance, he might yet have an opportunity to get a letter to Annie. "I reckon if you had a girl, you'd know—"

"I do." The boy's hand slipped away from his weapon, and empathy shone from his eyes. His brow scrunched, and he caught his lower lip with his teeth. He glanced over his shoulder as if assuring himself no one was listening, then turned back to Brock. "I'll do what I can," he whispered.

Chapter 19

A single large snowflake lit on Annie's dark wool cloak just as she glanced at the spot where it settled. The late-December sun glinted off the speck of moisture. For a brief instant, she glimpsed the intricate detail of the lacy flake. Its wondrous beauty struck her even as it disappeared beneath her warm breath.

She blinked away tears. God took the trouble to fashion elegance into a snowflake that might well have gone unnoticed. Walking toward the fort with the Dunbars, she gazed at the snow snaking across the worn path before the winter wind. How many such delicate works of God's hand made up the growing patches of white decorating the base of trees and the brown grass along the bottom of the fort's palisade? Yet the Almighty did not find it prudent to reach down and save Brock from the hangman's noose.

She tugged the heavy folds of the cloak closer around her, resentment swelling in her chest. God could make unnumbered snowflakes that doubtless few would appreciate, and some may even disdain. Yet hours and hours of prayers for Brock's life had gone unanswered. Since the letter she'd received from him in October, there had been no further word of his fate.

She held her Bible with the precious missive tucked safely within its pages close to her chest. The smudged words Brock had penned on the bits of tattered paper played over again in her mind.

My dearest Annie,

I have not the ink or paper to convey all that is in my heart. I must simply say that I am writing to express my love for you. I know now that I should have told you of my feelings months ago, and I greatly regret that cowardly omission. I

*pray that this letter finds you, so that at last, you may glimpse
the depths of my affection for you.*

*I have not yet stood for my court-martial as Colonel
Stryker has been away on campaign. Just this hour word has
reached me that he has returned to Newport Barracks, so my
trial may well be at hand. My incarceration has given me
much time to think, and I have thought a lot about what you
said about my soul. My dearest, if my life should be taken
from me I want to know I will one day see you again in
heaven. This day I fell on my knees and asked Christ to save
my soul, sorry as it is. I thank God every day for the sweet gift
of having known you. The example of your strong faith helped
lead me to salvation through our Lord. So my heart is eased,
knowing that one day we will meet again in heaven. I pray
daily for you and your babe, and that God will see fit that you
keep that land you hold such store by. Be assured that my last
thoughts on this earth will be of you, and your sweet name
will be the last utterance of my dying tongue.*

Forever your devoted,
Brock

As the group approached the fort's open gates, shame nipped
at Annie's conscience for her anger toward God. It was Christmas.
Like Brock, she should thank God for the gift of His Son that
bought them hope of one day reuniting in paradise.

Still, the sight of Katarina clinging to Johann's arm as the pair
entered the garrison house filled Annie's heart with regret and
her eyes with fresh tears. If only things had been different. If only
she and Brock, like Johann and Katarina, had been given another
chance to pledge their love and lives to each other.

Annie kept her head down, trying to hide her weepy eyes
beneath the hood of her cloak as she followed Bess and Obadiah
into the building. Since receiving Brock's letter, she'd cried enough
tears to fill both the White and Muscatatuck Rivers three times
over, it seemed.

Inside, she settled on the trestle board beside Bess. As her gaze roamed the room, she was reminded that hers was not the only grieving heart this Christmas Day. Several families had lost loved ones during the siege. And the Buxtons, Polly and Amos, still carried on their faces the shame and grief caused by their son's actions. Annie watched Ezra's mother, Polly, swipe at her thin, dried apple face. Though she tried to maintain a cheerful facade, her hollow eyes and slumped shoulders spoke of the toll her son's treachery had taken on her spirit. Not only had Ezra turned Brock in for the reward money, they learned that he'd headed out to the western wilderness without stopping by Deux Fleuves for so much as a parting word to his folks.

Seeming mindful of the sundry heartaches afflicting his flock, Obadiah's Christmas sermon encouraged his congregation to simply rejoice in the gift of salvation God sent to earth in the person of His Son.

The preacher's gaze touched briefly on Annie. A gentle smile softened the lines in his kind broad face. " 'To an inheritance incorruptible, and undefiled, and that fadeth not away, reserved in heaven for you,' " he read.

The scripture struck Annie full force. After her promise to Papa last February, nothing had seemed more important than keeping his and Jonah's inheritance.

As Obadiah led the congregation in singing a hymn, Annie ran her hand across the mound in her lap and smiled. Her precious babe answered her touch with a kick. Annie was indeed glad that her child had an opportunity to inherit the land that had meant so much to his father and grandfather. But over the past year she had learned how fragile such an inheritance could be. She finally understood that no scrap of land—nothing on this earth—could compete in importance with God's eternal inheritance. Though her heart moaned daily in grief for the loss of Brock, she rejoiced all the same that he had embraced Christ's salvation before it was too late.

A sudden gust of cold wind dried the tears on the cheeks. The singing faded until a hush fell over the room. She looked toward the door, wondering who could be so late for the service.

The soldier filling the doorway trained his gaze directly on her. A shower of snowflakes fell as he doffed his shako hat, and a gasp exploded from Annie.

Brock!

Annie.

Every muscle in Brock strained to dash to his beloved, sweep her up in his arms, and hold her fast against his pounding heart. But such an action would not be respectful during the Christmas worship service.

Instead, he nodded mutely toward a beaming Obadiah and slipped in beside Annie.

Her cinnamon eyes, brimming with tears and questions, gazed up at him unbelieving, while a tangle of emotions flashed across her pale, damp face.

Though he longed to tell her all that had transpired, there would be ample time for that later. He took her hand in his and gently squeezed her warm fingers. They trembled against his palm as he joined the congregation in the singing of a hymn.

After Obadiah's benediction, Brock surrendered to his longing and embraced Annie in a tender hug, whispering her name over and over.

Blissful moments passed as he reveled in the warmth of her embrace. Her bonnet slipped back, and he pressed his face against her thick, mahogany tresses, inhaling the sweet scent of her.

She clung to him as closely as her growing child allowed. Her muffled sobs against his chest tore at his heart even while they sped its pounding to triple-time cadence. In the arms of his beloved, winter melted into spring, his heart sang like the long-absent robin, and hope bloomed. If God called him home this moment, he could die a happy man.

The next moment he was set upon by the Dunbars, Johann and

Katarina, as well as a dozen or so other curious folk bombarding him with a barrage of questions.

With reluctance, he relinquished his precious captive, but only to a point, keeping an arm around her waist. He'd come close enough to death to smell its fetid breath. For the past three months, Annie's touch had been something he only dreamed about. He would not give it up lightly.

"It was not right, then, Ja?" Johann's confused but happy face peeked around Obadiah. "Ezra's paper, it was. . ." His broad brow scrunched as if searching for the right word. "*Fehler.* How you say—"

"Mistake." Katarina, clinging tightly to Johann's arm, supplied the English word.

"Yes, it was something like a mistake," Brock murmured the half truth, careful to not look at Obadiah. Or Annie. They had to know he would tell them everything in good time, but this was not the time or the place to do so.

Nodding, Johann gazed down upon Katarina fondly. "*Sehr gut! Mein Frau.* . .wife, know the English better."

Brock seized upon his friends' good news, eager to offer congratulations on their marriage while diverting attention from himself. But Johann would not be dissuaded from his questioning.

"Why then you wear the clothes of soldier?" Johann asked after Brock had pumped his hand and placed a congratulatory kiss on Katarina's cheek. It was the question he knew must be buzzing in everyone's minds, and the question he most dreaded.

"I'm sure Brock has many exciting tales to tell by the fireside this winter," Obadiah broke in, herding the group toward the door and earning Brock's silent thanks. "But Christmas dinner awaits." He patted his stomach. "And I've never been a man to leave roast fowl languishing."

Brock bid his German friends good day and good Christmas, allowing them to ponder the details of his release. It would doubtless provide interesting conversation at the Hoffmeier clan's Christmas dinner table.

When the well-wishers and curious had gone, Bess patted Brock's face and told him how peaked he looked. "Better come to our place for Christmas dinner. Me, Annie, and my girls have been cookin' and bakin' all week. We'll put some meat on them sorry bones o' yours so that uniform won't hang on you like you was a scarecrow."

"I will do that." Brock gave a little laugh, the first such sound of mirth he'd produced in a very long time. Bess's maternal fussing felt good.

Turning to Annie, he suddenly craved to hear her voice, but dreaded the inevitable subject of their conversation.

Without a word, Bess and Obadiah shooed their brood out of the fort while Brock and Annie lingered in the yard.

The snowing had slowed until only a few fluffy flakes dusted the shoulders and hood of Annie's dark cape. But the wind's icy gusts whipped at the folds of her cloak and made her cheeks rosy beneath the sprinkling of golden freckles. At least he attributed the color in her face solely to the cold temperature. He should get her into the warmth of the Dunbars' cabin as soon as possible.

An odd mixture of sadness and pride registered in her eyes as she examined him in his uniform. When she finally spoke her voice cracked, breaking his heart. "I got your letter." Her brown eyes glistening with tears, she slipped a soiled and tattered envelope from her Bible. His heart throbbed, imagining her reading over and over the tender words he'd penned to her months ago.

A brave smile quavered on her rosebud lips. "My heart rejoices at your salvation, and I praise God for whatever miracle has brought you safely back to me." A tear escaped its lovely confines and slipped unheeded down her cheek. "But you are not staying, are you, *mon amour?*"

Chapter 20

Annie sat beside the blazing fireplace, her fingers busily working the white linen thread and tatting shuttle. Yet it was not the crackling fire that warmed her through, but the rich tenor of Brock's voice.

With Christmas dinner cleared away and the last pot cleaned and hung, she'd been left with no outlet for her nervous energy. A swarm of wild emotions surging through her would not allow her to be still. So she tatted around the collar of the baby gown she'd made last week.

The moment Brock appeared in the garrison house doorway, she knew her prayers had been answered. Somehow God had found a way to save him. But at the same time the uniform he wore told her God had not saved him to be with her. She'd known the answer to her question before she posed it to him. No, he would not be staying. She wanted to believe she'd seen regret in his eyes, but sorrow and perhaps a touch of guilt was all she could honestly attest to.

Even as Brock regaled them over the dinner table with the fantastic tale of his deliverance, knowing he'd soon be leaving had blunted Annie's joy.

The incredible occurrences that had set him free remained the singular topic of conversation long after Bess sent the children to bed in the loft rooms above them.

"I'd say it was nothin' less then Providence that kept Colonel Stryker from presidin' over your trial." Obadiah looked up from his whittling, the carving knife becoming still against the little piece of wood in his hand. He shook his head. "Now, do not take me wrongly. Far be it from me to rejoice in any man's suffering. But it seems to me that by allowin' the colonel to be wounded in battle, the Almighty, in His infinite wisdom and mercy, found a way to

140

save both your life and the colonel's."

"Yes." Brock gave a solemn nod as he reached down and patted Cap'n Brody, snoozing at his feet. "It was indeed a blessing that Colonel Rodgers, an impartial, fair-minded man, replaced Colonel Stryker as post commander, and so became my court-martial judge. But it was Private Buchanan's testimony that saved me." His voice became thick, and he focused his attention on the dog as if he desired to avert his features from those around him. "I never imagined that the boy I saved from Driscoll's beating had lingered in the shadows and saw all that transpired."

"But why didn't he come forward sooner?" Bess's forehead knit together as tightly as the yarn she worked around the two long wooden needles in her hands.

"Said he was scared." One side of Brock's mouth lifted in a crooked grin. "Can't say I blame him. He said when he heard I'd be standing for court-martial and might be hanged, he felt compelled to come forward and bear witness to what he'd seen the evening of Lieutenant Driscoll's death."

"So you were cleared of the murder." Obadiah resumed scraping the wood with the knife. "But what about the desertion charges?"

Brock grinned. "I suppose in part, the war helped. The army needs every soldier they can get. Colonel Rodgers said he understood why I ran and took into account my years of unblemished service to the army and my action in going after help to break the siege here. Said as long as I returned to duty, he reckoned my good service mitigated my desertion."

"So when will you be leaving Deux Fleuves?" Annie strove to make her voice sound flat and indifferent. But judging by Brock's wince, she'd failed miserably.

"I must return to Newport Barracks by the first of January and serve another full year to make up for my time away from the army. After that I can either stay in the army or take a general discharge." Brock's gaze slid from hers, and Annie's hopes of him returning to Deux Fleuves after his required year of service melted like a snowflake beneath a puff of breath. Had he truly meant what he'd written in his letter to her? Or were those sentiments simply the outpourings of a doomed man and regretted now that life and freedom beckoned? The thought clawed at her heart.

A pounding on the cabin door shattered her melancholy reverie and yanked Cap'n Brody up from his snooze, instantly alert. Setting his carving aside, Obadiah rose with a grunt and crossed to the front door. He opened it, letting in a rush of frigid wind that swirled snow around a bewhiskered stranger in fringed buckskins and a dark beaver-fur hat. The man cradled a long rifle in the crook of one elbow.

"Don't mean to interrupt your Christmas celebratin'." The big man dragged his furry cap off long gray-brown hair that straggled about his shoulders. Clutching the cap to his chest, he made an awkward attempt at bows toward Bess and Annie.

"You are interrupting nothing, friend. We celebrate our Lord daily here. Come in and warm yourself at the hearth." Obadiah ushered the man in the room and toward a stool near the fireplace.

"I won't bother long," the stranger said as he leaned his long rifle against the wall by the fireplace. He settled himself on the stool and with murmured thanks, accepted the cup of hot sassafras tea Bess handed him while declining her offer of victuals. "Thank you kindly, Missus, but I just came from the Buxton cabin where the good wife there fed me to near bustin'."

He cleared his throat. "My name is Bartholomew Pickett, and I was told that the tale I have to tell would be received with interest by them herein." His dark eyes shining from the midst of his weathered face held an intense look.

Obadiah made the introductions, and Bartholomew's keen gaze swept the group, lingering with interest on Brock's uniform.

Aside from his rough appearance, which was not so different from many who regularly came through Deux Fleuves, Annie found nothing especially alarming about him. Yet the man's presence caused a foreboding to stir inside her. She did, however, derive comfort from both Brock's presence and Cap'n Brody's unconcerned posture. After investigating the stranger with a few sniffs, the dog slumped back to his place at Brock's feet where he yawned, then lay down and commenced thumping his tail on the floor as if to avow that the newcomer presented no threat.

Bartholomew took a healthy swig of the tea. He crossed his feet, which were clad in high-top moccasins that came nearly to his knees. The soft hide cut in decorative fringes around the boots' tops bounced with his every movement.

"Like I said, I jist came from Amos and Polly Buxton's place. It only seemed right to tell them first. Hard." He shook his grizzled head. "It's a hard thing I have to tell, and on Christmas, all the worse. But 'tis my duty." He shot a quick grim smile at Brock. "Somethin' I'm sure you understand, soldier."

The uneasy feeling twisted harder inside Annie, and she wished the man would just get out what he'd come to say.

The flickering firelight burnished the man's silhouette with an eerie glow.

Bartholomew glanced around at his audience as if assuring himself that all eyes were focused on him and all ears were keenly attuned to his words. He took a deep breath and began.

"It was a couple months ago—way down in October—when young Ezra Buxton joined up with me and four other fellers headin' out West to trap along the Mississippi." The mountain man's eyes took on a distant look, as if he were seeing something the others in the room could not see. "We never made it to the great river, though. We'd just crossed the Wabash some miles north of Vincennes when we was set upon by a fierce band of Miami braves. For several hours we carried on a right valiant battle, but in the end all perished but me."

Annie gasped as a deep sorrow for Amos and Polly gripped her. She agreed with Bartholomew's earlier words. How awful for the Buxtons to learn of their boy's death on Christmas night.

Bess clucked softly. "Poor Polly. I must visit her tomorrow."

Obadiah, too, voiced his desire to comfort Ezra's folks.

When the interruptions faded to silence again, Bartholomew resumed his narrative.

"Thing is, young Buxton didn't die right off. He lingered for some time after the Miami left us." He cast apologetic looks toward Annie and Bess. "Pardon me for sayin' so, ladies, but they took his hair."

Bess gasped, Obadiah sighed, and Brock groaned. Annie simply sat stunned, trying not to allow the picture Bartholomew had painted with his words to form in her mind.

The man forged on. "When I seen we was outnumbered and had no chance, I hid in underbrush, hopin' the savages didn't take time to count. When they'd gone, I went to see about the others in my party and found none save the boy still breathin', and him jist barely."

Bartholomew bent forward as if relishing this part of the story. "The boy grabbed the front of my shirt with his bloody hand and pulled me down so's I could hear, then commenced to bare his soul before he went to meet his Maker." Bartholomew clutched at his deerskin shirt, and in the firelight, Annie could make out a dark brown stain. Ezra's blood?

"He made me promise to come here to Deux Fleuves and repeat what he told me. He asked God's forgiveness and begged the Almighty to take his soul to heaven. Then he asked his pa and ma to forgive him for leavin' like he did."

Bartholomew's gaze flitted between Annie and Brock. "Ma'am, he said he wanted to ask your forgiveness for the wrong he'd done Mr. Brock Martin, here. . . . Said you'd know."

Annie nodded. With his mouth set in a grim line, Brock also gave his head a quick bob of acknowledgment. She could only wonder what emotions must be rolling through him, learning that the reward money Ezra had collected for turning Brock in had taken Ezra to his death.

The mountain man's piercing gaze pivoted to Annie where it settled. "The last Ezra had to say was to you, ma'am, and a most remarkable confession it was."

Annie abandoned the needlework to her lap as the quivering in her midsection increased.

"Ezra said after the Good Lord, he craved most desperate your and your dead husband's forgiveness for his heinous crimes. Said to tell you it was him what shot your man with an arrow from a quiver a Shawnee brave traded at his pa's post."

"But why?" The breathless words puffed from Annie. Had Ezra killed Jonah out of pure jealousy? But that didn't make sense. He must not have been that smitten with her, for after she refused to sell the land, his interest in her had seemed to fade.

"Somethin' about land and wantin' to sell it for the money to outfit him for an expedition. Said you'd understand." Bartholomew's statement made chilling sense of Ezra's actions.

A quick and deep sorrow for the boy she'd once intended to marry struck Annie. How tortured he must have been about what he'd done, especially finding it was for naught. She said a silent prayer for Ezra's soul, hoping that like the dying thief who petitioned Christ, he was taken to the Father's bosom in paradise.

Bartholomew shook his head sadly. "I don't condone what the boy did, but reckon some men'll do 'bout anything so's not to be bound to one place." He drained his cup, then rose and set the empty vessel by the hearth. "Thank you kindly for the warm drink," he said as he retrieved his firearm. "Night will be comin' on soon, so I reckon I'd best be headin' back to the fort. I beg your pardon for bringin' such grievous news on Christmas."

He turned his intent gaze on Obadiah. "If it eases your mind any Rev'rend, though I don't consider myself an especially pious man, I prayed for the salvation of the boy's soul as it left his body."

Obadiah stood and reached out his hand to grip Bartholomew's. "Thank you, friend. That means a lot to me, and to Ezra's folks, too, I'm sure."

Brock rose. "I'll be staying the night at the fort as well, Mr. Pickett. So if you don't mind my company, I'll walk back with you."

Cap'n Brody wakened, stretched, and yawned, but didn't follow Brock. Instead the big dog loped over to Annie and settled down at her feet.

Brock gave Bess a hug and shook Obadiah's hand. "Thank you

for the fine meal. I bid you good evening and happy Christmas."
He turned to Annie, and his intense look smoldered like a hot coal,
burning all the way to her soul.

"Happy Christmas, Annie. I should like to call tomorrow if it
be convenient."

Annie managed to make her head bob in a wooden nod.

After Brock and Bartholomew left, she sat numbly, unable
to fully soak up all the astounding revelations of the past hours.
Brock had made it clear that his visit tomorrow was specifically
to see her. To say his final adieus? Bartholomew's words echoed
hollowly in her ears. *Reckon some men'll do 'bout anything so's not to
be bound to one place.*

Chapter 21

"Don't fuss so. I will not have this child today." Gripping Brock's arm, Annie waddled to the wagon, wishing she could make her steps quicker. She'd scarcely slept all night, at once longing for and dreading this moment when she and Brock might have some time alone. But with the six Dunbar children squabbling and racing about, creating the tumult that generally held sway over the Dunbar household, no niche within the cabin offered seclusion for an intimate conversation. So when Brock arrived for his visit this morning as promised and mentioned he planned to stop by her cabin to visit Johann and Katarina Arnholt, Annie, against both Brock's and Bess's objections, had insisted on joining him. If they were to say their final farewells, she wanted it to at least be in private.

His strong arm linked with hers, Brock bent closer as if to shield her from any gusting breeze. "I am not convinced a drive in an open wagon is a good idea. Bess is right. It could be dangerous should you take a chill or become overtaxed."

Annie glanced up at the sun shining from a cloudless sky and glinting off the skiff of snow that decorated the frozen ground. "Bess is sometimes too much the mother hen. It is a lovely day, I have a good warm cloak, and the cabin is only a mile away. There is no reason I should not go with you to visit Katarina and Johann." She'd spent a sleepless night and waited agonizing hours for this chance at time alone with Brock. At this moment, a team of horses couldn't drag her back into the Dunbars' cabin. "I am eager to see what Katarina has done with my cabin."

After the siege, with winter and her laying-in time drawing near, Annie had finally acquiesced to Bess and Obadiah's insistence that she move in with them until spring. In the meantime, she'd offered Johann and Katarina Arnholt her cabin until Johann and the Hoffmeier men could build the couple one of their own.

She grasped the wagon and began to climb, forcing Brock to help her up.

"Besides," she said as she settled herself on the wagon seat and tugged on her woolen cloak to arrange its folds around her, "Indian women work up until the moment their time comes." She couldn't help thinking of Yellow Bird, who had surely given birth to her own child by now and wondered how the Shawnee girl who'd called Annie "sister" fared.

Brock climbed to the wagon seat that creaked and rocked gently with his movements as he sat down beside her. For several minutes, silence fell between them, broken only by the jangling of the harness, the squeak of the spring beneath the wagon seat, and the clop of the horse's hooves plodding over the frozen road toward her land.

Her land.

She gazed over the fields decorated with yesterday's snowfall. Beneath the sun, the rolling landscape sparkled as if it were encrusted in jewels.

Together, she and Brock had kept her promise to Papa and Jonah. The babe, whom she'd already begun referring to as Jonah Gerard, having no doubts it would be a son, kicked her as the wagon bumped in and out of a frozen rut.

She stole a sideways glance at Brock. His strong, angular jaw displayed only a hint of the russet stubble he'd allowed to grow into a fiery beard during the siege.

Her heart ached. She looked out across the white field and blinked hard, knowing it was not the sun reflecting brightly off the snow that generated her tears. Last spring she would never have agreed to give up her land—her mérite des ancêtres—for anyone. But now she would give it up in an instant if doing so would keep Brock here with her.

As the ache in her heart deepened, a flash of anger ignited inside her. The tender words of love he'd written to her from his jail cell remained etched on her heart. Every evening she removed the precious pages from her Bible and read them over again to keep the sweet sentiments fresh in her mind. But since his return scarcely twenty-four hours ago, Brock had yet to utter the first endearment to her. As she'd feared last night, he had obviously found it easy to pen such words of love and devotion when he thought he would never be required to prove them with any commitment.

"Johann says Hermann Hoffmeier's boy, Ernst, wants to join the army." Brock's sudden words shattered the silence, assaulting Annie's senses like the gusts of winter wind that stung her nose and cheeks. His approving tone rankled.

"You may think that a life spent in the army, fighting gallant battles and constantly moving from place to place, is a fine way to live," Annie didn't even try to blunt her sharp tone, "but I doubt Ernst's family is pleased with his decision. Mr. Pickett, I think, was right in what he said last night. Some men will do anything rather than be bound to one place." She couldn't keep the bitterness from her voice.

Brock yanked back on the reins hard, stopping the wagon so abruptly that Annie had to grab the side of the seat so as not to topple over.

The muscles in his jaw worked as he shoved the wagon brake in place and wrapped the reins around it. Then he turned such a fierce look toward her that she quaked. His knuckles whitened on the tops of his thighs, and his whole body seemed to quiver with a powerful emotion. Fury. . .or something else?

"You think I want to stay in the army, don't you?"

"You never said different." Hating the renegade tears sliding down her cheeks, Annie defiantly jutted out her quavering chin that would not behave.

Brock heaved a deep sigh that seemed to deflate his whole body. "Annie." Her name snagged as his voice cracked. He took her hands in his, and his eyes searched hers. "I told you in my letter how I feel about you. Why would you think I wouldn't want to come back?"

"You've been back here since this time yesterday, and you've never said one word about wanting to return after you serve your time in the army, or about wanting to be with. . .me. I know you have no interest in farming or in keeping the land—" Now the tears streamed, but Annie was past caring.

"Annie." Brock heaved another great sigh. His eyes held a pleading look. "I crave nothing more in this world than to stay right here with you, to make you my wife, and never leave this land Uncle Jonah left to us. But there is a war on, Annie. I might not make it back. I don't want to make you a widow a second time."

"And you decided this all by yourself without giving me a chance to say how I feel, or what *I* want?"

"What *do* you want, Annie?" He tenderly took her face in his hands and with his thumbs, gently brushed the wetness from her cheeks.

"I want you, Brock. I want you, me, and"—she glanced down at her distended belly—"this baby to make a family. . .a life together on our land."

She pulled away from him and raised her chin higher. "You have used the excuse of not wanting to make me a widow again long enough." Hugging herself to slow her trembling, she glared her challenge. "God has kept us safe thus far, and I have faith that He did not go to all the trouble to save you from the Shawnee and the hangman just to have you die in battle. So what say you to that, Brock Martin?"

He shook his head and chuckled softly. "I say Gerard Blanchet and Jonah Martin were wise men to put their inheritance in the hands of a woman with faith and pluck many times greater than her stature."

He wrapped his arms around her and drew her close. His breath quickened, warming her frozen nose and cheeks and sending delicious tingles through her entire body. His voice grew husky, setting the blood pulsing in her temples.

"I say," he continued in a low, almost fierce tone, "any man who would allow a woman like you to slip through his fingers is a fool indeed. And I am no fool. So I say, Annie Martin, will you make me the happiest man on earth and agree to marry me this very day?"

Happiness exploded inside her. Mustering both a stern look and tone, she fought to not giggle with glee. "Oui. It took you long enough to ask, mon amour! I feared when we got to the cabin, I would have to get Jonah's old brown Bess and hold it on you to make you say the words."

He laughed—a deep, rich rumble that filled her with joy. "Like I told you once before, you'll never need a musket to get a man's attention, Annie Martin."

She opened her mouth to argue, but before she could utter a word he lowered his head, his mouth capturing hers.

Epilogue

Pére. Can you say Père, Jonah?"

Annie hefted her fifteen-month-old son higher on her left hip and gazed at the wooden grave marker, weathered silver-gray.

The air smelled of blossoms, newly turned soil, and spring sunshine.

Jonah squirmed in her arms, seeming unimpressed with both the April morning and his mother's attempt at teaching him the French word. With the fingers of one pudgy hand, he clutched a wad of calico material at the bodice of her dress and with the other pointed at a robin tugging a worm from the soft, moist earth.

"Bur, bur. . . ," he mumbled, his bright brown eyes fixed on the rusty-breasted bird.

Annie chuckled indulgently. "Yes, mon amour, it is a bird." She leaned back to gaze at her child and her heart swelled to near bursting. From the moment last January tenth when Bess first laid Jonah Gerard in Annie's arms, an immeasurable love she'd never imagined could exist filled her and grew daily.

She brushed away a whirligig maple tree seed that had landed on her baby's soft dark curls—curls that matched hers almost exactly. Though he'd inherited his mother's hair and eye color, she could tell already that her son's broad forehead and big build would, in time, mimic his father's.

"How proud your father would be of you. . .and your grand-papa, too."

Jonah puffed his rosy cheeks up and began blowing bubbles, a trick he'd recently learned.

Annie stepped away from the graves and turned toward the newly plowed fields. True to his word, Johann Arnholt had saved enough seed corn to plant five acres again this year.

"Lord willing, one day you will plow and plant this land, Jonah. It will be yours, then your son's and your grandson's, just as your father and grandfather wanted."

Jonah squealed and bounced in excitement, pumping his chubby legs, which dangled from beneath the hem of his brown linsey-woolsey dress. "Cap, Cap, Cap!"

The big dog bounded up and lifted his muzzle to lick the bottom of Jonah's bare foot, making the boy giggle and bounce harder.

Annie laughed and widened her stance to steady herself against the buffeting by the exuberant dog and her wiggling son. "I am trying to teach Jonah his grandfather's language, Cap'n Brody, and you are not helping."

As she focused her attention on the dog, Jonah's weight was lifted from Annie's arms.

"Pa. . .Pa. . . ," Jonah babbled as he wrapped his stubby arms around Brock's neck.

"Easy there, big fellow. You and Cap'n Brody are not fair odds against your mother." Brock lifted the boy up and down against the bright blue sky until Jonah laughed so hard he gasped for breath.

When her husband had nestled their son in the crook of one arm, Annie stepped into the embrace of his other. Resting her head against Brock's strong chest, she gazed out over the rolling acres of dark rich land and marveled at all the blessings God had wrought in their lives. Once again her heart uttered its silent prayer of thanks that the week after her son's first birthday, her darling husband returned home safely from the war.

As if reading her mind, Brock drew her closer. "It is a fine heritage, Annie. One our little Jonah can treasure."

"It is. And I hope that he will one day appreciate it."

She angled a smile up at him. "But I also hope to teach him what we both learned. That the inheritance truly worth keeping is the one we have in heaven through Christ."

His mouth warm against her hair, Brock breathed a soft "Amen."

Ramona K. Cecil is a wife, mother, grandmother, freelance poet, and award-winning inspirational romance writer. Now empty nesters, she and her husband make their home in Indiana. A member of American Christian Fiction Writers and American Christian Fiction Writers Indiana Chapter, her work has won awards in a number of inspirational writing contests. Over eighty of her inspirational verses have been published on a wide array of items for the Christian gift market. She enjoys a speaking ministry, sharing her journey to publication while encouraging aspiring writers. When not writing, her hobbies include reading, gardening, and visiting places of historical interest.

The Magistrate's Folly

by Lisa Karon Richardson

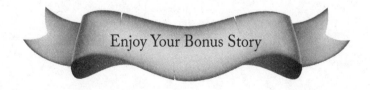

Enjoy Your Bonus Story

Prologue

February 6, 1773
London, England

From his perch above the fray, Graham Sinclair eyed his courtroom. The shabbiness of his domain mocked his dreams of justice. The cracksman he had just bound over for trial was two-thirds drunk and staggering. It wasn't justice. It was farce.

"Next case." He kneaded the bridge of his nose and shut his eyes. The usual shuffles and thumps were accompanied by the usual muted uproar from the waiting mob. These few moments between cases always reminded him of a scene change at the theater. Would comedy or tragedy play out next?

He sighed. He had his role to perform just as the other players in the drama.

He opened his eyes and sought Connor. His old friend and assistant nodded, and Graham cleared his throat. Connor slid a document before him.

"Mrs. Paget." Graham glanced from the brief in his hands to the accuser, a woman in middle years who wore a pinched expression as if her stays were too tight. As he regarded her, she sniffed and raised a handkerchief to her nose with excessive delicacy. The venomous glance she cast at the noisy throng of victims and vagabonds, constables and criminals milling on the other side of the railing might have wilted the lot—had they noticed.

Graham lifted his gaze to the raised dock directly before him. He blinked and looked again. A slight figure stood there, head held high. Surely he knew that auburn hair and those fiercely determined brown eyes.

His finger ran down the document as he sought the name of the accused. "Merry Lattimore." He whispered the name aloud as he read it. He dropped the paper, making no move to catch it as it fluttered to the ground.

He sought her face once more, searching for something, anything, that would put the lie to her claim of identity. She seemed not to recognize him. But then it had been years since they had last seen each other.

Connor placed the retrieved document before him and gave him an odd look.

Graham cleared his throat. "Are the accusers present?"

"We are, Your Honor." The plaintiffs' singsong chant sounded like a chorus of smug Eton lads.

"Of what does the prisoner stand accused?"

"Theft from her mistress," Connor said in his official voice.

Graham looked again at the prosecution bench. "You are Mrs. Paget?"

"Yes, Excellency."

"*Your Honor* will do."

The woman came perilously close to shrugging.

"You stand as accuser of this young woman?" His severest frown, which had quailed hardened cutthroats, had no marked effect on her.

"Yes, Your Honor."

"State your case."

The woman's chin jutted out farther. "This morning I discharged Merry Lattimore from my employ. I gave her time to pack her belongings. I then retired to the drawing room to recover my nerves from the unpleasant scene she made." She paused a moment as if to gauge his reaction.

"A few moments later, my son came to me and stated that he had seen her sneaking from my room. I assure you she had no cause to be in my chambers. I went in search of her and apprehended the little baggage as she was about to leave the house. She claimed her valise contained only her things. Indeed, she acted as if I were in the wrong." Outrage turned her voice brittle.

She sniffed and raised a handkerchief to her nose. "As soon as my son opened it, I found several pieces of my jewelry right there on top."

"Is that all you have to say?"

She looked confused, as if wondering what other proof he could possibly desire. "Yes."

"Have you any other witnesses to call?"

"My son, Lucas."

Lucas Paget took his mother's place.

Graham could not quite name why the man should be so off-putting. He looked like any of a thousand other louts with more money than sense. His pea-green jacket was embroidered with wildflowers; his pale satin breeches shone. His lace cuffs dripped over his hands, as languid as their wearer.

He recounted his tale of seeing Merry sneaking from his mother's room.

"Why was Miss Lattimore discharged from employment?"

Scarlet suffused the young man's face. "Immoral conduct."

Graham narrowed his eyes. Not the Merry he'd known. She had her faults. He knew that more than most, but she would not easily thrust aside her virtue. "And those scratches on your cheek? Where did they come from?"

"I don't see that it has any bearing on the theft." Paget took a pinch of snuff from an enameled box and sniffed.

"I can see why you might think so." Graham fought to keep the contempt from his tone. He'd have laid money that Merry had discouraged an unwanted advance. That was the real cause of her dismissal. But then why the accusation of theft? It made no sense. Unless she had taken the items in misguided retribution for getting the boot.

Paget's lips compressed into an ugly sneer.

"Have you anything else to add?" Graham said.

"No."

The constable who had taken Merry in charge was called, and he attested to being summoned to the house and seeing the jewelry in Miss Lattimore's bag.

Graham groaned inwardly. The Pagets' case was strong. What possible explanation could Merry produce to excuse herself? He had to find some way to help her. He owed her father that much.

In the curve of her lips and arch of her brow he again saw the carefree girl he had known. How had she been reduced to such circumstances?

Two spots of crimson burned brightly in her otherwise pale cheeks, and he could see the white of her knuckles as they clutched the railing. She stood unmoving in the dock. Was it possible that she had not moved since the proceedings started?

"Have you anything to say in your defense, Miss Lattimore?" He smiled. Nodded. *Come along, girl. Exonerate yourself.*

She met his gaze without flinching. Still he saw no hint of recognition in her eyes. Had he changed so much? Mayhap it was his stiff, white judicial wig. It tended to obscure the man beneath his office.

"I took nothing from the Pagets. Indeed, I was leaving without even the wages I had earned."

"And would you happen to know how Mr. Paget received the injuries to his face?"

The carmine blotches in her cheeks bled into the rest of her face. "Yes." The answer was little more than a whisper.

He had expected as much. "Please explain."

Merry closed her eyes and inhaled deeply, as if she needed the fortification of extra breath in her lungs. When she opened her eyes again, the color in her cheeks had drained, leaving her skin ivory pale.

"I caused the injuries in the course of discouraging his advances."

An outraged murmur issued from the plaintiff's bench, and Graham held up his hand for silence.

"How do you explain the presence of the jewelry in your case?"

"I cannot explain it. I don't know how it came to be there."

"Did you pack the bag yourself?" Silently he willed her to give him something to work with.

"I did."

A muscle in his jaw ticked. "And was it in your possession until you attempted to leave the house?"

"No."

Ah, finally the first ray of hope. "Please explain."

"I placed my bag on the table in the foyer as I went to say farewell to some fri—" Merry's gaze flickered toward Mrs. Paget. "Fellow servants in the kitchen before I departed."

"How long was your bag unattended?"

"A few moments."

"Were there other people about?"

"Yes, Your Honor."

"Is it possible that someone else placed the jewelry in your bag?"

"It's possible. Indeed, it is the only explanation, but I don't know who would do such a thing. At least. . ." Her voice sank, and she seemed to be talking half to herself. "Surely it was enough to see me out the door?"

Graham quieted the impulse to rub his temples. Was she intent on a visit to Tyburn's gallows?

"Did you see anyone near your valise when you came to retrieve it?"

"No sir."

Graham sighed deeply. There was no help for it now. He had tried to aid her, but he had no choice. There wasn't a scrap of evidence to support her.

His throat seemed suddenly as parched and dusty as a volume on legal ethics. "Merry Lattimore, I hereby bind you over for trial before the Sessions Court. You are to be committed to Newgate gaol until such time as your case is heard." The single crack of his gavel sounded as final as a blow from the executioner's ax.

With a grimly satisfied smile, Mrs. Paget flounced from his courtroom, followed closely by her son.

Merry remained motionless. The horror on her face cut Graham to the quick. "Your imprisonment won't last long. The Sessions are to be held in but three days."

Her eyes narrowed and she leaned forward, brow furrowed. A constable took her arm and escorted her from the dock. She accompanied him without protest, but shot one more look over her shoulder as she was pulled away. Their gazes met for an instant, and Graham knew she had finally recognized him.

Chapter 1

May 12, 1773
Yorktown, Virginia Colony

Had Merry arrived in Virginia under different circumstances she might have been charmed. The bustling port told of prosperity. Sailors and porters jostled one another with cargoes of Caribbean sugar, British silver, and East Indian teas. The sun graced the town with a loving favor it never seemed to shower on London.

Despite the predawn hour, the breeze held only a hint of coolness and coaxed her cloak from her shoulders for the first time in months. Flowers blossomed in all directions, declaring spring and new hope.

The irony wasn't lost upon her.

She took a half-dozen steps toward a tree with enormous, glossy, dark leaves and large, sweetly scented white flowers. Her physician father had instilled in her a love of all things botanical, along with an understanding of their medicinal properties. What healing powers might these new species contain?

A sailor's calloused hand snatched her up short. "Where do you think you're going? You've an appointment in Williamsburg." He laughed.

She was shackled in line with seventy-three other prisoners and herded through Yorktown and into the countryside. The forced march made her legs and lungs burn. She hadn't had so much exercise in ages. Yet, even the indignity of the manacles could not quite dim her curiosity. Magnificent oaks draped with some sort of feathery, ethereal plant stood like guardians on either side of the road. Was that some sort of moss? Her fingers itched to search one of Father's old books for the plant's name.

The man in front of her staggered, jerking her attention to him.

She steadied him with a hand to his elbow while trying not to trip over his floundering limbs. The prisoner behind her thumped into her back.

For the first time since their landing, Merry took notice of her fellow captives. Scant food and the fetid air belowdecks had enfeebled them. Most shambled forward, heads down, faces distorted with filth and despair. She glanced back at the man who had bumped her. His eyes were so glazed he seemed barely aware of his own movement, much less his surroundings.

She had only been saved from the same fate through the friendship of Sarah Proctor. They had grown close in Newgate when Merry nursed Sarah through a bout of malignant quinsy. She missed Sarah's practical company now. But her friend, though a convict, had had money set by. Sarah had paid for them both to share a small cabin and receive edible food. And now she had paid her own ransom, and would not have to suffer the indignity of an indenture. She had offered to pay Merry's ransom as well, but Merry could not bring herself to saddle Sarah with her upkeep, too. Now Merry questioned that decision.

At last a cluster of whitewashed houses, gleaming in the sun, heralded the beginning of a neat little town. Far from the crudeness Merry had expected, the town was built in fashionable style. Large clapboard homes with numerous windows watched over tidy streets. The town felt crisp and new, completely unlike London's jaded urbanity.

Passersby eyed the long file of prisoners, but without the derision they had endured in London. Here they were worthy of neither scorn nor compassion—no more or less than livestock for sale.

They were driven to a market green at the heart of the town. Most of the prisoners collapsed to the ground. They sounded miserable as they gasped for air. The guards had given them no water all morning.

Merry found the six other women from the ship, and they huddled together.

A stream of well-heeled customers flowed around them like

water surrounding an island. Despite the warmth of the day, Merry nearly took refuge beneath her cloak. But the guards would only have taken it from her. It was plain they wanted the wares on display, though the scrutiny of the strolling men stripped her to the core.

How had she been reduced to this?

Why?

Her tongue swelled in her mouth and her cheeks burned. Torn between the desire to disappear and the desire to shout her accomplishments, so as to obtain a good place, she trembled and sat still.

For the first time in months she muttered a prayer. A last resort. But she could summon no conviction. And the supplication dribbled away as Merry's grief lodged in her throat.

The heat wilted all but the strongest of the convicts. Dust stirred up by dray horses and carts and a thousand feet rose into the air, clogging her nose and mouth. Merry fanned herself with her free hand, but there was no relief to be had.

An elderly man some ten feet from Merry was the first to faint. Two others soon followed.

A wealthy tradesman wearing a violently purple waistcoat poked the man with his cane. "Weak stock."

His companion nodded as if soaking in words of wisdom.

Merry shot to her feet, irons jangling. Sarah had taught her how to handle importunate men. " 'Ere now, cully, you leave us be, or I'll scratch yer eyes out." She glared at the man with all the impotent fury she had nursed in the last three months.

The man's eyes widened. "How dare you."

"Get." Lips pulled back in a snarl, Merry jerked her head toward the street.

"Hoyden! You'll regret this display." The man led his friend away to the captain. His gesticulations and furtive glances made it clear he was reporting her behavior.

Merry continued to stand, head held high, though her heart pounded in her throat.

The captain stalked toward her. "What's all this then?"

"Sir, that gentleman was most offensive." Without giving him time to offer a rebuke she continued. "Pray tell, do you wish to make a profit on this human cargo?"

The question and her genteel accent seemed to confuse the man.

Merry went on, "I ask because you have done yourself a disservice. These people will be more lively and active if they are given some water. And that can only translate into more money for your coffers. If you wish, I would be willing to draw and distribute the water."

He eyed her for a long moment as if trying to comprehend what fraud she was plotting. At last he gave a short jerk of his head. "Very well. But a guard will go with you."

Merry nodded. It was no more than she had expected.

With the guard at her side, Merry took her place in the line for the pump. She filled a bucket to the brim and drank deeply. Even warm, the water felt glorious as it swept away the grit. Arms wrapped around the bucket, she hefted it up. She staggered and water sloshed over her, drenching her bodice.

Trying not to spill any more of the precious liquid, she hauled it back to the cluster of prisoners. They drank gratefully, greedily—slurping at the water and sighing as if they had never tasted anything so sweet. They soaked their kerchiefs in it and wiped their faces, eyes closing in delight.

Merry moved to the next person in the row and then the next. She refilled the bucket twice more and succeeded in giving them all a drink before her guardian insisted she return to her place. She put her hands to her aching back. Kneeling and bending with the bucket had become tedious long ago.

No sooner had she settled among her fellows again than the auction began. One by one the prisoners were led to the block. Merry turned away, stomach churning.

Inevitably, her turn came. She hesitated in climbing onto the block, and the guard prodded her forward. Her hands were damp, her throat dry again.

Men and women milled about the square, some looking prosperous, others mercenary. Most seemed to be in search of a specific type of servant. They gossiped and debated with friends until the convict they wished to bid for was put up.

The auctioneer's voice boomed preternaturally loud by her ear. "Name: Merry Lattimore, transported after conviction for larceny. Term of indenture is to be seven years. Former employment: governess. Can read and write and do sums. Some knowledge of herbs and physic. Age: twenty-two years. She is in good health. Unmarried. No children."

Merry cringed to be reduced to such a paltry accounting.

"Bidding will start at ten pounds."

Less than a good dray horse.

"Ten pounds."

Merry ripped her gaze from the ground. She knew that voice. It was the tradesman in the purple waistcoat, and he had a nasty gleam in his eye.

Connor made a sharp gesture, catching Graham's eye. After seeing the lad before him led away in manacles, Graham rose and rubbed his eyes. For an instant, as the door opened and the boy stepped outside, all Graham could see was Merry Lattimore's slight form as she had passed through those same doors. The two months since her ship had sailed for America had helped not a whit. The memory of her wounded gaze haunted him.

Retreating to his office, he placed his wig on its pedestal. The door behind him opened, and he turned to see Connor. His friendship with the former thief had begun when Graham had taken his part in a brawl with one of the local bully boys, but had deepened immeasurably since Connor had attended a Methodist meeting, given up theft, and come to work for Graham.

"What is it?" Graham hung his judicial robe on its hook.

"You remember them Pagets what had some jewelry stolen a couple months back."

Graham stiffened and turned to face his friend. "Yes."

"It's gone missin' again."

Graham gaped as if the report had been spouted in Dutch. "What?"

Connor smirked, a disquieting expression on his pugnacious features. "Thought that girl got to you. You've been sulking ever since you heard her case. Not your usual pleasant self, one might say."

Graham wished heartily that he could protest, but it was true. "I knew her father. . . ."

"So you said." Connor shrugged and turned to the door. "I can send one of the lads to look into the matter."

Drat the man. "No. I'll investigate." Graham snatched his waistcoat and shoved in his arms.

A wicked grin curved Connor's mouth until it resembled a devil's horns. "I thought as much. I told the constable we'd be over straightaway."

It didn't take long to find the pawnbroker who had bought the jewels and determine that Lucas Paget had been behind the theft. Graham had the weasel brought to the office for questioning.

Tears poured from the fellow as if someone had primed a pump. "I fell into a game of high stakes with a group of, well, they were no gentlemen." He sniffled into his handkerchief.

"Get on with it."

"The blackguards would not take my offer of payment with my next allowance. They wanted the blunt and threatened. . .extreme measures if I did not procure it right away."

Graham narrowed his eyes. "Beau traps will usually give more grace."

Paget refused to meet his gaze, and a dull red blanketed his features. "They somehow got the idea I was trying to gull them by sleight of hand."

"So they caught you cheating and ordered you to pay up or else."

Paget nodded miserably.

"Why didn't you simply ask your mother for the where-withal?"

"And listen to her bleating on about it until the end of time?"

"So you determined to stage a burglary."

"I was going to buy it all back next month when my quarterly allowance comes in. It would have been no loss to her."

Something Paget had said swirled to the forefront of Graham's thoughts. "It was you!" He grasped his hands behind his back to keep himself from throttling the rogue.

"I. . .yes, I admit I took the jewelry."

"No, I mean you were the one who put the jewelry in Merry Lattimore's bag. With your sleight of hand tricks you slipped the things inside as you opened it."

Paget licked his lips.

Graham's hands balled into fists. "She could have been sent to the gallows. And all because she did not allow you to defile her?"

"It wasn't that," Lucas wailed. "She found out I had been gaming. She'd have told mother of my. . .problems at the table. I had to discredit her."

The image of Merry answering the accusations put to her, head high and eyes snapping with wounded dignity, rose before Graham then faded into a red haze.

"C'mon. Graham, let 'im go."

Graham blinked, and Connor's face sprang into his line of sight.

"Let 'im go. He'll get his in Newgate."

Graham released Paget, and the wretch fell back into his chair, choking and whimpering.

"Take him away, Connor." Graham collapsed into one of the other chairs before the fireplace. "I cannot hear his case. Take him to Bow Street."

Connor led a defeated Paget away, one hand on his collar.

Graham stared into the fire. He had taken part in condemning Merry Lattimore unjustly. The guilt of it nearly bent him in two. He slid to his knees. Dear Lord, she was a thousand miles from home, at the mercy of heaven only knew what kind of master. What had he done? He put his head in his hands. "God, help me to make it right."

Chapter 2

Merry breathed in through her nose. *No. No. No.* Her gaze met the tradesman's. One side of his nose ticked up in a sneer.

"I have ten pounds from Mr. Cleaves."

She hunched in on herself as if someone had punched her in the stomach. She was going to be hauled away by the vindictive little man and worked to death in tobacco fields.

Or worse.

A fly buzzed around her, and she focused on it. The tiny creature was incredibly ugly—no doubt he would be swatted by one of the men present, and still his future seemed brighter than her own.

"Eleven pounds."

The cool, female voice slid over Merry, as refreshing as her first drink of water by the pump. She raised her head, eyes searching for the speaker. Against her will a flicker of hope ignited.

"Twelve." A querulous note raised Cleaves's voice.

"Thirteen."

This time Merry found the speaker. A petite, elegantly clad woman near the rear of the crowd. A tall slave woman stood at the lady's side holding a parasol over her perfectly coifed hair.

"Fifteen." Blotches of red stained Cleaves's cheekbones.

"Eighteen."

"Twenty."

"Twenty-five."

The crowd murmured.

Cleaves's nostrils flared. His lips twitched, but he said nothing.

"Twenty-five pounds, once. . .twice. . .to Mrs. Benning for twenty-five pounds."

The auctioneer nudged Merry and jerked his thumb toward the left. Knees trembling so that she nearly toppled from the platform, she shuffled toward a clerk who sat behind a small table, filling out the legal documents of indenture and accepting payment. The swish of skirts made her turn.

Her new mistress approached, her gaze focused not on Merry but on the man at the table. Mrs. Benning discussed payment arrangements for a long moment before suddenly turning and prodding the manacles that bound Merry's wrists. "I don't think we will need these, do you, Merry?"

Merry licked her lips. "No madam."

The shackles were removed and clunked down among the documents, nearly upsetting the clerk's inkpot.

Merry chaffed her wrists. She kept her eyes downcast, unsure of the etiquette of such a situation. "I am grateful for your kindness."

Mrs. Benning made no sign she had heard. Half-bent over the table, she wielded the quill with a flourish, signing the document presented to her. With a curt nod toward Merry and her slave woman she marched away from the market green, leaving them to scurry after her.

A landau awaited Mrs. Benning just outside a tidy brick church. A young black man in handsome livery perched in the coachman's seat. He scrambled down at their approach and swung the door open for Mrs. Benning. She climbed in without a word, and the lad closed the door behind her.

Uncertain what to do, Merry halted in midstep. Was she expected to walk? The Negress met her gaze for the first time and indicated with a jerk of her chin that they were to sit on the board at the back, where in London a footman might have stood.

"Home, Crawford."

"Yes'm." The coachman hopped back up to his place and whipped the horses into a canter.

The carriage lurched forward, and Merry snatched at the side before she slid right off her precarious seat. Her paltry bundle of belongings skidded toward the edge, and the Negress snatched it back. She seemed unaffected by the movement.

The meager contents of Merry's stomach sloshed about, making her regret the water she had drunk. She swallowed, and swallowed again. She could not disgrace herself. Her knuckle showed bone white as her hands gripped the seat.

In truth, she couldn't say if it was the motion of the cart or apprehension that unsettled her. What lay in store for her next? Was the ordeal drawing to a close or merely beginning?

Swaying slightly, Merry clambered from her seat to face an enormous white house on a broad, well-kempt street. No neighbors squashed up next to it as they were prone to do in London. Instead, she could see the edge of a garden and several outbuildings behind the main structure. Black shutters framed wide, arched windows. Gray shingles ran up the mansard roof, parting to allow four dormer windows to peek out over the street.

Merry stared at the imposing facade. She felt as if all her emotions had been forced through a strainer, leaving only a leaden, remote sort of apathy.

Mrs. Benning turned at the top step and glanced around. She caught Merry's gaze and made an impatient come-here motion with two fingers. As if the imperious gesture had broken some sort of spell, Merry found her legs capable of movement and followed her new mistress inside.

Mrs. Benning led the way into an elegant room painted a cheerful green. She settled onto a divan. "I imagine you would like to know a bit about your new situation."

"Yes madam. If you please." Merry stood in the center of the room, hands knit loosely in front of her.

"I believe you would do well as a nanny. My Emma is five and John, three. They are bright, precocious children, but they require firm guidance."

"Yes madam."

"You will teach them to read and write and some basic arithmetic. I will expect them to be clean and well-fed, their days to be regulated. But don't forget that they are children."

Merry nodded, not trusting herself to open her mouth. So many questions were piled in her head that if she spoke one would surely tumble out.

"The Benning name is respected throughout the colonies. We have high standards. I had not intended to indenture a convict when I went to market today."

"Why did you?" The words were out before Merry could blink. She would have given her last shilling to recall them.

Mrs. Benning's cool blue eyes surveyed Merry, and the slightest smile quirked one corner of her mouth before disappearing. "I saw you."

Merry frowned. What was she to make of that?

"I saw you tending the other convicts."

A blush heated Merry's face. "I. . .the heat." She failed to keep the defensiveness from her tone. "They needed water or—"

"I am not critical. Your kindness recalled to mind the story of Rebekah watering all those camels. I felt all at once as if I must purchase your indenture. That, and I detest Thomas Cleaves—dreadful man."

A jumble of new questions rendered Merry speechless.

"That being said, I must make some inquiries. The charge of which you were convicted was larceny?"

"Yes." Merry looked away. She would ever be bound by the accusation, whether physical chains chaffed her wrists or not.

"Please tell me about it."

Merry did, as concisely as possible. Mrs. Benning's mouth quirked again, but not with a smile, when she heard Merry's protests of innocence. No doubt every convict in Virginia heralded their innocence. At least her new mistress had the consideration not to laugh.

When Merry came to the end of her recital, Mrs. Benning regarded her for a long moment. Could she see anything beyond the filth of the convict hulk?

Was there anything else anymore?

"My woman, Jerusha, will show you what is expected."

The slave woman led the way from the sitting room. Acutely aware of her grubbiness, Merry licked her lips and smoothed her skirts. Nervous fingers tried to push the stray locks of hair back from her face, but without a glass it was difficult to say whether she was making matters better or worse.

On the third floor the slave woman swung open a door. "Here's the nursery. You'll sleep in here with the children." She indicated a thin pallet in the corner.

Jaunty yellow walls were broken by a series of tall windows that allowed light to stream in. Two narrow beds were covered with white coverlets and fluffy bolsters. A spindly chair sat between the beds. In the middle of the room a tiny table complete with miniature tea service sat atop a pretty floral carpet. A dollhouse sat in one corner near a rocking horse. Toy soldiers were scattered about, apparently where they had fallen in battle.

"This is very nice," Merry said.

"I'll see about finding you something to wear." Jerusha patted Merry's arm.

The human contact was almost more than Merry could bear. Tears welled in her eyes. "Thank you."

She took a seat in the rickety chair, which held up better than she had feared. Absently she stroked the soft coverlet. Mayhap the staff would disapprove of the notion of placing impressionable children in the charge of a convicted felon.

In her heart, she scarcely blamed them. Who could be expected to embrace a thief?

With Jerusha's help, Merry found new clothing and water for a bath.

Delight of delights.

Merry scrubbed with lye soap until her skin was raw and her fingers shriveled. It took an age, but at last she felt as if she had rid herself of the gaol's stink. Between the bath and Jerusha's kindness she felt nearly human again.

She turned as a slight slave girl shepherded the Benning children into the nursery, though she was little older than they.

The children had the same brown hair and gray eyes as their mother, but vivacity gave them a unique comeliness.

Gentle hands turned the children to face Merry. "Emma, John, this is Merry. She's gonna take care of you."

"I don't want her, Hattie. I want you." Little John whirled back to the girl with outstretched hands.

Graham stood on the deck of the *King's Favor*, staring back at Portsmouth's harbor. His fingers clutched the ship's rail as Merry's had clutched the railing of the dock.

Was he utterly daft? He had asked the question of himself at least twice a day since deciding on this rash course of action. Even as he had made the many preparations required before abandoning his magistracy to a temporary replacement.

Despite the most diligent search, he had been unable to determine much of Merry's fate. The intelligence had left him little choice; the hunt could not be picked up on this side of the Atlantic. But rather than search for a reliable agent to continue the quest in Virginia, Graham had known with a certainty that defied explanation that he must finalize the matter. He would never rest until his error had been made right.

His mind drifted to the last time he had planned a meeting with Merry. Yes, that last visit to the Lattimore house still rankled. Mrs. Lattimore had skewered him with a glare as sharp as a surgeon's scalpel even as her lips bent in an unwilling smile.

"I'm sure you understand, Mr. Sinclair. I have my heart set on this match. As a true friend of this family I know you will also want the best for Merry."

In the pocket of his waistcoat the ring he had purchased so hopefully seemed to singe his flesh right through the cloth. It gave rise to a painful flush that scalded his cheeks as if he were a schoolboy guilty of some monstrous prank.

She continued. "Lord Carroll and his father, the earl, have been more than willing to talk terms. Merry and Dr. Lattimore are down at the Dabney estate in Kent even now, and as you know, her father has determined to settle a very handsome dowry on her when she marries."

Her fan stirred the air, and dust motes scattered to escape the vortex she created. Graham focused on those tiny points of light, trying to maintain his sanity as she prattled.

"I thought you ought to know what was happening. I've noticed how she has led you on. But really the two of you would never have made much of a match. You can see that, I'm sure. She's set her cap for Lord Carroll, and in time you'll be as happy for her as I am." Her voice had turned as pointed as her gaze. "I'm sure you will do nothing to mar her chances. This will mean everything for her." She broadened her smile. "Won't you stay for tea?"

He croaked some reply and all but stumbled from the house in his haste to be away.

He blinked. Even now it pained him that Merry's mother had fended off his advances, as if he weren't a friend but some overeager fellow who needed to be beaten off with a stick.

"You're not brooding again."

"Not at all." Graham rounded on his companion. Trust Connor to hit the nail on the head. Particularly if it was aimed at something sensitive.

Connor placed a heavy hand on his shoulder. "You're doing the right thing."

Graham breathed deep, sucking in the freshening breeze. "My thanks, friend." He smiled. "There is still opportunity for you to turn back if you wish."

"Not I. Who would keep you on the straight and narrow if I'm not there?"

"You make an excellent point." Graham slapped him on the back.

As the last bit of land disappeared from the horizon, Graham led the way belowdecks. What would Merry say when she saw him again?

Chapter 3

September 2, 1773
Williamsburg, Virginia Colony*

Merry sat on the edge of the bed, holding a porcelain bowl near John's small, flushed face. Abigail Benning bent over her son, her face a study in worry as she administered a dose of ipecacuanha.

The emetic worked quickly, and Merry handed Abigail a clean linen towel, which she used to wipe his mouth. His languor clenched at her heart even more than the flush that bruised his cheeks an ugly purple-red. Everything had been done. He'd been bled; wrapped in cool, damp flannels; sweated; and purged, yet nothing seemed to loosen the fever's hold. That morning they had undertaken the journey from the Bennings' plantation, where they spent summers, back to town in the hopes that a change of air would affect an improvement.

Another fit of the miserable, whooping cough pushed him forward beneath its weight. Merry glanced up and met Abigail's gaze. "We must resort to the laudanum."

Mrs. Benning raised a hand to rub her forehead, but she nodded.

Merry hurried to the large closet that had been set aside as a stillroom. She had brewed the laudanum in anticipation, though she had hoped not to need it. Her hand shook as she took up the dark brown bottle.

In the nursery, Abigail took the bottle in hands that trembled even more than Merry's. She dosed her son then collapsed in the chair between the beds, looking from one child to the other and back again. Her lips moved soundlessly in prayer, as if her fear was so deep she could not bring herself to utter it aloud.

Emma's dinner tray was brought in, and Abigail waved Merry

away, busying herself with helping her daughter eat. Perhaps it was just as well Merry had never been graced with her own family. The naked ache in Abigail's eyes was too raw to endure. Merry didn't know if she could have survived such grief.

Merry opened the jar of garlic salve and rubbed a generous amount onto John's wrists and feet, wrapping them in strips of cotton so the virtue would not be lost. The laudanum had already proved effective. He slept through her ministrations. His breathing was easier, and he seemed in a deep sleep. The coughing was noticeably absent. A good thing. His little body needed rest.

Emma fell asleep after eating a portion of gruel. Her mother knelt by the bed and stroked the girl's soft cheek. As if the weight of her own head had grown too heavy, Abigail leaned her elbows against the counterpane and dropped her head down against her balled fists.

"I can't do it." She turned her haggard face toward Merry.

"Ma'am?"

"I cannot lose another child." The harshness of her tone lanced the sickbed silence of the room like wind sweeping away a fog.

Merry knelt beside Abigail, wishing, longing to be able to comfort her in some way, but she could not find the words. Could not offer hope when she held so little herself. She smoothed the stray hair away from Abigail's face, much as the woman had so recently done for her daughter.

"We will do all we can and leave the rest to God." A hard fate as far as Merry was concerned, but Abigail needed to hear something.

October 6, 1773
Williamsburg, Virginia Colony

Merry rubbed her forehead with the heel of her hand. The danger had passed, but her body ached as if she had been in a bare-knuckle ring with the disease and taken a beating.

Emma held out her slice of bread. "I want jam."

"I don't think so, sweet. It wouldn't sit well, and you don't want to be sick again."

Emma pursed her lips, obviously weighing the matter. Her thin little shoulders heaved in a sigh. "When?"

Merry tapped her bottom lip. "Perhaps tomorrow if you are strong enough."

"Promise?"

"I promise to try to make sure you're well enough."

"I want jam, too." John's lower lip pushed forward, and Merry welcomed the sight. He hadn't had the strength to be pugnacious in days, poor lamb.

She reached out to stroke his hair. "I shall make the same terms I made with your sister. No more, no less."

His lips pursed for a moment; then he nodded. "Tell us a story."

"Which one would you like to hear?"

" 'The Lion and the Mouse.' "

"Very well then." Merry resettled in her chair and smoothed her skirts.

From out in the hall came a rustle and a thump. Merry turned her head toward the noise. Someone must have stumbled and dropped something.

John tugged on her sleeve.

"Once upon a time there was a mighty lion—the king of the jungle. One day he was out hunting when he captured a tiny little mouse."

A strangled sob and hissing whispers pricked Merry's ears. She put up a hand. "Just a moment."

She padded on silent feet to the door and eased it open. Jerusha's son, Daniel, stood in the hall, head bent close to Hattie's. Misery weighed down his features, making him look a wizened old man, rather than a thirteen-year-old boy.

"What's all this?"

They whirled to her, faces etched with terror. Merry glanced down the hallway in both directions. "Come in here, both of you."

Hattie's shoulders still shook, but she and Daniel did as bidden.

"Now, tell me what's wrong."

"Mas. . .Master Benning." Hattie hiccuped. "He's selling Daniel."

Merry covered her mouth with her hand. "When did you hear this?"

Hattie bent over, hand covering her mouth to stifle her sobs.

Daniel took up the story. "Master and Missus were in the garden, and Mama sent Hattie to take Mrs. Benning a shawl. She overheard them arguin' 'bout it." Merry could well identify with the pain that brimmed in his eyes.

How would Jerusha bear it? This boy was her life's blood. If he was sent off somewhere, they might never see each other again. It would kill her.

"Does your mama know?"

He nodded, and then his chin began to tremble and he dissolved into tears. John and Emma came in behind her and clutched at her skirts, staring at the older children. Merry had thought her tears were spent, but apparently this was one thing the Lord meant to pour into her with abundance.

John and Emma began to cry then, too, though they did not know the reason. Gathering all four children to her along with the shreds of her emotions, Merry murmured meaningless soothing noises, until the worst of the storm passed.

The old questions that had plagued her sprang back to mind, poking and prodding. How could God allow such a thing to happen?

As the children subsided into hiccuping and sniffling, she settled them all around the nursery table with milk and biscuits. If Mr. Benning found the slaves eating and drinking in common with his own children, she would likely be sent to the tobacco fields, but it mattered not. They were all children in need of comfort.

"Daniel, where is your mother?"

The boy shrugged. "Slaves' hall maybe."

"Children, I'll be back in a bit. Be good and obey Hattie."

Merry found Jerusha in the slaves' hall, sitting stock-still in an old, oft-mended rocking chair. Her gaze was trained out the window, past the gardens and woods, out to the tobacco fields that stretched to the horizon. She was not weeping, but her eyes were red-rimmed, and she held a sopping wet handkerchief in a claw-like grip.

A bevy of slave women outside the hall tried to prevent Merry's intrusion, but she insisted that she must see her friend. In the five months since she had arrived in Virginia, it had been Jerusha who had kept her sane. The woman had sheltered and taught and helped Merry as she found her footing in this new land and station in life. Jerusha had made the staff accept her by sheer force of will. Without her, Merry was certain she'd have succumbed to despair.

"Jerusha." The single word seemed to get lost in the gulf of grief that surrounded the slave woman, even though she was only a few feet away.

Merry ventured another step into the room. "Daniel told me what's happened. What do you want to do about this?"

The question turned her head. "Do? What can I do? My boy. . ." Jerusha bent over her knees. The bones and tendons of her fingers stood out in stark relief as she dug into the material of her skirt.

Merry approached and knelt by the rocking chair, encircling Jerusha with one arm and offering her free hand. Jerusha clutched it, hanging on as if it were the whipping post. Faced with another mother about to lose her child, Merry once more found herself unable to speak. She could only be there to hear the words when, and if, they came.

When the torrent of sobs finally quieted, Jerusha released her hand and buried her eyes within her handkerchief. Hand hidden in a fold of her skirt, Merry flexed her fingers. They would be bruised later.

"I never thought this would happen. Not to me and my boy." Shredded by mourning, Jerusha's voice rasped.

Merry remained where she was, unspeaking and unmoving.

Jerusha crumpled the sopping handkerchief. "We're good workers. Never complain. . ." Her eyes had a dreamy quality to them as if she were speaking from a great distance.

Merry covered Jerusha's hand with her own, wanting to anchor her somehow.

Jerusha pulled away as if the contact hurt. "I see now how hate can crawl into a person's heart. It just finds the cracks from where it's been broken." She turned her face away, returning her gaze to the window. Desperation gleamed in her eye, and she gripped Merry's arm in talon-like fingers. "I can't lose him."

Merry rose on her knees until she was face-to-face with Jerusha. "You've told me that God works everything to good. You hold on to that. In the meantime, we have to think."

"Think about what?"

"I've heard that the Quakers of Pennsylvania have no heart for slavery."

Jerusha sat back as if she had been slapped. "What are you saying?"

Merry hardly knew herself. It was mad, impossible. Dangerous. For a moment the words wedged in her throat, too treacherous to be allowed voice. She thought of the children sobbing in the nursery, and the words spilled out of their own volition. "Take Daniel and run away."

A jolt of the cart nearly knocked Merry from her perch. She clutched at the seat and the precious parcel of medicines as she righted herself, but not before her wild gaze caught sight of a familiar face. She shook her head. Mayhap she was going mad. Graham Sinclair could not possibly be in Williamsburg.

But surely there could not be another such as he. His features had burned themselves into her memory with the intensity of a branding iron on a convict's thumb. His russet hair and dark eyes had been designed to melt an impressionable girl's heart. Hers had never stood a chance; and indeed, she had never attempted to guard it from him, but had welcomed his friendship and hoped for more.

When she was twelve and had found a bird with a broken wing in the garden, he had helped her tend it, and thus had sealed his heroic stature in her eyes. He had been Jason of the Argonauts, Sinclair the Great, and William the Conqueror rolled into one. She had believed him infallible and conformed every thought and opinion so that it mirrored his. At least, until he had abandoned her to care for her ailing father by herself, and then condemned her in his courtroom.

Merry blinked away the memories. She couldn't have seen him; therefore, it had just been nerves. She had a great deal to do, much of which could land her back in gaol for abetting a runaway. She pushed away thoughts of a phantom to focus on the task at hand.

In the morning she would claim that Jerusha and Daniel had come down with scarlet fever and insist they be quarantined in one of the outbuildings. She would see them away and keep up the pretense of treating them over the next week or so. Then she would pretend to discover their absence. That ought to give them plenty of time to evade a search party.

She inhaled deeply and nodded to herself. It should work.

It *would* work.

It had to.

Sunset splashed the city with the day's leftover color as the cart rattled up behind the mansion. The white walls glowed pink and orange, looking as if the house were blushing at some indiscretion.

She couldn't find it in her to pray for her own predicament, but for Jerusha. . . What could it hurt? *Lord, help Jerusha and Daniel. Help them to be free.*

Chapter 4

Graham grabbed Connor's arm and pointed. "That was Merry!"

Connor squinted after the open cart. "Yep."

In a trice they were sprinting after the cart. She was in his sights. He could not let her slip away again. He dodged a strolling couple and landed ankle deep in one of the puddles of wastewater that punctuated the street. It would be a miracle if he could salvage his boots. No matter. If the expense of a pair of boots was all it took to shift the weight of guilt this very night, he would pay it and gladly.

The cart turned and he lost sight of it. Redoubling his pace he swung around the corner with Connor hard on his heels. His side began to ache, and he gasped for breath. He pushed on in dogged pursuit, but the trotting cart horses were outpacing him.

He straggled to a walk when the cart turned down a street lined with prosperous homes. He turned and found Connor a few paces behind him.

Breathless, hands on his knees, he gasped, "I think it's safe to assume that they must be going home." A laugh burbled up from his belly. "I can't think why I was in such a rush to follow."

Connor mopped his face. "I can." The big bruiser's mouth turned down, but then the laugh he had repressed bounced to the surface.

Graham put a hand on Connor's shoulder and bent over, laughing and trying to catch his breath. "Connor, you are supposed to keep me from being ridiculous."

"No man can make water run uphill."

"You wound me, brother. You wound me."

"Not mortally. You look thoroughly disreputable."

Graham glanced down at himself and realized the truth of

it. His boots and breeches were splashed with effluvia from the street. His shirt was soaked through with perspiration and his neckcloth hopelessly disarranged.

Ought he return to his lodging for a change of linen? He could not bear the thought. His goal was within his grasp. In the brief glimpse he had of Merry, she had looked distinctly solemn. What if she suffered ill-use in that fine mansion? Could he live with himself if he allowed it to go on a moment more than necessary? He groaned. There was no way he was turning back at this point. He would see his task completed this very evening. "Come on."

Together they marched down the quiet street and turned in at the Benning gate. He had decided that he should tell Merry first, so he went around to the back entrance, where it would be more acceptable for a servant to receive someone. He raised his hand to knock, but hesitated, licking his lips.

"You want me to do this?" Connor stood at his elbow as always, supporting him by his mere presence.

Graham inhaled and knocked. "No."

A dignified black man answered the door, and Graham summoned a weak smile. "I would like to speak to Merry Lattimore."

The children were sleeping soundly by the time Merry returned from the apothecary. She went out to the kitchen for a bite of supper.

Cookie greeted her with a wave of her spoon. "Hello, Merry. Glad yer back, child. There's ham in the vittles today."

Merry bent over the pot. "Mmm, smells good." She heaped a pile into a bowl. "To what do we owe the honor?"

"Company. Mr. Benning's shipping partner, Mr. Fraser, is up from Charles Towne for a visit."

"Merry?"

Merry glanced up to find Mr. Benning's man, Isaiah, standing at the base of the stairs. "Isaiah, is everything well?"

"Yes ma'am. You have a visitor."

Unreasoning panic hit her like a punch. Who could it be? Had someone gotten wind of her plan? It wasn't possible. She hadn't even begun to act on it.

"Do you know who it is?"

"Mr. Sinclair—says he's a magistrate."

Merry slumped back onto the stool, face and hands suddenly clammy. "That is impossible. He's in London." Her words came out as a raspy whisper.

"He claims it's urgent."

"I have no wish to see him." Pushing to her feet she hurried from the kitchen.

Graham smiled and stepped forward as the manservant returned to the door. He had his hat half-off when the man held up a hand.

"I'm afraid Merry does not wish to see you."

"Pardon?"

"If I may say so, she seemed upset."

Graham merely blinked, hand suspended in the act of removing his hat. This could not be happening. It was simply too ridiculous. He had come halfway around the world to tell the minx that he had obtained her pardon, and she would not deign to see him?

The servant stepped back and the door shut firmly in Graham's face.

He whipped his hat the rest of the way off and ran a hand through his hair. Crushing the hat in his other hand, he slapped it against the doorframe.

"This is insufferable!"

Connor's lips were compressed in a manner that suggested he might be restraining a laugh. "Why don't you just mail the blooming papers, and I'll go book passage for home?"

Graham clapped his hat back on his head and stepped away from the door. "What we are going to do is set watch on this house until Merry Lattimore steps foot outside, and once she does, I am going to slap these papers in her hand and then bid her adieu and a pleasant life."

Merry tossed on her pallet bed until she thought she might go mad. What was Graham doing here? He belonged in London, pronouncing judgment on the masses. Or possibly at some country home, courting a squire's daughter. He belonged anywhere but here.

She put her hands to her cheeks, feeling the heat. She closed her eyes. Oh, there had been a day when she had longed for his arrival—waited, watched for it like an eager puppy. Nose pressed to the windowpane, her eyes had roamed over the foot traffic in the street. Watching, watching for a tall, lithe form in a bottle green coat and buff breeches. Russet hair tied back with a neat black ribbon. Dark, playful eyes that made her stomach flop like a landed fish.

Her fingertips brushed cool glass, reaching toward him when at last he appeared. She whirled to bound down the stairs in greeting only to find her mother standing in the doorway of her room.

"This will not do."

"What?"

"Flinging yourself after Mr. Sinclair in such a profligate manner."

Her cheeks ached as if they had been pinched a thousand times. Humiliation pulsing dull and sharp at the same time. "I just want to see him. He has been away so long."

"You haven't the sense of a nanny goat. Ladies do not wish to see men. Men wish to see us. I have told you this before."

"But—"

"Now, remember yourself, and for once act as a lady."

Mother ushered her from her room and down to the drawing room, a stiff hand on Merry's back both propelling her forward and restraining her. She took her place on the settee, hands gripping her embroidery hoop, but she couldn't make a stitch. Her eyes brimmed with tears, blurring the colored thread like a chalk drawing in the rain.

The door opened and Father ushered Graham in. Despite the weight of her mother's disapproval, Merry couldn't resist looking up, seeking his eyes. His delighted smile lit a glow in her, melting the reserve her mother's chilly words had iced around her heart.

She thrust aside her sewing and rushed to him, hands outstretched. They had a lovely afternoon.

And then he had never returned.

Father's health had begun to decline, and Graham disappeared, taking with him her hopes of love.

Merry started awake and pressed her fingers against her eyes. She had to find a way to banish these memories.

Abigail Benning had given her leave to borrow books from the library. Mayhap now was the time to avail herself of the privilege. Anything would be preferable to dwelling on her hurts or basking in dread of the errand she would have to perform that evening.

She slipped from the nursery and downstairs. The door to the parlor stood open, and conversation and laughter spilled out into the hallway.

She started to slip past, but the sound of her name brought her up short.

"Merry, we were just speaking of you, please come meet everyone."

She closed her eyes briefly. She had been so close. Straightening her spine, she turned back and entered the brightly lit drawing room. "Yes madam?"

Mrs. Benning sat next to a handsome youth. The lad was well formed with an unmistakable air of the master about him. Indeed, Mr. Benning must have looked just like him as a young man. Abigail patted the lad's arm. "This is Raleigh, my eldest son. He's been visiting with our friends the Frasers these many months. I'm so very happy to have him home." Her smile was brighter than the lamps that lit the room.

Another well-dressed couple sat among the family circle.

"And this is Mr. and Mrs. Fraser. They are good friends and partners with our family."

Mr. Benning hung back, standing behind the settee. A smile turned up the corners of his mouth, but it was as stiff and artificial as wooden flowers. Unlike the others who looked at her as if she were a performing monkey, his troubled gaze rested on Mr. Fraser.

Merry jerked her attention back to what Mrs. Benning was saying.

"Merry has proven to be a most adept stillroom maid. I don't know what I would have done without her help this past month."

Mr. Benning raised his glass. "To Merry Lattimore and her physics."

The fine folk raised their cups and laughed, tossing off the drinks in a go. Merry resisted the urge to smooth her apron.

Mrs. Benning embraced Master Raleigh again. "The children will be so pleased to see their brother if they are awake still."

"I'm sorry, madam, they were fatigued and went to sleep directly. Do you wish me to rouse them?"

Mrs. Benning looked to her son then shook her head. "No, I suppose not. He will see them in the morning."

The conversation swirled on, and Merry slipped away unnoticed. Thank goodness she had not been asked to wake the children. It would have been a battle to get them to sleep again. And she had plans for the evening.

Her fingers trembled at the thought of sneaking away in the night. At least the presence of guests meant that Mrs. Benning would be less likely to check on the children every few minutes as she had been wont to do in the past few days.

Merry selected a book at random from the library and returned to the refuge of the nursery. When at long last the rustles and murmurs faded into the quiet of night, she cracked open the nursery door and slipped into the hall.

A floorboard creaked, and she flattened herself into the shadow below the curve of the stairs. Master Raleigh stomped from his father's study, his face a study in scowling frustration.

Back pressed against the wall, she could feel his heavy tread reverberate through the house, just as his displeasure reverberated through the atmosphere.

Merry glanced at the front door. She was so close, and yet, what if someone discovered her absence? They could add time to her sentence, or even tie her to the whipping tree. Her heart stuttered at the thought. She closed her eyes. Why must she always borrow trouble?

Then she pictured Jerusha's red-rimmed eyes as she stared out the window into nothingness. She owed Jerusha a great deal, and she had promised herself that she would never sit back idly while injustice prevailed.

Licking her lips, Merry crept from the safety of the deep shadows. There would be no return.

It was time to hie himself home. Darkness had long since fallen, and Graham was beginning to fear he would fall asleep in his discreet vantage point. It was too late for Merry to stir tonight. He would return in the morning to renew the watch.

He stood and pushed his fists into the small of his back. By his count, and he had counted it over several times in the last few hours, they were nearly even. True, she had been wrongly transported, but she had caused him almost enough trouble to make up for it. The thought of the feather tick awaiting him rose in his mind. It was most certainly time to head for bed.

A tiny creak drew his attention. He turned in time to see a small figure slip into the street. He knew that frame. Moonlight crawled from behind a cloud to illuminate her delicate features. What was she up to?

Graham hurried from the shadows to follow. Merry paused every so often as if to get her bearings, but she always started again, aiming for some, as yet unknown, goal. Had she some tryst planned? Or perhaps she was trying to sneak aboard a boat headed back to England. Pure folly. Any convict caught returning before they'd completed their term faced an automatic death sentence.

She skirted the market green and entered another area of residences and shops. Then around the edge of the College of William and Mary and into a district chockablock with gin pits, gambling dens, and bawdy houses. At last she stopped in front of a tall, thin house. A porch lined each floor, but only on the side of the house, making it look like a debutante glancing coyly over her shoulder.

Merry approached the house and knocked on the door. It opened, and after a moment she was admitted. What could the girl be about?

He slipped into the narrow alley between a chandler's shop and a cartwright's paddock and settled in for another wait. He would find out what she was up to if it killed him.

Merry ought to have worn a cloak. Though ostensibly a private home, Sarah's business was all too public to risk being seen here.

At last the manservant who had admitted her returned and motioned her up the stairs. "Mistress Proctor will see you."

She followed him and was led into a small sitting room. Sarah rose to greet her. "Merry! It seems an age since I have had the pleasure of your company."

Merry embraced her friend and smiled. "You are looking well."

Indeed, she was. Gone was the gaudy dress she'd worn in Newgate. The gown she wore now was undoubtedly costly, but much more demure. And adorned by a single necklace of good quality. Her hair was piled high in an elaborate coiffure designed to show off her long, graceful neck. Everything about her bespoke taste and refinement.

"You tutored me well. And this new world has proven most lucrative. I may stay even after my term has expired. Come and sit. I must know how you are faring."

"I've come to beg a favor."

"Name it. I'm mistress here, and if it's in my power you shall have it."

"I need to borrow fifteen pounds."

Whatever Sarah had expected, this was not apparently it. Her eyebrows flew up in astonishment.

Merry rushed on. "I offer myself as surety. If I do not repay the debt, I shall indenture myself to you, though I must beg you to wait until my term of service with the Bennings is completed."

"What trouble have you found that you need such funds?"

Should she tell? Sarah knew as much about bondage as anyone. "A friend of mine is in desperate straits. Master Benning intends to sell off her son."

"Are you proposing to buy him? Fifteen pounds shan't prove sufficient."

Merry shook her head.

"Then what?" Eyes narrowed, Sarah stepped back, looking Merry over as if she did not know her. When her eyes reached Merry's face for the second time, she gasped and raised a hand to her mouth. "You intend to help them run away, don't you?"

Merry said nothing.

Her friend gripped her arm and leaned in close. "Are you mad? If you are caught. . . They do not treat such matters lightly here."

"I know."

Sarah's gaze searched her face. "I suppose if I don't agree to aid you in your folly, you will simply find some other means to obtain the funds?"

"You know me too well." Despite her weariness, Merry smiled.

Sarah shook her head. She looked as if she were about to refuse.

"I would not ask it for myself, Sarah. Please, I cannot sit by and see this boy torn from his mother. They. . . I must do this."

Sarah closed her eyes, her shoulders sagging. "You shall have what you ask, but"—she clutched both Merry's hands in hers—"I beg you to be careful."

"I swear I will be."

Sarah gazed into her eyes, searching for something. A promise that all would be well, perhaps. Merry could offer no such pledge. Matters had gone awry for her all too frequently.

Her friend pulled away. "I'll be back in a moment."

Merry sank onto the settee, absently caressing the smooth arm. The satiny finish glowed in the candlelight. Everything about this house and its furnishings spoke of luxury. Sarah's dubious profession had at least provided the means to live well. Merry could not begrudge her success, and yet how was it that Sarah had prosperity and independence, while Merry's struggle to do right had landed her in naught but trouble?

Sarah returned with a small leather purse.

"Here it is, in silver. They wouldn't be able to pass off gold without being questioned. As it is there could be difficulties. Hard currency is not easily obtained in these colonies."

Merry stood and took the weight in her hands. "Thank you."

"Won't you reconsider?"

"I wish I could."

"Then take it, and do as you will." Sarah sounded petulant as she placed a hand on Merry's shoulder. "I'll pray for you."

Merry could not quite prevent her eyebrows from leaping for her hairline. "You will pray for me?"

Sarah grinned and gave her a push. Her old accent snuck into her voice. "Even if He don't take much notice of baggage like me, I figure it won't do any 'arm."

Merry hugged her. "I must go before I'm missed. Take care of yourself."

"And you."

Merry slipped back down the stairs and out the door. The weight of the purse made her feel conspicuous. If it should be stolen. . . Summoning her courage, Merry breathed a prayer. She really ought to have brought a cloak, and to the devil with the rain.

She tiptoed down the porch steps and out to the street, one hand on the purse to keep the coins from jangling. She knew the way now though. It oughtn't take long to get home.

A parcel of black-gowned students from the college swung around the corner, and she darted into an alley. The boisterous pack launched into a drinking song. Window sashes clattered open, and sleeping householders hurled invectives. One of the disgruntled neighbors may have thrown something, too, judging from the loud grunt and slurred guffaws.

Merry shivered in her hiding place and wrinkled her nose. With her usual good sense, she had hidden next to someone's privy. She sighed and willed the inebriated scholars to pass on. At last they did so, and she emerged into the street.

A misty rain crowded in, both miserably wet and curiously dry. Merry hunched forward. She'd be lucky to survive this night's outing. Water leached into her shoes, turning her feet clammy. The soles had been worn through since arriving in Virginia, and she had not the funds to replace them, or was that the Bennings' duty?

It did not matter at the moment. All that mattered was that the water from the streets was soaking through her stockings. She shivered. Behind her she heard the sound of another step.

Her heart skipped a little as if encouraging her to speed up. Suddenly cold in addition to wet, she sped up to a trot.

There it was again. Was someone following her or merely traveling in the same direction? Again, Merry picked up her pace, hurtling through the narrow streets in search of sanctuary.

A hand gripped her shoulder. She opened her mouth to scream.

Chapter 5

"M erry, it's me."

Strangling the cry for help, Merry turned to face Graham Sinclair. He loomed above her in the night, tall and lean. Handsome face clean and gleaming, his hair neatly tied behind with a black bow. If he had the sense of a gnat, he would fear her. She curled her fingers into her skirts to keep from striking him.

"Why are you skulking about so late at night?" she demanded.

"I could ask the same of you."

He held up a hand. "Miss Lattimore, I know I must not appear to be your greatest friend, but I have been working diligently on your behalf."

"Oh yes, I know." Her nostrils flared as if she smelled something even worse than Newgate. "You saw me committed to the blackest hole in England, with nothing to look forward to but death."

The force of her anger scored his brow with deep ridges. "Miss Lattimore, I did no more than my duty."

"Have you come to gloat then? I confess I do not understand it. My family and I were ever kind to you."

His other hand joined the first in a placating gesture, though his voice grew harsh. "I had no choice in the matter. The evidence against you was too strong."

Her skin flamed beneath his scrutiny. Clinging to the tail of her anger, she held her arms out wide as if modeling a new gown. "Allow your eyes to drink their fill. I have been brought low by the Pagets and your false sense of duty. I hope you are proud of all you have accomplished."

She could see the bob of his Adam's apple despite his stock. The furnace of humiliation churning within her made even her eyes burn. He stepped back. His outstretched palms made him appear a supplicant. "I have no interest in seeing you brought low. Indeed, I owe your father too much for me to rejoice at your plight. I came to Virginia to find you."

"Surely you didn't assume I would desire your acquaintance after all that transpired. And why would you wish mine? I am nothing but a thief to you."

"Quiet." Graham held a finger to his lips. "Are you trying to draw the attention of the watchmen?"

She turned on her heel. "I did not desire this conversation at all. You accosted me."

"I know you didn't steal the jewels."

It was perhaps the only thing that could have made her stop and turn back. "You know?"

"Near the end of May the jewels turned up missing again. Upon investigation it was discovered that Lucas Paget had stolen them. It seems he was also the one to place them in your valise."

"Did he hate me so much?"

"It seems he feared you would tell his mother of his gambling debts."

Merry shook her head. "His debts? Surely, she already knew?"

"Not their full extent, I think."

"Do you mean to say that he purposely made it appear as if I had stolen those gems in order to discredit anything I might have told his mother?"

Graham shrugged.

She inhaled, fighting down a rage that stole her breath and blinded her. How could anyone be so depraved? So...so heedless of how their actions injured another person? She reached for a nearby wall to anchor herself. White-hot energy pulsed through her. The way she felt at the moment she could swim back to England and administer the thrashing Paget deserved.

Graham stepped closer. His eyes held a depth of understanding that prodded at her vitals. She closed her eyes against his sympathy. Despite herself she had been trying to salvage some sort of meaning from the madness. But no. It had all been senseless. A tragic waste. She shook off the gentle hand he placed on her arm and bared her teeth in a snarl.

"Have you come all this way to tell me that I'm innocent?"

"No." He whipped off his hat and ran a hand through his hair. "I've come because I have obtained a pardon for you."

"What?" Merry took a step back. The world spun and contracted.

"When I discovered the truth I petitioned the king and obtained a pardon."

"You did that for me?"

"Contrary to what you seem to think, I believe in justice and honor."

Tears stung her eyes. "I do not know what to think."

"You used to think me a friend." His voice was as gentle as the mist. He opened his jacket and pulled out an oilskin-wrapped packet, which he extended toward her.

Merry took it in trembling fingers. Home. She could go home. She could not speak. Tears spilled over onto her cheeks. Mayhap they would mix with the rain and he would not notice in the dark.

"Everything you need should be in there. If you wish, I will come to the Benning home tomorrow and explain it all. They may not want to let you go after having paid for you."

She opened her mouth to thank him when a sick feeling settled in her stomach. If she left the Bennings now, there would be no way she could help Jerusha and Daniel. Her hands began to tremble. "That will not be necessary."

The weight of the money pouch tugged at the waist of her skirt. She could forget that any of this had ever happened. Just book passage on the next ship leaving Virginia.

Graham was looking at her with an intensity that unnerved her. Could the man read her mind? She cast about for a means of explaining her reluctance. "They have been very good to me. Once they see the documents they will be just."

He gazed down at her, searching her face. "Are you certain? It would pain me a great deal to have gone to all this trouble and then for you to remain trapped here."

"By all means we must be certain that you are spared any pain."

He pulled back, the moon glinting on the hurt in his eyes.

Merry swallowed hard. "I'm sorry. I ought not to have said that. But I prefer to handle this matter myself."

"Then I bid you adieu." Stiffly he turned away.

"Mr. Sinclair?"

"Yes?"

"I. . . Thank you. You have accomplished something I never dreamed possible."

He stepped back to her side and took her hand in his. "Miss Lattimore, I am so dreadfully sorry for all that has befallen you, and for my part in it."

The warmth of his hand encircling hers sent a shiver up her spine. She looked up, searching his face, but shadows hid his eyes.

"My father said you had the most finely honed sense of honor he ever encountered."

He chuckled. "Of late, it has caused me a great deal of trouble." He took her hand and laid it on his bent arm. "Please allow me to see you back to the Benning house." He made no move to lead her away.

Merry could not seem to move or even to tear her gaze away from his. Almost dreamily he raised a hand and cupped her cheek. "You've not been harmed, have you?"

"No."

"You relieve my mind greatly." As if suddenly realizing the inappropriateness of his proximity he turned and strolled with her as if they were on the Strand in London rather than the backwater of Williamsburg.

The loss of his warmth was a kind of bereavement, but Merry attributed her desire for closeness to the chill of the rain.

Her foot slipped in something thick and viscous, and the coins in Sarah's pouch clanked. He glanced at her sharply but didn't comment, and she chose not to explain. It was not his affair. He would likely interfere if she confided in him. What he did not know, he could not divulge.

"Mrs. Paget's lady's maid, Grace, gave me your valise. I have it in my lodgings. Will you receive me if I bring it to you tomorrow?" His playful tone covered a wounded note.

It was Merry's turn to ignore what she did not wish to confront. "You've seen Grace? How was she? I was so concerned when I left."

"She seemed hale and hearty. I doubt any of them were surprised to see Lucas Paget come to a bad end."

He fulfilled her desire for news from England, describing every detail he could recall of his interviews with the Pagets' servants. He even made her laugh as he described Lucas's ignominious arrest.

Merry would never have dreamed that she would find herself in such a situation, and yet here she was, walking in the rain in the middle of the night with Graham Sinclair, and nearly enjoying herself.

Having reached the Benning home, Merry left Graham at the gate and continued on alone. She slipped in the same door she had left by and bolted it behind her. She crept up the stairs. No one stirred, though she thought she saw the gleam of Daniel's eyes as she passed his pallet in the hall.

She breathed more easily once she slipped into the nursery. Hastily she hid Sarah's purse and the documents regarding her pardon.

Then she gladly changed out of her wet dress and donned a dry nightgown. She towel dried her hair and lay down on her pallet. It felt so good to lie flat. She stretched out and sighed, listening to the rain that had picked up pace until it drummed in steady cadence against the roof.

In just a few days this would all be over, and she could go home to England. She practiced saying it aloud. "England."

Somehow the notion had become ephemeral, as difficult to conceive as the drops of water in the ocean. She shifted on her pallet, kneading the straw inside into more comfortable lumps.

Despite the chill in the air, she broke into a sudden sweat.

No. Oh no. What had she done? In borrowing money for Jerusha, she had offered herself as surety. It had all seemed so distant and tenuous. Jerusha would have found the means to repay the debt before Merry's years of service were completed with the Bennings. But now...

Perhaps they could get by on less. It mightn't be as easy for them to escape, and especially for them to start a new life, but they were used to handling difficulties. Certainly they were more used to poverty than stewardship.

Merry rolled over again, the metallic taste of shame on her tongue.

Had exposure to crooks and ruffians robbed her of her sense of justice? And yet, what benefit had justice ever provided her? Why should she not grasp at her opportunity for freedom?

"To do justly, and to love mercy." As if in a hazy mirror, an image of her father's face rose to the forefront of her mind. She shook her head to banish the vision. He had loved to speak of ideals, but there were no ideal situations, only chasms of chance to be avoided. It seemed that if she did not fall into this one, there was another nearby, yawning wide to swallow her.

A rustle, a murmur, a clatter in the hall. Chewing on her lip guiltily, Merry sat up. She swept back the coverlet, tiptoed to the door, and opened it a scant few inches.

Jerusha stood in huddled conversation with Daniel on the other side. She glanced up as Merry peeked out. "Master's ill. Come quick."

Merry nodded and slipped through the door, as quietly as possible so as not to disturb the children.

A cluster of slaves and visitors stood in the hall outside the master's room. They opened a path for her, and she entered to find Abigail Benning clinging to her husband's hand. The room stank of the vomit that befouled the bedding and floor. Red welts splotched Mr. Benning's face and chest. He opened his mouth to speak, and his features contorted. Veins corded his neck and stood out in stark relief at his temples.

Tears streamed down Abigail's cheeks. "Help him, please." The terror in her eyes tugged Merry forward.

"We need to stop him from vomiting," Jerusha said.

His eyes rolled back in their sockets. "Angel." He reached a hand toward Merry.

"No." Merry put a hand on Abigail's arm to draw her attention from her husband's agony. "The vomiting is good. His body is trying to purge itself of some evil humor."

Abigail looked deeply into her eyes for a moment and then nodded. "Listen to what she says."

"Has a physician been summoned?"

Jerusha stepped forward. "I sent Daniel."

"Hattie, I need towels and water. Jerusha, I will need marshmallow."

Both slaves sped from the room, their skirts whipping up a breeze.

Merry took Mr. Benning's wrist, trying to find the speed of his pulse.

Harsh and pointed, the blood pounded through his vessels in angry surges. The skin was flushed and hot, and carmine blotches blossomed on his arms and hands. His eyes fluttered shut. She opened the lids to find they had rolled back in his head.

She had seen something like it once when her father had been summoned to tend to an emergency while they had been on an outing together. Surely this could not be the same thing? She shook her head.

Not poison.

Someone handed Merry the water and towels she had requested. She soaked one of the towels in the basin and wrapped it around the master's neck. She spoke soothingly and wiped the sweat from his forehead with another dampened towel.

Jerusha returned with an entire basket of medicinal herbs from the garden, each labeled and preserved in its own paper packet. She had also thought to bring the mortar and pestle and the bloodletting kit from the stillroom.

"You are ahead of me, Jerusha. Thank you."

Jerusha took the towel from her hand. "I'll do this."

Merry met her gaze and nodded. "I need some lukewarm rose tea."

"I'll get it." Isaiah hurried from the room.

Merry flipped through the packets until she found the marshmallow. She unfolded the packet, tapped some into the mortar, and began to grind the dried leaves into powder.

The voices in the hall escalated in timbre.

Isaiah appeared at her side with a pitcher of tea.

She mixed a dose of powdered marshmallow into the tea.

"Help me hold his head."

Jerusha and Isaiah held his head still as Merry put the cup to his lips and slowly tipped in a sip. He gurgled and gasped. His eyes popped open.

Abigail murmured soothing noises. The rigidity in his frame relaxed slightly when his gaze found her.

"Angel." Again that single strange word.

The night spun out in jerky starts, as if time were a spool of yarn fitfully unwound. The marshmallow seemed to curb the violence of the purging, but his pulse remained hard and driven. With Jerusha's help, Merry made a tincture of hawthorn and administered it.

Another shifting in the hall and Dr. de Sequeyra arrived. "What is this then?"

Abigail dissolved into incoherent tears.

The slaves pulled back, looking to Merry. She outlined the symptoms she had observed and the physic she had administered. "I had thought to bleed him, but the pulse was so forceful I feared he would lose more than necessary."

The dignified physician nodded and opened his bag. He pulled out a lancet and scalpels. "Very right. He seems to be resting more comfortably now." He picked up his instruments and turned to the bed.

"The writhing has slowed," Merry said, racking her tired brain to provide all the details her father would have required in the same circumstance.

"You did well. Perhaps you could assist me further?"

"Yes sir. My father was a physician." She glanced up to find the good doctor regarding her approvingly.

He nodded directly. "See what you can do about relieving us of our audience."

Licking her lips, Merry did as she was bidden. Only Abigail refused to be shooed away. She stayed at her husband's side, never releasing her grip on his hand.

Dr. de Sequeyra kept Merry moving throughout the night as they fought for Reginald Benning's life. Somewhere around dawn, bloody spittle began to dribble from his mouth.

Merry quickly dabbed it away and glanced up to see if Abigail had seen.

They had lost.

By midmorning, he was dead.

The sun spread the town with a butter-colored glow. Graham led Connor around to the back entrance of the Benning home. He breathed in deeply, feeling a hundred pounds lighter. True, Merry hadn't initially reacted as he would have liked, but she had softened by the time he had seen her home. It wouldn't take long to convince her to return with him. It wasn't as if she had a great number of options at her disposal.

Merry's valise banged against his leg. The return of her things might even beguile a smile from her.

He knocked on the frame of the open door. Connor came up beside him, as stiff and alert as a bird dog on the scent. Graham's smile withered as he took in a more careful account of the house and grounds.

Not one servant bustled through the exposed corridor. The house was silent, with neither the murmur of voices nor the clatter of activity.

His boot scraped the bricks, and he turned around. No one toiled in the garden nor drew water at the well. He knocked again, his knuckles stinging from the sharp blows.

A coltish young maid shuffled from a side hall, saw them at the door, and approached. Her eyes were red-rimmed. Her face haggard. "Yes sir?"

"I wish to speak to Merry Lattimore."

"Yes sir. Come in and wait if you please." She sounded infinitely weary.

Removing their hats, Graham and Connor followed her into the hall.

Heavy silence blanketed the house and muffled every other sense as well. Though it was approaching lunchtime he could smell nothing from the kitchen. And the curtains were drawn tightly shut in most every room, leaving the house in gloomy shadow. He and Connor exchanged a wary glance, but neither could bring themselves to shatter the odd quiet. What might they find lying beneath?

Merry descended a narrow back stairwell on silent, slipper-shod feet. The black smudges beneath her eyes and pallor of her features confirmed his worst suspicions.

"Miss Lattimore."

"Good afternoon, Mr. Sinclair. Thank you for bringing my things." She held her hand out for the bag.

What could have happened? He lowered his voice and stepped closer to her. "Is everything well?"

"Mr. Benning died this morning."

"Do you have a moment?"

"I must get back to the children. I dislike leaving them. They are understandably upset."

"Of course." Graham handed the valise over, feeling at loose ends. "Perhaps I might call on you later, to make sure you are well?"

She nodded listlessly. "As you wish." Once more her tone held almost no inflection. Was she struggling with grief. . .or fear?

The appearance of a constable in the drawing room nearly paralyzed Merry with the certainty that she would be dragged to gaol. Heart galloping, she pulled the children close.

She breathed deeply through her nose, trying to still the surge of anxiety. She would not crumble into helplessness. The children needed her and so did Mrs. Benning. Their world had overturned like a phaeton in a strong wind. They needed someone to comfort, not drain them of their few remaining resources.

"So sorry for your loss. A great gentleman." Tricorn in hand, the constable delivered condolences to the room at general.

"Thank you, Mr. Harold." Abigail motioned for the man to be seated. He did so after a moment's hesitation and a brief swipe at the back of his pants with one hand.

"Such a shocking loss. So sudden."

Abigail's delicate nostrils flared as if she were fighting back more tears. She managed to retain control, though the struggle turned her voice high and tight. "Yes it was." She tried to turn to business. "I am not certain yet when we will best be able to accommodate the inventory."

"Oh yes, ma'am, we will stay out of the way of the family. I thought I would ask Mr. Geddy to help, since I know little about shipping and whatnot."

"That seems prudent."

"Thank you, ma'am. Could you direct me to Dr. de Sequeyra? He asked to speak to me."

"I offered him the use of a guestroom so that he could wash and rest before riding home. Jerusha will show you the way."

"Thank you, ma'am." The constable dropped his hat and bent to pick it up with a quick, awkward motion. He backed from the room, head bobbing like a turkey's as he bade his farewell.

The sober, diminished conversation of a house in mourning resumed as the man left.

"I am glad we could be here with you at such a terrible time." Catherine Fraser reached a hand to pat Abigail's arm. "I cannot imagine how it would be to go through all this alone. I hope you will allow us to do all we can to help." Her darkly elegant gown and quiet voice were perfectly modulated to mourning.

"I am grateful to have good friends around at such a time." Abigail sounded weary beyond human endurance. Red-rimmed eyes set in a chalky white face seemed to burn through the conventions and reduce the others in the room to fumbling.

Mrs. Fraser rallied and tried again. "Mr. Fraser will manage the funeral of course. You oughtn't to worry with such matters. And of course, I can do whatever needs to be done to keep the household running smoothly."

Abigail stood, swaying slightly. "Would you excuse me please? I feel. . .unwell."

Merry stood and hurried to brace her. She looked over her shoulder. "Children, find Hattie, please, while I help your mama to her room."

Wide-eyed they nodded, fear patent in their swollen eyes.

"Excuse me, ma'am."

Everyone in the room turned to find the constable in the door again. If possible he looked even more ill at ease, shifting from foot to foot, hands revolving his hat.

"Yes?" Abigail leaned more heavily into Merry as if the weight of trepidation were too much to bear.

"May I speak with you. . .privately?"

"Let us go into my closet." She took a step and reached back for Merry's hand, her grip as cold as a November fog. "Come with me, dear."

Safely ensconced in the small room where she handled household affairs, Mrs. Benning collapsed in a chair, and Merry stood beside her with a hand on her seat back assuring her of her presence and support.

"It's this way, ma'am. Dr. de Sequeyra found Mr. Benning's death a bit strange."

Mrs. Benning shook her head. "Strange?"

"He suspects poison."

Her features blanched even further. "What?"

The constable held up a hand. "Most likely it was an accident. This sort of thing happens. Something gets picked with the dinner herbs."

Abigail shook her head back and forth. "No. No. I'm. . . There must be some mistake."

"The doctor believes the illness was caused by lily of the valley. According to him it doesn't take long to take effect. I just need to interview the staff to see who picked it and how it got into your supper."

Merry frowned. "It was not in the supper or others would have been ill as well." The words sprang of their own accord from her lips. She winced and drew back a step as if she could distance herself from her own outspokenness.

The constable looked at her reproachfully, and even Abigail glanced up at her with lowered brows.

The constable sniffed and returned his attention to Abigail. "It might have been in any number of things. Dr. de Sequeyra says that even water from a vase that had held lilies would be enough to poison a man."

Abigail shook her head. "I don't recall picking any lilies recently."

The constable pushed his lips out in an exaggerated pucker. His head bobbed again in comedic fashion, though Merry felt no desire to laugh. "I'll need to speak to your cook and see what else Mr. Benning might have eaten, and who prepared it, and so on."

Tight little lines radiated around Abigail's mouth. "Do what you must." She rose. "I must see to my childr. . ."

Her hand reached for the chair but missed, and she swayed toward the fireplace.

Merry grabbed hold of her and guided her back down into the seat. "Pray wait here, ma'am. I'll fetch the doctor."

She shooed the constable before her and hurried in search of Dr. de Sequeyra. He prescribed immediate bed rest, and Mrs. Benning was bundled upstairs. Jerusha and Merry helped her out of the restrictive day dress she wore and into her nightdress. The doctor once again checked her pulse then administered a sleeping draught.

With Jerusha installed in silent vigil, Merry hurried in search of the children. She found them sitting mournfully in bed, their solemn little faces drained of their usual vitality. She checked them each for signs of returned fever. They seemed cool enough, despite their listlessness. When none of their toys captured their interest, she settled in to read to them.

They burrowed close, seeking the comfort of contact. Their innocent bewilderment broke her heart. They sensed the household's sorrow, but could not truly grasp the cause. They had never before been faced with such a loss. Her eyes stung with exhaustion and the dreadful dryness that remains when tears have been shed. Emma sighed. Nestling her head against Merry's arm, the rigidity in her little frame eased into the limpness of sleep. Merry stroked the girl's hair. She leaned her head back against the wall and allowed her eyes to drift closed.

The fire in the grate of her family's drawing room in London drew her close, and she stretched her hands toward it. She glanced at the clock on the mantel. Father would have been interred by now. Her tears hissed as they hit the hot bricks of the hearth.

The incessant snick of her mother's lace tatting needles grated against her nerves. Her self-satisfied conversation grated even more. "At least now you can marry Lord Carroll. He's been very gracious in not demanding your answer because of your father's illness."

Her jaw clenched against a rush of indignant words. "I have given him a response. More than once."

"Nonsense. You'll see differently now that your father is gone."

"I shall not." The whispered words were nearly swallowed in the crackle of flames. Where, oh where, was Graham? Not a word, not a note from him in months. She had believed, hoped, that Graham loved her and would offer for her. But then he had disappeared at almost the same time Father had become so ill. Now Father was dead, and still he made no appearance. She would never have believed he would abandon

her at the hour of her greatest need.

"You shall, or you shall not have a dowry."

Merry whirled. "No, Mother! I will not marry that man. He is loathsome."

Her mother looked up from her lacework. She narrowed her eyes, a calculating gleam lending her a venal appearance. "You'll marry him, or you'll not stay under my roof another night."

She was running. Fleeing. Cold wind hurtled past her, whipping her hair into tangles that blinded her. She stumbled. Fell.

Falling.

Merry jerked awake. A chilly breeze raised gooseflesh on her arms. Night had crept up on her. She rubbed at her eyes and then her temples where a dull throb pulsed. If only she could stretch out and sleep for a week.

Instead she slid carefully from between the still-sleeping children. Tenderly she tucked them under their coverlets. Blinking back tears, she retrieved Emma's doll from the floor where it had fallen and settled it in the crook of the girl's arm.

In the kitchen, Cookie tended some sort of stew as it hung over the fireplace.

"Are you all right?"

Cookie spun around as if she had been branded. "Lands, you scared me."

"I'm sorry. I just wondered how you are faring."

Tearstains ravaged the older woman's face. "I never thought I'd see the day, and that's the truth. I can't hardly believe it."

Merry sat at the table. "He seemed so. . .invincible."

Cook's eyebrows drew together in a bemused frown. "I'm not talkin' 'bout the master. Everyone has to die sometime."

"Then wha—"

"They took Jerusha away. Said as how she murdered 'im."

Chapter 6

For the second night in a row, Merry slipped away from the house as the shadows sank into midnight. She'd learned her lesson and wore a cape with a hood that disguised her features. Better to have anonymity than the freshness of a breeze on her face.

Once again she fingered the scrap of paper on which she had scrawled the address. She could not afford to mistake her location.

Shadows shifted before her, deepening as she drew near. The rustle of desiccated leaves sounded as if a woman in bombazine was hard on her heels. Despite herself, Merry glanced over her shoulder.

She picked up her pace, scurrying through the heart of Williamsburg as if she were an escaped convict.

Perhaps she was.

From the bowels of the night she heard a scrape and scrambled for cover behind a rain barrel. She licked her lips as she crouched in the dark. A night watchman appeared around the corner swinging his lantern.

"One o'clock and all is well. Fair night out. No clouds to tell."

Merry leaned her forehead against the rough oak barrel. Her eyes slid closed and she sighed. Only the ache in her legs got her moving again. She swayed slightly as she rose, placing a hand on the barrel to steady herself. The faster she completed her errand, the faster she could get to bed.

She found the house and pulled her hood farther down to hide her features. Breathing deeply she rapped hard on the door. No sound stirred within. She tried again, pounding for a long moment.

At last a woman dressed in a wrapper and nightcap answered. She appeared frightened. "What is it?" She asked in a hiss.

"I must speak to Mr. Sinclair. It is urgent."

The woman glared at her through narrowed eyes. "Come back in the morning."

Merry had the presence of mind to shove her foot in the door. "Fetch him now."

"Get out before I call the watch."

"He has already passed. I apologize for the disruption, but if you wish to return to your slumber you would do well to call for Mr. Sinclair."

The woman stepped closer, outrage in her eyes. "Listen here—"

"Thank you, Mrs. Bartlesby, but I am awake."

The goodwife turned to the voice at the head of the stairs. "Do you know this. . .young person?"

"I do, and I am certain she would not disturb the household unless the matter was of great import." Looking somber, Graham appeared in the narrow slice of interior Merry could see. Worry lines framed his eyes.

"I assure you, it is," Merry said, removing her now bruised foot from the door.

The landlady harrumphed and departed for her bed.

Graham edged the door open. The concern in his eyes made Merry's heart stutter from its usual rhythm.

"If you have sought me out, it must be a matter of dire concern."

"I don't know where else to turn." It was true. If this did not work. . . Merry's fingers pleated the edge of her apron as she awaited his verdict.

"Come in."

He led the way into a small drawing room and motioned for her to be seated. "I am sorry I have no refreshments to offer."

Merry shook her head. She continued to fold her apron between fidgety fingers. It would be best to be out with it. "The authorities believe Mr. Benning was poisoned."

"Poisoned?" Graham sat forward in his seat.

"At first they seemed to believe it was an accident, but later they took Jerusha into custody."

"Who is Jerusha?"

"A slave woman. My friend."

He waited.

"She had no reason to kill him."

"Then why do they believe she did?"

Unexpected tears stung Merry's eyes, and her breath caught in her throat. If she told him of their plans and he wrapped himself in his justice's robe, she could lose her freedom once again. All it would take was his word against hers just as with Lucas Paget. Could she face that fate?

She rubbed her burning eyes with trembling hands. If only she weren't so tired. Mayhap she had made a mistake coming here.

"Miss Lattimore." His gentle voice coaxed her to look at him. "Whatever you say I shall keep in confidence. But you must tell me what the trouble is so that I may help." His hand covered hers, warm and powerful.

She lifted her head to meet his gaze. Sincerity shone in his eyes, and something else, some deeper regard. A hint of the young man who had helped her bind a broken bird's wing so many years ago.

She swallowed and forced a tremulous smile. She had not been mistaken. "I know Jerusha did not kill Mr. Benning. They will say that she did it because he intended to sell her son away to a man from another colony. But we—*I* had a plan. I intended to help them escape. So you see, if she had another means of averting her worst fear, she would have no cause to take his life."

"You intended to abet a runaway slave?" Horror lanced his voice, reducing it to a sibilant hiss. "The slaves of Virginia are no less people than anyone else, and yet they are reduced to mere chattel." Merry shook her head vehemently. "I have been so reduced, and I can tell you that humanity is lost more often when power over another is gained than the reverse."

He placed a finger under her chin and nudged it up until he met his gaze again. "I do not question your morals in this matter, only your sense. Do you realize how dangerous—"

Merry's spine straightened as if infused with iron. She jerked her chin from his gentle grip. "It was all planned and would have meant only a minimal amount of danger for me."

"You could be hanged. Must you tempt fate again?"

She scooted to the edge of her chair. "*I* tempt fate? The circumstances that led to my downfall were hardly of my manufacture."

"I did not imply it was your fault, simply that you should be careful."

"You act as if I have no acquaintance with the ways of the world, when it was through your 'kind' offices that I was locked in with every manner of wastrel and criminal. I may have been naive upon entering Newgate, but I was not so when I emerged from that school of vice."

Graham paled, his mouth drawing into a thin line. "I have done all in my power to remedy my mistake." The words were as sharply severed as if they had met with the guillotine.

Merry gritted her teeth. She had endured much greater insult than he had offered and hardly blinked an eye. She breathed deeply.

"I told you of our plans so you would understand that Jerusha had no cause to murder her master. She had found other means of solving her dilemma."

"And what do you wish me to do with this information?"

Was he determined to make this as difficult as possible? I have come to ask you to represent Jerusha in the courts."

Surely he had been expecting such a thing? Yet he sat back with narrowed eyes.

"Do you seriously believe that a slave could use as her defense the notion that she intended to run away?"

Merry closed her eyes and looked down at her hands. "I—she did not—"

"I have never practiced law in this colony."

"Surely it cannot be so difficult. Nearly every lawyer in Williamsburg sat at the Middle Temple for instruction, just as you did." Her desperate hope was slipping away.

"I had intended to return to England on the first available packet."

Merry gritted her teeth. Time to discard her pride. "I beseech you, Mr. Sinclair. I know that Jerusha did not do what she is accused of. I also know how highly you prize the ideal of justice." She raised a hand to her stuttering heart. Perhaps a dash of guilt would help him to decide. She opened her mouth to remind him of the mistake he had made in her case.

But he spoke before she did. "You are correct. I love justice." He offered her a rueful smile. "I am also coming to value mercy. I will speak to Jerusha, but. . ."

Merry held her breath and met his gaze steadily.

"You must understand that this will not be easily settled."

"I understand that Jerusha will die unless someone does something to help her."

He rubbed his face wearily. "I shall undertake to see her tomorrow."

He looked so worn that Merry softened. She placed a tentative hand on his sleeve, feeling the warmth of him through linen and brocade. "Thank you." The words came out close to a whisper. "This means a great deal to me. More than I can say."

"Tell me all you know." His free hand covered hers as it rested on his arm, his gaze seared hers with a look at once unfathomable and unguarded. A scalding flush rose through her neck and into her cheeks. She caught her breath.

At last she could bear the weight of his regard no longer and pulled her hand from beneath his.

She cleared her throat, making an effort to sound normal. Carefully she recounted all she could of Mr. Benning's illness and all that had been done to save him.

Graham proved a good listener. His questions incisive. "Who brought the medicines?"

"Jerusha."

"Is it possible she tampered with them?"

"There wasn't time. And besides, he had already been poisoned, though I did not wish to think it at the time."

"How was the diagnosis of poison made?"

"I cannot answer for Dr. de Sequeyra, but it occurred to me

almost immediately. Mr. Benning was covered by a virulent red rash. And he said the word *angel* twice. That combined with the intensity of his pulse and vomiting called to mind a case my father treated." Despite the gravity of the discussion, Merry almost smiled. Her mother would have been appalled to hear this conversation. And yet Graham seemed not so squeamish. Perhaps all her mother's pronouncements had been her own opinion, and not truly representative of his feelings at all. He seemed genuinely interested in her opinion—in this matter at least.

"Why the word *angel*?"

"The toxin in lily of the valley can cause a person to see a halo around objects or people."

"When was it administered?"

Merry stared into the fire. "I don't know. It would not take long for the poison to act. It must have been shortly before he went to bed."

"Did Jerusha have opportunity to dispense the poison?"

Merry swallowed and then nodded. "She took both Mr. and Mrs. Benning their evening's draught each night before bed."

Graham sighed and sat back in his seat. "Matters are not promising. Jerusha had the means and the opportunity to commit this murder."

"I swear she did not. She would not. As I told you, we had it all planned."

He held up a quieting hand. "We must face the realities if we are to overcome them. Your own case might have been decided differently if you had understood the weight of the evidence against you."

She could scarce argue with that. "What do you intend? I checked. We have only three days before the hustings court convenes."

"I shall ask questions. Luckily, my friend Connor has accompanied me, and I will enlist his aid. I swear to you that I will do everything in my power to absolve her. You can return to England in peace, knowing you have done all you can in aid of your friend."

Merry cocked her head. "I have no intention of proclaiming my innocence until this matter has been resolved."

He stiffened and frowned, eyebrows drawing together. "Why-ever not?"

She clenched her jaw. This was more like the Graham Sinclair she'd known of late. "I have grown fond of the children and of Mrs. Benning. They do not need more upheaval in their lives at this time. And besides, if Jerusha did not kill Mr. Benning, someone else did. Surely the most effective means of proving Jerusha's innocence is to discover who is guilty. I am perfectly placed in the household to search for evidence of the true killer."

"This is far too dangerous." He stood. "I forbid it."

Merry stood as well. "You can forbid me nothing. You are not my guardian."

He sighed heavily. "Don't be fatuous. Investigation is dangerous work. If you intend to go through with this, then perhaps I shall withdraw as Jerusha's counsel."

Merry shrugged out of her cloak and draped it over one arm, her chill gone. "Then it is even more imperative that I discover who really committed the murder. And I shall start with Mr. Fraser."

He ran a hand through his hair. "Then I shall be forced to present myself to Mrs. Benning and inform her of your good fortune myself."

She breathed in through her nose. Once. Twice. "I don't think you would do anything so ridiculous. You are more a gentleman, and more intelligent, than that. But if you do, I will destroy the proofs and claim not to know you, and you shall look like an imbecile."

Chin high, Merry managed to sweep from the house before she began to cry. It was no wonder he had never married. Who could bear with such a manner?

Grumbling under his breath, Graham shrugged out of his robe. Drat the chit. There were times she had not the sense of a goat.

Hadn't he already warned her of the dangers of walking about at night? She had either the hardest head in Williamsburg or the thickest.

He had no time to go upstairs in search of his boots. And yet there was something valiant about her heedless courage. Sighing, he slipped from the house, taking care to secure the door behind him.

There was no fathoming women. He scanned the street searching for a hint of her passing. Which direction had she taken? In fact, how had she found him in the first place? The situation seemed to sum her up, a bundle of competence and naivete.

He set off in the direction that would lead most quickly to the Benning house. Trotting in double time he soon spied a small figure ahead of him. It could only be Merry. He picked up his pace until he was no more than a block behind. He opened his mouth to call out, but thought better of it. No woman would want her name heralded through town in the middle of the night. Come to think of it, after her tantrum, it might be best to lag behind and simply watch to make certain she made it home.

A shadow disengaged from its brothers and lurched toward Merry.

Graham sprang forward. A yell as savage as an Indian war cry tore from his throat.

The shadow reached for her. Snatched at her shoulder and spun her around. Sprinting, Graham tucked in his chin and lowered his shoulder to barrel into the attacker.

His shoulder hit naught but air, but his knee and shin caught on something that sent him tumbling. He threw out his hands to catch himself, grunting at the bite of gravel against his palms. In clumsy haste he rolled over, prepared to parry an attack.

But no attack followed. The only sound was a low groan. A man knelt in the street rocking slightly, his shoulders hunched.

Well, that explained what he had tripped over, but what in heaven had happened?

Merry stood over him, her face as fierce as an avenging angel in the moonlight. The light of recognition dawned, and her hands dropped to her sides.

Graham sat up. "What did you do?"

"Something my friend Sarah taught me." She looked smug as she offered him a hand up. "What are you doing?"

"I'm picking gravel from my palms. You might have warned a fellow."

"I meant why are you here?"

"I followed to make sure no harm came to you."

If possible she looked even smugger. "As you can see I am perfectly well."

"I see." He squinted at her. Mayhap there was less naivete in her makeup than he had guessed. "Do you know this fellow? Do you wish to call the watch?"

The smugness fled, to be followed by wide-eyed horror. "Heavens no. I don't wish to be found out of the house this evening."

He clambered to his feet. Eyes still narrowed, he offered his arm. "I've come this far, perhaps you would not mind if I saw you home."

After a moment's hesitation she accepted. "As you wish, but we cannot make a habit of this."

Graham looked over his shoulder to find the dark figure still crumpled like a dirty handkerchief. He nodded and restrained the desire to administer a good kick of his own.

Merry flicked a sidewise glance up at him. "Are you wearing house slippers?"

Despite himself he flushed. "I did not want to miss catching you."

She shook her head, but the caustic comment he expected did not emerge. "I appreciate your concern."

This was his chance to repair the offense he had caused. "It was the same impulse that prompted my earlier remarks. I care for your safety, though perhaps I could express it in a less heavy-handed fashion."

"That would be a pleasant change. If you think you can manage it."

Ah, there was the biting repartee.

He halted, drawing her to a standstill as well, and offered his best bow. "I can but try. Perhaps you will do me the honor of keeping me humble? You are so good at it."

She turned her face away, but not before he caught the ghost of a smile flicker across her features.

Chapter 7

Merry woke to find herself wedged between two small bodies. Sometime in the night the children had climbed from their beds to cuddle on her pallet. Dried tearstains still streaked John's downy cheeks. She traced the path with the pad of her thumb. Poor baby.

He sighed in his sleep and turned on his side. Gently, Merry edged from between the children and stood. What she wouldn't give for a few more minutes of sleep. Temptation pulled at her as inexorably as gravity. She yawned. Stretched. There was much to be done.

Yawning again, she coiled her hair up and covered it with her mobcap. In a few moments she was in the kitchen inquiring about breakfast for the children.

The other slaves had already eaten, and Hattie was in the scullery, so she found herself alone with Cookie. Merry stood with her bowl of mush and watched her for a moment. Despite her age, the old slave woman moved about her tasks with economical grace.

"Cookie?"

"Yes, honey?" She scarcely looked up from the dough she was kneading.

"You don't think Jerusha did this, do you?"

Cookie stopped then and studied her for a long moment. "No." She returned to pummeling the dough. "No, I don't."

"Then someone else must have."

"Don't know nothing 'bout that." She stared doggedly at the dough she worked.

"What do you know of the Frasers?"

"Nothin' I ain't already told you."

Merry put her palms flat on the worktable. "They're the only newcomers to the household. Unless someone else came to see

221

Mr. Benning late in the evening." She reached a tentative hand out to touch Cookie's arm. "I don't think she did it either. I want to help her."

Tears welled in Cookie's eyes. "Ain't nothin' can help her now." Her features crumpled, and she felt for a chair.

"I don't believe that." Merry moved closer and put an arm around the woman.

Cookie's shoulders heaved, and she raised her apron to conceal her face. Merry's own eyes stung from unshed tears and her throat ached, but she could not give way to sentiment. If she had any hope of helping Jerusha, she had to keep her emotions under control, and as Graham had suggested, find evidence. At long last, Cookie lifted her face and swiped at her eyes. Without a glance for Merry she stood and settled back into the rhythm of her work.

"How long had Mr. Benning and Mr. Fraser done business together?" Merry asked.

"Sixteen, seventeen years. Long as Master Raleigh been alive. They met while Missus was expecting."

"Do you know what sorts of business interests they have in common?"

"I don't know nothing 'bout business."

"Have they visited before?"

Cookie sniffed, sighed, and turned back to her dough. "Once a year usually. They sail up from Charles Towne on one of their ships and stay for a month or so."

"How long have they been doing that?"

"Oh, ten years, maybe."

"Has this visit been different than any others?"

"Don't know. I don't see much of the family 'cept for Mrs. Benning. I'd say she and Mrs. Fraser are polite, but they ain't never been great friends. You'd do better to ask Jerusha or Isaiah."

"I'll do that." Merry pushed away from the table and stood. "Cookie, I will do everything I can to make sure justice prevails."

The old woman nodded, but didn't meet Merry's eyes.

With the children's breakfast tray balanced on her hip, Merry padded down the hall. Through the door of the morning room she heard the sound of the young master's voice raised against the softer timbre of what could only be his mother's voice. Merry paused, glancing to make sure she was alone in the corridor.

"I care not. I am nearly a man."

Merry could not make out Abigail's reply. She stepped closer to the door, taking care not to rattle the crockery.

". . .what your father wanted, Raleigh."

"Then it is small wonder I am glad he is dead!" The pounding of boots warned Merry, and she scooted down the hall before it was flung open by the red-faced, tearful young man. He rushed past her, hardly seeming to notice her presence.

In the vacuum of his anger she could hear his mother weeping.

Merry bit her lip, the desire to comfort Abigail at war with the knowledge that she should not intrude. Abigail Benning had been a gentle and generous mistress, but that did not make them friends. It was no good thinking of what might have been if the circumstances had been different. Merry was a convict, and she'd do well not to forget it. At least, not until she could put her pardon to use.

She headed up the stairs and was about to enter the nursery when Mrs. Fraser's woman sidled into the hall, closing the door behind her as if it were made of porcelain.

Merry hoisted her tray higher and nodded a greeting. "Good morning. You're Nellie, aren't you?"

The woman raised her gaze from the ground as if startled to be addressed. "Mornin'."

She was a handsome woman with tawny skin, but some weight seemed to pull at her, grinding her shoulders down into a stoop.

Merry cast about for a means of prolonging the encounter. "Do you know where everything is? Do you need anything?"

The other woman paused. "I'm fine." She spoke quietly, almost furtively, as if unused to being addressed.

"You must have been here before."

She nodded. "The family has been coming here for years, and I've come with 'em ever since Mrs. Fraser made me her woman."

"Do you enjoy the visits?"

"It's a nice place. 'Course this time hasn't been the same, what with poor Mr. Benning being killed."

Nellie glanced side to side as if worried about eaves-droppers. "I feel real bad for poor Master Raleigh. Mrs. Fraser heard him having a big fight with his daddy right before he took sick. He's a good boy, but that kind of guilt can eat a boy up. Don't do nobody any good."

"Do the Frasers ever bring their children?"

"Don't have none. I best be getting Mrs. Fraser's morning tea. She don't like to be kept waiting."

"Of course. It was nice to meet you."

Merry shifted the breakfast tray again and entered the nursery. Something Nellie had said niggled at her, but she could not bring the thought into full bloom.

The children stirred as she entered, and she set the tray down gingerly.

She must find time to speak to Isaiah. He could tell her about Mr. Benning's business dealings. He might even be willing to tell her if there was bad blood between Mr. Benning and Mr. Fraser, provided she could find the right leverage.

Graham rubbed a damp palm on his breeches as he approached the Benning home. He'd grappled with the decision all night, just as Jacob had grappled with God. Merry might never speak to him after this, but he had to see her safe.

He half expected to be turned away as the house was in mourn-ing, but Mrs. Benning agreed to see him, and he was shown into the drawing room.

He bowed over her hand and took the proffered seat.

"I understand that you have been bereaved, Mrs. Benning.

I offer my sincerest condolences. I assure you I would not have intruded were it not important."

She was gracious, but grief seemed to have worn her thin as a tissue-paper doll. "Thank you, Mr. Sinclair. Isaiah said you have some news for me?"

"Yes madam. It's in regards to Miss Merry Lattimore. I believe she is indentured to this household?"

"Yes." A wary light glinted in her eyes. "I'm afraid she is not for sale. Mr. Cleaves has been most persistent, but I cannot—will not—part with her."

Graham held up a hand. "No madam, that is not my intent. I've come from London." He explained his part in Merry's conviction and the subsequent discovery of Paget's guilt.

Almost in spite of herself, she seemed drawn into the tale. She nodded as he explained the circumstances of Paget's capture.

"Then she was not guilty at all."

"She was not. You can imagine my feelings at this discovery."

She nodded, as intent on the story as a small child.

"I have obtained a pardon from the king on her behalf. She is a free woman."

"We must tell her." Mrs. Benning nodded to a young slave boy standing at unobtrusive attention in the corner, and he scurried from the room.

In a few moments, Merry entered the drawing room. She looked much as usual until she saw him seated near Mrs. Benning. The color drained from her face in a rush, and she stumbled slightly.

Abigail Benning rushed to her side. "Oh my dear. I ought to have warned you. I know you do not associate this gentleman with entirely pleasant memories, but I assure you, he has rendered you a great service. Come. Come and sit with us."

Merry pulled back, shaking her head. "Ma'am, I could not."

"Nonsense. Oh, I have muddled this. Perhaps you ought to explain matters, Mr. Sinclair."

Graham stood until both Merry and Mrs. Benning had seated themselves.

Merry's lips were tipped up in a stiff smile, but her glare ate like acid.

He swallowed. "It's a long tale, but the essence is that your innocence is known, and I have obtained a full pardon on your behalf."

Her jaw clenched so tightly he could nearly hear the grinding of her teeth. He cleared his throat. He had known she would be furious. Even so a sense of loss swept through him, and he realized how much he desired to reclaim her regard. And how unlikely it was.

Perhaps one day she would find it within her to forgive him. For everything. He squared his shoulders. If not, at least he would have the comfort of knowing that he had done what he could for her.

Heedless of the tension between them, Mrs. Benning embraced Merry. "Oh my dear, I am so happy for you. It is all so wonderful. You will stay with us of course, won't you? As my guest? I could not bear to lose you just now. And the children. . ."

Merry blinked and then smiled broadly. Her eyes glittered with triumph as she gazed at him over Mrs. Benning's shoulder. "Of course, I shall stay with you as long as you wish. I could never leave at such a time."

He gritted his teeth. *Blast it all anyway!* He ought to hire a berth on the next outbound ship, no matter its destination, simply to be away from her. Did she not see that her mission could be dangerous? He knew something of investigation, and it was not for the faint of heart.

Not that Merry was in any way faint of heart.

He stifled a sigh. He would simply have to talk some sense into her. In the meantime, he had promised to take on the slave woman's cause.

Heaven help him when he confessed to Connor.

"Mr. Sinclair, won't you stay and have some refreshments?" Mrs. Benning's features were animated now, and her smile seemed genuine.

He winced. "You are most kind, Mrs. Benning. But I don't wish to tax your strength. Nor could I enjoy your hospitality under false pretenses."

Her smile melted into confusion.

He fumbled for words. "I have been asked to defend your slave woman against the charge of murder."

"What?"

"Do you believe her guilty?"

The color in her cheeks went the way of her smile. "I have known Jerusha all my life. She could never have done this. No one— It had to have been an accident. Nothing else makes any sense."

"Mrs. Benning." The sonorous voice of the elderly butler brought conversation to a halt.

"Yes, Isaiah?"

"Mr. Cleaves is here to see you, ma'am."

She sighed then squared her shoulders. "Show him in."

Merry shifted in her seat, but Mrs. Benning placed a hand on her arm. "Stay with me, dear."

Cleaves marched into the drawing room with a jaunty stride that spoke of a man who expected to get his way. "Mrs. Benning, I'm sure sorry to hear of your fine husband's passing. It's a sad day for Virginia. A sad day."

"Thank you, Mr. Cleaves." She pointedly did not invite him to sit.

His eyes flickered from Mrs. Benning's face to Merry's beside her to Graham. And then jerked back to Merry.

"Did you need something else, Mr. Cleaves?" Mrs. Benning's voice was frigidly polite.

"I just— That is. . ." His Adam's apple bobbed reflexively. "I've heard tattle about this young woman here. I thought, what with your husband's death and all, that you shouldn't be burdened with a rebellious and forward servant." Mrs. Benning's chilly stare seemed finally to penetrate his understanding, and his final words trailed off uncertainly. "I came to offer for her. . . ."

"Yes, well. I note your concern, but you need not fret on my account. Good day."

Befuddled, Cleaves clapped his hat back on his head. "Good day."

"And Mr. Cleaves. Please do not return in regards to this matter. Miss Lattimore's innocence has been acknowledged, and she has been pardoned. While she remains in Williamsburg, she will be my guest."

His nod was a single short jerk of his chin. "Good day." His stride was clipped and precise as he departed.

"Thank you." Merry reached for Mrs. Benning's hand.

"Think nothing of it, my dear. I am more than glad to see the back of that man." She smiled and touched the edge of Merry's apron. "We must see to making you look like a lady."

Graham smiled secretly. Abigail Benning was stronger than he would have credited. He would be leaving Merry in good hands.

Mrs. Benning turned to him. "Mr. Sinclair, I will be most grateful if you will defend Jerusha. Find out what really happened so that my husband may rest in peace."

Merry was sucked into a tempest of gowns and ribbons, frills and furbelows the moment Graham departed. Two maids worked on her hair while Abigail regarded her critically. They made a wall of skirts around her, hemming her in before the vanity.

With the backs of her fingers, Merry caressed the silk dressing gown she wore, taking care not to catch the fine thread with her work-roughened hands. It had been years since she had worn anything so fine. Merry recognized the impulse driving Abigail. In the wake of her father's death, Merry had taken on any number of new projects. Anything to find distraction from her loss.

It was an altogether different prospect to be on the other end of such attention.

At least she'd had the satisfaction of seeing the look on Graham's face when she had been invited to stay in the house. It nearly made up for his conniving. Why had he suddenly assumed responsibility for her well-being? Where had he been for the last five years, when she could have used a friend? She shook off the frisson of resentment.

For now, the most important thing was that she could continue to try to discover who had really murdered Mr. Benning.

Would the slaves speak to her now? It would look odd if she continued to haunt the slave hall.

Hattie pulled her hair and she grimaced.

"Sorry, miss."

Merry raised a hand. There it was. The formality—the distance. It may already be too late to get any information from the staff.

On the other hand, her new status gave her greater license with the family and guests. She could ask questions of them now that might have gotten her punished for impertinence as a servant.

"Thank you for your kindness, Mrs. Benning. I am most grateful to you, especially at such a time."

"I am only sorry you've had to suffer so in the first place. I feel as if I've contributed to the injustice by buying your indenture." Abigail patted her shoulder.

"Oh no. You saved me. If Cleaves—" She shuddered. "I just wish there were something I could do to repay your kindness. I would remove your burden if I could."

Tears lurked in Abigail's eyes. "Thank you, but grief can only be healed by time."

"At least Master Raleigh is home. That must be a comfort."

"Poor Raleigh. He is so like his father." She reached forward and plucked a curl from its confines and placed it at Merry's temple. "I am not sure Charles Towne was altogether good for him. He seems not himself since he returned."

"Perhaps it is a symptom of grief, or simply a process of maturing?"

"Perhaps. Hopefully he will settle once classes resume at the college. He did very well last year. But his father wanted him to go to England and study law."

"He does not care for law?"

"He does not care for England."

Merry blinked, unsure whether she ought to be affronted on behalf of her homeland.

"He fell in with a group of agitators while at school. They are sowing discord all up and down the coast. They seem to set out each day looking for offence. Though from what I understand there have been some legitimate grievances. I do not follow politics, but I fear there is trouble brewing in these colonies."

"Was his father sending him to England to tear him away from unsuitable friends?"

"Oh no, I don't think so. He simply felt that law would be the best field for Raleigh."

"Mr. Sinclair passed the bar at the Middle Temple. I'm certain he has fond memories of his time there. Perhaps he could be prevailed upon to speak to Master Raleigh. That is, if you intend to encourage him to follow his father's wishes."

"That may be just the thing Raleigh needs. He is so headstrong at times."

Abigail pinned a final ribbon in the back of Merry's hair then patted her shoulder. "You look lovely."

For the first time since being plunked down in front of the glass, Merry focused on her image. Her hair was piled high, though mercifully not powdered. Between that and her fine gown, she bore little resemblance to the bedraggled woman who arrived in Virginia aboard a convict hulk.

She raised a tentative hand to her cheek. "I hardly know myself."

"Oh my dear. Fate has played on you so unfairly. It is time that something good should happen." A playful smile crossed Abigail's features. "Now you must tell me about Mr. Sinclair. I think there must be more to the story than I have been privy to."

The click of heeled shoes stopped by the open door. "The funeral must be starting now." Mrs. Fraser's observation brought instant tears to Abigail's eyes.

Merry shot the woman a hard glare. Could she not let Abigail forget about her loss even for a few moments? No, she must dredge it all back up and then top it with a dose of guilt.

"I wish I could be there with Raleigh. He's young to bear such a burden." Abigail looked down, her fingers plucking at invisible bits of lint on Merry's shoulder. "And I would have liked one more chance to bid Reginald farewell. I don't know how we shall all get on without him."

"That would hardly be fitting. You do best by staying decently with your children and allowing the gentlemen to attend to such ghoulish duties. My husband will take great pains to ensure that Raleigh is comforted." Catherine Fraser's brisk tone held no understanding.

Abigail straightened as if she'd been doused with a bucket of rainwater. "We are lucky you have been with us at this time."

Merry watched Abigail closely. If there was any irony in the comment it was so well hidden as to be indiscernible.

They repaired to the parlor for a genteel tea, and as the ladies talked over their memories of Mr. Benning, Merry's mind wandered to her earlier conversation with Abigail. She had been given much to consider.

If Master Raleigh had fallen in with a crowd of political troublemakers, was it possible his newfound convictions were so strongly held that he would do anything to avoid consorting with the enemy?

Graham inhaled and wished he hadn't. The prison's stench was thick with the pungent musk of despair. His eyes adjusted slowly from the brightness of the Virginian sun.

"Jerusha?"

He heard a scrabble in the corner and finally saw her, hunched in so deeply on herself that he had missed her presence.

"Yes sir." Her voice rasped as if she had been coughing, or perhaps crying, a great deal.

"My name is Graham Sinclair."

"Yes sir. I know you."

"I have obtained permission to speak in the yard. Would you care to step outside?"

The prisoners' yard was a pitiful little brick-and-stone court-yard perhaps ten feet wide and fifteen feet long. Its only advantage was that it allowed them to speak away from the ears of the other prisoners.

She squinted in the light, and her reddened eyes bore witness that his surmise of recent weeping had been correct.

"Miss Lattimore has been busy on your behalf."

The comment coaxed an almost-smile from the woman. "She's a loyal girl, and kind."

"But perhaps a bit naive?" Graham completed the sentiment she could not seem to bring herself to voice.

Jerusha shrugged.

"I'm a lawyer. She has requested that I take on the defense of your case."

She looked up at him sharply. "Is that allowed?"

"There is no law preventing it."

She looked at him askance, as if realizing he had not exactly answered her question.

"Do you know anything about this murder?"

She shook her head adamantly. "I don't know nothing about it."

He eyed her steadily. "Jerusha, you know the household, you know the people. Servants hear a great deal of the most intimate discourse. You are privy to more about your mistress than even most of her family. You must have heard or seen something."

"No sir. I don't take account of nothing that ain't my business."

Graham restrained a sigh. She had to say it of course; she could not admit to hearing the conversations that whirled about her. Slaves had been flogged to death for repeating gossip about their masters. But the keeper would be back in a few moments to send him about his business.

"Jerusha, I don't have much time. You must tell me if you saw or heard anything suspicious."

"Mr. Sinclair, sir, I learned long ago it don't do to speak ill of white folk. I don't know no reason anybody'd want to kill Master."

Time to try a different tack. "Had he been acting differently of late?"

"Not that I recall. He was just himself. Except. . ."

He latched onto it. "Except what?"

She glanced around again and lowered her voice. "He seemed worried. He and Mister Fraser were at odds. Don't ask me. I don't know why. I take care of Miz Benning, and the gentlemen didn't say anything quarrelsome in front of the ladies. They just weren't as friendly-like as they used to be. And then there—" Once more she skidded to a stop, midsentence.

He took her arm, perhaps a bit more roughly than he intended since she winced. She did not pull away though, accepting the pain as if it were to be expected. He loosened his grip.

A key scraped in the courtyard's gate.

"You must tell me whatever you know."

"Mr. Benning's been upset with Master Raleigh. It was silly, an argument, no more. They would have made up in a few days, and things would have gone back to normal."

The keeper appeared, blowing his nose into a large, grayish handkerchief. "Time's up."

Jerusha reached a hand toward him and then snatched it back. "Is my Abigail well?"

Graham nodded. "She is holding up, though I think the loss has wounded her deeply."

Tears pooled in her eyes and spilled over onto her cheeks. "I didn't kill 'im. Please tell her."

The turnkey cleared his throat pointedly.

"She doesn't think you did." He would have liked to offer some sort of comfort, but could think of no hope to extend her.

Merry swept into the dining room on Raleigh Benning's arm. As she took her seat, she peeked up at him through demure lashes.

Though only seventeen, he had his father's elegant leanness and stood half a head taller than she. His eyes came straight from his mother however. Now they were stormy, though he troubled to offer her a smile.

They were a small party, just the household and Mr. Sinclair. It would not be fitting to entertain at such a time. Still, Merry's fingers returned again and again to caressing the lush brocade of her skirts, and her nose quivered at the tantalizing smells of roasted meat, fine sauces, and freshly baked bread. Smells she had sought to ignore for months so as not to be driven mad with longing.

Despite the witness of the looking glass, Merry could not quite reconcile herself to the notion that she was no longer a servant. She felt at once both small and grubby, and overlarge and clumsy. A spectacle, that's what she was. The only saving grace was that there were not many spectators.

Mr. Fraser's eyes raked her from stem to stern. "My wife told me of your good fortune, Merry." He welcomed her as if he were the host rather than a guest himself. "I'm sure we are all pleased at your extraordinary luck."

Merry's cheeks tingled, and she withdrew her hand from his grip. To still use her given name, so informally. He acted as if she were not innocent all along, but had simply wriggled through some fantastical loophole.

"Thank you, Mr. Fraser." She managed to incline her head with a measure of dignity. She at least knew how to conduct herself.

Graham leaned forward across the table slightly. "Miss Lattimore"—was it just Merry or had he stressed the appropriate form of address?—"has been through a great ordeal. I for one am most relieved that her reputation has been fully restored."

Mr. Fraser pursed his lips, and the line of his jaw tightened. An instant later the expression disappeared into a toothy grin. "Hear, hear." Mr. Fraser raised his glass. "To Miss Lattimore."

The others had no choice but to follow suit, though it hardly seemed in the best taste to be toasting at dinner when Mr. Benning had been buried that afternoon.

"I imagine you will be returning to England now that you are at liberty?" Mrs. Fraser's smile looked as thin as Merry's felt.

Mr. Fraser flourished his knife, spattering the table with sauce from his squab. "I believe the sloop in port at Yorktown will be sailing within the week."

Despite his apparent goodwill, Merry could not find it within herself to like the gentleman. She watched with distaste as he shoveled another bite into his maw, no more mannered than one of the convicts with whom she had been caged.

"It has all happened so quickly that I hardly know what to do. Indeed, I do not even know what my options are."

"Surely you do not mean to say that you would consider staying here?" Mrs. Fraser dabbed at the corners of her mouth with her napkin.

Abigail looked up from her plate. "Oh, I wish you would."

The houseboys presented the next course with the unobtrusive precision of a well-executed minuet.

Merry smiled at her. "I would not leave you at such a time in any event. There is time enough for me to return to England."

"Then we shall have the pleasure of your company for a while longer." Mr. Fraser lifted his glass, and for a moment Merry feared he would propose another toast. He merely drank deeply and followed with a too-large bite of roasted beef.

"Mr. Sinclair, do you have any notion how long your obligations will keep you here?" Merry was desperate enough to turn the conversation away from herself that she had no compunction in throwing Graham to the wolves.

"Williamsburg will miss the presence of such a polished, handsome gentleman." Mrs. Fraser sounded as distressed at the notion of Graham leaving as she had at the thought that Merry might be staying.

He cleared his throat. "I am not certain my business will be so neatly concluded. Matters of law can often be complicated by unforeseen circumstances."

"A lawyer, eh?" Mr. Fraser held his glass up for Daniel to refill.

Graham inclined his head. "A barrister. Although I have not practiced in a good while. I am compelled by circumstance to return to my old occupation."

Mr. Fraser's eyebrows lifted in exaggerated inquiry. "I took you for a solicitor. I suppose it must be a personal matter, if you would prolong your stay here. Perhaps you are considering establishing a business in Williamsburg. We are flourishing."

A calculating gleam entered Graham's eye, and his chin tilted, oh so slightly. Merry had seen that look on any number of occasions, from considering a horse for purchase, to crafting a strategy to confound one of his professors. It generally preceded something outrageous.

"Actually, sir, I have committed to defend the slave woman, Jerusha, against the charge of murder."

Mrs. Fraser spluttered and coughed into her glass. Graham turned to her, offering his napkin. Her husband paid no mind. He half stood. "You presume on Mrs. Benning's kindness! I will ask you to leave, sir."

At Merry's side, Raleigh Benning also rose. "Mr. Fraser, this is not your household that you can—"

Abigail raised a hand in a gesture as peremptory as a general's signal. "Mr. Fraser, you will not speak to a guest at my table in such a manner." Her voice brooked no quibbling. "Raleigh, Mr. Fraser is also our guest. Now, I assure you both that I wholly support Mr. Sinclair's efforts. I do not for a moment believe Jerusha killed my husband. There has been some mistake."

Mr. Fraser resumed his seat, his mumbled apology less than convincing. Brow furrowed, he stared at his plate as if he had forgotten what he had been in the midst of doing.

Mrs. Fraser had overcome her coughing fit, though her voice sounded strained. "But slaves are well known for their scheming. It wouldn't be the first time one poisoned their master. The penchant is well documented."

Merry sought Daniel. He stood by the sideboard, his eyes staring into nothingness. Did she not realize that Jerusha's son was at hand?

Raleigh spoke for the first time. "Not Jerusha." Scarlet spots seared his cheekbones in asymmetrical splotches. His glare dared anyone to argue with him.

Head held high, Abigail stretched her lips into a smile. "I do appreciate your concern for our family, Mr. Fraser. Perhaps we could turn the conversation to less painful topics? Mr. Sinclair, we are most pleased to have your company for as long as possible."

Graham inclined his head. "Thank you, madam."

Merry regarded Abigail as she shepherded the conversation through the next course. A formidable spirit lived within her delicate frame. She had to look closely to notice that the skin around Abigail's eyes was pulled taut with strain, and her mouth was ringed with a tense white line. Her eyes were dry, but reddened, and she blinked often. She ought to rest, but seemed unable to accord herself the luxury.

Merry turned her attention to her plate. She had not eaten so well in many months. Despite dreaming of such a moment, she found she was ill equipped to stomach the bounty. Indeed, she was growing queasy. She pushed the remaining food around, like a child hoping that a detested vegetable will disappear if prodded enough.

Her flagging attention was brought back to the conversation by Mr. Fraser's raised voice.

"I wonder at your obstinacy, young sir." Mr. Fraser tossed his napkin on the table.

Raleigh Benning regarded the older gentleman from beneath lowering brows. The smoldering rage in his eyes sent a chill up Merry's spine. Such bitterness...

"I shall thank you not to presume too much upon our acquaintance, sir. You are not my father."

Fraser's eyes widened and his nostrils flared. "You should be glad of that, my boy. If a child of mine treated a friend of the family, who only sought his good, with such impertinence I should have him horsewhipped."

"I shall count my blessings then." Raleigh shoved away from

the table. "Mother, ladies, I bid you good evening." He offered a perfunctory bow before marching from the room.

"You will have to take that boy in hand." Mr. Fraser was not yet done putting a damper on the meal. "He will require a step-father to keep him in line. I understand that he ran with a most unpleasant crowd while at William and Mary. We kept him from such things while in Charles Towne of course. But now that he has been returned, he will need watching. A devotee of Patrick Henry, of all people. Those fellows are all rabble-rousers. Mark my words." He stabbed the table with a forefinger. "You will need to marry again soon. It will require a man's strength of will to keep that lad in check."

Abigail sat so still that she might have been carved of alabaster. Only her eyes snapped with fiery outrage. Even Mr. Fraser must have sensed that he had gone too far. Uncomfortable silence settled over the table.

"Mr. Fraser." Abigail's voice held an edge like sharpened iron. "I shall be most grateful if you would refrain from such comments. My husband was only buried this morning. I do not care to be married off again so soon, nor do I wish my son upset further with talk of being sent away. I am sure you understand."

Merry was sure of no such thing.

Clearing his throat, Fraser wiped his mouth with the napkin he had tossed aside earlier. "Apologies. Meant no offense. I'm merely advising you as I know Reginald would have wished me to."

"I appreciate your concern, and I will call upon you as I have need." As regal as any duchess, Abigail stood. "Ladies, perhaps it is time we withdraw and allow the gentlemen to enjoy some port."

More than happy to leave the table, Merry stood and hurried to the door then stepped aside to allow Mrs. Benning and Mrs. Fraser to precede her. She glanced back hoping to catch Graham's eye. Instead, she found Mr. Fraser staring at her with a narrowed, calculating gaze.

Chapter 8

M r. Sinclair." Merry pulled her wrap more tightly around her shoulders. She glanced furtively around. "Mr. Sinclair," she hissed again.

He stopped and turned to her, retracing his steps along the oyster-shell path. "If we are going to continue these midnight assignations, you may as well call me Graham."

"This is no assignation."

"What do you call it, pray tell?"

"I. . ." Merry sucked in a calming breath. "Have you matured at all since nineteen?"

He flashed a grin. "Some."

"I fail to see it." She waved an impatient hand. "There is little time for games. I wanted to share what I have discovered."

"Yes, that dinner was perhaps the least successful I have ever attended." He drew closer. "And yet it provided a most interesting glimpse into the relationships of these characters."

"They are not characters. They are people."

"Poor Miss Lattimore, has life used you so cruelly that you have abandoned all the joy and whimsy I always associated with you?"

Her cheeks flamed in irritation, and it was an effort to keep her voice lowered. "Yes, they have abandoned me. Now, will you please listen?"

At last chastened, he nodded. "Let us step away from the house at least."

Hand on her elbow he steered her beneath a graceful old oak. They stood close together in the gloom of the overarching branches, curiously intimate in their seclusion from the rest of the world.

Merry's breath seemed overly loud all of a sudden. The heat radiating from Graham's body seeped into her, and she relinquished her grip on her wrap. She closed her eyes briefly. What would it be like to relinquish control of herself as well? To just be held? To let him stroke her hair and tell her it would all be well?

"Well?"

Merry blinked. Now it was she distracted by foolishness. "I apologize, I'm woolgathering."

"Is it possible that Raleigh Benning killed his father?"

She shook her head. "Don't be daft."

"Did you not hear the passion in him? The notion of going to London fills him with dread."

"I'll grant you that he does not care for the idea, but I cannot credit he would deliberately kill his father."

"Perhaps in the heat of an argument he lost his head and lashed out in desperation."

"If Mr. Benning had been killed by a blow to the head I might be able to credit your theory, but he was poisoned. That requires deliberation."

"He does not seem much affected by the death."

If only she could see Graham's face she could read his intentions better. Was he playing devil's advocate, or did he really think Raleigh Benning might have murdered his father? "I think he is more grieved than he appears. He masks his pain in anger."

"His grief could contain a large measure of remorse."

"I am convinced of it, but not because he killed his father, merely because they argued before he died."

He cocked his head to the side. "Aren't you taking a great deal on trust?"

"Perhaps you have never felt such a degree of fury. I have. I know what it is like to be angry enough to kill, and yet not to strike out. I learned it was possible just before I left London."

His voice softened. "Merry—"

She held up a hand to ward off the words, though he probably couldn't see it. "Can you look into Mr. Fraser's business relationship with Mr. Benning? He is my choice of suspect. I have been unable to learn a thing about their dealings. It's not the sort of matter they discussed with their slaves. Though the servants know about almost everything else."

"I already have Connor looking into things. But do not close your mind to other possibilities." He leaned a shoulder against the oak. "Have you considered Mrs. Benning?"

"Abigail? Why?"

"A great number of murders are committed by the spouses of the victim. And I saw a formidable strength of will in her."

Merry shook her head. "Absolutely not. Abigail had nothing to do with his death. I would swear to it."

"How can you be so certain?"

"I know her. She is not capable of murder. Certainly not that of her husband. They were in love."

"We must at least consider her. If you truly want to see Jerusha freed, we must consider someone."

"I tell you she did not do it." She dropped her voice to a feathery hiss. "I realize that people are capable of the foulest deeds, but Abigail Benning had no reason to kill her husband. She loved him more now than when they first married."

He cleared his throat. "What if he had. . .betrayed that love?"

"The slaves would know."

"Do not be blind to the possibility." Stiffening, he peeled himself away from the tree and gripped her arms. "You must be on guard at all times. If you were to slip and let someone know that you are trying to discover the murderer, you could be in grave danger." He shifted even closer and raised a hand to cup her cheek.

She longed to see his face better, to read the message his eyes contained. Her heart pounded, sending the blood rushing pellmell through her veins and scattering her thoughts.

She had craved this since leaving England. A comforting arm. Someone to rely on other than herself. How nice it would be to simply turn over all responsibility and allow Graham to handle matters.

A flutter of panic plucked at her chest. She would never again make the mistake of blindly trusting that matters would work out simply because it was just. If things were going to be set right for Jerusha, it would be because Merry made certain it happened. Graham might do what he could, but he might just as easily change his mind. After all, he'd left her when she needed him.

The delicateness of Merry's cheekbone cradled in the palm of Graham's hand made his heart constrict. Had she eaten anything since leaving England?

She seemed to lean into him, and he inhaled the lilac scent of her hair. She was no longer the girlish miss of his memory, but fully a woman. A groan stuck in his throat as he fought the instinct to draw her closer, crush her to his chest, to feel the press of her body against his.

What would she do if he lowered his mouth over hers? He blinked.

She stiffened, straightened, pulled away. Perhaps she could discern his thoughts.

He cleared his throat of confusion. "I promise to do all I can for your Jerusha. But you must promise to be cautious. I cannot bear the notion of you being in danger again."

His arms hung at his sides, empty.

"I need to get back to the house." Her voice held a wistful note. Mayhap she did not want to leave?

What was he thinking? He had condemned this woman to horrors he couldn't imagine. It was scarcely a recipe for courtship.

She slipped away from him as quiet as a wraith in the darkness. "Thank you. I know this is not what you intended when you left England. I hope you are able to return as soon as you wished." She whirled, lifted her skirts, and darted for the house.

Graham sighed. It was entirely possible he had taken on more than he could handle with this case. He rubbed a hand over the stubble forming on his chin and turned toward his lodgings.

Upon entering, he found that Connor had waited up for him.

"Learn anything?" Graham sat on his bed with enough force

that the ticking on either end went airborne, as if the feathers had not forgotten how to fly.

"A bit."

"Spill it, Connor. I'm exhausted." Graham pulled off a boot and allowed it to thud to the floor.

"There isn't much to spill. Fraser and Benning were partners in several ventures. They jointly owned three different ships transporting cotton, rice, indigo, and tobacco from the colonies to England and returning with tea, woolens, and the trappings of civilization."

"What else?"

"An auction house and a silver smithy. Their plantations are separately held, and each has other sole holdings."

"Any hint of shady dealings?"

"Not a whisper, but I'm just getting started. If there are any grubs under the rocks, I'll dig 'em up."

"We may have to begin looking at the son."

"He's young, isn't he? Just a lad?"

"Seventeen or so. Seems he's cast his lot in with the rabble-rousers who have been putting His Majesty's nose out of joint."

"Seems a leap from there to murdering his own father."

Graham worked at his other boot. "His father wanted him to go to the Middle Temple to study law. Zealotry is a strange creature. It can blind an otherwise reasonable person to his own folly. He finds all manner of justification for his behavior."

"But this is a poisoning. Lads strike out in anger. They don't usually have the foresight to employ poison."

"Poison is a woman's weapon?" Graham paused and glanced up.

Connor shrugged. "Did you consider the wife?"

"I tried." Graham immediately regretted the acerbity of his tone. "Merry is decidedly opposed to the notion that it is even possible."

"*Merry* is it?"

"Not to you." Graham let his other boot fall, though he would have preferred to heave it at Connor's smug smile. "She will not dictate whom we can investigate. I intend to save Jerusha's life, but I very much fear it may be a Pyrrhic victory."

Afternoon sun streamed through the drawing room windows, setting the dust motes aglitter. Merry watched as they swirled and glided in unending dance. The need to yawn niggled at the back of her throat, and she inhaled through her nose as deeply as she could, trying to forestall the inevitable.

She plunged her needle back through the fine muslin secured in her hoop and formed another tiny stitch. Out on the lawn she heard John's throaty giggle and smiled. Despite the blow of their father's passing, the children were fully recovered from their illness.

A bit of iron from her busk poked her in the side and she shifted.

Mrs. Fraser's too-refined voice carried on in seeming perpetual soliloquy. "The royal governor wrote personally to thank me for my support. He said that without such support as mine, the museum never would have been founded. It's the first in the colonies, you know. I feel quite humbled to know I had a hand in it. I always say it is important to be civically minded. Our countrymen can learn a good deal by studying culture. It will raise the moral tone. Of course, I quite understand that Williamsburg is a smallish place. It would be difficult to organize something so ambitious here—"

"Oh, I don't know," Abigail broke in, a smile crinkling the fine skin around her eyes. "We have managed to complete the Public Hospital. I'm told it will open any day."

"Yes, well, a hospital such as that is scarcely a bastion of culture and good taste." Mrs. Fraser set aside her sewing and reached for her snuffbox.

"Too true, but it does speak to the compassion of our House of Burgesses, and it will provide a valuable benefit to our citizens."

Mrs. Fraser took a delicate pinch of snuff. "My dear Abigail, it is to house mental incompetents. Not really the sort of place one would want one's name associated with. Now, if you turned your attention to patronizing the arts—"

"Oh dear," said Abigail.

"Is something the matter?" Mrs. Fraser dabbed at her nose with a filmy white handkerchief.

"I seem to have run out of black ribbon."

Merry shifted her aching shoulders. "I would be pleased to run to the milliner's."

Abigail looked up from her handiwork. "Would you?"

"Of course."

"Well, if you do not mind. There are one or two other trifles I could use. Have them put on our account." Abigail busied herself with writing out a list of the required items.

Merry neatly folded up her sewing and put it away.

With a conspiratorial wink, Abigail handed her the list. "It is a beautiful afternoon, my dear. Take your time."

A corresponding smile burst from Merry as she understood. Poor Abigail, she could not save herself from another tedious afternoon with Mrs. Fraser, but she could fall on her sword and give Merry leave to save herself.

Abigail waved her away. "And do take one of the slaves to carry things."

Merry inclined her head. "Yes ma'am." She had just the person in mind.

She found Isaiah in the butler's pantry polishing the silver. "I'm going to the milliner's to fetch some things for Mrs. Benning. Would you come with me?"

"Yes ma'am." He wiped his hands on the apron he wore to protect his clothing and slipped it over his head. "You want me to fetch the cart?"

Merry blinked. She hadn't been offered the use of a carriage for her convenience in. . .ever. The offer sounded ludicrous in its luxury. But they would have more time to converse if they were on foot. Regretfully she declined the offer.

Isaiah retrieved a large basket, and they set out.

"How long did you serve Mr. Benning?"

"Oh, I was his man since we was just striplings."

"It must be strange to think he is gone."

"That it is, miss. I never thought I'd see the day. . . ." He shook his head.

"Do you believe Jerusha poisoned him?"

He hesitated. "That's what they's sayin'."

Merry cocked her head, looking up at him sideways. "I don't believe a word of it. Jerusha would no more harm the Bennings than you. Mrs. Benning agrees."

His mouth sagged open a touch, and his eyebrows pulled together. "Mrs. Benning said that?"

Merry nodded.

"I surely am glad to hear it." His dark eyes bored into her. "Do you think there's hope for Jerusha?"

Merry paused. She didn't want to provide false expectation, but neither did she wish to dash the tentative hope she saw in his eyes. "Our belief in her innocence means little. We must find the means to prove it."

"How you goin' to do that?"

"What can you tell me of Mr. Benning's business dealings? Particularly as they relate to Mr. Fraser?"

"I don't know as there's much I *can* tell. Mr. Benning's clerk, Mr. Porter, would know all 'bout that—"

A commotion down the street snatched at Merry's attention, and she turned her head.

It couldn't be. What was he doing now?

Graham grabbed for his hat as it tumbled from his head. He whirled to face the culprit. "Apologize, sir!"

Mr. Cleaves crossed his arms. His nose turned up in a caricature of disgust. "It only stands to reason that a man who would choose to advocate for a Negress should be undressed in public."

Three ruffians, either sons or apprentices, closed in hard by the man's shoulder.

Graham narrowed his eyes. "Have you a quarrel with me, sir?" He felt Connor taking up position at his own shoulder.

"Why? Do you intend to call me out?"

"Perhaps. Do you intend to continue being an insufferable lout?"

Cleaves flushed, his arms dropped to his sides, and he stepped closer. "We don't need the likes of you coming to Virginia and stirring up trouble among the slaves."

The louder Cleaves became, the more passersby stopped to watch.

Graham looked down the end of his nose at the tradesman. "Treating your slaves with a modicum of decency will do more toward dampening unrest than rushing to judgment." He held up the tip of his walking stick while discreetly redistributing his weight and bending ever so slightly at the knee. "But I shall make allowances for your error. A mere bully boy cannot be expected to understand deeper considerations."

A hoot of laughter went up from the men surrounding the tavern door.

Cleaves rushed forward, his fist raised.

Graham braced for the attack. He was in no mood to be trifled with, and the jackanapes would get the beating he so clearly required.

"There you are!" A flurry of flowered, beribboned femininity inserted itself between Graham and the charging bull.

The latter stumbled to a stop.

Graham blinked and looked down to find Merry Lattimore dressed in the finest Williamsburg could offer and looking lovely. Her smile might well have been spread on with a trowel, however, for it did not reach her eyes, which snapped with fury.

"I have been looking everywhere." She looped her arm through his. "Good afternoon, gentlemen." She tossed a rosy smile over her shoulder in coquettish fashion then led him away, prattling on about an errand at the milliner's shop.

Graham glanced over his shoulder. Her manservant and

Connor flanked them, while the befuddled tradesman still stood with his arm raised.

Graham's fingers clenched into fists. "What do you think you are doing?"

"I'd ask you the same," she hissed. "Brawling in the street like some urchin? Such behavior does not befit the dignity of a magistrate. . .or a barrister. And it will win you no friends among the gentlemen of this city."

She was right of course, but he itched to pound something, and Cleaves would have done nicely.

Raleigh Benning appeared at his side. "I saw that."

Graham glanced at him. "Yes?"

"That was Thomas Cleaves. Don't listen to a thing he says. He thinks that because he is rich he can do anything he wants."

"Oh yes?"

Raleigh nodded. "There are many of his type around the college. They beat their servants and families and think they are big men. I say they are small men with small minds. They know nothing of the principles of liberty."

Graham looked sidewise at the lad. "On that we are agreed."

Raleigh Benning offered him a cocky smirk. "Many nations suffer the same lack of understanding, I think."

Graham returned the smile and touched the brim of his hat, acknowledging the young man's score.

Raleigh nodded, and his expression softened into a genuine smile. "Had it come to open battle, I would have joined your side. Jerusha would never hurt my father, and that means someone else did. I would consider it a service to my family if you find the person responsible."

Graham halted to turn and look Raleigh in the eye. He placed a hand on the young man's shoulder. "I give you my solemn oath to do everything in my power."

"Thank you, sir." Moisture flooded Raleigh's eyes, and he cleared his throat. "I must be off." He tipped his tricorn. "Miss Lattimore, gentlemen."

He hastened down a side street leaving Graham to stare after him.

"If that lad killed his father, I'll eat my stockings," Connor said.

Graham turned to him. "Hardly evidence worthy of the court's consideration."

"Don't mean it's not worthy of ours."

"Miss Lattimore, may I present Connor Cray, the most contrary man in the world, and the best friend."

Merry dipped into a curtsey as she extended her hand to Connor. She was regaining the unconscious grace she had carried as a young girl. Perhaps there was hope that her experiences had not damaged her beyond repair.

"Mr. Cray, I am delighted to make your acquaintance."

"Oh, we met before, miss. Back in Mr. Sinclair's magistrate's office."

Her cheeks bloomed as red as a peony, and Graham caught a flash of white as she briefly caught at her lip with her teeth. But then she swallowed. "Then I am pleased to meet you again in better circumstances."

"And I you. Gra—Mr. Sinclair was as testy as an old goat until he obtained your pardon. He couldn't think of anything else."

Merry glanced up at Graham, and their gazes collided. "Indeed?"

Her coffee dark eyes held his.

"Yes ma'am. He couldn't sleep for weeks."

Graham cleared his throat. "May we escort you somewhere?"

"I am on my way to the milliner's." At last she broke her gaze.

Graham drooped. Ben Franklin's electrical experiments might be advanced exponentially if he could harness the power in Merry Lattimore's eyes.

Chapter 9

Merry turned her face away from the street and adjusted her veil. Her reputation had just been restored, no sense in inviting recognition. She rapped on the door to Sarah's fine house.

Her fingers tapped a restless tattoo against her skirt. She raised a fist to the door again. It swung in before she could strike, and she stepped forward involuntarily. She adjusted her veil again. "Is Mrs. Proctor home?"

"She's sleeping." The maid's bleary eyes and disheveled hair suggested that she had been doing the same.

Merry plastered on a cajoling smile. "I am sorry for disturbing you, but it is most urgent that I speak with her."

The maid sighed, but stepped back, allowing Merry just enough room to squeeze through into the house.

"I'll go ask if she will receive you."

Merry nodded. Fair enough. She toyed with the fringe on her reticule as she waited for the maid to return. Had Graham been as upset by her sentencing as Mr. Cray implied? Could it be that she had been as harsh as he in her judgment. Or perhaps even harsher. She swallowed hard against the notion.

"This way."

Merry jumped at the break in her reverie and followed the maid upstairs. She found Sarah still abed.

Her friend extended a languid hand, but retracted it to smother a yawn.

"What is it, Merry?"

"I'm afraid I have another favor to beg."

Sarah shifted her covers. "More money?"

"No. In fact, I've brought your coin back." Merry plopped the heavy purse onto the mattress.

"Then what?"

"The friend I told you of has been taken up for murder."

Sarah's eyes widened, and she put a hand to her mouth. "What happened?"

In terse sentences, Merry sketched out the details. She could not sit still, and found herself wearing a trough in Sarah's Wilton carpet.

Sarah shook her head. "It's terrible, but I don't see that your Jerusha has a hope."

"She did not do it."

"She is a Negress. Her trial will have even less to do with justice than mine would if I were accused of murder."

"I refuse to believe that justice can only be afforded to the well-to-do."

Sarah shook her head. "Don't be naive." Her tone was a lash, bringing blood stinging into Merry's cheeks. "Money is only one factor. I have coin enough, but in many respects I am as much a slave as Jerusha. I am bound by my occupation as surely as she is fettered by the color of her skin. Neither of us will ever be given the benefit of the doubt."

"If we provide evidence that someone else committed the crime, they will have to listen to reason."

Again, Sarah shook her head, her pretty lips turned up in a resigned half smile. "What do you wish of me?"

"The *Nyriad* is in port. It was owned by Mr. Benning and his partner. If any of the crew come to your house, would you endeavor to discover whether they have ever heard of any dubious dealings?"

"That ought to be easy enough."

"Be discreet."

"My dear, men say women are gossips, but once you get a man gabbing there is no stopping him."

"Thank you, Sarah."

"Think nothing of it, my girl." Sarah offered a genuine smile now, her pique evidently forgotten or at least forgiven. "Shall I send round a note if I learn anything?"

"Yes, that shouldn't be a problem now."

"Ah, then now we can discuss what interests me." Sarah plucked at the fine linen of Merry's skirts. "Where did you get these new togs? Not to mention the wherewithal to come a-visiting in the morning?"

Graham pushed away from the table and rubbed his eyes. He needed a drink. Law texts were so dry they sucked the moisture right out of a man. His lamp flickered, and he reached to the sideboard for his mug. Tepid lemon water would not have been his first choice, but he would make do. He quaffed the drink and smacked his lips at the tartness.

The piled books glared at him like a pack of disapproving dons. He ground his teeth. He left Oxford years ago, but it had never left him.

Kneading the back of his neck with one hand he flipped the page of the enormous text before him. Hmm. Perhaps if he appealed to the Virginians' notion of the principles of property ownership. He dipped his quill in the inkpot and began sketching out his defense.

Merry's image rose before his mind's eye. Her eyes had haunted him for months now. He would not fail her.

The knob rattled, and Connor stepped over the threshold.

Hungry for the distraction, Graham turned to him. "What news?"

"You owe me two quid."

Making a show of grousing, Graham dug in his pockets and counted out the sum in the smallest denominations he could find. "I hope I got my money's worth."

"I think you'll be pleased."

"Would you care to elaborate?"

Connor's rigid stoicism cracked, and a grin split his features. "I thought you'd never ask." He settled onto his bed and loosened his stock.

Graham smiled back and shook his head. "Out with it, man!"

"All right, no need to shout." The great lout stifled a chuckle and narrowly averted a bloody nose by beginning, "I couldn't turn up a hint of scandal 'bout Mrs. Benning. Seems a lady of blameless and upright habits. 'Course I ain't talked to her servants. Miss Lattimore chased me away 'fore I could strike up any interesting conversations. She told me she'd speak to you later."

That should be an enjoyable conversation. "Is that it?"

Connor slid him a sly sidewise glance. "Not by a long shot. There is a lad what works at the warehouse Mr. Benning owned. I loosened him up with a couple of pints of ale over at Chowning's Tavern, and when we were friendly, he tells me as how Mr. Fraser has taken over care of the books in the last two years. He also found as how there were two different insurances taken out on the same cargo. One here in Williamsburg in the firm's name, and one in only Fraser's name, taken out by a company down in Charles Towne.

"He would never have known, but for coming across a copy of the policy once when Mr. Fraser was here last year. Seems this ship in question, the *Phoenix*, sank in a sudden gale. Apparently it was a real shame. She was fully laden, on a return trip from England, and went down within a couple leagues of the port in Charles Towne."

Graham straightened in his chair. He'd known there was something off about Fraser. Merry would be delighted. "How convenient."

"Wasn't it just."

"Did he have the policy, or can he get it?"

"Wouldn't clap to the notion, I'm afraid. Doesn't want to be out of a job."

"I suppose he'll not testify then."

"Nope. Looked like a vicar at a bull-baiting when I asked him about it ever so gentle-like."

Graham rested his chin on his knuckles. "It's a start. If there was this, there will be more." He glared at the wall before him as if the answers he sought might suddenly be written there.

They had a good deal of investigation yet to do. Preventing the exposure of a fraud might be enough to drive a man to murder, but who was to say Benning hadn't been in on the deal? Still, the second policy in only Fraser's name was suggestive. He needed to speak to Benning's clerk as soon as possible.

"Do you think—" His question was interrupted by a snore. Connor had changed clothes and gone to bed.

Graham blew out the lamp and stood, stretching.

It mightn't work, but at least he now had a strategy.

Merry closed her eyes and raised her face to the sun's caress. The rich smell of the soil and sun-warmed herbs seemed almost another personality working alongside her and Abigail.

"It is beastly out here. I don't know how you both can stand it." Perched gingerly on a cushioned seat, Mrs. Fraser swatted at a bumblebee droning lazily near her ear. "Pay attention, you foolish girl."

Nellie started to attention and shifted the enormous parasol she held so that no bit of Mrs. Fraser's person should be exposed to the sunlight.

Pink faced and smudged, Abigail looked up from her weeding next to Merry. "But it is such a lovely day, Catherine. Just smell the flowers. Surely such scents are as beautiful as incense wafted before the Lord."

"Don't be blasphemous, Abigail." Mrs. Fraser raised a lace-edged handkerchief to her nose. "All this aggravates my summer catarrh. I'm sure it can't be good for you to be mucking about in the dirt all day. It certainly does your complexion no favors."

"I hardly think that matters. I no longer have anyone to impress." Abigail attacked the root of a weed, driving her trowel deep into the soil and extracting it with a tiny grunt of triumph.

"Dr. de Sequeyra agreed that fresh air and exercise would be beneficial." Merry would not see Abigail driven indoors before she was good and ready.

Head bowed over her work, Abigail's gaze slid toward Merry,

and she gave her a wink.

Isaiah approached. "'Scuse me, miss, you have a visitor."

Mrs. Fraser brushed a stray blade of grass from her skirt. "Inform them I will be there in a moment."

"Not you, missus. The guest is for Miss Lattimore."

"Well." Catherine reclined in her seat and took another pinch of snuff from an enameled box.

Abigail settled back on her haunches. "I wonder if it is Mr. Sinclair? I think he is quite taken with you, Merry."

Merry shook her head. "That is unlikely."

"Catherine, I could use a respite. Why don't we have tea and biscuits in the shade over there?"

Merry hurried inside, brushing dirt from the knees of her gown. Graham Sinclair had seen her looking far worse, but an odd reluctance rose within her to allow it to happen again.

She pounded up the stairs to her spacious guest room and with Hattie's help slipped into a clean day dress. Within a few moments she was respectably attired and progressing sedately down the front stairs.

Sarah whirled at her entrance. "You have landed in clover, haven't you?"

A flicker of disappointment skittered through Merry at Graham's absence. But then she smiled. "For the time being." Sarah's presence meant she must have learned something of import.

"Well, come here and let me tell you what I've uncovered."

They settled on a settee and Sarah bent close. "Last night the first mate of the *Nyriad* came a-visiting."

Eyes wide, Merry waited.

"It seems he was aboard a different ship, the *Phoenix*, a year or so ago. They were just a few miles from port when Mr. Fraser comes out to meet the boat in his cutter. He tells them there is plague in the town, and they should put in at a little island along the coast until the all clear is given. He goes ahead and pays the sailors their wages and gives them their liberty while the ship lies to the lee of the island. Three days later a bit of a squall came up.

There were only two or three men aboard the ship, and when the weather cleared, the *Phoenix* had disappeared. Mr. Fraser and the captain, one Asa McKelvy, claimed to have seen her sink."

Merry latched onto the odd phrasing. "Claimed?"

"Yes, it seems no trace of her was ever found, except a few barrels of salt pork from the hold and part of the masthead."

"Were any hands lost?"

"No. The men who stayed to guard her all swore she sank, but my first mate said that none of them ever worked a deck again, but set themselves up in trade."

Merry's brow furrowed. "He believes the ship did not actually sink then?"

"It is his idea that the ship's goods were unloaded, and then she was taken out just ahead of the storm and scuttled."

Merry tapped her lip. "It seems far-fetched."

Sarah's face fell like a child denied a treat.

"But it is something, when before I had nothing at all. I wonder what Mr. Fraser would do if I asked him about it?"

"Oh Merry, don't." Sarah put an urgent hand on her arm. "I have asked about him in the town. He has a reputation as a harsh taskmaster. Rigid as a pike and twice as sharp. It could be dangerous to cross him. Especially if you think him capable of murder."

"Something needs to be done."

"Leave well enough alone. He would swat you like a fly if you get in his way." Terror widened Sarah's eyes.

Merry cocked her head. "You are truly frightened of him, aren't you?"

"Indeed I am, and you would be, too, if you knew what was good for you."

With a swish of skirts, Merry stood. "Come with me. I'd like to introduce you to someone."

Graham's eyes blinked open involuntarily at the click of the door, and immediately clamped shut again.

"Excuse me, Mr. Sinclair. You have visitors." The houseboy sounded far too energetic.

Suppressing a groan, Graham risked opening a single eye. "Who is it?"

"Sorry, sir. Mrs. Bartlesby admitted the ladies and sent me to fetch you. I didn't hear their names."

"What time is it?"

"Nearly noon, sir."

Graham inhaled a fortifying breath. "All right. I shall be down shortly." With a great deal of effort he relinquished his hold on his pillow and sat up. In the next bed, Connor rolled over to face the wall.

A yawn wrenched Graham's jaws apart, and he stood. He reached for his breeches and administered a sharp kick to Connor's bed. Connor continued to feign sleep, but Graham knew better.

"I sense that I shall need your assistance with this interview."

Connor stiffened then flopped over. "You are a cruel, cruel man."

"Stop your grousing and get dressed. There are ladies waiting."

They emerged a few moments later. Graham's cravat was pitifully mauled and his shaving had been haphazard, but at least he could claim the virtue of speed.

He thrust through the parlor door and sketched a brief bow. Merry Lattimore sat on the settee. Her color was high, and her hands fidgeted in her lap. Golden light flared in her dark eyes when she looked at him, and all of a sudden his stock felt too tight. He ran a finger under it to loosen its stranglehold.

"Pardon me, ladies. I was not expecting such charming guests." He crossed to Merry, made his honors, and took her hand.

Merry smiled politely and withdrew her hand. "Sarah, may I introduce Mr. Graham Sinclair. Mr. Sinclair, Miss Proctor is a dear friend of mine and has some information that may well be key to the answer we seek."

Graham turned to the other woman. She was a pretty piece, but compared to Merry a bit flashy. Her hair was piled atop her

LISA KARON RICHARDSON

head and powdered as fashion dictated. Her gown was also rigidly à la mode. But unless he missed his guess, she had not been born a gentlewoman.

Nevertheless, he bowed over her hand. "Miss Proctor. I am most interested to hear what you have to impart."

Connor clomped into the room. It was Graham's turn to perform introductions.

For a moment it seemed Connor blushed as he bowed over Miss Proctor's hand. No. Graham doubted his stalwart companion had ever blushed in his thirty-odd years on the earth. It didn't bear thinking of.

Merry looked as fidgety as a child forced to sit through a Sunday sermon. She might burst if they did not get to the matter at hand.

Miss Proctor soon confirmed his guess as to her background as she recounted the tale she had heard from the first mate. It all fit quite nicely with what Connor had uncovered. Merry had been uncommonly savvy to enlist the aid of her pretty friend. Come to think on it, she'd been far more successful in her attempts at investigation than he would ever have credited.

Graham sat back, forming a pyramid of his fingers. He nodded for Connor to describe what he had learned.

At the end of Connor's recitation, Merry jumped to her feet and began pacing the room, forcing him and Connor to stand as well. "This is it. He has committed murder to cover his fraud."

Graham shook his head. "We must have proof. To accuse a man without evidence opens us to charges of libel and will do nothing for Jerusha."

"They have no more than this sort of innuendo by which to hold Jerusha. Surely everything we have learned leads to him?"

"Even granting that he is guilty of fraud, there is not necessarily a connection to this murder. We have no proof that Mr. Benning was aware of his machinations. For all that, he may have been a party to the fraud."

The pulse in Merry's neck stood out in stark relief, and her mouth was ringed with a white line. "What must we do?" Her words held the same tightly controlled quality that laced a man's voice in the instant before he issued a challenge.

"We must establish not only why he might have done it, but that he had the means and the opportunity to commit the crime. And then we must find proof that he did so. I am afraid that without proof, there is very little chance of seeing Jerusha freed."

Merry marched home. Truly, Graham Sinclair was the most insufferable man on earth. Why was it they needed no real proof to convict someone, but they must have rock-solid evidence to free them? And he wouldn't even try. Well Merry would find proof, and if she had to, she would shove it down the magistrate's throat.

She thrust open the door to the Benning mansion herself rather than wait on a slave to perform the office for her. She had marched home without pause. Panting, she pounded up to her room and sank into a chair. She dropped her head in her hands.

Unbidden tears stung her eyes. How was she to prove Jerusha innocent? She hadn't even been able to accomplish that feat for herself. If only Father were still alive, none of this would ever have happened. She would be safely home in England, blessedly oblivious to all the ugliness the world could hold.

She closed her eyes tight, trying to check the tears. If she gave way just once she might never stop crying again. She gasped for breath. Her throat burned with the need to scream invectives and hurl blame. She slid to her knees; her forehead brushed the floor. Harsh keening broke from her lips.

Why?

Why?

Why had God done this?

Where had she failed?

The temptation to pray tugged at her.

She had dreamed of vindication. Thought that the restoration of her reputation would restore everything else in her life to its proper place, but it wasn't to be. Her spirit had a hollow space within that she could not fill, and it seemed to be growing larger.

She needed to forgive Graham. He had done everything in his power to correct his mistake. But what if he left again? If she released the last of her resentment, what would she use to guard her heart?

She tried to stifle her sobs. She did not want to be heard. To be found. To have to explain her despair.

Lord, where are You?

At last the great racking spasms passed, and she lay upon the floor, spent.

A cool breeze drifted through the window and caressed her flushed, damp cheeks.

Jerusha would have been accused of murder even if Merry had never arrived on these shores. Mayhap Merry could find purpose in that. True, she had been unable to save herself, but didn't that give her more reason to see that someone else did not suffer a similar fate?

Jerusha needed her. It was time to get to work. She sat up and dampened a handkerchief with water from the guglet on her dresser. She washed her face and rubbed lavender oil into her temples to becalm the headache her sobs had created.

Her face was still red and puffy, but the house was in mourning. It should scarcely be called into question. As she looked at herself in the glass she nearly fell to weeping again. A chasm was growing within her, pulling at her. Her very person seemed held together by nothing more substantial than the lacings of her stays. Her hands clenched around the wooden lip of the dressing table.

She could fall apart after she saw Jerusha freed. But first, justice.

"Master Benning." Graham raised his arm to hail the young man. It had taken long enough to pick the lad out from his identically robed comrades.

Raleigh turned, and a smile ghosted across his features. He

took leave of his companions and turned aside to where Graham stood.

"Mr. Sinclair, I had not looked for the pleasure of your company today."

"Would you have a few moments to speak?"

"Certainly, I do not have to attend Mr. Wythe for another hour."

"It pertains to your father's murder."

Raleigh nodded. "I thought it might."

Graham led the way from the campus to a nearby tavern. "Perhaps you'd care for a bite. It's near the lunch hour."

Raleigh accepted, and they were soon seated at a table.

"Can you tell me anything of your father's last night? I understand you met with him quite late."

The boy reddened and stared into the contents of his mug. When he at last looked up tears brimmed in his eyes. "My father and I had a falling out. We were both upset when I left."

"May I ask what caused the rift?" Graham kept his voice low. No use allowing the boy's business to become public.

"He wanted to send me to school in England. He felt that my friends are advocating measures against the crown that come perilously close to treason."

"You did not agree."

"How can it be treason simply to desire a voice in the Parliament that governs and taxes us? Are we lesser English-men simply because we are removed by an ocean from our fellows? His Majesty and Lord North have nothing to fear if they but treat us fairly." Raleigh was becoming more voluble. His eyes glinted with fervor, and for the first time Graham began to understand what motivated the radicals.

"What happened next?"

"I left. He asked me to. He wouldn't listen to sense, and I was too angry."

"Did you see anyone about when you left?"

"Not a soul."

"Did he eat or drink anything while you were together?"

Raleigh pursed his lips in thought. "Not that I recall."

"Did he mention feeling ill?"

Raleigh shook his head. "He seemed his usual self."

Graham sought for some straw of useful information. "Perhaps he mentioned problems he was having with someone else?"

Raleigh snorted indelicately. "He was too focused on the problems he was having with me."

Graham nodded in commiseration. "I had the opposite problem. My father refused to allow me to enter the Middle Temple and train for a barrister. He and my mother wanted to send me into the church."

For the first time Raleigh put down his mug and met Graham's eye. "Why the law?"

Graham considered. "I suppose that I felt about the law much as you do."

"Me?"

"Of course, you were just speaking of governments and liberty. Laws can restrict freedom or grant it. Can empower the common man and check a king. Can be wielded for good or evil. It only requires men of passion and honor to pursue justice."

Raleigh leaned forward. "I never considered it in such a fashion."

The clock on the mantel pinged the hour, and the boy started.

"I had no idea it was so late. Please excuse me. I must hurry." He stood and trotted away only to return an instant later, half-breathless. "I've just remembered. As I was leaving, Father muttered something about having to have another unpleasant conversation with Mr. Fraser. Does that help?"

Graham's eyebrows rose. "It might. It just might at that."

Chapter 10

Merry tracked down Mr. Porter to his small office. Mr. Benning's clerk scrambled to his feet at her entrance, offering her the seat he had occupied while his underlings disappeared so quickly they might never have been there at all.

"You all right, miss?"

Merry closed her eyes briefly, and then opened them again, allowing the tears to resurface. "I'm greatly distressed about Jerusha."

Mr. Porter turned away, rummaging with a teapot and clay mug. "I've got some tea."

"I don't think she is guilty."

His hands paused in their deft movement. He half turned his head toward her. "I can't say as I agree with you. Though it's sure sad." His words were low and rough as if they cost him something to say. "Truth be told, it don't matter a great deal what either of us thinks."

"Perhaps not, but what really happened matters a great deal. As does catching the real killer. I need you to tell me all you can of Mr. Fraser."

He shook his head. "That won't help."

"You cannot know that." She raised her gaze to him in earnest supplication. "Please."

"Naw, miss. I think you'd best just leave this sort of thing to the officials. You don't need to trouble yourself."

Merry's patience had nearly run its course. If she could, she would have snatched the knowledge from his head by force. Instead she forced a sweet simper. "I hope you understand that I am here at the direct request of Mrs. Benning. She is most unsettled in her mind about all that has happened and will be evaluating all of the employees most carefully, now that the responsibility for the estate has fallen on her shoulders."

He sank back into his seat across from her, looking as resentful as if he had been bested in a prizefight. "What do you want to know?"

"Had there been a break between Mr. Fraser and Mr. Benning?"

"How did you know 'bout that?"

The answer was there, just beyond her grasp. "What happened?"

"I don't know for sure. Mr. Benning was troubled 'bout something and wrote to ask Mr. Fraser to come right away. They don't usually come till later in the year when the House of Burgesses meets."

"Then the matter was urgent."

"Must've been. Mr. Benning took whatever it was hard. He even started taking a draught to help him sleep at night. That's what poisoned him, you know. That draught Jerusha took him."

"That is what the sheriff believes." She could not allow herself to be diverted into an argument. "Would you say this all happened suddenly? It wasn't frustration that had been building?"

"Sudden as a kick in the pants, I'd say. Mr. Benning was fine; then he read his post and was in a tearing hurry. He tore up his study looking for some report or other about a ship. Took me near a week to get everything filed away again."

"What ship? Do you remember the name?"

His lips pursed, and he looked into the middle distance. "I don't rightly recall. It was *Furnace* or *Feen*..."

Merry's eyes widened. "*Phoenix*."

"If you already know the story, why are you bedeviling me?"

"I'm sorry, Mr. Porter, I don't know the story. It was just that that particular ship has come up before. Did Mr. Benning find what he was looking for?"

"It was right where it was supposed to be. He was just too upset. I pulled it out straightaway when he called me in to help."

"Do you know what it was?"

"A letter of appraisal on the *Phoenix* needing repairs."

That wasn't what she had expected. It certainly didn't seem to be the sort of document worthy of such a frenzied search. She must be missing something.

"What sort of repairs?"

"From what I can recollect, 'bout near everything. There were the usual small things, but they said she needed a new copper bottom. She was hulled once in an action and never did get patched up good. Caused lots of problems. Worse yet, her knees were all but useless, and they'd have had to replace them."

"Is that expensive?"

"It's nearly cheaper to build a whole new ship than do repairs like that."

A glimmer of an idea poked through Merry's confusion. "But she was insured?"

"Oh yes. All the ships and goods are insured. Mr. Benning was no fool."

"Insurance wouldn't pay for routine repairs though. Only if the ship were lost?"

"That's right."

Merry sat back. It explained a great deal. If Fraser received the same report, he may have just grabbed at the chance to make as much profit as he could. By offloading the cargo, he was paid for it several times, once by the private insurance he obtained, once by the joint policy, and once by whomever he had eventually sold it to. And he did not have to pay for any costly repairs for the *Phoenix*. It must have seemed the perfect opportunity.

But then somehow Mr. Benning had figured it all out and summoned him to Williamsburg. Fraser must have known his time was limited.

"Do you have the letter of assessment?"

He shook his head. "Mr. Benning took it somewhere."

"Where?"

"I don't know."

"Would you recognize it if you saw it again?"

"Probably."

"Do you know if Mr. Benning confronted Mr. Fraser?"

"I doubt it. There wasn't much time for one thing. Mr. Benning was a gentleman. He wouldn't have said anything in front of the ladies."

"Did they meet privately that night?"

"I think Mr. Benning meant to meet Mr. Fraser in the morning. He'd have plenty of time to sort out business." He leaned forward, resting his elbows on his knees. "Look here, Miss Lattimore. I don't see what this has to do with anything. Mr. Fraser is wealthy in his own right. Even if he and Mr. Benning parted ways, he wouldn't be ruined. He could find someone else to partner up with if he wanted."

Merry looked into the clerk's deep-set little eyes. "You are probably right. I have been thinking too hard."

Mr. Porter blew a gust of air out. "I guess it's been a nasty shock for you ladies."

"Yes, well thank you, Mr. Porter. I can see that I have taken up too much of your time. I do apologize." Merry stood and offered a guileless smile.

Merry found Abigail in the parlor listening to Emma practice on the pianoforte. John sat on the floor at her feet playing with his tin soldiers. The moment he spied Merry, he tugged her down to join him.

"You be the French."

John led a whinnying, snorting cavalry charge designed to decimate her forces.

"I'm Colonel Washington," he crowed.

Great swathes of her soldiers fell, and even the artillery could not prevail against such dashing horsemanship.

Emma's piece ended and Merry clapped enthusiastically. Flushed with success, the little girl began a new selection. John, his tongue protruding slightly between his teeth, concentrated on forming new battle lines.

Merry turned to Abigail. "Where is Mrs. Fraser this afternoon?"

"I'm afraid she has a headache. She is resting."

"It's good to see the children so full of vitality."

"God has been so gracious to bless me with them. I was so afraid while they were ill. And then Reginald..." The tip of Abigail's nose turned red as did her eyes. She plucked a handkerchief from her sleeve and dabbed at her eyes. "Excuse me."

Merry placed a hand on her arm in silent commiseration. She had no words that could heal Abigail's grief. Not when she could not even stem the tide of her own sorrow.

She lowered her voice. "Have you or one of the servants come across any papers that Mr. Benning might have hidden somewhere? Particularly anything to do with a ship named the *Phoenix*?"

Abigail cocked her head to one side. "No. I don't think so. Surely the man to ask would be Mr. Porter?"

"I've spoken to him, and these papers are no longer in the office."

"Do you think it has aught to do with his murder?"

"It could. I do not know, and I would not ruin your good opinion of a man without just cause. Are you certain that nothing odd has turned up?"

"When you phrase it that way, something very odd turned up indeed." From the table beside her Abigail plucked a key wrapped tightly in a bit of paper. She held it out to Merry, who unwound the paper to discover that it was a receipt from Lorring's Tavern for the amount of twenty shillings. A note in the upper left hand read,

Nth Rm, Sep Prv Ent.

"Isaiah brought it to me yesterday. He found it in the pocket of Reginald's best waistcoat. I cannot make heads nor tails of it. Lorring's is far from the best tavern in town, nor is it convenient."

Merry's mind worked as busily as a gristmill as it ground through possibilities. Could Lorring have agreed to hold the papers for Mr. Benning? But then he might as easily have requested a friend do the honor for free and with surer certainty of discretion.

"Mr. Benning did not frequent Lorring's then?"

"Almost never."

The receipt by itself could merely have been for an evening's entertainment, except that it did not itemize the fare or drinks, as would have been mandated by town regulations. And then of course, why the key?

Merry looked at the slip more closely. *Nth Rm, Sep Prv Ent.*

Could it be that *Rm* stood for room? Tavern owners had to provide lodging at set rates for travelers. Perhaps Mr. Benning had stayed there? But that made no sense either. The cost was beyond exorbitant, and he had been on his plantation or at home; he had not stayed at some tavern, nor would he have in such a small town, where gossip would have been rife.

Merry gnawed at her lower lip and allowed her troops to be soundly thrashed again by Colonel Washington.

Tavern keepers also rented out meeting rooms. What if Mr. Benning had obtained one of those for the long term—a place to keep the documents he wanted to secure? Somewhere away from his own household, where he knew Mr. Fraser would be staying. Somewhere with no clear relation to him. Somewhere safe.

What if the receipt referred to the North Room of Lorring's Tavern? Was it possible that the room had a separate, private entrance? An entrance granted by the key growing warm in her clenched fingers?

Graham settled his hat and left the clerk of court's office. He'd made good headway. The man was certainly knowledgeable in any event. And not just about the law.

He picked up his pace. Connor would be waiting at Chowning's. He needed a bit of something to eat. A nice veal pie and a suet pudding. His mouth watered. He could practically smell it, though it was unlikely he'd find any. These colonials seemed to eat naught but pork.

His feet flew out from under him as rough hands hauled him into the shadow of a narrow alley. An arm clenched tight around his neck. A harsh whisper rasped against his ear. "Let the Negress swing, or you'll be sorry."

Graham stomped on the man's instep, eliciting a howl. A sharp backward thrust of his elbow made the attacker gasp. Grabbing the arm around his neck, Graham twisted in a long, fluid motion, freeing himself and spinning the other man until Graham stood behind him and had the attacker pressed face-first against the wall.

A blow to Graham's lower back made him grunt in pain. Another pair of hands took him by the arms and hauled him backward.

The first man recovered and spun to deliver a sharp kick.

Graham threw his head back, striking the man who held him in the face. The grip on his arms loosened, and Graham wrenched free, but a blow to his stomach expelled the air from his lungs in a whoosh.

He staggered and would have fallen except that a steadying hand righted him. The attackers fled.

He glanced up to find Connor at his shoulder.

"Let's go after them."

Connor shook his head. "They'll have already disappeared. If this was London, I could track them anywhere in the city, but I haven't found my depth here yet."

Graham eased himself onto a packing crate, rubbing his stomach. "Not that I'm ungrateful, but what brings you this way? I thought we were to meet at Chowning's."

Connor grinned. "Seems I've come across some information that might be helpful."

"You're acquainted with the sorts of documents Mr. Benning's business required, aren't you, Isaiah?"

"Yes miss."

"Would you recognize one?"

"I can read, miss. And I know Mr. Benning's hand as well as anyone."

"Then I need your help after supper. I believe Mr. Benning hid some documents away from where Mr. Fraser could easily get at them. We must retrieve those papers. If anyone asks, I will say I am performing a commission for his widow in fetching some papers she needs in regards to his estate."

Isaiah nodded.

"Has Mr. Fraser been in Mr. Benning's office?"

"Every day, miss. And he don't want no help. Locks himself in in the morning and don't come out for meals half the time."

"Mr. Benning was a wise man to move those documents away from his home. If Mr. Fraser should emerge from his seclusion, you must keep him occupied if you can. Find some pretext to distract him from the trial tomorrow. I don't want him thinking to look elsewhere for the report on the *Phoenix*."

"Yes miss. I can do that sure enough."

"Good." Merry sighed. "Then I am going to see Jerusha before dinner. I'd like to give her reason to hope."

Chapter 11

Merry barely kept from sneering at the turnkey. She handed over a shilling and forced one foot in front of the other until she was ushered into the miniscule space that passed for an exercise yard. The sound of the key grating in the rusted lock sent a bolt of panic so strong up her spine that she jerked.

Dread gagged her as the gaol house odors seeped into her pores. She raised a scented handkerchief to her nose, trying to block the stench.

If only she could blot out the memories. Her hands shook so that she nearly dropped the handkerchief. She had not bargained for this welling terror, this absolute certainty that she would never be allowed to leave.

She tried to swallow but could not.

Jerusha appeared, and Merry focused on her face. She seemed to be at the end of a long tunnel. Everything spun and shifted, making Merry dizzy, but if she could focus on Jerusha's face, she could stay upright.

"Miss Merry. I'm right glad to see you."

With a supreme effort of will, Merry unlocked her jaw. "Are they treating you well?"

Jerusha shrugged. "As well as can be expected."

Merry took her arm and pulled her nearer the wall, as far as she could get from the gaoler. Turning away from him, she lowered her voice.

"I believe Mr. Fraser is the murderer. I hope to have proof tonight, and then Mr. Sinclair will be able to present it at the trial tomorrow and have you acquitted."

"Don't you go and get in any trouble on my account. I'll be getting out of this prison, one way or the other."

Merry blinked. She leaned even nearer. "Do you understand what I've told you?"

"You think you might be able to catch the real murderer and get them to let me go."

"How can you be so...calm?"

Jerusha patted her arm. "Time in a cell goes slow. Gives a body plenty of space to think on things. I figure it like this. God holds my life. These folks only think they do. Joseph went through slavery and prison, but it made him a better man. If I hadn't been brought to this country, I never would have learned about Jesus, and I wouldn't have my son."

Merry shook her head. How could Jerusha cling to a God who allowed the innocent to be condemned? If He loved justice so much, why didn't He do something to prevent injustice?

A lump wedged solidly in Merry's throat again. It must be the circumstances stirring up painful memories. Just being in this gaol made her want to scratch through the walls with her fingernails.

"Well, I am here to see that you are not convicted for something you did not do."

"And who put you here, child?" A gentle smile played at Jerusha's lips, but her eyes were probing.

Merry's face felt suddenly cool as the blood drained away. The significance of Jerusha's words resonated within her like a church bell.

"You blame Him for it. I thank Him," Jerusha said.

"How can you be so certain?"

"Even the good Lord was accused of something He didn't do, and they murdered Him for it. Should I expect to have an easier time of it? Nope. He never offered me an easy life, just a redeemed one."

Merry sniffed and dabbed at her eyes. She had never been so prone to sentiment. Jerusha drew her into a warm embrace, patting her back and stroking her hair.

The sobs Merry had suppressed all afternoon were suddenly clawing at her again, along with that sensation of being split in two. But now she knew she must make a choice if she were to be free, whole. She clung to Jerusha as tears streamed down her cheeks.

"There, there, child. It's not so bad as all that. He's protected you, hasn't He? Kept you from real hurt. You can see it now when you look back."

The turnkey entered the tiny courtyard. "Here now, none of that. None of that."

Merry pulled back and mopped at her face with her handkerchief. "I came to comfort you, but seem to have done a poor job of it."

A fresh round of tears interrupted her, but these were gentler, the residue of a heavy storm. When she had regained her composure she continued. "I have to forgive, don't I?"

Jerusha nodded. "If you want to be free." She lifted the hem of her skirt to reveal the manacles around her ankles and the bruised, swollen flesh. "These chains hang on to my body, but they can't touch my spirit. So I'd say yep, you gotta forgive, but also trust. Rest in His purpose. God showed Joseph the reason for his suffering years later."

Merry looked down at her wadded handkerchief. For the first time in a great while a light kindled in her soul. The warmth radiated outward, inching away the coldness of prison that had settled around her heart like a dense fog.

"I think I felt as if God owed me something for my years of living as a dutiful Christian. Never have I taken a moment to consider what He might be trying to teach me." She smiled then and offered a tearful little laugh. "It may have aught to do with humility."

"How is my Daniel?" The question sprang from Jerusha as if she could no longer restrain it.

Heavens. Merry had been so focused on her own heartache she hadn't given a thought to Jerusha's. She took hold of her friend's hand. "He is doing well. Understandably concerned for you. I swear to you, that whatever happens I will do my best to see him freed."

Graham crushed a scuttling roach beneath the heel of his boot. "Are you certain this is where she said to come?"

Connor nodded. "She gave me the name. Said most of the clerks end up here when money runs low."

"I suppose we'll not get away without ordering a couple of pints." Graham settled into a grimy booth, pulling his coattails onto his lap.

Connor's sly grin said clearly that he thought Graham too nice by half.

"Just go order for us, will you?"

Connor made his way to the bar, leaving Graham to sit alone in the squalor and take note of the surroundings. In the afternoon sun, the gin house, den of iniquity though it was, looked more jaded and anemic than evil. But there was no doubt as to the moral character of the occupants. Vice flowed as freely as the alcohol.

Connor returned and plunked down two tankards.

Graham was ready. "I noticed that you could scarce take your eyes off Miss Sarah Proctor this morning. Could it be that the untouchable Connor Cray has been brought low by a convict doxy?"

Connor colored the dull red of terra-cotta. "Watch yourself, boy'o. Miss Proctor has a good heart. Why else would she agree to help a beak like you?"

So his shot had struck home. Graham had suspected something was amiss when Connor had returned to their shared apartments actually whistling. Now his infatuation had been confirmed.

Connor took a slug from his cup. "At least Miss Proctor don't hold me responsible for her transportation."

Graham winced as an image of Merry rose unbidden. Even if she wasn't still outright furious with him, she remained aloof.

Time for a change of subject. "Is the fellow expected?"

"They couldn't say for certain. He comes in most nights, but not always."

"Then we shall have to hope for the best." Graham picked up

the grubby tankard before him, eyed the contents, and set it aside.

They passed the next hour and a half in desultory chatter as the crowd in the tavern grew.

At last, the man in question wandered in with a few of his cronies. His short, whip-thin frame and deep-set eyes marked him out as the right fellow, as surely as did his ink-stained fingers among this lot of sailors and journeymen.

Graham jerked his chin toward the man, and Connor approached him with alacrity. For such a big fellow he could move with the swiftness of a wolf when he wished.

Hand resting lightly on the back of the man's neck, Connor steered him away from his comrades.

Graham slid his untouched tankard in front of the man. "Have a seat, Mr. Porter."

"Can I help you gentlemen?" The clerk's fingers closed around the cup greedily, but he still managed to sound superior.

Graham reclined in the booth, using his own posture to put the man at ease. "I believe you can."

Porter could restrain himself no longer. He raised the tankard to his lips and drained it off in a long swallow. Graham gestured for Connor to get the man another round.

"I need you to tell me all you can of Mr. Benning's business dealings with Mr. Harland Fraser."

"I know 'bout you. You're defending the slave woman. Not the kind of work what's going to earn you any friends round these parts, I can tell you."

Graham retained his slouch, but allowed an edge to creep into his voice. "I do not care to curry your friendship. I simply require information."

Porter sniffed, but accepted the second tankard Connor shoved in front of him. "Ain't nothing to tell."

"Had there been a falling out between the two?"

"Why can't you people simply accept that the Negress done for him?"

Graham narrowed his eyes. "What do you mean, *you people?*

Have other people been asking?"

"Yeah, that Miss Lattimore what weaseled her way into the household. She's a slick one. She was asking about poor Mr. Fraser just this afternoon. Didn't find nothing out though. Had to admit he were an upright gentleman."

Miss Merry was in a fair way to becoming quite the investigator. He needed to talk to her about not trampling the field before him, however.

Graham plucked a couple of sovereigns from his pocket and allowed Porter to see the gleam of gold. He rubbed his thumb over the topmost coin, and Porter licked his lips.

"Think hard. Did Mr. Benning act strangely in any way before his death? Change any of his habits? Anything?"

Porter's gaze followed the coins as Graham placed them deliberately on the table with a definitive clink.

"There was one thing."

"Yes?"

"He rented a meeting room from Lorring's Tavern for a whole month. His nicest one, too, with a private entrance. No one but Mr. Benning was to go in or out."

"How did you learn of this?"

"I um. . .happened to see him going in one night and asked around a bit."

"He was not simply entertaining a wench?"

"He never stayed in there for long. And nobody else ever came or went. At least not that I knew. I mean, there weren't but the one key."

"Can you think of anything else?"

Porter held up a hand. "Not a blessed thing. He was a very regular gentleman."

Graham slid the coins toward Porter a half inch, and the man scooped them up, grabbed his tankard, and bolted.

What could Benning have been about in that meeting room? And how was Graham going to gain entrance?

Merry's late-night forays through Williamsburg had nearly grown mundane. So much so that when the night watchman's lantern momentarily blinded her, she was able to summon the aggravated hauteur necessary.

" 'Ere now, where you goin'?"

"I hardly think it's any concern of yours where I go."

"It ain't safe for a lady to be out this time of night. There's bad'uns about what would try to take advantage of a pretty piece on the loose." His lantern swayed slightly, and gin fumes wafted her way.

Isaiah stepped closer to her shoulder, entering the circle of light.

The watchman sniffed. "This fella yours?"

"As you can see I am well protected. Now please allow us to pass."

The man shambled aside, and Merry swept past, her heart pounding in her throat.

A wispy fog settled into the streets, as if Williamsburg were self-conscious of its taverns and gin houses and trying to hide them from view.

"Maybe I ought to lead the way, miss." Isaiah spoke in a hushed tone, looking over his shoulder as if expecting to be set upon.

Merry licked her lips. "Yes, I believe you are right."

Within moments they stood before Lorring's Tavern. Isaiah led the way around the back. Merry produced the key and handed it to him. He inserted it in the lock, and it turned smoothly.

Despite her bravado, there was a chance that someone would disbelieve her tale of an errand from the Widow Benning. The threat of being sent to gaol struck her anew, paralyzing her. She inhaled and closed her eyes tight.

She had made her decision. She would have to trust God to see her through the next step, even if she couldn't see the way herself.

Swallowing the acrid taste of dread, she crossed the threshold. Her heartbeat pulsed in her ears as she surveyed the scene. The very ordinariness of the narrow chamber settled her nerves a bit.

A table, a handful of chairs, a sideboard, and a small secretary occupied the room. Even the walls were spartan, containing only a map of the colonies over the fireplace mantel and a few wall sconces decked with half-burned tallow candles.

Isaiah moved toward the lamp on the table.

"No," Merry whispered. "Make certain the curtains are drawn first."

He did as bidden. His tug on the drapery sliced the moon's light from the room.

Merry groped forward. Her toe cracked against the table leg, and she swallowed a howl.

"You all right, miss?"

Her affirmative came out as more of a whimper.

The light flared, and she found him eyeing her with concern.

"Stubbed my toe. I'll be fine." She turned to the secretary and pulled it open.

For several moments the only sound was the rustling of paper. The letter of assessment, whatever had spurred Mr. Benning's summons, it had to be here—somewhere. She refused to believe differently. But the moments sped past. They had to hurry.

Lord, please help us find these things. Grant that justice is done in this matter. The prayer tumbled through her, and with it came a sudden release of the worst of her tension. The responsibility for this endeavor did not lie solely with her. Jerusha had been right. Even if she failed, God's plan would not be thwarted. Even if she never understood the purpose of the suffering, God knew, and in the end His judgment was the only one that would matter.

Fingers no longer trembling, she paged through the last of the documents. They were all as dull as drainage ditches. Nothing.

"Isaiah, perhaps you could search the sideboard."

Gnawing at her lip, she sat back in the seat and surveyed the narrow wooden desk. With all its cubbyholes and crannies, it reminded her of her father's desk. She bolted upright.

Could it be possible?

Her fingers groped beneath the shelves. Father's desk had had a secret compartment that would open only if one knew the trick. Her fingers brushed the edges of each nook.

"Ouch!"

Isaiah looked up as if wondering how she had possibly managed to injure herself while sitting still. "Miss?"

She pulled her finger from her mouth. "Splinter."

He nodded and turned back to the sideboard.

"It must be here somewhere." She stood and turned. Her eyes measured and noted every inch of the room. This secret office was too coincidental not to play some significant part.

She stopped in her perusal and turned back to the map on the wall. Was it the uncertain flicker of candlelight, or was there a bulge in the map's canvas?

She crossed to it and eased it from the wall. A thin leather folio dropped from behind the map and thunked to the floor.

A scraping sound from outside snapped their heads up as sharply as the wind tugging at laundry on a line. Their gazes met and Isaiah bent to blow out the lamp. He scrambled behind the curtains while Merry snatched up the folio, dropped to the floor, and crawled beneath the table.

She pulled her knees up to her chin, making herself as small as possible. The door swung inward, allowing a tiny slice of moonlight in with it.

Her ears strained to the bursting point, alert to every rustle and scrape. The intruder was quiet, but her sensitive fingertips detected his approach by the give in the floorboards. Her own breathing rasped unnaturally loud in her ears.

He rounded the table, and she realized that there were at least two of them. One on each side of the table. She was trapped.

"The lamp is hot." The whisper sounded taut. "Someone has been here."

How many of them were there? Merry shrank farther in on herself. Maybe she could crawl out the other side and through the door before they noticed her.

No such luck. The lamp leaped back into life, illuminating the chamber. It might as well have been broad daylight.

A chair slid away from the table, and a man sat down, his knee nudging her.

Merry scrabbled for the other side of the table, but a hand had hold of the back of her skirt and dragged her inexorably backward.

The intruder hauled her clear of the table, and she landed on her backside with a thump.

Graham jumped back, rapping his elbow sharply against the table. "Merry!"

"Graham?"

"What in the devil were you doing under there?"

"Hiding. What are you doing here?" She struggled to untwine her feet from her skirts and stand.

He grimaced. "You must know. I'd venture you are here to the same purpose."

She thawed a bit. Her chin lowered and a sheepish smile flirted with the corners of her lips. "I believe we have just discovered the documents we sought."

"We?"

Isaiah stepped from behind the curtains. Just two feet away from where the man had been hiding, Connor sucked in a choked gurgle.

Graham turned back to Merry, and she cast a superior smile in his direction and held up a thin portfolio.

In the wavering lamplight, Graham fumbled with the string holding the documents closed.

"C'mon." Connor flapped a hand, urging haste.

At last he had it. He unfolded the stiff leather and removed several sheets of parchment.

The heads around him bent even closer. Merry pressed against his side, her hair so close he could smell lavender. The desire to slip a hand around her narrow waist and draw her even closer blinded him for a moment.

What was he doing? He yanked his attention back to the matter at hand with brute force. The first document proved to be a letter of assessment for the *Phoenix*, produced by a shipbuilder in Norfolk.

"This is it." The warm whisper of Merry's words caressed the nape of his neck, and he swallowed hard.

He turned to the next page. "What is this?" The penmanship was childish at best, blotched and nearly unrecognizable.

Dear Sir,

I have knowlige that may be of use to you. There is a more to the sinkin of yor ship then you been told. If you are intrested maybe we can reach turms. I will call at yor convenince.

Jim Nash

Behind this was an affidavit drawn up, signed, and even properly notarized.

They all hunched forward to read it.

Merry gasped as she came to the end of it. She looked to Isaiah. "Fraser turned the *Phoenix* into a pirate ship."

Graham rubbed the back of his neck and chuckled. Now this was motive for murder. What a devious mind the man must have to dream up such a scheme.

"Then they didn't scuttle the ship?" Connor said.

"No. He must have used his ill-gotten gain to refit her and put her into service terrifying his competition along the South Carolina coast." Graham grimaced at the man's audacity. "A nearly perfect plan. If the ship were ever hauled to, he could deny any knowledge. As far as he knew, it had sunk."

Merry picked up the thread of the story. "But this Jim Nash had been a mate on the *Phoenix* and knew her top to bottom. He recognized her and brought the story to Mr. Benning. Surely now we have Fraser."

She turned to face him, and Graham's chest tightened. He

couldn't think clearly when he was so near her. He backed away a step. "We are certainly a good deal closer. Connor, we need to find this Jim Nash."

"Yes sir."

"We must determine how Fraser managed to introduce the poison. I have pondered the problem all afternoon and have been unable to discover a satisfactory conclusion."

"It seems doubtful it was introduced during dinner." Merry ticked off one finger. "And I have not discovered that they met afterward." She looked back at Isaiah.

"That's right, miss."

"Nor did they meet before dinner. I spoke to Master Raleigh today, and he said that his father mentioned an unpleasant interview he would be having with Fraser. But he didn't say when."

"That's right, sir," Isaiah said. They hardly have time to say 'good day' to each other before dinner. Mr. Benning would have waited for a better time to conduct business."

"What does that leave us with?" Graham had to distance himself from Merry's warmth and sweet smell. He took to pacing the narrow confines of the room, a finger raised thoughtfully to his lips. As if he could think of anything but pulling Merry close to him.

Connor pushed himself away from the wall he had been holding up. "When did the Frasers arrive?"

Isaiah rubbed at the stubble on his chin. "The morning before the family got home."

Merry tilted her head. "We took the children out to the plantation for a few days. We were supposed to be home a couple days earlier. But didn't arrive until the same day you did."

Perhaps they'd gotten the wrong end of the stick. If the poison had not been introduced that day. . . Graham whirled on the old slave. "Did Mr. Fraser have the use of Mr. Benning's study during that time?"

"Yes sir."

"And Mr. Benning was already upset with him?"

"Yes sir."

"One more question. Did Mr. Benning habitually take anything in the evening? A glass of brandy or port?"

Isaiah shook his head. "No sir. I mean, he did sometimes, but not regular-like."

Graham hung his head. Blast. Mr. Benning had been known as a man of regular habits. Surely it was likely that the murderer had counted on that foible to execute his plan. Nothing else made sense.

"There was his tincture though."

"What?"

"A patent medicine Mr. Benning swore by. Said he'd never had a day's sickness since takin' that stuff."

"Had he been taking this medicine long?"

The corner of Isaiah's mouth quirked up. "At least five years. He hid it in his study though, and took it before bed each night 'cause Missus didn't like it. She said it was quackery, and it'd kill 'im one day."

"And it did." Graham smacked his hands on the desk. "Fraser must have known the jig was up and set out from Charles Towne with murder in his heart. Things worked perfectly to his purposes. He was familiar with Benning's habits. All he need do was place the poison in the medicine and then wait for Benning to poison himself."

"If we find the bottle, perhaps an apothecary or chemist can discover if it yet contains poison." Merry's eyes glittered so brightly with hope that it hurt to look at her. What if he should yet fail?

"Surely Fraser will have destroyed it," Connor said.

"We must at least look," Merry said.

Graham held up a hand. "Merry, if you find it, bring it to me before court in the morning. If I do not hear from you, I will assume it was destroyed. Connor will search for this Jim Nash. By the grace of God, we will save an innocent life."

Chapter 12

Merry bounced impatiently from one foot to the next as she waited for Isaiah to produce the tincture.

A grin nearly split her face in two as he pulled a small green bottle from the very back of the desk drawer.

Professor Cardew's Tincture for the Restoration of Health and Spirits.

"We have him." It was only then she looked up to find Isaiah frowning. "What is it?"

"This here's empty. He weren't even halfway through his last one. I knows 'cause I always bought the new ones for him."

Her spirits plummeted like a pheasant hit by a fowling piece. "I had so hoped." Sighing, she pressed the bottle tight. "Perhaps the chemist will be able to swab it out and get enough to test." She tried to smile.

"I'll be praying on it, Miss Merry. You can be sure of that."

"Thank you, Isaiah."

She trudged up the stairs to her room. Thank heavens for Graham. At least he would do all he could for Jerusha. She could not ask for a more valiant defender. Her cheeks warmed at the thought of his head bending nearer as he inhaled the scent of her hair. In decency she ought to have pulled away, but she couldn't. He had seen her at disadvantage so often that she could not refuse the opportunity to be attractive in some measure.

She unpinned her hair and rang for Hattie to help doff her finery.

The memory of his shock at finding her beneath that desk brought a smile to her lips. He had looked fit to faint. How ironic that his breaking in to a tavern had proven to her he was a man of principle, just as her father had always believed.

Lighting a candle required too much effort. Once Hattie had

helped her from her bodice and skirts, Merry slipped into her nightdress and headed for bed. Even if she could not fall asleep, it would be nice to stretch out and close her eyes. It was almost over.

The sheets were cool as she slid between them. She rested her head on the feather pillow and allowed her eyes to drift shut.

Her foot nudged something and she froze. A bed warmer gone cold?

Something shifted. Slithered. Searing pain sliced through her foot. She screamed. Flailing against the covers that seemed to pin her in place, she rolled from the bed, landing with a thud on the floorboards. Tears stung her eyes. Her foot throbbed. She couldn't stand. She crawled away.

Her door was flung open, and Daniel rushed in. Hard on his heels, Abigail, the Frasers, and several of the slaves poured through the door in search of the commotion.

Merry pointed with a shaky hand to the bed. "Snake."

Snatching up the tongs from the fire, Daniel prodded the bedclothes. Abigail joined Merry on the floor, wrapping her in an embrace. "Are you injured?"

Merry held out her foot.

Abigail covered her mouth in horror. "Dear Jesus."

Daniel pulled the writhing snake from the bedding. Its scales glinted in the candlelight, streaks of tan and brown and cream. About a foot and a half long, it twisted this way and that, heaving its body in hopes of escape. Its hiss filled the room as all other sounds died away in the awful horror of watching it.

"It's a copperhead." Daniel's round eyes and fearful somberness hit Merry as if he'd struck her in the stomach. How long did she have? Would the venom kill her quickly and painfully? Or slowly and painfully?

Tears rained down her cheeks. There were so many things she should have done. She ought to have apologized to Graham. She needed to see him one last time, to tell him how much his help had meant to her.

Abigail dabbed at the twin wounds on Merry's foot, but the

trickle of blood could not be staunched. The skin around the bite was puffed and swollen already. Where was the poison? Had it found its way to her heart?

The snake continued its frantic gyrations as Daniel backed from the room. With a dry rasp of scales it broke free and landed in a writhing mass on the floor. The onlookers screamed and scattered. Abigail grabbed Merry's hand to help her scoot out of the way.

Isaiah struck it and then struck again with a poker until the creature stopped its movement.

Quiet descended on the room. Merry couldn't stop shaking. She breathed in for what seemed like the first time in several minutes. Abigail removed her own shawl and wrapped it around Merry's shoulders.

At the forefront of the spectators, Mr. Fraser inspected the snake's carcass. "That's no copperhead. It's only a water snake. A good look-alike, but you can tell by the banding."

"Then it's not poisonous?" his wife asked.

"Not at all. The bite will hurt like the devil, but it won't kill her." He addressed his comment to Abigail, as if Merry weren't in the room.

It didn't matter. Merry drew in a breath and clasped her hands together to still their trembling. It wasn't poisonous. *It wasn't poisonous. Thank You, Lord.*

"But how did it get in here?"

Mr. Fraser scratched at the stubble spotting his jaw. "Could've come in through a window. Probably just looking for a warm place to hole up for the night."

Merry didn't bother forcing away her grimace. Hopefully it would be chalked up to the pain in her foot. The effort of being courteous to this man would choke her. "I shall be checking my sheets after this, you can be sure."

The spectators drifted away, and Abigail gentled Merry into a seat. She washed and bound the wound with clean linen bandages. Daniel produced a cup of hot tea for each of them, and Abigail insisted Merry drink every drop before tucking her back in bed.

At last, Merry was left alone. Unwilling to stretch out fully in the bed, she pulled her knees up to her chest. She tossed and turned, unable to find a comfortable position. Unable to rid her mind's eye of the glistening image of the serpent. At last she stood.

Regarding the bed with distaste she licked her lips. *Dear Lord, help me.* With a jerk at the covers she dislodged them. Determined to prove to herself that nothing else lurked beneath the blankets, she pulled all of the bedding away from the mattress.

She remade the bed, smoothing the sheets into place and tucking the edges beneath the mattress so that nothing else could crawl in. She replaced the quilt as well and, hands on hips, stepped back to admire her handiwork. Soft living hadn't yet robbed her of domestic skill.

Her gaze caught on a scrap of fabric peeking from under the frame of the bed, and she bent to retrieve it. It was a coarse linen sack with a gaping drawstring mouth. Where had it come from? There had been several people in the room earlier. She had not noticed anyone carrying a sack, but mayhap one of them had dropped it. But then why not retrieve it?

What if the snake had been in the bag? If the opening had been left slightly open the creature would have slithered out, leaving the bag to get caught up in the bedclothes. It must have felt threatened and lashed out when she climbed into the bed. But all that required a planner, someone who had found that snake and deliberately placed it in her bed.

Her extremities went cold again, and the trembling returned. Had they known it was essentially harmless, or did that malevolent hand believe it to be a copperhead?

Graham scrubbed at his face with the palm of his hand as he stepped from Mr. Benning's secret office. The poor man had no doubt known in part that he was up against a dangerous adversary.

But it seemed he had never anticipated the depths of his partner's selfish malice.

Of course, Fraser probably saw it as a matter of self-preservation. If news of his fraud and piracy became public, his life was forfeit.

With a clap on Graham's shoulder in farewell, Connor departed to make the rounds of the taverns in search of Jim Nash. The idea of bed and a good night's sleep called to Graham. He had a case to organize, however.

He passed from the narrow alley he had taken by way of shortcut to find an eerie glow smudging the sky before him. Anxiety plucked at the pit of his stomach. He picked up his pace. A whiff of smoke scratched his throat, and he hurried faster. Somewhere down the street the night watchman's bell began to ring.

Above his head, shutters were flung open and footsteps pounded.

He was racing now. In his gut he knew even before he rounded the final corner that it was Mrs. Bartlesby's home on fire. He had never considered that he might be bringing trouble down on her head with his quest for justice.

As he neared the house a spray of sparks flared from the roof over the kitchen. Soot and hot ash rained down like the snow of hell. The slaves were salvaging what they could. Others had formed a bucket brigade and worked feverishly to douse the kitchen wing and keep the fire from spreading.

Graham dashed in through the front door and bounded up the stairs. Smoke swirled about him, making his eyes stream and his breath hitch in his throat. In his room he tossed everything that came to hand into his trunk and dragged it out to the safety of the street. He made another trip, forcing himself up the stairs two by two. If this fire had been set because of his presence in the household, the least he could do was save what he could for his landlady.

His eyes watered, and he covered his mouth with his forearm to block the smoke. Another flight and he flung open the window sash. They would never get it all out by the stairs. It was time to find a quicker route.

First to go were the linens and bolsters. Graham flung them through the window and watched as they plummeted to the ground. Hopefully they would make a bit of padding for other things.

He caught the attention of the houseboy and began to toss down more fragile items.

Dark figures whirled and cavorted below in frenzied activity. More windows were opened and household goods flapped and fluttered through the sky. Orange flames glistened off the windows and water doused on the buildings.

Through the swirl of light and haze and the confusion of frantic movement, Graham spied a figure standing perfectly still. The fire flared, illuminating the form of Cleaves, looking like a giant beetle in his round hat and too-shiny coat.

"Surely you don't mean to go to that vulgar trial?"

Merry glanced up from her porridge at Mrs. Fraser. "It had been my intention."

"Why would a lady desire to mingle with the uncouth rabble? I think it most unseemly."

Abigail met Merry's gaze, her eyes pleading. "I should be most grateful if you would stay with me. Catherine has convinced me of the impropriety of attending a criminal trial, unless called upon by the law."

Merry dropped her spoon with a clatter and gritted her teeth. Catherine Fraser had to be the most interfering, pompous woman in all the colonies. Had it not been for Abigail she would have flouted the woman simply for the fun of it. As it was, she inclined her head. "As you wish."

"Thank you, my dear," Abigail said.

Merry stood and pushed away from the table. "Do you mean to work in the garden this morning?"

"That's a wonderful idea. I need to do something that will keep my mind from all that is occurring."

"I shall join you soon." First she had to find Daniel and ask him to convey the patent medicine to Graham along with her hopes that the dregs could be analyzed.

She hastened to her room and quickly changed from her morning gown to something more suitable to gardening. Her fingers fumbled with the pins as she secured a voluminous apron in place.

She reached for the tincture bottle but stopped short. It wasn't there. Heart pounding in her ears, she tried to convince herself not to panic. Mayhap it had been knocked to the ground during the commotion last night.

She knelt and peered under the wardrobe.

Nothing.

Not even a dust ball.

On hands and knees she twisted to peer under the bed. She investigated every corner of the room. It had to be here somewhere.

But no. It had disappeared.

She sat on the floor and covered her face. Fraser could not have placed the snake in her bed in order to obtain the tincture, but perhaps he had spied it during the confusion and taken the opportunity to snatch it.

She remembered Fraser's oh-so-helpful advice about the snake. He was a master at turning situations to his advantage.

Even if she could find the tincture now, there would be no time to have it tested.

She had failed.

"Step forward, sir, and be admitted to the bar."

Graham did as bidden. He had provided his credentials to the clerk of courts the day before and now all that remained was the ceremony.

He passed through the swinging gate in the half rail and was granted the privilege of arguing cases before the court. He could not resist a glance back at the door. Where was Connor? Had he found Jim Nash?

"I must tell you, Mr. Sinclair. It is most unusual for a slave to be granted benefit of counsel." The plump, official gentleman formed a steeple of his forefingers. His half-moon spectacles and balding pate made him resemble Benjamin Franklin.

"I am certain that is because there are rarely such serious circumstances involved. Most do not require benefit of counsel, but in such a case. . ." Graham waved a hand as if his argument were self-evident. "There is more than usual reason to be cautious."

"I am not certain I fully appreciate your case. Do you mean to imply some sort of uprising if this Negress is denied counsel?"

Graham had meant to imply just that, but he had the sense to deny it. Playing to one of the greatest fears of a plantation owner had to be done cautiously. "The clerk of courts and I have searched the archives, and there is no charge against it."

"Neither is there precedent or provision for it. I cannot tell you the last time we had a lawyer appear in hustings court."

"Yes sir, I know criminal matters are usually tried in the court of Oyer and Terminer. However, since the accused is a slave, this venue is her only recourse. You gentlemen have the final say as to her sentence."

The semicircle of solemn gentlemen nodded.

"Gentlemen, this is not the usual petty matter you must decide where the complainant is no more schooled in the law than the defendant. Consider the implications. Justice would be made a mockery if the crown is permitted the representation of counsel in the person of the prosecutor, but an unlettered and defenseless slave woman has no one to speak for her. That, gentlemen, is not sound English justice. It is murder by another name."

Had he gone too far? These speeches must be judged to a nicety. His cheeks burned and he longed to loosen his stock. He dabbed at his brow with a handkerchief, and yet when had he last felt so alive? His magistracy had left him jaded. It felt good to be able to throw himself wholeheartedly into a cause.

The chief magistrate seemed to be waiting for Graham's next argument, so he continued. "Consider it in this fashion. Say she was said to have killed not her owner, but another man. Would not her owner have the right to protect his property by obtaining counsel on her behalf? I would think that if you precluded this basic right that the plantation owners of this country might have a word to say. You colonists are notoriously protective of your rights."

The magistrate's bench put their heads together in murmured conversation.

The chief magistrate finally settled back in his seat. "I fear you shall have a difficult time convincing a group of Virginians to acquit. We are likely to err on the side of caution. It would never do to allow slaves to think they can get away with murder. However, I find that if a lawyer is intent on wasting his time, I have no cause to prevent him—no matter how futile his cause. I shall grant your request."

Graham bowed his head. "Thank you, sir."

"Return after the noon hour, and we shall hear out this matter."

Graham half sprinted from the courtroom. Where was Connor? Had he found Nash or not? He peered up and down Duke of Gloucester Street.

Jerusha's son, Daniel, barreled around the corner of Chowning's Tavern, prompting outraged squawks from the men loitering there as they awaited their chance to be heard in the courtroom.

"Whoa there, lad." Graham placed a hand on the panting boy's shoulder. "Did she find the tincture? Do you have it?"

The lad swallowed, trying to find his voice. "Miss Merry—"

Graham nodded. "Yes?"

"She." He gasped again, kneading his side as he tried to find his breath. "She found it."

Triumph shot through Graham, a hot burst of flame that made him want to crow like a rooster.

"This morning. . .gone."

The thrill was quenched as surely as if someone had dunked him in a rain barrel.

"Tell me all of it."

In short, gasping sentences, Daniel poured out the tale of the snake and subsequent loss of the tincture.

Graham's lips compressed together as if each word were a vice. He had to put an end to Fraser before he attempted to harm Merry again.

A dray cart pulled to a rumbling stop beside him, and Connor heaved himself from the back. With a tip of his hat he called his thanks to the driver, and the cart ground forward again.

"Where have you been all night?"

"Had to go out to Yorktown."

"Well?"

"It's bad news, I'm afraid. Nash is dead. Drowned, a week ago."

Graham could hear nothing above the buzzing in his ears. Fraser was going to get away with murder and an innocent woman was going to hang.

Connor's brow bunched. "What else has gone wrong? And don't bother to deny it. Your eyes are as bloodshot as an old hound."

"Our lodgings nearly burned to the ground last night. Merry was bitten by a snake in her bed, and the tincture has been taken."

For once he had managed to astonish his laconic friend. Too bad he could derive no enjoyment from this particular situation.

Beside Graham, Daniel stiffened and went tearing across the street. Graham reached to snatch him back, but missed.

"Mama!"

Pressed between two turnkeys, hands manacled in front of her, Jerusha appeared haggard. As they neared the courthouse, colonists clumped around her, both men and women, jeering and taunting. A rock hurtled through the air striking her cheek only an inch or so below her right eye. Blood spurted, and she staggered between the guards.

Graham elbowed his way through the mob until he stood in front of her. She was on her knees now. Garbage and rotten vegetation pelted her. Daniel clung to her, trying to shield her with his body. Graham held up his hands.

"This is unworthy!"

At the sight of his well-dressed form and authoritative manner, the crowd quieted somewhat.

"I say, this is unworthy. I had heard that Virginia is a colony that values justice and the rule of law. How is it that the poorest and most wretched among you can be denied it at the very steps of the courthouse?"

"Murderess." The shout came from somewhere at the back of the mob and renewed the rumbling.

"That is not for you to decide. It may be true, or may not. But her fate will be determined by the King's justice. It is the envy of the world. Why would you seek to circumvent it? Walk worthy of your heritage."

Daniel and Connor helped Jerusha to her feet.

Graham glanced back to ascertain her condition. Blood streamed from the gash on her cheek. It blotched and spotted her pinafore and dress, a gruesome badge of her station in life. His nostrils flared, and his jaw went rigid.

Connor stood at his back, protecting him from assault on that side. God bless the man.

Graham turned back to the mobs, and with his gaze, dared them to make another move. Invariably, the eyes he met turned downward, and the person shifted. With awful slowness the crowd dispersed. When the last of the men had turned tail, he swiveled on his heel.

"Get her into the courthouse quickly." Graham pressed his handkerchief into her hand.

She lifted it to her cheek. "Thank you, sir."

"I'll see you free yet."

Her gaze lifted to meet his, for perhaps the first time in their acquaintance. "I know you'll try. You're a good man." And then she was gone, swept away like street refuse by the turnkeys. Daniel trailed in their wake, his cheeks streaked with tears.

Breathing in through his nose, Graham tried to recover his equilibrium. His fingers ached with the need to pummel something.

But Jerusha did not need his skills as a fighter, she needed his skills as a lawyer. Fraser would not win. There had to be a way.

"You did not accept all that bilge about it being unseemly did you?" Merry's spade bit into the earth with extra force.

Abigail looked sheepish. "No, indeed. I would have gone, but...the truth is, I could not bear the thought of seeing Jerusha in such circumstances. Even if she is guilty, I...I just could not."

"Surely you have not come to believe she is guilty?"

Abigail dropped her trowel in her lap and sat back on her heels. "Oh Merry, I don't know what to believe. My mind keeps coming back to the thought that if it is not Jerusha, it was someone else I know and care for. She was terribly upset at the thought of Daniel being sold. She was certain he'd be put to work in the tobacco fields or the rice paddies and die within the year, even though I assured her that he would be sold as a houseboy."

Catherine Fraser strolled near and waited as her slave woman set out a little folding bench. With a graceful sweep of brocade skirts she took her place, holding her parasol so that it shielded her face from the sun. Her handmaid stepped back two paces, near enough to be at hand, not so near that she intruded on the conversation.

"I do declare, all you ladies think of is this garden," Catherine said.

Merry hacked at a stubborn weed. "It is not all we think of. We've just been discussing the trial. We don't believe Jerusha is guilty."

Catherine Fraser's smile died away, leaving her looking as if she had smelled something noxious. "Of course she did it. Don't be silly."

Struggling to keep her dislike from showing, Merry strove for a civil tone. "I lost all tendency for silliness when I was accused of a crime I did not commit and torn from my home."

"I'm afraid her race is prone to lying and sneaking about in order to get their own way."

Merry met the woman's gaze. "I have found every race prone to that particular failing. Even men who by most standards have more than they could ever need have been prodded into crimes by greed."

The barb seemed to strike home. Mrs. Fraser paled and then flushed angry scarlet. "Surely you would not malign a dead man in front of his widow."

"Oh no, not Mr. Benning. I am fully persuaded that he was a most honorable gentleman. Indeed, he was killed precisely because of his virtue."

"Merry. . ."They both ignored Abigail's tentative voice.

"Then what do you mean to imply?" Catherine exuded haughtiness like a stale perfume. Her manner reminded Merry of Mrs. Paget.

Merry's fingers curled around the spade's handle. Not again. An innocent woman would not be condemned while a pompous, self-righteous prig of a woman could not even be brought to face the truth about her own family.

"Surely you knew that your husband defrauded the insurance company and lined his pockets with the proceeds of turning the *Phoenix* into a pirate ship. He killed Mr. Benning to keep the truth from coming out."

All pretense of amiable complacency disappeared as Catherine tore to her feet. "No." The single word dripped with venom. "It was that slave woman. She placed the poison in Benning's tincture because he meant to sell her mewling brat."

Merry's spine stiffened, and she dropped the spade. She gazed at Catherine Fraser with new eyes. Of course!

Graham listened intently as John Randolph, the attorney general, outlined the crown's case against Jerusha. Despite the fact that the normal course of Randolph's duties saw him practice at the General Court before the governor, no hint of distaste at appearing before the hustings court marred his demeanor.

He kept his message straightforward and easy for the untrained magistrates to grasp, even if he had no proof. According to the prosecution, Jerusha had been in danger of losing her son and had decided to try to end the transaction by committing petty treason, in this case, by poisoning Mr. Benning's evening draught.

Graham would have a great deal more difficulty in holding their attention, much less persuading them to adopt his theory.

"I would like to call Mr. Harlan Fraser to appear before the court." With a courtly gesture, Randolph gestured for the man to step up to the bar.

Graham turned to watch as Fraser took his place. The gentleman duly took his oath and waited politely for the attorney general to commence. His hands rested lightly on the bar. The brass buttons on his bottle green coat gleamed. His tricorn nestled under one arm. His periwig sat squarely in place, but had been so freshly powdered that when he moved it seemed to snow about his shoulders.

"Mr. Fraser, you are a guest at the Benning home, am I correct?"

"Yes sir."

"Indeed, you shared various business interests with Mr. Benning."

"Yes."

"And you were a member of the household when this foul murder occurred."

"Yes sir."

"Thank you, sir. Isn't it also true that on the night in question, you met this Jerusha in the hall?"

"Yes sir. The look she gave me would have flayed a cat."

"Did she act in any way insubordinate?"

"Refused to make her courtesy."

A grumble stirred through the spectators.

"Was she carrying anything at the time?"

"A tray with a pair of glasses on it."

"What time was this?"

"Eight thirty or nine o'clock."

"What did she do with the tray?"

"I could not undertake to say. She carried it into Benning's chamber, and I never saw it again."

"Thank you, sir, for your testimony."

Fraser stepped back from the railing and the attorney general turned to the chief magistrate. "If it please Your Honor, I will now call Dr. de Sequeyra."

With consummate skill, the prosecutor extracted the good doctor's testimony regarding the diagnosis of poisoning.

"Had you any reason to suspect poisoning before your arrival?"

"Oh no. Good heavens, a simple case of acute gastritis I thought. But the symptoms—well, there was really very little doubt you see. They would be recognizable to any competent physician."

The doctor described the symptoms and the steps taken to aid the dying man. "I'm afraid there just wasn't much to be done. Their stillroom maid had already taken steps and administered the correct draughts, but the poison had advanced too far."

"Can you opine as to when the poison had been administered?"

The doctor scratched his nose. "Based on the understanding that the first onset of symptoms was at approximately eleven thirty, I would estimate that the poison had to have been given between eight and ten o'clock."

More rustling and murmuring from the onlookers.

Dr. de Sequeyra might just have lit the tinder that would consume Jerusha.

Chapter 13

I t was you!"

Catherine's lips twisted into a snarl. "What are you gabbling on about?"

"You murdered Mr. Benning."

"Merry!" Abigail scrambled to her feet, and the three formed a taut triangle. "How could you say such a thing?"

"All this energy we have wasted in speculation about your husband's fraudulent dealings, and it was you all along."

Catherine's face burned crimson, but she sniffed. "I think you ought to see the girl to bed, Abigail dear. It is obvious she is suffering from overexposure to the sun. Either that or she is unhinged and ought to be taken to your precious Public Hospital."

Merry's lips curved in a sour smile. "It shan't work, Catherine."

"Really, Abigail, you must do something about your little... protégé. I'd hate to have to bring a libel suit against her."

Abigail stood gaping, her head swinging back and forth to take them both in.

"I finally have the right end. You had as much to lose as your husband. Your dowry is long since gone, and with the extravagant debts you two have acquired it is no wonder he had to set to theft in order to meet the demands upon him."

"Shut your mouth, you venomous little wretch." All trace of good manners and breeding had been stripped away from her demeanor. Her balled fists and belligerent stance were as common as any fishwife's.

"It wasn't about money for you though, was it?" Merry narrowed her eyes, closing the distance between them by one small step at a time. "At least it wasn't the primary concern. For you it was about your status. The grande dame of Charles Towne."

"Be silent!"

"Won't they all be surprised to know your whole life was a facade?"

Catherine's face twisted in torment, and she covered her ears with her hands.

Merry's stomach roiled. But she had to do this. She had to provoke the woman into admitting her crime if there was to be any hope of saving Jerusha. "No more parties, no more credit. They'll all know you are no better than the indentured convicts working in their fields."

"No." A howl of rage surged through the refined woman like a wild creature clawing its way free of a cage. She leaped at Merry, and they toppled together into the freshly turned dirt of the garden.

Merry had tried to force a confession, but she wasn't prepared for the ferocity of the attack. Catherine Fraser was stronger than she appeared.

They grappled on the ground, scratching and tearing at each other.

Abigail stood over them, trying to pull first Catherine and then Merry away. She turned to Catherine's slave woman. "Go get help!"

Nellie looked as if her eyes might pop from her skull. It took her a moment to respond. Merry could spare them little attention. Catherine's fingers had become talons intent on scratching out her eyes.

With every ounce of strength she possessed, Merry held the woman at bay. She brought her knee up between them as Sarah had shown her and heaved Catherine off, flipping her over her head. Merry scrambled to her feet and whirled to face Catherine again, fingers flexed into claws, ready to defend herself.

Panting, Catherine staggered to her feet. Her wig had toppled to the ground, and sparse, mousy brown hair straggled in her face. Her gown was dirtied. Uglier by far was the maniacal gleam in her eye.

"I will kill you, too. By all rights you should already be dead."

"You put the snake in my bed?"

Catherine gave an ugly snort. "That wretched Indian. He assured me it was a copperhead. Can you believe he thought I wanted to eat the creature?"

Her gaze flickered past Merry, settling just over her left shoulder, and something new flitted across her features.

Merry glanced over her shoulder. Several people were hurtling toward them from the house and grounds.

She turned back to confront Catherine with the imminence of her capture and try to reason with her, but the woman had taken to her heels.

Graham straightened his notes. *God help me.*

He stood, allowing the gravitas of silence to descend on the courtroom and hush the onlookers. It worked more effectively than any request for quiet.

He half turned to Jerusha. "How long have you served Mrs. Benning?"

Her eyes widened and she started. Indeed, it was the first time she had been addressed during the proceedings. "Since she was nine or ten."

"And how old were you?"

"I was thirteen or thereabouts."

"She brought you with her when she married because she did not wish to be parted from you."

"Yes sir."

"Would you characterize Mrs. Benning as a good mistress?"

"Yes sir."

"She was kind to you?"

"Yes sir."

"Did Mrs. Benning get along well with her husband?"

Her gaze cast about the room as if looking for a way to escape answering the question.

The attorney general shot his cuffs. "Your Honor, I fail to see the relevance of this inquiry."

Graham held up a palm. "Sir, if Mrs. Benning is known to have treated this slave woman with great kindness, and she also was on good terms with her husband, does it not stand to reason that she would have exerted her influence on behalf of her servant?"

At the magistrate's nod, he repeated his question. "Did she get along well with Mr. Benning?"

"Yes sir. They were very happy together."

"Do you believe that Mrs. Benning would have advocated for your son?"

"What, sir?"

"Would she have spoken on Daniel's behalf?"

"Oh yes, sir."

The attorney general nearly toppled his chair in his haste. "Your Honor, this is outrageous speculation. Mr. Sinclair invites the Negress to perjure herself with such questions. No witness ought to be so constrained."

"I withdraw the question."

Nodding sharply, Randolph resumed his seat.

Graham walked Jerusha through her activities of that fateful evening. As they had discussed, she answered truthfully, but as shortly as possible.

The crowd in the courtroom was growing restless, shifting from one foot to the other as the testimony continued.

It was time to tread more dangerous territory.

"So in essence, the case that the prosecution has built for Your Honors is based not on fact, but on mere conjecture as to what might have happened. Is this the basis of His Majesty's justice? I say no, a thousand times no."

As his oratorical pace began to accelerate, the crowd once more quieted. He clasped his hands behind his back and paced before the magistrate.

He had only this one opportunity.

Merry lifted her skirts and sprinted after Catherine's fleeing form. For a sedentary gentlewoman, she was as fleet as a deer. Merry's foot shrieked its disapproval of her hurry. The path curved around the corner of the house, and Catherine disappeared from sight.

The tumult of pursuers reached her ears, and Merry glanced over her shoulder. They were not far behind. She charged around the corner in time to see Catherine snatch John up from where he was playing on the lawn and hold him to her.

He wriggled in her grasp, but she tightened her grip until he howled. She bent her head and whispered something in his ear that stilled his protest but set tears flowing down his cheeks.

Dear Lord, what did the woman mean to do? Merry skidded to a halt. John held his little hands out to her. She had to anticipate what Catherine might do. Breathing a prayer, Merry took a single cautious step forward.

She raised a hand as if her fingers could touch John's. She spoke, taking care to sound calm and reasonable. "Catherine, let John go. He's just a little boy."

Catherine backed away a pace. "I don't want to hurt him, but if you make me, I'll snap his neck like a chicken's."

Renewed sobs coursed through the little boy, and Catherine shook him. "Hush."

Merry took another step forward.

"Catherine." Abigail's horrified whisper at Merry's back signaled that the others would be mere seconds away.

Merry stretched out her hand. "It's over, Catherine. There are too many who know."

"Slaves." She spat the word as if it tasted bitter. "They can't testify against me."

"I can." Abigail's firm voice surprised Merry. The woman moved nearer to Catherine, her hands outstretched toward her child. "Let my son go."

"You've always had everything." Hate scored Catherine's words.

"Don't be absurd."

The hue and cry died as the pursuers rounded the corner and witnessed the drama unfolding.

"That's just like you, always so patronizing. *'Don't be absurd','*" Catherine mimicked.

Abigail shook her head. "I mean only that you are blessed. You have wealth, health, and intelligence. What more could you ask?"

"I have nothing." The cry wrenched from her throat was so ragged it hurt to hear. "But you. You had a husband who doted on you, three healthy children, even the devotion of your staff." Her face crumpled with self-indulgent tears. "My husband will chase anything in a skirt, my five children died stillborn, and my slaves all try to run away. The only thing I have is my standing in the community. Your husband wanted to steal that from me, too."

One eye on Abigail for any sort of signal, Merry continued to edge closer to the distraught woman.

"You're right, Catherine. I ought to have been more compassionate. I have been a thoughtless friend not to see that you have been troubled. Don't punish Johnny for my sins."

Catherine's grip seemed to loosen ever so slightly.

"Mama," John wailed.

Catherine blinked as if waking from a dream. Her grip tightened again as she clutched the boy to her chest. "No! Stop where you are or I will kill him."

Just four or five more paces. As Abigail drew Catherine's attention, Merry inched toward her. Now the woman reeled to her right, brandishing Johnny like an amulet to ward off evil.

"Stay back."

Behind the deranged woman, Merry saw the door to the slaves' hall ease open ever so slightly. She had to draw the woman's attention. "Catherine, you must know that you cannot get away with this. We've caught you."

The door opened a touch more.

"You? You are no better than a doxy. Parading yourself in front of my husband and all society as if you are a lady. It is ridiculous."

Isaiah's head appeared from behind the door and just as quickly disappeared.

Merry eased forward another step. "Not just I. There are too many who have seen your behavior today."

With a guttural cry, Isaiah barreled through the door. Flinging himself from the stoop he wrapped his arms around Catherine's waist and carried her to the ground. John flew free. Catherine screamed and writhed, scratching and biting.

Merry reached John first. He was bawling, but appeared uninjured. Abigail took him, cradling him close to her chest as she quieted his sobs with the comfort of her presence.

The other slaves piled into the fray, and in a moment they had Catherine Fraser's hands trussed behind her back.

She ranted at the servants, swearing and lashing out with her feet.

Merry hobbled away from the melee. Her injured foot hurt abominably. She leaned against a tree and took the weight off it.

Daniel rounded the house, his eyes going wide and his jaw slack as he took in the scene.

Good Lord. What time was it? Merry straightened and lurched toward Abigail. "We must get her to the courthouse. Jerusha could be condemned at any moment."

"Gentlemen, the widowed Mrs. Benning stands to suffer a doubly grievous harm in this instance. She has already lost her husband, and now she is to be faced with the loss of the services and comfort of her faithful handmaid of many years standing."

Mr. Randolph sniffed.

"Can we bear to allow that to happen on such flimsy evidence as has been presented here? I tell you that I could pick a man from this very room and make a stronger case against him." His palms were damp with sweat, but Graham did not stop his discourse to obtain permission for his little demonstration.

"Mr. Fraser, you were at the Benning house and have testified on behalf of the prosecution. I understand that you were Mr. Benning's business partner and confidant?"

Fraser nodded gravely.

"And yet I could easily suggest that you had access to his bottle of patent medicine, and thus opportunity to place the poison. You had as easy access to lily of the valley as anyone else in this courtroom, and thus the means of committing the crime. To complete a case against you there remains only the reason you might do so." He paused dramatically as if he hadn't thought of that aspect.

A laugh filtered through the small courtroom.

"Yes, that could be a problem." He paused again and then flourished a finger. "But no, I can provide even that. Mr. Benning planned to break off the partnership and expose you because he had discovered you guilty of fraud and in league with pirates."

A collective gasp filled the courtroom, and every head pivoted to peer at Fraser. He seemed rooted to the spot, as if turned into a pillar of salt by the accusation. A scowl deformed his lips as his face turned red and then purple, and at last he sputtered in impotent fury.

"Your Honor." Mr. Randolph sprang up from his bench. "Mr. Sinclair cannot make such accusations without proof. This is the merest calumny. Slander in order to distract this court from his own client."

"Oh, I have proof." Graham held up Jim Nash's affidavit and the letter of assessment. He passed the documents to the clerk of courts.

An expectant hush settled over the crowd as the chief magistrate received the documents. He placed his spectacles on the end of his nose and perused them. After a long moment he turned a speculative gaze on Fraser.

Graham remained as still as if he were confined to the stocks.

The chief magistrate passed first one and then the other document to his colleagues. He lowered his glasses.

"It appears that charges may indeed be forthcoming against

Mr. Fraser. However, I do not find that these documents constitute proof of murder."

Avid whispers swirled through the court as spectators nudged and pointed.

"And nor should you, Your Honor. As I said, these documents are proof merely of motive. And yet the case built by the crown against my client is even weaker."

A clamor sounded outside the courtroom, and several heads turned to the noise.

"I am afraid, sir, that we are beyond the stage of looking for further suspects. Have you any proof that this Negress did not commit the crime?"

Graham's heart sank. "Sir, I have further witnesses who were scheduled to appear—"

The courtroom door burst in before a tidal wave of noise. Shouts and curses surged through the courthouse as more people pushed their way into the room.

The sheriff added to the clamor by banging his tipstaff vigorously, but to no avail.

Sitting on the bar, Graham swung his legs over and grabbed Jerusha's arm. He pushed her behind him. Any mob intent on hanging her would have to go through him first.

He caught sight of Merry near the heart of the tumult, and his heart clenched. What on earth?

As fierce as an avenging angel, Abigail Benning strode beside her. She marched straight to the bar. Jerusha's shackles clanked as Abigail thrust little John into her arms. She fixed the chief magistrate with her glare. "Your Honor, I must speak." Her imperious tone sounded nothing like her usual gentle courtesy.

Like the waves on a beach, the crowd receded, and Graham realized that Merry was holding the arm of a bound Catherine Fraser. They both looked as bedraggled as inmates fresh off a convict ship.

"Widow Benning, I do not deny your right to address us in the matter of your husband's murder, but I do not thank you for this disruption to the court's dignity."

"You have my sincere apologies, Your Honor. However, I believe you will find my actions forgivable. I am come to prevent a serious miscarriage of justice."

The chief magistrate merely raised an eyebrow.

Obviously taking this as permission to continue, Abigail sailed on. "Mrs. Catherine Fraser has admitted to myself and to Miss Merry Lattimore that she murdered my husband."

Graham's jaw fell open, as did the magistrate's.

The crowd surged. Shouts of outrage and peels of laughter mingled with gasps of horror and chagrin.

The only people seemingly unaffected by the pronouncement were Abigail, Merry, and Mrs. Fraser herself. She stared at the wall as if she were alone in the room. Her face grimy and her hair toppled, but not a tear streaked her face.

When his efforts to quell the mob failed to restore order, the chief magistrate gestured to his sheriff. "Clear the courtroom."

When the doors had been shut and barred against the crowd, only the interested parties remained standing before the justices. Fraser stared at his wife as if he had never seen her before.

"You make grave accusations, Mrs. Benning. Indeed, you have opened yourself to a charge of libel if you cannot support these claims."

Abigail outlined the events of the morning. "I still don't know how Miss Lattimore knew to condemn her, but her reactions proved the veracity of the charge."

The magistrate turned to Merry next. "How is it that your suspicions rested on Mrs. Fraser?"

Merry had turned as pale as her fichu, and one hand moved to smooth her hair into place, but she remained composed as she responded. "I had been privy to much of Mr. Sinclair's investigation, and therefore knew that Mr. Fraser had much to answer for in his dealings with Mr. Benning. Indeed, I believed him guilty of the murder.

"This morning, however, whilst working in the garden we were in conversation with Mrs. Fraser, and she mentioned that the poison had been administered in Mr. Benning's patent medicine. It was something Mr. Sinclair had deduced, but everyone else assumed it had been in the draught Jerusha poured. When I confronted her, her actions and words put the lie to her claim of innocence."

The magistrate turned to Abigail again, and the whole story of the afternoon's events came out.

Throughout the proceedings, Mrs. Fraser refused to speak. But she stared at Abigail Benning with a gaze so acid it might have burned a hole through her.

The chief magistrate asked the disheveled woman several questions, which she ignored. She made no movement at all until her husband sidled near and placed his hand on her elbow, urging her to respond to the magistrate. She yanked free of his touch as if he had been an adder.

The magistrate pursed his lips and motioned for his colleagues and the clerk of the court to draw closer. After a brief conference he straightened in his seat and cleared his throat. "It is hereby ordered that Mrs. Fraser be taken to the new Public Hospital for persons of insane and disordered minds."

"No!" Catherine's shriek raised the fine hairs on the back of Graham's neck.

She lunged away from her husband's restraining hands and hurtled toward the door despite the bonds that still secured her hands and arms. With her disheveled hair flying wildly, her face contorted in a grimace, and her eyes frantically darting side to side, she more than looked the part of a madwoman.

The sheriff scrambled from his perch and joined Mr. Fraser in trying to subdue his thrashing wife. The bailiff joined them, and together the three men hauled Mrs. Fraser from the room.

The justices stood, evidently having decided they had heard enough for the day.

Graham wasn't about to let them get away without assigning Jerusha's disposition. He pressed forward. "My Lords, I must ask for your judgment in the matter of this slave woman. Am I to understand that she has been fully acquitted?"

The chief magistrate turned back to him. His eyes held no warmth, but he nodded once. "The Negress is acquitted. Mrs. Benning, take her home and make sure she causes no more mischief."

Chapter 14

Heedless of the disapproving glare of the officials, Merry embraced Jerusha. They had done it. *Thank You, Lord.* An instant later her hands were shaking, and she wished for a place to sit down. They had done it.

If only it hadn't been so awful. Catherine Fraser was clearly unhinged. Still, Merry couldn't help but lay some of the blame at Mr. Fraser's door. His cold greed had led to much of his wife's desperation. Now they were both ruined.

Merry had expected to feel triumph, but she simply felt tired and disheartened.

Abigail turned to Graham. "Mr. Sinclair, I wish you would accompany me to my home. I have a request of you." Abigail held her hand out to Graham, allowing him to raise it to his lips.

There was something different about Abigail. Merry tilted her head, hoping a shift in perspective would reveal the source.

Abigail spoke again. "I fear that I have ignored unpleasantness because I have been too cowardly to face it. It is unseemly. I would most appreciate your assistance in straightening out my husband's affairs."

"Of course, madam."

Abigail nodded graciously and took her son back into her arms. Skirts swinging like a church bell, she turned and swept from the room.

The ride home was silent. The eyes of the townsfolk followed their progress with unwonted speculation. There were none of the heralded congratulations Merry might have expected at the unmasking of a murderer. Mr. Benning's true killer had been apprehended. And yet, looking into the grave gazes of the pedestrians they passed, Merry got the sense that they would have preferred that Jerusha had been found guilty of petty treason

311

and burned at the stake.

Merry ground her teeth. No doubt these good folk resented having their view of things disrupted. For all the recent clamor in the colony about freedom and justice, it seemed no one wanted to extend those things beyond their own social set.

Her heart clenched. Was the entire world the same? If it had not been for her own experiences, she might easily have accepted the status quo. Could it be that God really had brought her to Virginia for a greater purpose, not just to help Jerusha and Daniel, but to fight for justice on a larger scale?

She ruminated on the new thought, and her gaze found Graham's. She owed him an apology. She had known for some time that he was not at fault for her transportation. He had simply been a convenient scapegoat, someone upon whom she could focus her anger.

His gaze continued to hold hers. Could he understand? Would he forgive her manipulation in forcing him to help Jerusha?

Abigail ushered Graham into the drawing room, and once more he was struck with the elegant simplicity of the room.

He took the seat she offered and settled in comfortably.

"Mr. Sinclair, I fear that I have done nothing in the interests of my husband's estate since his murder. I. . .I had left it all in Mr. Fraser's hands, thinking him trustworthy and capable. Now, of course, there is a different complexion on matters, and I must know if he has managed things as I fear he has. Would you be willing to look into the matter for me?"

"I would be happy to do so, Mrs. Benning. It's wise to be concerned under the circumstances."

"I would also like you to prepare an order of manumission for Jerusha and Daniel."

He raised an eyebrow. "Do you think it will be granted?"

A small smile flickered over her features. "I shall see to it. You may leave that part to me. After what Jerusha has been put through, it is only fair and. . . Did you see the people in the street? They seemed not at all pleased that the real murderess has been captured. Had Jerusha been alone, they might still have strung her up on some pretext."

"I will certainly do so, but you realize that if she is freed, she will not be allowed to remain in Virginia."

"It will be difficult to let her go, but I will give her enough to get her to Pennsylvania. I have heard that freed slaves can make a life for themselves in that colony."

"It seems you have thought this all through."

"For the first time in a long while I am thinking for myself rather than gliding along the river of someone else's expectation." Her wistful smile was fleeting.

He nodded in sympathy. In some small measure he understood her regrets. He himself had been going through the motions of life for too long. This journey to Virginia, the pursuit of justice, had reminded him of his zeal for the law, and the joy to be found in seeing right prevail.

"There is one more thing I would ask you to consider, Mr. Sinclair."

"Yes?"

For the first time Abigail Benning looked away and seemed at a loss for words. When she turned her gaze back to him it was with an accompanying flush heating her cheeks. "Go to Merry. Confess your feelings for her."

The flush transferred itself to him. He tugged at his already straight waistcoat. "I. . .I do not. That is to say—"

She held up a peremptory hand. "Please, I would not ask you to expose your affection if I did not believe it might be returned. She is a lovely girl, and you might make each other very happy. If all of this has taught me anything, it is not to squander the opportunities we are given to love and be loved."

He could not move. The air in his lungs seemed suddenly insufficient.

"You will at least consider it?"

With an effort he forced a nod, and she smiled. "Ah, here is Hattie with refreshment. Would you care for tea, or perhaps you would prefer coffee?"

The children's squeals of laughter filled the air as they dashed about the lawn playing tag.

Merry smiled where she sat in the shade of the oaks. There was something infectious about their radiant joy. Beside her, Abigail continued an anecdote about Mr. Benning. Her grief at his death remained, but it was less raw. She seemed to draw a great deal of comfort from the happy memories they had shared.

A figure appeared around the corner of the house and sauntered toward them. Shading her eyes, Merry leaned forward. Her heart fluttered. It was Graham Sinclair. She had tried to find the chance to make amends, but though he had been by the house often in the last few weeks, they had never been alone.

Today she would grasp the opportunity. He would not leave until she had a chance to speak to him.

He neared and swept off his hat. "Good afternoon, ladies." His queue gleamed dark chestnut in the sun. His smile as catching as the children's.

"Mr. Sinclair—"

"Miss Lattimore—"

Trust her to blurt something out just as he was trying to speak. "I'm sorry. What did you wish to say?"

"What I have to say can wait." He seemed relieved.

Merry licked her lips. "Are you certain? I would not mind waiting." She turned to ask Abigail to excuse them for a moment, but she had disappeared. In for a penny, in for a pound. Merry sighed and waved toward Abigail's seat. "Won't you be seated?"

He complied.

"Mr. Sinclair, I. . ." Tears pricked her eyes. "I owe you an apology. Since my trial I have treated you terribly. I blamed you for all my wretchedness. And I was most unkind. I beg your forgiveness."

He shook his head and seemed about to speak, but she held up a hand.

"No, please. I was innocent, but matters certainly did not give credence to that fact. I shouldn't have held that against you. Particularly when you were so gallant as to secure my pardon and come all the way to the colonies to deliver it to me." She bit her lip. On with it. Confession would do her good. "And then I manipulated you into handling Jerusha's case, though I knew you must wish to return to your own life in England. I've acted wretchedly. I am so sorry."

"My dear girl. Your apology isn't necessary, but since you've made it, I accept it in the same spirit it was offered. If I'd been more discerning when you first appeared in my court, none of this would have happened."

Her gaze met his again. He had the kindest face. "My father was right to promote your passion for justice. I ought not to have said he wasn't."

"But you were right, too. I had forgotten myself. I was so bogged down by the cases I heard in my court that I gradually forgot that in every instance there were people's lives and livelihoods at stake. I don't know if I would ever have awakened to that realization but for you. Shall we consider it even?"

She smiled. He could be so adept at putting her at ease.

He stood and offered his arm. "Would you care to walk?"

Little bubbles of warmth effervesced through her. He helped her to her feet, and they walked toward the orchard. Fall had kissed the leaves, turning them every shade of red and orange and gold.

"I must apologize as well," Graham said. "In my attempts to find you, I spoke to your mother. She admitted that when she sent me away all those years ago, it had been without your consent. I allowed resentment—"

"What?" She stopped and tugged her hand free.

He looked bewildered. His mouth opened and then shut twice.

She closed her eyes and tears prickled the lids. "She sent you away?"

He nodded. "I thought you knew?"

She shook her head. Despite her effort at restraint, the tears spilled over. She covered her face with her hands. He hadn't abandoned her, he'd been sent away. All this time he'd been as hurt as she. The last few bands of iron that had constricted her heart tumbled free. "I thought you no longer cared."

He drew near, wrapping her in the warmth of his embrace. "I'm sorry. I'm so sorry," he murmured, his chin pressing gently against the top of her head.

At last she regained her composure. "I ought to have known. She was so determined to see me married off to that odious man."

"No, I should have spoken to you before just disappearing."

At last she stepped away, breaking the embrace. Arm in arm they strolled through the orchard. Their individual sides of the story tumbled out, leaving Merry shaking her head in wonder. Somehow God had orchestrated matters to see them reunited, their pain mended.

The sun flared as it touched the rim of the horizon.

Graham started as if waking from a dream. "I forgot why I've come." He smiled so warmly that something fluttered in her belly. "There is a ship in port. It will head for England before the month is out."

The sun must have plummeted from the sky. The world seemed immediately colder and darker. She tried to keep the regret from her voice. "You are leaving then?"

"I don't think so. Not yet at any event. I thought you might wish to return home." He leaned nearer. "To be honest I find myself enjoying the colonial life. There is an abundance of opportunity here for a man with initiative."

"Then you intend to stay?" She could not keep the note of hope from her voice.

"For a while at least. After your experiences, however, I thought that perhaps you might wish to return to England as quickly as possible."

The notion of returning home felt curiously flat. What was

there for her? Her mother cared not a whit for her welfare. There was no position waiting. What claim did England truly have on her? "I thought I wished to return to England, but now I find that the prospect holds little charm. I could make a nice life for myself here. Abigail or Sarah might agree to help me start a tearoom."

"Not tea."

She glanced up at him. "Pardon me?"

"Be a mantua maker or a milliner or open a coffeehouse, but do not go into the business of tea at a time like this."

"Why ever not?"

"Have you not heard of Parliament's Tea Act? People throughout the colonies are abstaining from drinking tea because of the duties imposed upon it, and I hardly blame them."

"Coffee then." She smiled at him. "Do I detect a note of sympathy for these colonists?"

He shrugged, but could not quite conceal his smile at having been caught. "I have been talking to young Raleigh. Though I don't agree with everything his Mr. Henry espouses, it appears that the colonists do have basis for their grievances."

"It sounds as if you propose to become one of these colonists yourself."

He stopped, halting their progress, and looked down at her for a long moment. "I suppose I do. Opportunities abound in this new world. Why should I not grasp mine? I could make a difference. I could fight for justice, for a better system of governance in this land."

Merry nodded. His passion conveyed through the pressure of his fingers on her arm and the smoldering heat in his eyes.

"Your case, and Jerusha's, have opened my eyes to much that is wrong with the current system. Why should people not be accorded the dignity of being presumed innocent? Surely it should be the government's duty, with its greater resources, to prove guilt, rather than for the individual to prove innocence. For an unlettered layman to be forced into proving a negative—it seems more than unfair when I consider the evils it has wrought." He sounded

317

almost angry as he ticked off his points.

"You can do it. With such passion driving you, you'll be able to help shape the course of the colony."

His hand moved to caress her cheek. "Then you believe in me—" His voice choked off, and he groaned, drawing her close.

"Merry. Merry," he whispered, burying his face in her hair. "I have not spoken. I feared you could never be brought to bear any affection for me, but now. . ."

She turned her face up to his. He gently cupped her face in his hands and lowered his lips over hers. She sank into the kiss, a thrill swirling down into her belly. He drew her even closer, and she went willingly, wrapping her arms about him.

When he at last broke away she was breathless, her knees as wobbly as a new foal's.

"Can you. . . Is it possible that you could have feelings for me?" His voice was raspy, as if he, too, was a bit short of breath.

"I've loved you since I was a girl and you helped me rescue that bird with the broken wing."

He laughed and pulled her close to him again. "You were so worried about that sparrow."

Her head fit perfectly in the hollow of his shoulder. She could stay like that forever. Safe and secure and. . .loved. Realization swept over her. God had seen that sparrow fall, and He had made provision for it through her. How much more did He love His children? All the time she had wallowed in the certainty that He and Graham had abandoned her, He had been working matters around to this place. She blinked against tears. No longer fettered, her heart seemed to swell in her chest, ready to burst with blessings. "I'm so unworthy."

Graham stepped back slightly to look in her face. "Not you, my gallant Merry. You are everything I could ever desire in a woman. If anything, it is I who am unworthy."

He cupped her cheek in the palm of his hand. "We can stay mired in our pasts, or we can look to the future."

Merry tipped her lips up for another long kiss. When she

pulled away again she was trembling.

Graham took hold of both her hands. "Merry, will you join your future to mine? I think we can make a real difference in this land. Change other futures, too. Will you become my wife?"

Merry's heart stuttered to a halt. Had she heard rightly? Could God truly be pouring out such blessings on her despite her many mistakes? Her gaze sought his, and the tender sincerity she found there warmed her to her toes. "Yes. Oh yes. Together we can do anything."

Lisa Karon Richardson is an award-winning author and a member of American Christian Fiction Writers. Influenced by books like *The Little Princess*, Lisa's early books were heavy on creepy boarding schools. Though she's mostly all grown-up now, she still loves a healthy dash of adventure in any story she creates, even her real-life story. She's been a missionary to the Seychelles and Gabon and now that she and her husband are back in America, they are tackling new adventures—starting a daughter-work church and raising two precocious kids.